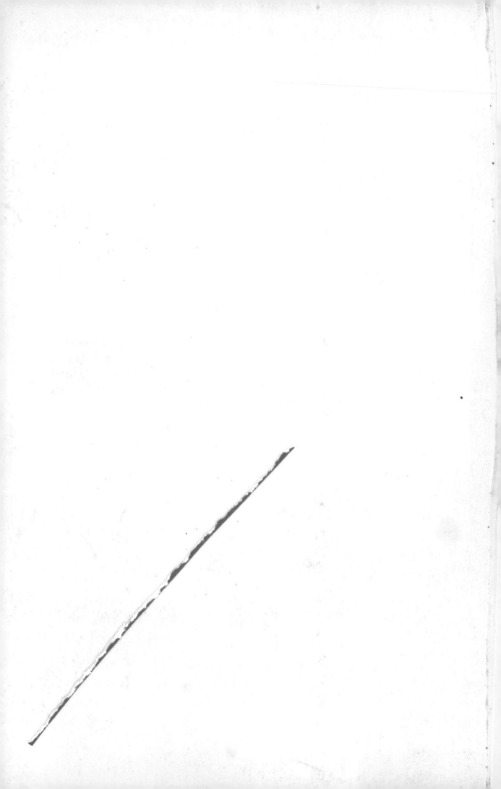

THE

INHERITANCE

GAMES

SHE CAME FROM NOTHING.

THEY HAVE EVERYTHING.

LET THE GAMES BEGIN.

THE INHERITANCE GAMES

JENNIFER LYNN BARNES

LITTLE, BROWN AND COMPANY

New York   Boston

Little, Brown and Company
Hachette Book Group
1290 Avenue of the Americas, New York, NY 10104
Visit us at LBYR.com

First Edition: September 2020

Little, Brown and Company is a division of Hachette Book Group, Inc.
The Little, Brown name and logo are trademarks of Hachette Book Group, Inc.

The publisher is not responsible for websites (or their content) that are not owned by the publisher.

Library of Congress Cataloging-in-Publication Data
Names: Barnes, Jennifer (Jennifer Lynn), author.
Title: The inheritance games / Jennifer Lynn Barnes.
Description: First edition. | New York: Little, Brown and Company, 2020. | Audience: Ages 12+ | Summary: "When a teen inherits vast wealth and an eccentric estate from the richest man in Texas, she must also live with his surviving family—a family hellbent on discovering just how she earned her inheritance"—Provided by publisher.
Identifiers: LCCN 2019054648 | ISBN 9781368052405 (hardcover) | ISBN 9781368053242 (ebook)
Subjects: CYAC: Inheritance and succession—Fiction. | Wealth—Fiction. | Puzzles—Fiction.
Classification: LCC PZ7.B26225 In 2020 | DDC [Fic]—dc23
LC record available at https://lccn.loc.gov/2019054648

ISBNs: 978-1-368-05240-5 (hardcover), 978-1-368-05324-2 (ebook)

Printed in the United States of America

LSC-H

Printing 11, 2022

For Samuel

CHAPTER 1

When I was a kid, my mom constantly invented games. The Quiet Game. The Who Can Make Their Cookie Last Longer? Game. A perennial favorite, The Marshmallow Game involved eating marshmallows while wearing puffy Goodwill jackets indoors, to avoid turning on the heat. The Flashlight Game was what we played when the electricity went out. We never walked anywhere—we raced. The floor was nearly always lava. The primary purpose of pillows was building forts.

Our longest-lasting game was called I Have A Secret, because my mom said that everyone should always have at least one. Some days she guessed mine. Some days she didn't. We played every week, right up until I was fifteen and one of her secrets landed her in the hospital.

The next thing I knew, she was gone.

"Your move, princess." A gravelly voice dragged me back to the present. "I don't have all day."

"Not a princess," I retorted, sliding one of my knights into place. "Your move, *old man*."

Harry scowled at me. I didn't know how old he was, really, and

I had no idea how he'd come to be homeless and living in the park where we played chess each morning. I did know that he was a formidable opponent.

"You," he grumbled, eyeing the board, "are a horrible person."

Three moves later, I had him. "Checkmate. You know what that means, Harry."

He gave me a dirty look. "I have to let you buy me breakfast." Those were the terms of our long-standing bet. When I won, he couldn't turn down the free meal.

To my credit, I only gloated a little. "It's good to be queen."

———◆———

I made it to school on time but barely. I had a habit of cutting things close. I walked the same tightrope with my grades: How little effort could I put in and still get an A? I wasn't lazy. I was practical. Picking up an extra shift was worth trading a 98 for a 92.

I was in the middle of drafting an English paper in Spanish class when I was called to the office. Girls like me were supposed to be invisible. We didn't get summoned for sit-downs with the principal. We made exactly as much trouble as we could afford to make, which in my case was none.

"Avery." Principal Altman's greeting was not what one would call warm. "Have a seat."

I sat.

He folded his hands on the desk between us. "I assume you know why you're here."

Unless this was about the weekly poker game I'd been running in the parking lot to finance Harry's breakfasts—and sometimes my own—I had no idea what I'd done to draw the administration's attention. "Sorry," I said, trying to sound sufficiently meek, "but I don't."

Principal Altman let me sit with my response for a moment,

then presented me with a stapled packet of paper. "This is the physics test you took yesterday."

"Okay," I said. That wasn't the response he was looking for, but it was all I had. For once, I'd actually studied. I couldn't imagine I'd done badly enough to merit intervention.

"Mr. Yates graded the tests, Avery. Yours was the only perfect score."

"Great," I said, in a deliberate effort to keep myself from saying *okay* again.

"Not great, young lady. Mr. Yates intentionally creates exams that challenge the abilities of his students. In twenty years, he's never given a perfect score. Do you see the problem?"

I couldn't quite bite back my instinctive reply. "A teacher who designs tests most of his students can't pass?"

Mr. Altman narrowed his eyes. "You're a good student, Avery. Quite good, given your circumstances. But you don't exactly have a history of setting the curve."

That was fair, so why did I feel like he'd gut-punched me?

"I am not without sympathy for your situation," Principal Altman continued, "but I need you to be straight with me here." He locked his eyes onto mine. "Were you aware that Mr. Yates keeps copies of all his exams on the cloud?" He thought I'd cheated. He was sitting there, staring me down, and I'd never felt less seen. "I'd like to help you, Avery. You've done extremely well, given the hand life has dealt you. I would hate to see any plans you might have for the future derailed."

"Any plans I *might* have?" I repeated. If I'd had a different last name, if I'd had a dad who was a dentist and a mom who stayed home, he wouldn't have acted like the future was something I *might* have thought about. "I'm a junior," I gritted out. "I'll graduate next year with at least two semesters' worth of college credit. My test scores should put me in scholarship contention at UConn, which has one of the top actuarial science programs in the country."

Mr. Altman frowned. "Actuarial science?"

"Statistical risk assessment." It was the closest I could come to double-majoring in poker and math. Besides, it was one of the most employable majors on the planet.

"Are you a fan of calculated risks, Ms. Grambs?"

Like cheating? I couldn't let myself get any angrier. Instead, I pictured myself playing chess. I marked out the moves in my mind. Girls like me didn't get to explode. "I didn't cheat." I said calmly. "I studied."

I'd scraped together time—in other classes, between shifts, later at night than I should have stayed up. Knowing that Mr. Yates was infamous for giving impossible tests had made me want to redefine *possible.* For once, instead of seeing how close I could cut it, I'd wanted to see how far I could go.

And *this* was what I got for my effort, because girls like me didn't ace impossible exams.

"I'll take the test again," I said, trying not to sound furious, or worse, wounded. "I'll get the same grade again."

"And what would you say if I told you that Mr. Yates had prepared a new exam? All new questions, every bit as difficult as the first."

I didn't even hesitate. "I'll take it."

"That can be arranged tomorrow during third period, but I have to warn you that this will go significantly better for you if—"

"Now."

Mr. Altman stared at me. "Excuse me?"

Forget sounding meek. Forget being invisible. "I want to take the new exam right here, in your office, right now."

CHAPTER 2

R ough day?" Libby asked. My sister was seven years older than me and way too empathetic for her own good—or mine.

"I'm fine," I replied. Recounting my trip to Altman's office would only have worried her, and until Mr. Yates graded my second test there was nothing anyone could do. I changed the subject. "Tips were good tonight."

"How good?" Libby's sense of style resided somewhere between punk and goth, but personality-wise, she was the kind of eternal optimist who believed a hundred-dollar-tip was always just around the corner at a hole-in-the-wall diner where most entrees cost $6.99.

I pressed a wad of crumpled singles into her hand. "Good enough to help make rent."

Libby tried to hand the money back, but I moved out of reach before she could. "I will throw this cash at you," she warned sternly.

I shrugged. "I'd dodge."

"You're impossible." Libby grudgingly put the money away, produced a muffin tin out of nowhere, and fixed me with a look. "You *will* accept this muffin to make it up to me."

"Yes, ma'am." I went to take it from her outstretched hand, but then I looked past her to the counter and realized she'd baked more than muffins. There were also cupcakes. I felt my stomach plummet. "Oh no, Lib."

"It's not what you think," Libby promised. She was an apology cupcake baker. A guilty cupcake baker. A please-don't-be-mad-at-me cupcake baker.

"Not what I think?" I repeated softly. "So he's not moving back in?"

"It's going to be different this time," Libby promised. "And the cupcakes are chocolate!"

My favorite.

"It's never going to be different," I said, but if I'd been capable of making her believe that, she'd have believed it already.

Right on cue, Libby's on-again, off-again boyfriend—who had a fondness for punching walls and extolling his own virtues for not punching Libby—strolled in. He snagged a cupcake off the counter and let his gaze rake over me. "Hey, jailbait."

"Drake," Libby said.

"I'm kidding." Drake smiled. "You know I'm kidding, Libby-mine. You and your sister just need to learn how to take a joke."

One minute in, and he was already making us the problem. "This is not healthy," I told Libby. He hadn't wanted her to take me in—and he'd never stopped punishing her for it.

"This is not your apartment," Drake shot back.

"Avery's my sister," Libby insisted.

"Half sister," Drake corrected, and then he smiled again. "Joking."

He wasn't, but he also wasn't wrong. Libby and I shared an absent father, but had different moms. We'd only seen each other once or twice a year growing up. No one had expected her to take custody of me two years earlier. She was young. She was barely scraping by. But she was *Libby*. Loving people was what she did.

"If Drake's staying here," I told her quietly, "then I'm not."

Libby picked up a cupcake and cradled it in her hands. "I'm doing the best I can, Avery."

She was a people pleaser. Drake liked putting her in the middle. He used me to hurt her.

I couldn't just wait around for the day he stopped punching *walls*.

"If you need me," I told Libby, "I'll be living in my car."

CHAPTER 3

My ancient Pontiac was a piece of junk, but at least the heater worked. Mostly. I parked at the diner, around the back, where no one would see me. Libby texted, but I couldn't bring myself to text back, so I ended up just staring at my phone instead. The screen was cracked. My data plan was practically non-existent, so I couldn't go online, but I did have unlimited texts.

Besides Libby, there was exactly one person in my life worth texting. I kept my message to Max short and sweet: *You-know-who is back.*

There was no immediate response. Max's parents were big on "phone-free" time and confiscated hers frequently. They were also infamous for intermittently monitoring her messages, which was why I hadn't named Drake and wouldn't type a word about where I was spending the night. Neither the Liu family nor my social worker needed to know that I wasn't where I was supposed to be.

Setting my phone down, I glanced at my backpack in the passenger seat, but decided that the rest of my homework could wait for morning. I laid my seat back and closed my eyes but couldn't sleep, so I reached into the glove box and retrieved the only thing of value that my mother had left me: a stack of postcards. Dozens of them. Dozens of places we'd planned to go together.

Hawaii. New Zealand. Machu Picchu. Staring at each of the pictures in turn, I imagined myself anywhere but here. Tokyo. Bali. Greece. I wasn't sure how long I'd been lost in thought when my phone beeped. I picked it up and was greeted by Max's response to my message about Drake.

That mother-faxer. And then, a moment later: *Are you okay?*

Max had moved away the summer after eighth grade. Most of our communication was written, and she refused to write curse words, lest her parents see them.

So she got creative.

I'm fine, I wrote back, and that was all the impetus she needed to unleash her righteous fury on my behalf.

THAT FAXING CHIPHEAD CAN GO STRAIGHT TO ELF AND EAT A BAG OF DUCKS!!!

A second later, my phone rang. "Are you really okay?" Max asked when I answered.

I looked back down at the postcards in my lap, and the muscles in my throat tightened. I would make it through high school. I'd apply for every scholarship I qualified for. I'd get a marketable degree that allowed me to work remotely and paid me well.

I'd travel the world.

I let out a long, jagged breath, and then answered Max's question. "You know me, Maxine. I always land on my feet."

CHAPTER 4

The next day, I paid a price for sleeping in my car. My whole body ached, and I had to shower after gym, because paper towels in the bathroom at the diner could only go so far. I didn't have time to dry my hair, so I arrived at my next class sopping wet. It wasn't my best look, but I'd gone to school with the same kids my whole life. I was wallpaper.

No one was looking.

"*Romeo and Juliet* is littered with proverbs—small, pithy bits of wisdom that make a statement about the way the world and human nature work." My English teacher was young and earnest, and I deeply suspected she'd had too much coffee. "Let's take a step back from Shakespeare. Who can give me an example of an everyday proverb?"

Beggars can't be choosers, I thought, my head pounding and water droplets dripping down my back. *Necessity is the mother of invention. If wishes were horses, beggars would ride.*

The door to the classroom opened. An office aide waited for the teacher to look at her, then announced loudly enough for the whole class to hear, "Avery Grambs is wanted in the office."

I took that to mean that someone had graded my test.

———————————

I knew better than to expect an apology, but I also wasn't expecting Mr. Altman to meet me at his secretary's desk, beaming like he'd just had a visit from the Pope. "Avery!"

An alarm went off in the back of my head, because no one was ever that glad to see me.

"Right this way." He opened the door to his office, and I caught sight of a familiar neon-blue ponytail inside.

"Libby?" I said. She was wearing skull-print scrubs and no makeup, both of which suggested she'd come straight from work. In the middle of a shift. Orderlies at assisted living facilities couldn't just walk out in the middle of shifts.

Not unless something was wrong.

"Is Dad..." I couldn't make myself finish the question.

"Your father is fine." The voice that issued that statement didn't belong to Libby or Principal Altman. My head whipped up, and I looked past my sister. The chair behind the principal's desk was occupied—by a guy not much older than me. *What is going on here?*

He was wearing a suit. He looked like the kind of person who should have had an entourage.

"As of yesterday," he continued, his low, rich voice measured and precise, "Ricky Grambs was alive, well, and safely passed out in a motel room in Michigan, an hour outside of Detroit."

I tried not to stare at him—and failed. *Light hair. Pale eyes. Features sharp enough to cut rocks.*

"How could you possibly know that?" I demanded. *I didn't even know where my deadbeat father was. How could he?*

The boy in the suit didn't answer my question. Instead, he

11

arched an eyebrow. "Principal Altman?" he said. "If you could give us a moment?"

The principal opened his mouth, presumably to object to being removed from his own office, but the boy's eyebrow lifted higher.

"I believe we had an agreement."

Altman cleared his throat. "Of course." And just like that, he turned and walked out the door. It closed behind him, and I resumed openly staring at the boy who'd banished him.

"You asked how I know where your father is." His eyes were the same color as his suit—gray, bordering on silver. "It would be best, for the moment, for you to just assume that I know everything."

His voice would have been pleasant to listen to if it weren't for the words. "A guy who thinks he knows everything," I muttered. "That's new."

"A girl with a razor-sharp tongue," he returned, silver eyes focused on mine, the ends of his lips ticking upward.

"Who are you?" I asked. "And what do you want?" *With me,* something inside me added. *What do you want with me?*

"All I want," he said, "is to deliver a message." For reasons I couldn't quite pinpoint, my heart started beating faster. "One that has proven rather difficult to send via traditional means."

"That might be my fault," Libby volunteered sheepishly beside me.

"What might be your fault?" I turned to look at her, grateful for an excuse to look away from Gray Eyes and fighting the urge to glance back.

"The first thing you need to know," Libby said, as earnestly as anyone wearing skull-print scrubs had ever said anything, "is that I had *no* idea the letters were real."

"What letters?" I asked. I was the only person in this room who didn't know what was going on here, and I couldn't shake the feeling that not knowing was a liability, like standing on train tracks but not knowing which direction the train was coming from.

"The letters," the boy in the suit said, his voice wrapping around me, "that my grandfather's attorneys have been sending, certified mail, to your residence for the better part of three weeks."

"I thought they were a scam," Libby told me.

"I assure you," the boy replied silkily, "they are not."

I knew better than to put any confidence in the assurances of good-looking guys.

"Let me start again." He folded his hands on the desk between us, the thumb of his right hand lightly circling the cuff link on his left wrist. "My name is Grayson Hawthorne. I'm here on behalf of McNamara, Ortega, and Jones, a Dallas-based law firm representing my grandfather's estate." Grayson's pale eyes met mine. "My grandfather passed away earlier this month." A weighty pause. "His name was Tobias Hawthorne." Grayson studied my reaction—or, more accurately, the lack thereof. "Does that name mean anything to you?"

The sensation of standing on train tracks was back. "No," I said. "Should it?"

"My grandfather was a very wealthy man, Ms. Grambs. And it appears that, along with our family and people who worked for him for years, you have been named in his will."

I heard the words but couldn't process them. "His *what*?"

"His will," Grayson repeated, a slight smile crossing his lips. "I don't know what he left you, exactly, but your presence is required at the will's reading. We've been postponing it for weeks."

I was an intelligent person, but Grayson Hawthorne might as well have been speaking Swedish.

"Why would your grandfather leave anything to me?" I asked.

Grayson stood. "That's the question of the hour, isn't it?" He stepped out from behind the desk, and suddenly I knew *exactly* what direction the train was coming from.

His.

"I've taken the liberty of making travel arrangements on your behalf."

This wasn't an invitation. It was a *summons.* "What makes you think—" I started to say, but Libby cut me off. "Great!" she said, giving me a healthy side-eye.

Grayson smirked. "I'll give you two a moment." His eyes lingered on mine too long for comfort, and then, without another word, he strode out the door.

Libby and I were silent for a full five seconds after he was gone. "Don't take this the wrong way," she whispered finally, "but I think he might be God."

I snorted. "He certainly thinks so." It was easier to ignore the effect he'd had on me now that he was gone. What kind of person had self-assurance that absolute? It was there in every aspect of his posture and word choice, in every interaction. Power was as much a fact of life for this guy as gravity. The world bent to the will of Grayson Hawthorne. What money couldn't buy him, those eyes probably did.

"Start from the beginning," I told Libby. "And don't leave anything out."

She fidgeted with the inky-black tips of her blue ponytail. "A couple of weeks ago, we started getting these letters—addressed to you, care of me. They said that you'd inherited money, gave us a number to call. I thought they were a scam. Like one of those emails that claims to be from a foreign prince."

"Why would this Tobias Hawthorne—a man I've never met, never even heard of—put me in his will?" I asked.

"I don't know," Libby said, "but *that*"—she gestured in the direction Grayson had gone—"is not a scam. Did you *see* the way he dealt with Principal Altman? What do you think their agreement was? A bribe...or a threat?"

Both. Pushing down that response, I pulled out my phone and connected to the school's Wi-Fi. One internet search for Tobias Hawthorne later, the two of us were reading a news headline: *Noted Philanthropist Dies at 78.*

"Do you know what *philanthropist* means?" Libby asked me seriously. "It means *rich*."

"It means someone who gives to charity," I corrected her.

"So...*rich*." Libby gave me a look. "What if *you* are charity? They wouldn't send this guy's grandson to get you if he'd just left you a few hundred dollars. We must be talking thousands. You could travel, Avery, or put it toward college, or buy a better car."

I could feel my heart starting to beat faster again. "Why would a total stranger leave me anything?" I reiterated, resisting the urge to daydream, even for a second, because if I started, I wasn't sure I could stop.

"Maybe he knew your mom?" Libby suggested. "I don't know, but I do know that you need to go to the reading of that will."

"I can't just take off," I told her. "Neither can you." We'd both miss work. I'd miss class. And yet...if nothing else, a trip would get Libby away from Drake, at least temporarily.

And if this is real... It was already getting harder *not* to think about the possibilities.

"My shifts are covered for the next two days," Libby informed me. "I made some calls, and so are yours." She reached for my hand. "Come on, Ave. Wouldn't it be nice to take a trip, just you and me?"

She squeezed my hand. After a moment, I squeezed back. "Where exactly is the reading of the will?"

"Texas!" Libby grinned. "And they didn't just book our tickets. They booked them *first class*."

CHAPTER 5

'd never flown before. Looking down from ten thousand feet, I could imagine myself going farther than Texas. Paris. Bali. Machu Picchu. Those had always been *someday* dreams.

But now . . .

Beside me, Libby was in heaven, sipping on a complimentary cocktail. "Picture time," she declared. "Smoosh in and hold up your warm nuts."

On the other side of the aisle, a lady shot Libby a disapproving look. I wasn't sure whether the target of her disapproval was Libby's hair, the camo-print jacket she'd changed into when she'd ditched her scrubs, her metal-studded choker, the selfie she was attempting to take, or the volume with which she'd just said the phrase *warm nuts*.

Adopting my haughtiest look, I leaned toward my sister and raised my warm nuts high.

Libby laid her head on my shoulder and snapped the pic. She turned the phone to show me. "I'll send it to you when we land." The smile on her face wavered, just for a second. "Don't put it online, okay?"

Drake doesn't know where you are, does he? I bit back the

urge to remind her that she was allowed to have a life. I didn't want to argue. "I won't." That wasn't any big sacrifice on my part. I had social media accounts, but I mostly used them to DM Max.

And speaking of...I pulled my phone out. I'd put it in airplane mode, which meant no texting, but first class offered free Wi-Fi. I sent Max a quick update on what had happened, then spent the rest of the flight obsessively reading up on Tobias Hawthorne.

He'd made his money in oil, then diversified. I'd expected, based on the way Grayson had said his grandfather was a "wealthy" man and the newspaper's use of the word *philanthropist*, that he was some kind of millionaire.

I was wrong.

Tobias Hawthorne wasn't just "wealthy" or "well-off." There weren't any polite terms for what Tobias Hawthorne was, other than really insert-expletive-of-your-choice-here filthy rich. Billions, with a *b* and plural. He was the ninth-richest person in the United States and the richest man in the state of Texas.

Forty-six point two billion dollars. That was his net worth. As far as numbers went, it didn't even sound real. Eventually, I stopped wondering why a man I'd never met would have left me something—and started wondering how much.

Max messaged back right before landing: *Are you foxing with me, beach?*

I grinned. *No. I am legit on a plane to Texas right now. Getting ready to land.*

Max's only response was: *Holy ship.*

>———◄

A dark-haired woman in an all-white power suit met Libby and me the second we stepped past security. "Ms. Grambs." She nodded to me, then to Libby, as she added on a second identical greeting. "Ms. Grambs." She turned, expecting us to follow. To my chagrin, we both did. "I'm Alisa Ortega," she said, "from McNamara, Ortega, and Jones." Another pause, then she cast a sideways glance at me. "You are a very hard young woman to get ahold of."

I shrugged. "I live in my car."

"She doesn't *live* there," Libby said quickly. "Tell her you don't."

"We're so glad you could make it." Alisa Ortega, from McNamara, Ortega, and Jones, didn't wait for me to tell her anything. I had the sense that my half of this conversation was perfunctory. "During your time in Texas, you're to consider yourselves guests of the Hawthorne family. I'll be your liaison to the firm. Anything you need while you're here, come to me."

Don't lawyers bill by the hour? I thought. How much was this personal pickup costing the Hawthorne family? I didn't even consider the option that this woman might not be a lawyer. She looked to be in her late twenties. Talking to her gave me the same feeling as talking to Grayson Hawthorne. She was *someone.*

"*Is* there anything I can do for you?" Alisa Ortega asked, striding toward an automatic door, her pace not slowing at all when it seemed like the door might not open in time.

I waited until I'd made sure she wasn't going to run smack into the glass before I replied. "How about some information?"

"You'll have to be a bit more specific."

"Do you know what's in the will?" I asked.

"I do not." She gestured to a black sedan idling near the curb. She opened the back door for me. I slid in, and Libby followed suit. Alisa sat in the front passenger seat. The driver's seat was already occupied. I tried to see the driver but couldn't make out much of his face.

"You'll find out what's in the will soon enough," Alisa said, the words as crisp and neat as that dare-the-devil-to-ruin-it white suit. "We all will. The reading is scheduled for shortly after your arrival at Hawthorne House."

Not *the Hawthornes' house*. Just *Hawthorne House*, like it was some kind of English manor, complete with a name.

"Is that where we'll be staying?" Libby asked. "Hawthorne House?"

Our return tickets had been booked for tomorrow. We'd packed for an overnight.

"You'll have your pick of bedrooms," Alisa assured us. "Mr. Hawthorne bought the land the House is built on more than fifty years ago and spent every one of those years adding onto the architectural marvel he built there. I've lost track of the total number of bedrooms, but it's upward of thirty. Hawthorne House is... quite something."

That was the most information we'd gotten out of her yet. I pressed my luck. "I'm guessing Mr. Hawthorne was *quite something*, too?"

"Good guess," Alisa said. She glanced back at me. "Mr. Hawthorne was fond of good guessers."

An eerie feeling washed over me then, almost like a premonition. *Is that why he chose me?*

"How well did you know him?" Libby asked beside me.

"My father has been Tobias Hawthorne's attorney since before I was born." Alisa Ortega wasn't power-talking now. Her voice was soft. "I spent a lot of time at Hawthorne House growing up."

He wasn't just a client to her, I thought. "Do you have any idea why I'm here?" I asked. "Why he'd leave me anything at all?"

"Are you the world-saving type?" Alisa asked, like that was a perfectly ordinary question.

"No?" I guessed.

"Ever had your life ruined by someone with the last name Hawthorne?" Alisa continued.

I stared at her, then managed to answer more confidently this time. "No."

Alisa smiled, but it didn't quite reach her eyes. "Lucky you."

CHAPTER 6

Hawthorne House sat on a hill. Massive. Sprawling. It looked like a castle—more suited to royalty than ranch country. There were a half dozen cars parked out front and one beat-up motorcycle that looked like it should be dismantled and sold for parts.

Alisa eyed the bike. "Looks like Nash made it home."

"Nash?" Libby asked.

"The oldest Hawthorne grandson," Alisa replied, tearing her gaze from the motorcycle and staring up at the castle. "There are four of them total."

Four grandsons. I couldn't keep my mind from going back to the one Hawthorne I'd already met. *Grayson.* The perfectly tailored suit. The silvery gray eyes. The arrogance in the way he'd told me to assume he knew everything.

Alisa gave me a knowing look. "Take it from someone who's both been there and done that—never lose your heart to a Hawthorne."

"Don't worry," I told her, as annoyed with her assumption as I was with the fact that she'd been able to see any trace of my thoughts on my face. "I keep mine under lock and key."

The foyer was bigger than some houses—easily a thousand square feet, like the person who had built it was afraid that the entryway might have to double as a place to host balls. Stone archways lined the foyer on either side, and the room stretched up two stories to an ornate ceiling, elaborately carved from wood. Even just looking up took my breath away.

"You've arrived." A familiar voice drew my attention back down to earth. "And right on time. I trust there were no problems with your flight?"

Grayson Hawthorne was wearing a different suit now. This one was black—and so were his shirt and his tie.

"*You.*" Alisa greeted him with a steely-eyed look.

"I take it I'm not forgiven for interfering?" Grayson asked.

"You're nineteen," Alisa retorted. "Would it kill you to act like it?"

"It might." Grayson flashed his teeth in a smile. "And you're welcome." It took me a second to realize that by *interfering*, Grayson meant coming to fetch me. "Ladies," he said, "may I take your coats?"

"I'll keep mine," I replied, feeling contrary—and like an extra layer between me and the rest of the world couldn't hurt.

"And yours?" Grayson asked Libby smoothly.

Still agog at the foyer, Libby shed her coat and handed it to him. Grayson walked underneath one of the stone arches. On the other side, there was a corridor. Small square panels lined the wall. Grayson laid a hand on one panel and pushed. He turned his hand ninety degrees, pushed in the next panel, and then, in a motion too fast for me to decode, hit at least two others. I heard a *pop*, and a door appeared, separating itself from the rest of the wall as it swung open.

"What the..." I started to say.

Grayson reached in and pulled out a hanger. "Coat closet." That wasn't an explanation. It was a label, like this was any old coat closet in any old house.

Alisa took that as her cue to leave us in Grayson's capable hands, and I tried to summon up a response that wasn't just standing there with my mouth open like a fish. Grayson went to close the closet, but a sound from deep within stopped him.

I heard a *creak*, then a *bam*. There was a shuffling sound back behind the coats, and then a figure in shadow pushed through them and stepped out into the light. A boy, maybe my age, maybe a little younger. He was wearing a suit, but that was where the similarities with Grayson ended. This boy's suit was rumpled, like he'd taken a nap in it—or twenty. The jacket wasn't buttoned. The tie lying around his neck wasn't tied. He was tall but had a baby face—and a mop of dark, curly hair. His eyes were light brown and so was his skin.

"Am I late?" he asked Grayson.

"One might suggest that you direct that query toward your watch."

"Is Jameson here yet?" the dark-haired boy amended his question.

Grayson stiffened. "No."

The other boy grinned. "Then I'm not late!" He looked past Grayson, to Libby and me. "And these must be our guests! How rude of Grayson not to introduce us."

A muscle in Grayson's jaw twitched. "Avery Grambs," he said formally, "and her sister, Libby. Ladies, this is my brother, Alexander." For a moment, it seemed like Grayson might leave it there, but then came the eyebrow arch. "Xander is the baby of the family."

"I'm the handsome one," Xander corrected. "I know what you're thinking. This serious bugger beside me can really fill out an

24

Armani suit. But, I ask you, can he jolt the universe on and up to ten with his smile, like a young Mary Tyler Moore incarnate in the body of a multiracial James Dean?" Xander seemed to have only one mode of speaking: fast. "No," he answered his own question. "No, he cannot."

He finally stopped talking long enough for someone else to speak. "It's nice to meet you," Libby managed.

"Spend a lot of time in coat closets?" I asked.

Xander dusted his hands off on his pants. "Secret passage," he said, then attempted to dust off his pant legs with his hands. "This place is full of them."

CHAPTER 7

My fingers itched to pull out my phone and start taking pictures, but I resisted. Libby had no such compunctions.

"Mademoiselle…" Xander side-stepped to block one of Libby's shots. "May I ask: What are your feelings on roller coasters?"

I thought Libby's eyes might actually pop out of her head. "This place has a roller coaster?"

Xander grinned. "Not exactly." The next thing I knew, the "baby" of the Hawthorne family—who was six foot three if he was an inch—was pulling my sister toward the back of the foyer.

I was dumbfounded. *How can a house "not exactly" have a roller coaster?* Beside me, Grayson snorted. I caught him looking at me and narrowed my eyes. "What?"

"Nothing," Grayson said, the tilt of his lips suggesting otherwise. "It's just…you have a very expressive face."

No. I didn't. Libby was always saying that I was hard to read. My poker face had single-handedly been funding Harry's breakfasts for months. I wasn't expressive.

There was nothing remarkable about my face.

"I apologize for Xander," Grayson commented. "He tends not to buy into such antiquated notions as thinking before one speaks and sitting still for more than three consecutive seconds." He looked down. "He's the best of us, even on his worst days."

"Ms. Ortega said there were four of you." I couldn't help myself. I wanted to know more about this family. About *him*. "Four grandsons, I mean."

"I have three brothers," Grayson told me. "Same mother, different fathers. Our aunt Zara doesn't have any children." He looked past me. "And on the topic of my relations, I feel as though I should issue a second apology, in advance."

"Gray, darling!" A woman swept up to us in a swirl of fabric and motion. Once her flowy shirt had settled around her, I tried to peg her age. Older than thirty, younger than fifty. Beyond that, I couldn't tell. "They're ready for us in the Great Room," she told Grayson. "Or they will be shortly. Where's your brother?"

"Specificity, Mother."

The woman rolled her eyes. "Don't you 'Mother' me, Grayson Hawthorne." She turned to me. "You'd think he was born wearing that suit," she said with the air of someone confiding a great secret, "but Gray was my little streaker. A real free spirit. We couldn't keep clothes on him at all, really, until he was four. Frankly, I didn't even try." She paused and assessed me without bothering to hide what she was doing. "You must be Ava."

"Avery," Grayson corrected. If he felt any embarrassment about his purported past as a toddler nudist, he didn't show it. "Her name is Avery, Mother."

The woman sighed but also smiled, like it was impossible for her to look at her son and not find herself utterly delighted in his presence. "I always swore my children would call me by my first name," she told me. "I'd raise them as my equals, you know? But then, I always imagined having girls. Four boys later..." She gave the world's most elegant shrug.

Objectively, Grayson's mother was over the top. But subjectively? She was infectious.

"Do you mind if I ask, dear, when is your birthday?"

The question took me by surprise. I had a mouth. It was fully functioning. But I couldn't keep up with her enough to reply. She put a hand on my cheek. "Scorpio? Or Capricorn? Not a Pisces, clearly—"

"Mother," Grayson said, and then he corrected himself. "*Skye.*"

It took me a moment to realize that must be her first name, and that he'd used it to humor her in an attempt to get her to stop astrologically cross-examining me.

"Grayson's a good boy," Skye told me. "Too good." Then she winked at me. "We'll talk."

"I doubt Ms. Grambs plans to stay long enough for a fireside chat—or a tarot reading." A second woman, Skye's age or a little older, inserted herself into our conversation. If Skye was flowy fabric and oversharing, this woman was pencil-skirts and pearls.

"I'm Zara Hawthorne-Calligaris." She eyed me, the expression on her face as austere as her name. "Do you mind if I ask—how did you know my father?"

Silence descended on the cavernous foyer. I swallowed. "I didn't."

Beside me, I could feel Grayson staring again. After a small eternity, Zara offered me a tight smile. "Well, we appreciate your presence. It's been a trying time these past few weeks, as I'm sure you can imagine."

These past few weeks, I filled in, *when no one could get ahold of me.*

"Zara?" A man with slicked-back hair interrupted us, slipping an arm around her waist. "Mr. Ortega would like a word." The man, who I took to be Zara's husband, didn't spare so much as a glance for me.

Skye made up for it—and then some. "My sister 'has words' with people," she commented. "I have conversations. Lovely conversations. Quite frankly, that's how I ended up with four sons. Wonderful, *intimate* conversations with four fascinating men..."

"I will pay you to stop right there," Grayson said, a pained expression on his face.

Skye patted her son's cheek. "Bribe. Threaten. Buy out. You couldn't be more Hawthorne, darling, if you tried." She gave me a knowing smile. "That's why we call him the heir apparent."

There was something in Skye's voice, something about Grayson's expression when his mother said the phrase *heir apparent,* that made me think I had greatly underestimated just how much the Hawthorne family wanted that will read.

They don't know what's in the will, either. I suddenly felt like I'd stepped into an arena, utterly unaware of the rules of the game.

"Now," Skye said, looping one arm around me and one around Grayson, "why don't we make our way to the Great Room?"

CHAPTER 8

The Great Room was two-thirds the size of the foyer. An enormous stone fireplace stood at the front. There were gargoyles carved into the sides of the fireplace. Literal gargoyles.

Grayson deposited Libby and me into wingback chairs and then excused himself to the front of the room, where three older gentlemen in suits stood, talking to Zara and her husband.

The lawyers, I realized. After another few minutes, Alisa joined them, and I took stock of the other occupants of the room. A White couple, older, in their sixties at least. A Black man, forties, with a military bearing, who stood with his back to a wall and maintained a clear line of sight to both exits. Xander, with what was clearly another Hawthorne brother by his side. This one was older—midtwenties. He needed a haircut and had paired his suit with cowboy boots that, like the motorcycle outside, had seen better days.

Nash, I thought, recalling the name that Alisa had provided.

Finally, an ancient woman joined the fray. Nash offered her an arm, but she took Xander's instead. He led her straight to Libby and me. "This is Nan," he told us. "The woman. The legend."

"Get on with you." She swatted his arm. "I'm this rascal's great-grandmother." Nan settled, with no small difficulty, into the open seat beside me. "Older than dirt and twice as mean."

"She's a softy," Xander assured me cheerfully. "And I'm her favorite."

"You are *not* my favorite," Nan grumbled.

"I'm everyone's favorite!" Xander grinned.

"Far too much like that incorrigible grandfather of yours," Nan grunted. She closed her eyes, and I saw her hands shake slightly. "Awful man." There was a tenderness there.

"Was Mr. Hawthorne your son?" Libby asked gently. She worked with the elderly, and she was a good listener.

Nan welcomed the opportunity to snort again. "Son-in-law."

"He was also her favorite," Xander clarified. There was something poignant in the way he said it. This wasn't a funeral. They must have laid the man to rest weeks earlier, but I knew grief, could feel it—could practically *smell* it.

"Are you all right, Ave?" Libby asked beside me. I thought back to Grayson telling me how expressive my face was.

Better to think about Grayson Hawthorne than funerals and grieving.

"I'm fine," I told Libby. But I wasn't. Even after two years, missing my mom could hit me like a tsunami. "I'm going to step outside," I said, forcing a smile. "I just need some air."

Zara's husband stopped me on my way out. "Where are you going? We're about to start." He locked a hand over my elbow.

I wrenched my arm out of his grasp. I didn't care who these people were. No one got to lay hands on me. "I was told there are four Hawthorne grandsons," I said, my voice steely. "By my count, you're still down by one. I'll be back in a minute. You won't even notice I'm gone."

I ended up in the backyard instead of the front—if you could even call it a yard. The grounds were immaculately kept. There was a fountain. A statue garden. A greenhouse. And stretching into the distance, as far as I could see, *land*. Some of it was treed. Some was open. But it was easy enough, standing there and looking out, to imagine that a person who walked off to the horizon might never make their way back.

"If *yes* is *no* and *once* is *never*, then how many sides does a triangle have?" The question came from above me. I looked up and saw a boy sitting on the edge of a balcony overhead, balanced precariously on a wrought-iron railing. *Drunk.*

"You're going to fall," I told him.

He smirked. "An interesting proposition."

"That wasn't a proposition," I said.

He offered me a lazy grin. "There's no shame in propositioning a Hawthorne." He had hair darker than Grayson's and lighter than Xander's. He wasn't wearing a shirt.

Always a good decision in the middle of winter, I thought acerbically, but I couldn't keep my gaze from traveling downward from his face. His torso was lean, his stomach defined. He had a long, thin scar that ran from collarbone to hip.

"You must be Mystery Girl," he said.

"I'm Avery," I corrected. I'd come out here to get away from the Hawthornes and their grief. There wasn't a trace of a care on this boy's face, like life was one grand lark. Like he wasn't grieving just as much as the people inside were.

"Whatever you say, M.G.," he retorted. "Can I call you M.G., Mystery Girl?"

I crossed my arms. "No."

He brought his feet up to the railing and stood. He wobbled, and I had a moment of chilling prescience. *He's grieving, and he's too high up.* I hadn't allowed myself to self-destruct when my mom died. That didn't mean I hadn't felt the call.

He shifted his weight to one foot and held the other out.

"Don't!" Before I could say anything else, the boy twisted and grabbed the railing with his hands, holding himself vertical, feet in the air. I could see the muscles in his back tensing, rippling over his shoulder blades, as he lowered himself... and dropped.

He landed right beside me. "You shouldn't be out here, M.G."

I wasn't the shirtless one who'd just jumped off a balcony. "Neither should you."

I wondered if he could tell how fast my heart was beating. I wondered if his was racing at all.

"If I do what I should no more often than I say what I shouldn't"—his lips twisted—"then what does that make me?"

Jameson Hawthorne, I thought. Up close, I could make out the color of his eyes: a dark, fathomless green.

"What," he repeated intently, "does that make me?"

I stopped looking at his eyes. And his abs. And his haphazardly gelled hair. "Drunk," I said, and then, because I could sense an annoying comeback coming, I added two more words. "And two."

"What?" Jameson Hawthorne said.

"The answer to your first riddle," I told him. "If *yes* is *no* and *once* is *never*, then the number of sides a triangle has... is... *two.*" I drew out my reply, not bothering to explain how I'd arrived at my answer.

"Touché, M.G." Jameson ambled past me, brushing his bare arm lightly over mine as he did. "Touché."

CHAPTER 9

I stayed out back a few minutes longer. Nothing about this day felt real. And tomorrow, I'd go back to Connecticut, a little richer, hopefully, and with a story to tell, and I'd probably never see any of the Hawthornes again.

I'd never have a view like *this* again.

By the time I returned to the Great Room, Jameson Hawthorne had miraculously managed to find a shirt—and a suit jacket. He smiled in my direction and gave a little salute. Beside him, Grayson stiffened, his jaw muscles tensing.

"Now that everyone is here," one of the lawyers said, "let's get started."

The three lawyers stood in triangle formation. The one who'd spoken shared Alisa's dark hair, brown skin, and self-assured expression. I assumed he was the Ortega in McNamara, Ortega, and Jones. The other two—presumably Jones and McNamara—stood to either side.

Since when does it take four lawyers to read a will? I thought.

"You are here," Mr. Ortega said, projecting his voice to the corners of the room, "to hear the last will and testament of Tobias

Tattersall Hawthorne. Per Mr. Hawthorne's instructions, my colleagues will now distribute letters he has left for each of you."

The other men began to make the rounds of the room, handing out envelopes one by one.

"You may open these letters when the reading is concluded."

I was handed an envelope. My full name was written in calligraphy on the front. Beside me, Libby looked up at the lawyer, but he passed over her and went on delivering envelopes to the other occupants of the room.

"Mr. Hawthorne stipulated that all of the following individuals must be physically present for the reading of this will: Skye Hawthorne, Zara Hawthorne-Calligaris, Nash Hawthorne, Grayson Hawthorne, Jameson Hawthorne, Alexander Hawthorne, and Ms. Avery Kylie Grambs of New Castle, Connecticut."

I felt about as conspicuous as I would have if I'd looked down and discovered that I wasn't wearing clothes.

"Since you are all here," Mr. Ortega continued, "we may begin."

Beside me, Libby slipped her hand into mine.

"I, Tobias Tattersall Hawthorne," Mr. Ortega read, "being of sound body and mind, decree that my worldly possessions, including all monetary and physical assets, be disposed of as follows.

"To Andrew and Lottie Laughlin, for years of loyal service, I bequeath a sum of one hundred thousand dollars apiece, with lifelong, rent-free tenancy granted in Wayback Cottage, located on the western border of my Texas estate."

The older couple I'd seen earlier leaned into each other. All I could think was: ONE HUNDRED THOUSAND DOLLARS. The Laughlins' presence wasn't mandatory for the reading of the will, and they'd just been given one hundred thousand dollars. Apiece!

I tried very hard to remember how to breathe.

"To John Oren, head of my security detail, who has saved my life more times and in more ways than I can count, I leave the contents of my toolbox, held currently in the offices of McNamara, Ortega, and Jones, as well as a sum of three hundred thousand dollars."

Tobias Hawthorne knew these people, I told myself, heart thumping. *They worked for him. They* mattered *to him. I'm nothing.*

"To my mother-in-law, Pearl O'Day, I leave an annuity of one hundred thousand dollars a year, plus a trust for medical expenses as set forth in the appendix. All jewelry belonging to my late wife, Alice O'Day Hawthorne, shall pass to her mother upon my death, to be distributed as she sees fit upon hers."

Nan harrumphed. "Don't you go getting any ideas," she ordered the room at large. "I'm going to outlive you all."

Mr. Ortega smiled, but then that smile faltered. "To..." He paused and then tried again. "To my daughters, Zara Hawthorne-Calligaris and Skye Hawthorne, I leave the funds necessary to pay off all debts accrued as of the date and time of my death." Mr. Ortega paused again, his lips pushing themselves together. The other two lawyers stared straight ahead, avoiding looking at any member of the Hawthorne family directly.

"Additionally, I leave to Skye my compass, may she always know true north, and to Zara, I leave my wedding ring, may she love as wholly and steadfastly as I loved her mother."

Another pause, more painful than the last.

"Go on." That came from Zara's husband.

"To each of my daughters," Mr. Ortega read slowly, "beyond that already stated, I leave a one-time inheritance of fifty thousand dollars."

Fifty thousand dollars? I'd no sooner thought those words than Zara's husband echoed them out loud, irate. *Tobias Hawthorne left his daughters less than he left his security detail.*

Suddenly, Skye's reference to Grayson as the *heir apparent* took on a whole new meaning.

"You did this." Zara turned toward Skye. She didn't raise her voice, but it was deadly all the same.

"Me?" Skye said, indignant.

"Daddy was never the same after Toby died," Zara continued.

"Disappeared," Skye corrected.

"God, listen to you!" Zara lost her hold on her tone. "You got in his head, didn't you, Skye? Batted your eyelashes and convinced him to bypass us and leave everything to your—"

"*Sons.*" Skye's voice was crisp. "The word you're looking for is *sons.*"

"The word she's looking for is *bastards.*" Nash Hawthorne had the thickest Texas accent of anyone in the room. "Not like we haven't heard it before."

"If I'd had a son..." Zara's voice caught.

"But you didn't." Skye let that sink in. "Did you, Zara?"

"*Enough.*" Zara's husband stepped in. "We will sort this out."

"I'm afraid there's nothing to be sorted." Mr. Ortega reentered the fray. "You will find the will is ironclad, with significant disincentives to any who might be tempted to challenge it."

I translated that to mean, roughly, *shut up and sit down.*

"Now, if I may continue..." Mr. Ortega looked back down at the will in his hands. "To my grandsons, Nash Westbrook Hawthorne, Grayson Davenport Hawthorne, Jameson Winchester Hawthorne, and Alexander Blackwood Hawthorne, I leave..."

"Everything," Zara muttered bitterly.

Mr. Ortega spoke over her. "Two hundred and fifty thousand dollars apiece, payable on their twenty-fifth birthdays, until such time to be managed by Alisa Ortega, trustee."

"What?" Alisa sounded shocked. "I mean...*what?*"

"The hell," Nash told her pleasantly. "The phrase you're looking for, darlin', is *what the hell?*"

Tobias Hawthorne hadn't left everything to his grandsons. Given the scope of his fortune, he'd left them a pittance.

"What is going on here?" Grayson asked, each word deadly and precise.

Tobias Hawthorne didn't leave everything to his grandsons. He didn't leave everything to his daughters. My brain ground to a halt right there. My ears rang.

"Please, everyone," Mr. Ortega held up a hand. "Allow me to finish."

Forty-six point two billion dollars, I thought, my heart attacking my rib cage and my mouth sandpaper-dry. *Tobias Hawthorne was worth forty-six point two billion dollars, and he left his grandsons a million dollars, combined. A hundred thousand total to his daughters. Another half million to his servants, an annuity for Nan...*

The math in this equation did not add up. It *couldn't* add up.

One by one, the other occupants of the room turned to stare at me.

"The remainder of my estate," Mr. Ortega read, "including all properties, monetary assets, and worldly possessions not otherwise specified, I leave to Avery Kylie Grambs."

CHAPTER 10

This is not happening.
This cannot be happening.
I'm dreaming.
I'm delusional.

"He left everything to *her?*" Skye's voice was shrill enough to break through my stupor. "Why?" Gone was the woman who'd mused about my astrological sign and regaled me with tales of her sons and lovers. This Skye looked like she could kill someone. Literally.

"Who the hell is she?" Zara's voice was knife-edged and clear as a bell.

"There must be some mistake." Grayson spoke like a person used to dealing with mistakes. *Bribe, threaten, buy out,* I thought. What would the "heir apparent" do to me? *This is not happening.* I felt that with every beat of my heart, every breath in, every breath out. *This cannot be happening.*

"He's right." My words came out in a whisper, lost to voices being raised all around me. I tried again, louder. "Grayson's right." Heads started turning in my direction. "There must be some mistake." My voice was hoarse. I felt like I'd just jumped out of a plane. Like I was skydiving and waiting for my chute to open.

This is not real. It can't be.

"*Avery.*" Libby nudged me in the ribs, clearly telegraphing that I should shut up and stop talking about *mistakes.*

But there was no way. There had to have been some kind of mix-up. A man I'd never met hadn't just left me a multi-billion-dollar fortune. Things like that didn't happen, period.

"You see?" Skye latched on to what I'd said. "Even Ava agrees this is ridiculous."

This time, I was pretty sure she'd gotten my name wrong on purpose. *The remainder of my estate, including all properties, monetary assets, and worldly possessions not otherwise specified, I leave to Avery Kylie Grambs.* Skye Hawthorne knew my name now.

They all did.

"I assure you, there is no mistake." Mr. Ortega met my gaze, then turned his attention to the others. "And I assure the rest of you, Tobias Hawthorne's last will and testament is utterly unbreakable. Since the majority of the remaining details concern only Avery, we'll cease with the dramatics. But let me make one thing very clear: Per the terms of the will, any heir who challenges Avery's inheritance will forfeit their share of the estate entirely."

Avery's inheritance. I felt dizzy, almost nauseous. It was like someone had snapped their fingers and rewritten the laws of physics, like the coefficient of gravity had changed, and my body was ill-suited to coping. The world was spinning off its axis.

"No will is that ironclad," Zara's husband said, his voice acidic. "Not when there's this kind of money at stake."

"Spoken," Nash Hawthorne interjected, "like someone who didn't really know the old man."

"Traps upon traps," Jameson murmured. "And riddles upon riddles." I could feel his dark green eyes on mine.

"I think you should leave," Grayson told me curtly. Not a request. An order.

"Technically…" Alisa Ortega sounded like she'd just swallowed arsenic. "It's her house."

Clearly, she really hadn't known what was in the will. She'd been kept in the dark, just like the family. *How could Tobias Hawthorne blindside them like this? What kind of person does that to their own flesh and blood?*

"I don't understand," I said out loud, dizzy and numb, because none of this made any kind of sense.

"My daughter is correct." Mr. Ortega kept his tone neutral. "You own it all, Ms. Grambs. Not just the fortune, but all of Mr. Hawthorne's properties, including Hawthorne House. Per the terms of your inheritance, which I will gladly go over with you, the current occupants have been granted tenancy unless—and until—they give you cause for removal." He let those words hang in the air. "Under no circumstances," he continued gravely, his words rife with warning, "can those tenants attempt to remove you."

The room was suddenly silent and still. *They're going to kill me. Someone in this room is actually going to kill me.* The man I'd pegged as former military strode to stand between me and Tobias Hawthorne's family. He said nothing, crossing his arms over his chest, keeping me behind him and the rest of them in his sight.

"Oren!" Zara sounded shocked. "You work for this family."

"I worked for Mr. Hawthorne." John Oren paused and held up a piece of paper. It took me a moment to realize that it was his letter. "It was his last request that I continue in the employment of Ms. Avery Kylie Grambs." He glanced at me. "Security. You'll need it."

"And not just to protect you from us!" Xander added to my left.

"Take a step back, please," Oren ordered.

Xander held his hands up. "Peace," he declared. "I make dire predictions in peace!"

"Xan's right." Jameson smiled, like this was all a game. "The entire world's going to want a piece of you, Mystery Girl. This has *story of the century* written all over it."

Story of the century. My brain kicked back into gear because there was every indication that this wasn't a joke. I wasn't delusional. I wasn't dreaming.

I was an heiress.

CHAPTER 11

I bolted. The next thing I knew, I was outside. The front door of Hawthorne House slammed behind me. Cool air hit my face. I was almost sure I was breathing, but my entire body felt distant and numb. Was this what shock felt like?

"Avery!" Libby burst out of the house after me. "Are you okay?" She studied me, concerned. "Also: Are you insane? When someone gives you money, you don't try to give it back!"

"*You* do," I pointed out, the roar in my brain so loud that I couldn't hear myself think. "Every time I try to give you my tips."

"We're not talking tips here!" Libby's blue hair was falling out of her ponytail. "We're talking *millions*."

Billions, I corrected silently, but my mouth flat-out refused to say the word.

"Ave." Libby put a hand on my shoulder. "Think about what this means. You'll never have to worry about money again. You can buy whatever you want, do whatever you want. Those postcards you kept of your mom's?" She leaned forward, touching her forehead against mine. "You can go anywhere. Imagine the possibilities."

I did, even though this felt like a cruel joke, like the universe's way of tricking me into wanting things that girls like me were never meant to—

The massive front door of Hawthorne House slammed open. I jumped back, and Nash Hawthorne stepped out. Even wearing a suit, he looked every inch the cowboy, ready to meet a rival at high noon.

I braced myself. *Billions.* Wars had been fought over less.

"Relax, kid." Nash's Texas drawl was slow and smooth, like whiskey. "I don't want the money. Never have. Far as I'm concerned, this is the universe having a bit of fun with folks who probably deserve it."

The oldest Hawthorne brother's gaze drifted from me to Libby. He was tall, muscular, and suntanned. She was tiny and slight, her pale skin standing in stark contrast to her dark lipstick and neon hair. The two of them looked like they didn't belong within ten feet of each other, and yet, there he was, slow-smiling at her.

"You take care, darlin'," Nash told my sister. He ambled toward his motorcycle, then put on his helmet, and a moment later, he was gone.

Libby stared after the motorcycle. "I take back what I said about Grayson. Maybe *he's* God."

Right now, we had bigger issues than which of the Hawthorne brothers was divine. "We can't stay here, Libby. I doubt the rest of the family is as blasé about the will as Nash is. We need to go."

"I'm going with you," a deep voice said. I turned. John Oren stood next to the front door. I hadn't heard him open it.

"I don't need security," I told him. "I just need to get out of here."

"You'll need security for the rest of your life." He was so matter-of-fact, I couldn't even begin to argue. "But look on the bright side. . . ." He nodded to the car that had picked us up at the airport. "I also drive."

I asked Oren to take us to a motel. Instead, he drove us to the fanciest hotel I'd ever seen, and he must have taken the scenic route, because Alisa Ortega was waiting for us in the lobby.

"I've had a chance to read the will in full." Apparently, that was her version of *hello*. "I brought a copy for you. I suggest we retire to your rooms and go over the details."

"Our rooms?" I repeated. The doormen were wearing tuxedos. There were *six* chandeliers in the lobby. Nearby, a woman was playing a five-foot-tall harp. "We can't afford rooms here."

Alisa gave me an almost pitying look. "Oh, honey," she said, then recovered her professionalism. "You own this hotel."

I ... what? Libby and I were getting "who let the rabble in?" looks from other patrons just standing in the lobby. I could not possibly *own this hotel.*

"Besides which," Alisa continued, "the will is now in probate. It may be some time before the money and properties are out of escrow, but in the meantime, McNamara, Ortega, and Jones will be picking up the tab for anything you need."

Libby frowned, crinkling her brow. "Is that a thing that law firms do?"

"You have probably gathered that Mr. Hawthorne was one of our most important clients," Alisa said delicately. "It would be more precise to say that he was our *only* client. And now ..."

"Now," I said, the truth sinking in, "that client is me."

It took me almost an hour to read and reread and re-reread the will. Tobias Hawthorne had put only one condition on my inheritance.

"You're to live in Hawthorne House for one year, commencing

45

no more than three days from now." Alisa had made that point at least twice already, but I couldn't get my brain to accept it.

"The only string attached to my inheriting billions of dollars is that I *must* move into a mansion."

"Correct."

"A mansion where a large number of the people who were expecting to inherit this money still live. And I can't kick them out."

"Barring extraordinary circumstances, also correct. If it's any consolation, it *is* a very large house."

"And if I refuse?" I asked. "Or if the Hawthorne family has me killed?"

"No one is going to have you killed," Alisa said calmly.

"I know you grew up around these people and everything," Libby told Alisa, trying to be diplomatic, "but they are totally, one hundred percent going to go all Lizzie Borden on my sister."

"Really would prefer not to be ax-murdered," I emphasized.

"Risk assessment: low," Oren rumbled. "At least insofar as axes are concerned."

It took me a second to figure out that he was joking. "This is serious!"

"Believe me," he returned, "I know. But I also know the Hawthorne family. The boys would never harm a woman, and the women will come for you in the courtroom, no axes involved."

"Besides," Alisa added, "in the state of Texas, if an heir dies while a will is in probate, the inheritance doesn't revert to the original estate—it becomes part of the *heir's* estate."

I have an estate? I thought dully. "And if I refuse to move in with them?" I asked again, a giant ball in my throat.

"She's not going to refuse." Libby shot laser eyes in my direction.

"If you fail to move into Hawthorne House in three days' time," Alisa told me, "your portion of the estate will be dispersed to charity."

"Not to Tobias Hawthorne's family?" I asked.

"No." Alisa's neutral mask slipped slightly. She'd known the Hawthornes for years. She might work for me now, but she couldn't be happy about that.

Could she?

"Your father wrote the will, right?" I said, trying to wrap my head around the insane situation I was in.

"In consultation with the other partners at the firm," Alisa confirmed.

"Did he tell you..." I tried to find a better way to phrase what I wanted to ask, then gave up. "Did he tell you *why*?"

Why had Tobias Hawthorne disinherited his family? Why leave everything to *me*?

"I don't think my father knows why," Alisa said. She peered at me, the neutral mask slipping once more. "Do you?"

CHAPTER 12

Mother-faxing elf," Max breathed. *"Goat-dram, mother-faxing elf."* She lowered her voice to a whisper and let out an actual expletive. It was past midnight for me, and two hours earlier for her. I half expected Mrs. Liu to sweep in and snatch the phone away, but nothing happened.

"How?" Max demanded. "Why?"

I looked down at the letter in my lap. Tobias Hawthorne had left me an explanation, but in the hours since the will was read, I hadn't been able to bring myself to open the envelope. I was alone, sitting in the dark on the balcony of the penthouse suite of a *hotel that I owned*, wearing a plush, floor-length robe that probably cost more than my car—and I was frozen.

"Maybe," Max said thoughtfully, "you were switched at birth." Max watched a lot of television and had what could probably have been classified as a book addiction. "Maybe your mother saved his life, years ago. Maybe he owes his entire fortune to your great-great-grandfather. *Maybe you were selected via an advanced computer algorithm that is poised to develop artificial intelligence any day!*"

"Maxine." I snorted. Somehow, that was enough to allow me to say the exact words I'd been trying not to think. "Maybe my father isn't really my father."

That was the most rational explanation, wasn't it? Maybe Tobias Hawthorne *hadn't* disinherited his family for a stranger. Maybe I *was* family.

I have a secret.... I pictured my mom in my mind. How many times had I heard her say those exact words?

"You okay?" Max asked on the other end of the line.

I looked down at the envelope, at my name in calligraphy on the front. I swallowed. "Tobias Hawthorne left me a letter."

"And you haven't opened it yet?" Max said. "Avery, for fox sakes—"

"Maxine!" Even over the phone, I could hear Max's mom in the background.

"Fox, Mama. I said *fox*. As in 'for the sake of foxes and their furry little tails...'" There was a brief pause and then: "Avery? I have to go."

My stomach muscles tightened. "Talk soon?"

"Very soon," Max promised. "And in the meantime: Open. The. Letter."

She hung up. I hung up. I put my thumb underneath the lip of the envelope—but a knock at the door saved me from following through.

Back in the suite, I found Oren positioned at the door. "Who is it?" I asked him.

"Grayson Hawthorne," Oren replied. I stared at the door, and Oren elaborated. "If my men considered him a threat, he never would have made it to our floor. I trust Grayson. But if you don't want to see him..."

"No," I said. *What am I doing?* It was late, and I doubted

American royalty took kindly to being dethroned. But there was something about the way Grayson had looked at me, from the first time we'd met....

"Open the door," I told Oren. He did, and then he stepped back.

"Aren't you going to invite me in?" Grayson wasn't the *heir* anymore, but you wouldn't have known it from his tone.

"You shouldn't be here," I told him, pulling my robe tighter around me.

"I've spent the past hour telling myself much the same thing, and yet, here I am." His eyes were pools of gray, his hair unkempt, like I wasn't the only one who hadn't been able to sleep. He'd lost everything today.

"Grayson—" I said.

"I don't know how you did this." He cut me off, his voice dangerous and soft. "I don't know what hold you had over my grandfather, or what kind of con you're running here."

"I'm not—"

"I'm talking right now, Ms. Grambs." He placed his hand flat on the door. I'd been wrong about his eyes. They weren't pools. They were ice. "I haven't a clue how you pulled this off, but I will find out. I see you now. I know what you are and what you're capable of, and there is *nothing* I wouldn't do to protect my family. Whatever game you're playing here, no matter how long this con—I will find the truth, and God help you when I do."

Oren stepped into my peripheral vision, but I didn't wait for him to act. I pushed the door forward, hard enough to send Grayson back, then slammed it closed. Heart pounding, I waited for him to knock again, to shout through the door. *Nothing*. Slowly, my head bowed, my eyes drawn like magnet to metal by the envelope in my hands.

With one last glance at Oren, I retreated to my bedroom. *Open*.

The. Letter. This time, I did it, removing a card from the envelope. The body of the message was only two words long. I stared at the page, reading the salutation, the message, and the signature, over and over again.

> *Dearest Avery,*
> *I'm sorry.*
> *—T. T. H.*

CHAPTER 13

Sorry? *Sorry for what?* The question was still ringing in my mind the next morning. For once in my life, I'd slept late. I found Oren and Alisa in our suite's kitchen talking softly.

Too softly for me to hear.

"Avery." Oren noticed me first. I wondered if he'd told Alisa about Grayson. "There are some security protocols I'd like to go over with you."

Like not opening doors to Grayson Hawthorne?

"You're a target now," Alisa told me crisply.

Given that she'd been so insistent that the Hawthornes weren't a threat, I had to ask: "A target for what?"

"Paparazzi, of course. The firm is keeping a lid on the story for the time being, but that won't last, and there are other concerns."

"Kidnapping." Oren didn't put any particular emphasis on that word. "Stalking. People will make threats—they always do. You're young, and you're female, and that will make it worse. With your sister's permission, I'll arrange a detail for her as well, as soon as she gets back."

Kidnapping. Stalking. Threats. I couldn't even wrap my mind around the words. "Where is Libby?" I asked, since he'd made reference to her coming *back*.

"On a plane," Alisa answered. "Specifically, your plane."

"I have a plane?" I was *never* going to get used to this.

"You have several," Alisa told me. "And a helicopter, I believe, but that's neither here nor there. Your sister is en route to retrieve your things, as well as her own. Given the deadline for your move into Hawthorne House—and the stakes—we thought it best that you remain here. Ideally, we'll have you moved in no later than tonight."

"The second this news gets out," Oren said seriously, "you will be on the cover of every newspaper. You'll be the leading story on every newscast, the number one trending topic on all social media. To some people, you'll be Cinderella. To others, Marie Antoinette."

Some people would want to be me. Some people would hate me to the depths of their souls. For the first time, I noticed the gun holstered to Oren's side.

"It's best you sit tight," Oren said evenly. "Your sister should be back tonight."

⟫———————⟪

For the rest of the morning, Alisa and I played what I had mentally termed The Uprooting Avery's Life In An Instant game. I quit my job. Alisa took care of withdrawing me from school.

"What about my car?" I asked.

"Oren will be driving you for the foreseeable future, but we can have your vehicle shipped, if you would like," Alisa offered. "Or you can pick out a new car for personal use."

For all the emphasis she put on that, you would have thought she was talking about buying gum at the supermarket.

"Do you prefer sedans or SUVs?" she queried, holding her phone in a way that suggested she was fully capable of ordering a car with a mere click of a button. "Any color preference?"

"You're going to have to excuse me for a second," I told her. I ducked back into my bedroom. The bed was piled ridiculously high with pillows. I climbed up on the bed, let myself fall back on the mountain of pillows, and pulled out my phone.

Texting, calling, and DM-ing Max all led to the same result: nothing. She had *definitely* had her phone confiscated—and possibly her laptop, which meant that she couldn't advise me on the appropriate response when one's lawyer started talking about ordering a car like it was a *foxing* pizza.

This is unreal. Less than twenty-four hours earlier, I'd been sleeping in a parking lot. The closest I'd come to splurging was the occasional breakfast sandwich.

Breakfast sandwich, I thought. *Harry.* I sat up in bed. "Alisa?" I called. "If I didn't want a new car, if I wanted to spend that money on something else—could I?"

➤━━━━━━━━━━◄

Bankrolling a place for Harry to stay—and getting him to accept it—wouldn't be easy, but Alisa told me to consider it handled. That was the world I lived in now. All I had to do was speak, and it was *handled*.

This wouldn't last. It couldn't. Sooner or later, someone would figure out that this was some kind of screwup. *So I might as well enjoy it while it lasts.*

That was the number one thought on my mind when we went to pick up Libby. As my sister stepped out of *my* private jet. I wondered if Alisa could get her into the Sorbonne. Or buy her a little cupcake shop. Or—

"Libby." Every thought in my head came screeching to a halt

the moment I saw her face. Her right eye was bruised and swollen nearly shut.

Libby swallowed but didn't avert her eyes. "If you say 'I told you so,' I will make butterscotch cupcakes and guilt you into eating them every day."

"Is there a problem I should know about?" Alisa asked Libby, her voice deceptively calm as she eyed the bruise.

"Avery hates butterscotch," Libby said, like that was the problem.

"Alisa," I gritted out, "does your law firm have a hit man on retainer?"

"No." Alisa kept her tone strictly professional. "But I'm very resourceful. I could make some inquiries."

"I legitimately cannot tell if you are joking," Libby said, and then she turned to me. "I don't want to talk about it. And I'm fine."

"But—"

"I'm fine."

I managed to keep my mouth shut, and all of us managed to make it back to the hotel. The plan was to finish up a few final arrangements and leave immediately for Hawthorne House.

Things did not go exactly according to plan.

"We have a problem." Oren didn't sound overly bothered, but Alisa immediately put down her phone. Oren nodded to our suite's balcony. Alisa stepped outside, looked down, and swore.

I pushed past Oren and went out on the balcony to see what was going on. Down below, outside the hotel's entrance, hotel security guards were struggling with what appeared to be a mob. It wasn't until a flash went off that I realized what that mob was.

Paparazzi.

And just like that, every camera was pointed up at the balcony. At me.

CHAPTER 14

I thought you said your firm had this locked down." Oren gave Alisa a look. She scowled back at him, made three phone calls in quick succession—two of them in Spanish—and then turned back to my head of security. "The leak didn't come from us." Her eyes darted toward Libby. "It came from your boyfriend."

Libby's answer was barely more than a whisper. "My ex."

———◆———

"I'm sorry." Libby had apologized at least a dozen times. She'd told Drake everything—about the will, the conditions on my inheritance, where we were staying. *Everything*. I knew her well enough to know why. He would have been angry that she'd taken off. She would have tried to pacify him. And the moment she'd told him about the money, he would have demanded to tag along. He would have started making plans to spend the Hawthorne money. And Libby, God bless her, would have told him that it wasn't theirs to spend, that it wasn't *his*.

He hit her. She left him. He went to the press. And now they were here. A horde descended on us as Oren led me out a side door.

"There she is!" a voice yelled.

"Avery!"

"Avery, over here!"

"Avery, how does it feel to be the richest teenager in America?"

"How does it feel to be the world's youngest billionaire?"

"How did you know Tobias Hawthorne?"

"Is it true that you're Tobias Hawthorne's illegitimate daughter?"

I was shuffled into an SUV. The door closed, dulling the roar of the reporters' questions. Exactly halfway through our drive, I got a text—not from Max. From an unknown number.

I opened it and saw a screenshot of a news headline. *Avery Grambs: Who Is the Hawthorne Heiress?*

A short message accompanied the picture.

Hey, Mystery Girl. You're officially famous.

———◆———

There were more paparazzi outside the gates of Hawthorne House, but once we pulled past them, the rest of the world faded away. There was no welcome party. No Jameson. No Grayson. No Hawthornes of any kind. I reached for the massive front door— locked. Alisa disappeared around the back of the house. When she finally reappeared, there was a pained expression on her face. She handed me a large envelope.

"Legally," she said, "the Hawthorne family is required to pro- vide you with keys. Practically speaking…" She narrowed her eyes. "The Hawthorne family is a pain in the ass."

"That a legal term?" Oren asked dryly.

I ripped open the envelope and found that the Hawthorne family had indeed provided me with keys—somewhere in the neighbor- hood of a hundred of them.

"Any idea which one of these goes to the front door?" I asked. They weren't normal keys. They were oversized and ornately made. They all looked like antiques, and each key was distinct—different designs, different metals, different lengths and sizes.

"You'll figure it out," someone said.

My gaze jerked upward, and I found myself staring at an intercom.

"Cut the games, Jameson," Alisa ordered. "This isn't nearly as cute as you all think it is."

No reply.

"Jameson?" Alisa tried again.

Silence, and then: "I have faith in you, M.G."

The intercom cut off, and Alisa blew out a long, frustrated breath. "God save me from Hawthornes."

"M.G.?" Libby asked, bewildered.

"Mystery Girl," I clarified. "From what I've gathered, that's Jameson Hawthorne's idea of a nickname." I turned my attention to the ring of keys in my hand. The obvious solution was to try them all. Assuming one of these keys opened the front door, I'd get lucky eventually. But luck didn't feel like enough. I was already the luckiest girl in the world.

Some part of me wanted to deserve it.

I flipped through the keys, inspecting the designs on the handles. *An apple. A snake. A pattern of swirls reminiscent of water.* There were keys for each letter of the alphabet, in fancy, old-fashioned script. There were keys with numbers and keys with shapes, one with a mermaid and four different keys featuring eyes.

"Well?" Alisa said abruptly. "Do you want me to make a phone call?"

"No." I turned my attention from the keys to the door. The design was simple, geometric—not a match for anything on any of the keys I'd looked at so far. *That would be too easy,* I thought. *Too simple.* A second later, a parallel thought followed. *Not simple enough.*

I'd learned this much playing chess: The more complicated a

person's strategy seemed, the less likely an opponent was to look for simple answers. If you could keep someone looking at your knight, you could take them with a pawn. *Look past the details. Past the complications.* I shifted my focus from the handles of the keys to the part that actually went into the lock. Though the keys differed in size overall, the lock end was sized similarly from key to key.

Not just sized *similarly,* I realized, looking at two of the keys side by side. The pattern—the mechanism that actually turned the lock—was identical between the two. I moved on to a third key. *The same.* I began working my way through the ring, comparing each key to the next, one by one. *Same. Same. Same.*

There weren't a hundred keys on this ring. The faster I flipped through them, the surer I was. There were two—dozens of copies of the wrong key, dressed up to look different from each other, and then...

"This one." I finally hit a key with a different pattern from the others. The intercom crackled, but if Jameson was still on the other side, he didn't say a word. I moved to put the key in the lock, and adrenaline jolted through my veins when it turned.

Eureka.

"How did you know which key to use?" Libby asked me.

The answer came from the intercom. "Sometimes," Jameson Hawthorne said, sounding strangely contemplative, "things that appear very different on the surface are actually exactly the same at their core."

CHAPTER 15

Welcome home, Avery." Alisa stepped into the foyer and spun to face me. I stopped breathing, just for an instant, as I crossed the threshold. It was like stepping into Buckingham Palace or Hogwarts and being told that it was *yours*.

"Down that corridor," Alisa said, "we have the theater, the music room, conservatory, solarium...." I didn't even know what half of those rooms *were*. "You've seen the Great Room, of course," Alisa continued. "The formal dining is farther down, then the kitchen, the chef's kitchen...."

"There's a chef?" I blurted out.

"There are sushi, Italian, Taiwanese, vegetarian, and pastry chefs on retainer." The voice that said those words was male. I turned to see the older couple from the will's reading standing by the entry to the Great Room. *The Laughlins*, I remembered. "But my wife handles the cooking day-to-day," Mr. Laughlin continued gruffly.

"Mr. Hawthorne was a very private man." Mrs. Laughlin eyed me. "He made do with my cooking most days because he didn't like having any more outsiders poking around in the House than necessary."

There was no doubt in my mind that she was saying *House* with a capital *H*—and even less that she considered me an *outsider*.

"There are dozens of staff on retainer," Alisa explained. "They all receive a full-time wage but work on call."

"If something needs doing, there's someone to do it," Mr. Laughlin said plainly, "and I see that it's done in the most discreet fashion possible. More often than not, you won't even know they're here."

"But I will," Oren stated. "Movement on and off the estate is strictly tracked, and no one makes it past the gates without a deep background check. Construction crews, the housekeeping and gardening staff, every masseuse, chef, stylist, or sommelier—they are all cleared through my team."

Sommelier. Stylist. Chef. Masseuse. My brain worked backward through that list. It was dizzying.

"The gym facilities are down this hall," Alisa said, returning to her tour guide role. "There are full-sized basketball and racquetball courts, a rock climbing wall, bowling alley—"

"A *bowling alley?*" I repeated.

"Only four lanes," Alisa assured me, as if it was perfectly reasonable to have a *small* bowling alley in one's house.

I was still trying to formulate an appropriate response when the front door opened behind me. The day before, Nash Hawthorne had given the impression of someone who was out of here—yet there he was.

"*Motorcycle cowboy,*" Libby whispered in my ear.

Beside me, Alisa stiffened. "If everything's in order here, I should check in with the firm." She reached into her suit pocket and handed me a new phone. "I programmed in my number, Mr. Laughlin's, and Oren's. If you need anything, call."

She left without saying a single word to Nash, and he watched her go.

"You be careful with that one," Mrs. Laughlin advised the eldest Hawthorne brother, once the door had closed. "Hell hath no fury like a woman scorned."

That cemented something for me. *Alisa and Nash.* My lawyer had advised me against losing my heart to a Hawthorne, and when she'd asked me if I'd ever had my life ruined by one of them, and I'd said no, her response had been *lucky you.*

"Don't go convincing yourself Lee-Lee is consortin' with the enemy," Nash told Mrs. Laughlin. "Avery isn't anyone's enemy. There are no enemies here. This is what he wanted."

He. Tobias Hawthorne. Even dead, he was larger than life.

"None of this is Avery's fault," Libby said beside me. "She's just a kid."

Nash swung his attention to my sister, and I could feel her trying to fade into oblivion. Nash peered through her hair to the black eye underneath. "What happened here?" he murmured.

"I'm fine," Libby said, sticking her chin out.

"I can see that," Nash replied softly. "But if you decide you'd like to give me a name? I'd take it."

I could see the effect those words had on Libby. She wasn't used to having anyone but me in her corner.

"Libby." Oren got her attention. "If you've got a moment, I'd like to introduce you to Hector, who will be running point on your detail. Avery, I can personally guarantee that Nash will not ax-murder you or allow you to be ax-murdered by anyone else while I'm gone."

That got a snort from Nash, and I glared at Oren. He didn't have to advertise how little I trusted them! As Libby followed Oren into the bowels of the house, I became keenly aware of the way that the oldest Hawthorne brother watched her go.

"Leave her alone," I told Nash.

"You're protective," Nash commented, "and you seem like you'd fight dirty, and if there's one thing I respect, it's those particular traits in combination."

There was a *crash*, then a *thud* in the distance.

"That," Nash said meditatively, "would be the reason I came back and am not living a pleasantly nomadic existence as we speak."

Another *thud*.

Nash rolled his eyes. "This should be fun." He began striding toward a nearby hall. He looked back over his shoulder. "You might as well tag along, kid. You know what they say about baptisms and fire."

CHAPTER 16

Nash had long legs, so a lazy amble on his part required me to jog to keep up. I looked in each room as we passed, but they were all a blur of art and architecture and natural light. At the end of a long hall, Nash threw open a door. I prepared myself to see evidence of a brawl. Instead, I saw Grayson and Jameson standing on opposite sides of a library that took my breath away.

The room was circular. Shelves stretched up fifteen or twenty feet overhead, and every single one was lined completely with hardcover books. The shelves were made of a deep, rich wood. Spread across the room, four wrought-iron staircases spiraled toward the upper shelves, like the points on a compass. In the library's center, there was a massive tree stump, easily ten feet across. Even from a distance, I could see the rings marking the tree's age.

It took me a moment to realize that it was meant to be used as a desk.

I could stay here forever, I thought. *I could stay in this room forever and never leave.*

"So," Nash said beside me, casually eyeing his brothers. "Whose ass do I need to kick first?"

Grayson looked up from the book he was holding. "Must we always resort to fisticuffs?"

"Looks like I have a volunteer for the first ass-kicking," Nash said, then shot a measuring look at Jameson, who was leaning against one of the wrought-iron staircases. "Do I have a second?"

Jameson smirked. "Couldn't stay away, could you, big brother?"

"And leave Avery here with you knuckleheads?" Until Nash mentioned my name, neither of the other two seemed to have registered my presence behind him, but I felt my invisibility slip away, just like that.

"I wouldn't worry too much about Ms. Grambs," Grayson said, silver eyes sharp. "She's clearly capable of taking care of herself."

Translation: I'm a soulless, gold-digging con artist, and he sees straight through me.

"Don't pay any attention to Gray," Jameson told me lazily. "None of us do."

"Jamie," Nash said. "Zip it."

Jameson ignored him. "Grayson is in training for the Insufferable Olympics, and we really think he can go all the way if he can just jam that stick a little farther up his—"

Asterisk, I thought, channeling Max.

"Enough," Nash grunted.

"What did I miss?" Xander bounded through the doorway. He was wearing a private school uniform, complete with a blazer that he shed in one liquid motion.

"You haven't missed anything at all," Grayson told him. "And Ms. Grambs was just leaving." He flicked his gaze toward me. "I'm sure you want to get settled."

I was the billionaire now, and he was still giving orders.

"Wait a second." Xander frowned suddenly, taking in the state of the room. "Were you guys brawling in here without me?" I still saw no visible signs of a fight or destruction, but obviously, Xander had picked up on something I hadn't. "This is what I get for being the one who doesn't skip school," he said mournfully.

At the mention of *school*, Nash looked from Xander to Jameson. "No uniform," he noted. "Playing hooky, Jamie? Two ass-kickings it is."

Xander heard the phrase *ass-kicking*, grinned, bounced to the balls of his feet, and pounced with no warning, tackling Nash to the ground. *Just some friendly impromptu wrestling between brothers.*

"Pinned you!" Xander declared triumphantly.

Nash hooked his ankle around Xander's leg and flipped him, pinning him to the ground. "Not today, little brother." Nash grinned, then flashed a much darker look at the other two brothers. *"Not today."*

They were—the four of them—a unit. They were *Hawthornes.* I wasn't. I felt that now, in a physical way. They shared a bond that was impervious to outsiders.

"I should go," I said. I didn't belong here, and if I stayed, all I would do was stare.

"You shouldn't *be* here at all," Grayson replied tersely.

"Stuff a sock in it, Gray," Nash said. "What's done is done, and you know as well as I do that if the old man did it, there's no undoing it." Nash swiveled his head toward Jameson. "And as for you: Self-destructive tendencies aren't nearly as adorable as you think they are."

"Avery solved the keys," Jameson said casually. "Faster than any of us."

For the first time since I'd walked into the room, all four brothers fell into an extended silence. *What is going on here?* I wondered. The moment felt tense, electric, borderline unbearable, and then—

"You gave her the keys?" Grayson broke the silence.

I was still holding the key ring in my hand. It suddenly felt very heavy. *Jameson wasn't supposed to give me these.*

"We were legally obligated to hand over—"

"A key." Grayson interrupted Jameson and started stalking slowly toward him, snapping the book in his hand closed. "We were legally obligated to give her *a* key, Jameson, not *the* keys."

I'd assumed that I was being messed with. At best, I'd thought it was a test. But from the way they were talking, it seemed more like a tradition. An invitation.

A rite of passage.

"I was curious how she'd do." Jameson arched an eyebrow. "Do you want to hear her time?"

"No," Nash boomed. I wasn't sure if he was answering Jameson's question or telling Grayson to stop advancing on their brother.

"Can I get up now?" Xander interjected, still pinned beneath Nash and seemingly in a better humor than the other three combined.

"Nope," Nash replied.

"I told you she was special," Jameson murmured as Grayson continued closing in on him.

"And I told you to stay away from her." Grayson stopped, just out of Jameson's reach.

"So I see that you two are talking again!" Xander commented jollily. "Excellent."

Not excellent, I thought, unable to draw my eyes away from the storm brewing just feet away. Jameson was taller, Grayson broader through the shoulders. The smirk on the former's face was matched by steel on the latter's.

"Welcome to Hawthorne House, Mystery Girl." Jameson's welcome seemed to be more for Grayson's benefit than for mine. Whatever this fight was about, it wasn't just a difference of opinion on recent events.

It wasn't just about me.

"Stop calling me Mystery Girl." I'd barely spoken since the moment the library door had swung inward, but I was getting sick of playing spectator. "My name is Avery."

"I'd also be willing to call you Heiress," Jameson offered. He stepped forward into a beam of light shining down from a skylight above. He was toe-to-toe with Grayson now. "What do you think, Gray? Got a nickname preference for our new landlord?"

Landlord. Jameson was rubbing it in, like he could handle being disinherited if it meant that the heir apparent had lost everything, too.

"I'm trying to protect you," Grayson said lowly.

"I think we both know," Jameson replied, "that the only person you've ever protected is yourself."

Grayson went completely, deathly still.

"Xander." Nash stood, pulling the youngest brother to his feet. "Why don't you show Avery to her wing?"

That was either Nash's attempt to prevent a line from being crossed or an indication that one already had been.

"Come on." Xander bumped his shoulder lightly against mine. "We'll stop for cookies on the way."

If that statement was meant to dissipate the tension in the room, it didn't work, but it did draw Grayson's attention away from Jameson—for the moment.

"No cookies." Grayson's voice was strangled, like his throat was closing down around the words—like Jameson's last shot had cut off his air completely.

"Fine," Xander replied cheerily. "You drive a hard bargain, Grayson Hawthorne. No cookies." Xander winked at me. "We'll stop for scones."

CHAPTER 17

T
he first scone is what I like to call the *practice* scone." Xander stuffed an entire scone in his mouth, handed one to me, then swallowed and continued lecturing. "It is not until the third—nay, *fourth*—scone that you develop any kind of scone-eating expertise."

"Scone-eating expertise," I repeated in a deadpan.

"Your nature is skeptical," Xander noted. "That will serve you well in these halls, but if there is one universal truth in the human experience, it is that a finely honed scone-eating palate does not just develop overnight."

Out of the corner of my eye, I caught sight of Oren and wondered how long he had been tailing us. "Why are we standing here talking about scones?" I asked Xander. Oren had insisted that the Hawthorne brothers weren't a physical threat, but still! At the very least, Xander should have been trying to make my life miserable. "Aren't you supposed to hate me?" I asked.

"I do hate you," Xander replied, happily devouring his third scone. "If you notice, I have kept the blueberry confections for myself and given you"—he shuddered—"the *lemon*-flavored scones. Such is the depth of my loathing for you personally and on principle."

"This isn't a joke." I felt like I'd fallen into Wonderland—and then fallen again, rabbit hole after rabbit hole, in a vicious cycle.

Traps upon traps, I could hear Jameson saying. *And riddles upon riddles.*

"Why would I hate you, Avery?" Xander asked finally. There were layers of emotion in his tone that hadn't been there before. "You aren't the one who did this."

Tobias Hawthorne had.

"Maybe you're blameless." Xander shrugged. "Maybe you're the evil genius that Gray seems to think you are, but at the end of the day, even if you *thought* that you'd manipulated our grandfather into this, I guarantee that he'd be the one manipulating you."

I thought of the letter that Tobias Hawthorne had left me—two words, no explanation.

"Your grandfather was a piece of work," I told Xander.

He picked up a fourth scone. "I agree. In his honor, I eat this scone." He did just that. "Want me to show you to your rooms now?"

There's got to be a catch here. Xander Hawthorne had to be more than he appeared. "Just point me in the right direction," I told him.

"About that . . ." The youngest Hawthorne brother made a face. "There's a chance that Hawthorne House is just a tiny bit hard to navigate. Imagine, if you will, that a labyrinth had a baby with *Where's Waldo?*, only Waldo is your rooms."

I attempted to translate that ridiculous sentence. "Hawthorne House has an unconventional layout."

Xander did away with a fifth and final scone. "Has anyone ever told you that you have a way with words?"

➤———◄

"Hawthorne House is the largest privately owned residential home in the state of Texas." Xander led me up a staircase. "I could give you a number for square footage, but it would only be an estimate. The thing that truly separates Hawthorne House from other obscenely large, castle-like structures isn't so much its size as its nature. My grandfather added at least one new room or wing every year. Imagine, if you will, that an M. C. Escher drawing conceived a child with Leonardo da Vinci's most masterful designs...."

"Stop," I ordered. "New rule: You're no longer allowed to use any terminology for baby-making when describing this house or its occupants—including yourself."

Xander brought a hand melodramatically to his chest. "Harsh."

I shrugged. "My house, my rules."

He gawked at me. I couldn't believe I'd said it, either, but there was something about Xander Hawthorne that made me feel like I didn't have to apologize for my own existence.

"Too soon?" I asked.

"I'm a Hawthorne." Xander gave me his most dignified look. "It's never too soon to start trash-talking." He resumed playing the tour guide. "Now, as I was saying, the East Wing is actually the Northeast Wing, located on the second floor. If you get lost, just look for the old man." Xander nodded toward a portrait on the wall. "This was his wing, these last few months."

I'd seen pictures of Tobias Hawthorne online, but once I looked at the portrait, I couldn't look away. He had silver-gray hair and a face more weather-worn than I'd realized. His eyes were Grayson's, almost exactly, his build Jameson's, his chin Nash's. If I hadn't seen Xander in motion, I might not have recognized a resemblance between him and the old man at all, but it was there in the way Tobias Hawthorne's features pulled together—not the eyes or nose or mouth, but something about the shape in between.

"I never even met him." I tore my eyes from the portrait and looked at Xander. "I'd remember if I had."

"Are you sure?" Xander asked me.

I found myself looking back at the portrait. *Had* I ever met the billionaire? Had our paths crossed, even for a moment? My mind was blank, except for one phrase, looping through over and over again. *I'm sorry.*

CHAPTER 18

Xander left me to explore my wing.

My wing. I felt ridiculous even thinking the words. *In my mansion.* The first four doors led to suites, each of them sized to make a king bed look tiny. The closets could have doubled as bedrooms. And the *bathrooms!* Showers with built-in seats and a *minimum* of three different showerheads apiece. Gargantuan bathtubs that came with control panels. Televisions inlaid in every mirror.

Dazed, I made my way to the fifth and final door on my hall. *Not a bedroom,* I realized when I opened it. *An office.* Enormous leather chairs—six of them—sat in a horseshoe shape, facing a balcony. Glass display shelves lined the walls. Evenly spaced on the shelves were items that looked like they belonged in a museum— geodes, antique weaponry, statues of onyx and stone. Opposite the balcony, at the back of the room, was a desk. As I got closer, I saw a large bronze compass built into its surface. I trailed my fingers over the compass. It turned—*northwest*—and a compartment in the desk popped open.

This wing was where Tobias Hawthorne spent his last few

months, I thought. Suddenly, I didn't just want to look in the open compartment—I wanted to rifle through every drawer in Tobias Hawthorne's desk. There had to be something, somewhere, that could tell me what he was thinking—why I was here, why he'd pushed his family aside for me. Had I done something to impress him? Did he see something in me?

Or Mom?

I got a closer look at the opened compartment. Inside, there were deep grooves, carved in the shape of the letter *T*. I ran my fingers across the grooves. Nothing happened. I tested the rest of the drawers. Locked.

Behind the desk, there were shelves filled with plaques and trophies. I walked toward them. The first plaque had the words *United States of America* engraved on a gold background; underneath them, there was a seal. It took a little more reading of the smaller print for me to realize that it was a patent—and not one issued to Tobias Hawthorne.

This patent was held by Xander.

There were at least a half dozen other patents on the wall, several world records, and trophies in every shape imaginable. A bronze bull rider. A surfboard. A sword. There were medals. Multiple black belts. Championship cups—some of them *national* championships—for everything from motocross to swimming to pinball. There was a series of four framed comic books—superheroes I recognized, the kind they made movies about—authored by the four Hawthorne grandsons. A coffee table book of photographs bore Grayson's name on the spine.

This wasn't just a display. It was practically a *shrine*—Tobias Hawthorne's ode to his four extraordinary grandsons. This made no sense. It didn't make sense that any four people—three of them teenagers—could have achieved this much, and it definitely didn't make sense that the man who'd kept this display in his office had decided that *none* of them deserved to inherit his fortune.

Even if you thought *that you'd manipulated our grandfather into this*, I could hear Xander saying, *I guarantee that he'd be the one manipulating you.*

"Avery?"

The second I heard my name, I stepped back from the trophies. Hastily, I closed the compartment I'd released on the desk.

"In here," I called back.

Libby appeared in the doorway. "This is unreal," she said. "This entire place is *unreal.*"

"That's one word for it." I tried to focus on the marvel that was Hawthorne House and not on my sister's black eye, but I failed. If possible, the bruising looked worse now.

Libby wrapped her arms around her torso. "I'm fine," she said when she noticed my stare. "It doesn't even hurt that much."

"Please tell me you're done with him." The words escaped before I could stop them. Libby needed support right now—not judgment. But I couldn't help thinking that Drake had been her *ex* before.

"I'm here, aren't I?" Libby said. "I chose *you.*"

I wanted her to choose *herself*, and I said as much. Libby let her hair fall into her face and turned toward the balcony. She was silent for a full minute before she spoke again.

"My mom used to hit me. Only when she was really stressed, you know? She was a single mom, and things were hard. I could understand that. I tried to make everything easier."

I could picture her as a kid, getting hit and trying to make it up to the person who hit her. "Libby..."

"Drake loved me, Avery. I know he did, and I tried so hard to understand..." She was hugging herself harder now. The black polish on her nails looked fresh. *Perfect.* "But you were right."

My heart broke a little. "I didn't want to be."

Libby stood there for a few more seconds, then walked over to the balcony and tested the door. I followed, and the two of us stepped out into the night air. Down below, there was a swimming pool. It must have been heated, because someone was swimming laps.

Grayson. My body recognized him before my mind did. His arms beat against the water in a brutally efficient butterfly stroke. And his back muscles...

"I have to tell you something," Libby said beside me.

That let me tear my eyes away from the pool—and the swimmer. "About Drake?" I asked.

"No. I heard something." Libby swallowed. "When Oren introduced me to my security detail, I overheard Zara's husband talking. They're running a test—a DNA test. On *you.*"

I had no idea where Zara and her husband had gotten a sample of my DNA, but I wasn't entirely surprised. I'd thought it myself: The simplest explanation for including a total stranger in your will was that she *wasn't* a total stranger. The simplest explanation was that I *was* a Hawthorne.

I had no business watching Grayson at all.

"If Tobias Hawthorne was your father," Libby managed, "then our dad—*my* dad—isn't. And if we don't share a dad, and we barely even saw each other growing up—"

"Don't you dare say we're not sisters," I told her.

"Would you still want me here?" Libby asked me, her fingers rubbing at her choker. "If we're not—"

"I want you here," I promised. "No matter what."

CHAPTER 19

That night, I took the longest shower of my life. The hot-water supply was endless. The glass doors on the shower held in the steam. It was like having my own personal sauna. After drying off with plush, oversized towels, I put on my ratty pajamas and flopped down on what I was pretty sure were Egyptian cotton sheets.

I wasn't sure how long I'd been lying there when I heard it. A voice. "Pull the candlestick."

I was on my feet in an instant, whirling to put my back to the wall. On instinct, I grabbed the keys I'd left on the nightstand, in case I needed a weapon. My eyes scanned the room for the person who'd spoken, and came up empty.

"Pull the candlestick on the fireplace, Heiress. Unless you *want* me stuck back here?"

Annoyance replaced my initial fight-or-flight response. I narrowed my eyes at the stone fireplace at the back of my room. Sure enough, there was a candelabra on the mantel.

"Pretty sure this qualifies as stalking," I told the fireplace—or, more accurately, the boy on the other side of it. Still, I couldn't *not* pull the candlestick. Who could resist something like that? I wrapped my hand around the base of the candelabra. I was met with resistance, and another suggestion came from behind the fireplace.

"Don't just pull forward. Angle it down."

I did as I was instructed. The candelabra rotated, and then I heard a *click*, and the back of the fireplace separated from its floor, just by an inch. A moment later, I saw fingertips in the gap, and I watched as the back of the fireplace was lifted up and disappeared behind the mantel. Now at the back of the fireplace there was an opening. Jameson Hawthorne stepped through. He straightened, then returned the candle to its upright position, and the entry he'd just used was slowly covered once more.

"Secret passage," he explained unnecessarily. "The house is full of them."

"Am I supposed to find that comforting?" I asked him. "Or terrifying?"

"You tell me, Mystery Girl. Are you comforted or terrified?" He let me sit with that for a moment. "Or is it possible that you're intrigued?"

The first time I'd met Jameson Hawthorne, he was drunk. This time, I didn't smell alcohol on his breath, but I wondered how much he'd slept since the reading of the will. His hair was behaving itself, but there was something wild in his glinting green eyes.

"You're not asking about the keys." Jameson offered me a crooked little smile. "I expected you to ask about the keys."

I held them up. "This was your doing."

Not a question—and he didn't treat it like one. "It's a little bit of a family tradition."

"I'm not family."

He tilted his head to one side. "Do you believe that?"

I thought about Tobias Hawthorne—about the DNA test that Zara's husband was already running. "I don't know."

"It would be a shame," Jameson commented, "if we were related." He spared another smile for me, slow and sharp-edged. "Don't you think?"

What was it with me and Hawthorne boys? *Stop thinking about his smile. Stop looking at his lips. Just—stop.*

"I think that you already have more family than you can deal with." I crossed my arms. "I also think you're a lot less smooth than you think you are. You want something."

I'd always been good at math. I'd always been logical. He was here, in my room, flirting for a reason.

"Everyone is going to want something from you soon, Heiress." Jameson smiled. "The question is: How many of us want something you're willing to give?"

Even just the sound of his voice, the way he phrased things—I could feel myself wanting to lean toward him. This was *ridiculous.*

"Stop calling me Heiress," I shot back. "And if you turn answering my question into some kind of riddle, I'm calling security."

"That's the thing, Mystery Girl. I don't think I'm turning anything into a riddle. I don't think I have to. You are a riddle, a puzzle, a game—my grandfather's last."

He was looking at me so intently now, I didn't dare look away.

"Why do you think this house has so many secret passages? Why are there so many keys that don't work in any of the locks? Every desk my grandfather ever bought has secret compartments. There's an organ in the theater, and if you play a specific sequence of notes, it unlocks a hidden drawer. Every Saturday morning, from the time I was a kid until the night my grandfather died, he sat my brothers and me down and gave us a riddle, a puzzle, an impossible

challenge—something to solve. And then he died. And then..."
Jameson took a step toward me. "There was you."

Me.

"Grayson thinks you're some master manipulator. My aunt is
convinced you must have Hawthorne blood. But I think you're
the old man's final riddle—one last puzzle to be solved." He took
another step, bringing the two of us that much closer. "He chose
you for a reason, Avery. You're special, and I think he wanted us—
wanted me—to figure out why."

"I'm not a puzzle." I could feel my heart beating in my neck. He
was close enough now to see my pulse.

"Sure you are," Jameson replied. "We all are. Don't tell me that
some part of you hasn't been trying to figure us out. Grayson. Me.
Maybe even Xander."

"Is this all just a game to you?" I put my hand out to stop him
from advancing farther. He took one last step, forcing my palm to
his chest.

"Everything's a game, Avery Grambs. The only thing we get to
decide in this life is if we play to win." He reached up to brush the
hair from my face, and I jerked back.

"Get out," I said lowly. "Use the normal door this time." My
entire life, no one had touched me as gently as he had a moment
before.

"You're angry," Jameson said.

"I told you—if you want something, ask. Don't come in here
talking about how I'm special. Don't touch my face."

"You are special." Jameson kept his hands to himself, but the
heady expression in his eyes never shifted. "And what I want is to
figure out why. Why you, Avery?" He took a step back, giving me
space. "Don't tell me you don't want to know, too."

I did. Of course I did.

"I'm going to leave this here." Jameson held up an envelope. He laid it carefully on the mantel. "Read it, and then tell me this isn't a game to be won. Tell me this isn't a riddle." Jameson reached for the candelabra, and as the fireplace passage opened once more, he offered a targeted, parting shot. "He left you the fortune, Avery, and all he left us is *you*."

CHAPTER 20

Long after Jameson had disappeared into darkness and the fireplace door had closed, I stood there, staring. Was this the only secret passage into my room? In a house like this one, how could I ever really know that I was alone?

Eventually, I moved to take the envelope Jameson had left on the mantel, even though everything in me rebelled against what he had said. I wasn't a puzzle. I was just a girl.

I turned the envelope over and saw Jameson's name scrawled across the front. *This is his letter*, I realized. *The one he was given at the reading of the will.* I still had no idea what to make of my own letter, no idea what Tobias Hawthorne was apologizing *for*. Maybe Jameson's letter would clarify something.

I opened it and read. The message was longer than mine—and made even less sense.

Jameson,
 Better the devil you know than the one you don't—or is it? Power corrupts. Absolute power corrupts absolutely. All that glitters is not gold. Nothing is certain but death and taxes. There but for the grace of God go I.

Don't judge.
—Tobias Tattersall Hawthorne

<hr />

By the next morning, I'd memorized Jameson's letter. It sounded like it had been written by someone who hadn't slept in days—manic, rattling off one platitude after another. But the longer the words marinated in the back of my brain, the more I began to consider the possibility that Jameson might be right.

There's something there, in the letters. In Jameson's. In mine. An answer—or at least a clue.

Rolling out of my massive bed, I went to unplug my phones, plural, from their chargers and discovered that my old phone had powered down. With some hefty pushes on the power button and a little bit of luck, I managed to cajole it back on. I didn't know how I could even begin to explain the past twenty-four hours to Max, but I needed to talk to someone.

I needed a reality check.

What I got was more than a hundred missed calls and texts. Suddenly, the reason Alisa had given me a new phone was clear. People I hadn't spoken to in years were messaging me. People who had spent their lives ignoring me clamored for my attention. Coworkers. Classmates. Even *teachers*. I had no idea how half of them had gotten my number. I grabbed my new phone, went online, and discovered that my email and social media accounts were even worse.

I had *thousands* of messages—most of them from strangers. *To some people, you'll be Cinderella. To others, Marie Antoinette.* My stomach muscles tightened. I set both phones down and stood up, my hand going over my mouth. I should have seen this coming. It shouldn't have been a shock to my system at all. But I wasn't ready.

How could a person be ready for this?

"Avery?" A voice called into my room—female and not Libby.

"Alisa?" I double-checked before opening my bedroom door.

"You missed breakfast," came the reply. Brisk, businesslike—definitely Alisa.

I opened the door.

"Mrs. Laughlin wasn't sure what you like, so she made a bit of everything," Alisa told me. A woman I didn't recognize—early twenties, maybe—followed her into the room carrying a tray. She deposited it on my nightstand, cut a narrowed-eyed glance my way, then left without a word.

"I thought the staff only came in as needed," I said, turning to Alisa once the door was closed.

Alisa blew out a long breath. "The staff," she said, "is very, very loyal and extremely concerned right now. That"—Alisa nodded to the door—"was one of the newer hires. She's one of Nash's."

I narrowed my eyes. "What do you mean, she's one of Nash's?"

Alisa's composure never faltered. "Nash is a bit of a nomad. He leaves. He wanders. He finds some hole-in-the-wall place to bartend for a while, and then, like a moth to the flame, he comes back—usually with one or two hopeless souls in tow. As I'm sure you can imagine, there's plenty of work to be had at Hawthorne House, and Mr. Hawthorne had a habit of putting Nash's lost souls to work."

"And the girl who was just in here?" I asked.

"She's been here about a year." Alisa's tone gave nothing away. "She'd die for Nash. Most of them would."

"Are she and Nash…" I wasn't sure how to phrase this. "Involved?"

"No!" Alisa said sharply. She took a deep breath and continued. "Nash would never let anything happen with someone he had any kind of power over. He has his flaws—a savior complex among them—but he's not like that."

I couldn't take the elephant in the room any longer, so I dragged it into the light. "He's your ex."

Alisa's chin rose. "We were engaged for a time," she allowed. "We were young. There were issues. But I assure you, I have no conflict of interest when it comes to your representation."

Engaged? I had to actively try to keep my jaw from dropping. My lawyer had planned to *marry* a Hawthorne, and she hadn't thought that merited a mention?

"If you'd prefer," Alisa said stiffly, "I can arrange for someone else from the firm to work as your liaison."

I forced myself to stop gawking at her and tried to process the situation. Alisa had been nothing but professional and seemed almost frighteningly good at her job. Plus, given the whole broken engagement thing, she had a reason *not* to be loyal to the Hawthornes.

"It's okay," I said. "I don't need a new liaison."

That got a very small smile out of her. "I've taken the liberty of enrolling you at Heights Country Day." Alisa moved to the next item on her to-do list with merciless efficiency. "It's the school that Xander and Jameson attend. Grayson graduated last year. I'd hoped to have you enrolled and at least partially acclimated before news of your inheritance broke in the press, but we'll deal with the hand we've been dealt." She gave me a look. "You're the Hawthorne heiress, and you're not a Hawthorne. That's going to draw attention, even at a place like Country Day, where you will be far from the only one with means."

Means, I thought. How many ways did rich people have of not saying the word *rich*?

"I'm pretty sure I can handle a bunch of prep school kids," I said, even though I wasn't sure of that. At all.

Alisa caught sight of my phones. She squatted down and plucked my old phone from the ground. "I'll dispose of this for you."

She didn't even have to look at the screen to realize what had happened. What was *still* happening, if the constant, muted buzzing of the phone was any indication.

"Wait," I told her. I grabbed the phone, ignored the messages, and went for Max's number. I transferred it to my new phone.

"I suggest you strictly regulate who has access to your new number," Alisa told me. "This isn't going to die down anytime soon."

"This," I repeated. The media attention. Strangers sending me messages. People who'd never cared about me deciding we were best friends.

"The students at Country Day will have a bit more discretion," Alisa told me, "but you need to be prepared. As awful as it sounds, money *is* power, and power is magnetic. You're not the person you were two days ago."

I wanted to argue that point, but instead, my mind cycled back to Tobias Hawthorne's letter to Jameson, his words echoing in my mind. *Power corrupts. Absolute power corrupts absolutely.*

CHAPTER 21

You read my letter." Jameson Hawthorne slid into the back seat of the SUV beside me. Oren had already given me the rundown on the security features of the car. The windows were bulletproof and heavily tinted, and Tobias Hawthorne had owned multiple identical SUVs for times when decoys were needed.

Going to Heights Country Day School apparently wasn't one of them.

"Xander need a ride?" Oren asked from the driver's seat, catching Jameson's eyes in the mirror.

"Xan goes to school early on Fridays," Jameson said. "Extracurricular activity."

In the mirror, Oren's gaze shifted to me. "You okay having company?"

Was I okay in close quarters with Jameson Hawthorne, who'd stepped out of a fireplace and into my bedroom the night before? *He touched my face—*

"It's fine," I told Oren, squelching the memory.

Oren turned the key in the ignition and then cast a glance back over his shoulder. "She's the package," he told Jameson. "If there's an incident..."

"You save her first," Jameson finished. He kicked a foot up on the center console and reclined against the door. "Grandfather always said Hawthorne males have nine lives. I can't possibly have burned through more than five of mine."

Oren turned back to the front and put the car in drive, and then we were off. Even through the bulletproof windows, I could hear the minor roar that went up when we passed outside the gates. Paparazzi. There'd been at least a dozen before. Now there were twice that number—maybe more.

I didn't let myself dwell on that for long. I looked away from the reporters—and toward Jameson. "Here." I reached into my bag and handed him my letter.

"I showed you mine," Jameson said, playing the double entendre for all it was worth. "You show me yours."

"Shut up and read."

He did. "That's it?" he asked when he was done.

I nodded.

"Any idea what he's apologizing for?" Jameson asked. "Any great and anonymous wrongs in your past?"

"One." I swallowed and broke eye contact. "But unless you think your grandfather is responsible for my mom having an extremely rare blood type and ending up way too low on the transplant list, he's probably in the clear."

I'd meant that to sound sarcastic, not raw.

"We'll come back to your letter." Jameson did me the courtesy of ignoring every hint of emotion in my tone. "And turn our attention to mine. I'm curious, Mystery Girl, what do you make of it?"

I got the feeling that this was another test. A chance to show my worth. *Challenge accepted.*

"Your letter is written in proverbs," I said, starting with the obvious. "*All that glitters is not gold. Absolute power corrupts absolutely.*

He's saying that money and power are dangerous. And the first line—*better the devil you know than the one you don't*—or is it?—that's obvious, right?"

His family was the devil that Tobias Hawthorne had known—and I was the devil he hadn't. *But if that's true—why me?* If I was a stranger, how had he chosen me? A dart on a map? Max's imaginary computer algorithm?

And if I was a stranger—why was he sorry?

"Keep going," Jameson prompted.

I focused. "*Nothing is certain but death and taxes.* It sounds to me like he knew he was going to die."

"We didn't even know he was sick," Jameson murmured. That hit close to home. Tobias Hawthorne had apparently been a champion at keeping secrets—like my mother. *I could be the devil he doesn't know, even if he knew her. I would still be a stranger, even if she wasn't.*

I could feel Jameson beside me, watching me in a way that made me wonder if he could see straight inside my head.

"*There but for the grace of God go I,*" I said, returning to the letter's contents, intent on following this to the end. "With different circumstances, any of us could have ended up in anyone else's position," I translated.

"The rich boy can become a pauper." Jameson took his feet down from the center console and turned his head wholly toward me, his green eyes catching mine in a way that made my entire body go to high alert. "And the girl from the wrong side of the tracks can become..."

A princess. A riddle. An heiress. A game.

Jameson smiled. If this was a test, I'd passed. "On the surface," he told me, "it appears that the letter outlines what we already know: My grandfather died and left everything to the devil he didn't know, thereby reversing the fortune of many. Why? Because power corrupts. Absolute power corrupts absolutely."

I couldn't have looked away from him if I'd tried.

"And what about you, Heiress?" Jameson continued. "Are you incorruptible? Is that why he left the fortune in your hands?" The expression playing at the corners of his lips wasn't a smile. I wasn't sure what it was, exactly, other than magnetic. "I know my grand-father." Jameson stared at me intently. "There's more here. A play on words. A code. A hidden message. *Something.*"

He handed my letter back. I took it and looked down. "Your grandfather signed my letter with initials." I offered up one last observation. "And yours with his full name."

"And what," Jameson said lightly, "do we make of that?"

We. How had a Hawthorne and I become a *we*? I should have been wary. Even with Oren's assurances—and Alisa's—I should have been keeping my distance. But there was something about this family. Something about these boys.

"Almost there." Oren spoke from the front seat. If he'd been fol-lowing our conversation, he gave no sign of it. "The Country Day administration has been briefed on the situation. I signed off on the school's security years ago, when the boys enrolled. You should be fine here, Avery, but do not, under any circumstances, leave the campus." Our car pulled past a guarded gate. "I won't be far."

I turned my mind from the letters—Jameson's and mine—to what awaited me outside this car. *This is a high school?* I thought, taking in the sight outside my window. It looked more like a college or a museum, like something out of a catalog where all the students were beautiful and smiling. Suddenly, the uniform I'd been given felt like it didn't belong on my body. I was a kid playing dress-up, pretending that wearing a kitchen pot on her head could turn her into an astronaut, that smudging lipstick all over her face made her a star.

To the rest of the world, I was a sudden celebrity. I was a fascination—and a target. But here? How could people who'd grown up with this kind of money see a girl like me as anything but a fraud?

"I hate to puzzle and run, Mystery Girl...." Jameson's hand was already on the door handle as the SUV pulled to a stop. "But the last thing you need on your first day at this school is for anyone to see you getting cozy with me."

CHAPTER 22

Jameson was gone in a blink. He disappeared into a crowd of burgundy blazers and shiny hair, and I was left still buckled into my seat, unable to move.

"It's just a school," Oren told me. "They're just kids."

Rich kids. Kids whose baseline for normal was probably "just" being the child of a brain surgeon or hotshot lawyer. When they thought *college*, they were probably talking about Harvard or Yale. And there I was, wearing a pleated plaid skirt and a burgundy blazer, complete with a navy crest embossed with Latin words I didn't know how to read.

I grabbed my new phone and sent a message to Max. *This is Avery. New number. Call me.*

Glancing at the front seat again, I forced my hand to the door. It wasn't Oren's job to coddle me. It was his job to protect me—and not from the stares I fully expected the moment I stepped out of this car.

"Do I meet you back here at the end of the day?" I asked.

"I'll be here."

I waited a beat, in case Oren had any other instructions, and then I opened the door. "Thanks for the ride."

Nobody was staring at me. Nobody was whispering. In fact, as I walked toward the twin archways marking the entrance to the main building, I got the distinct feeling that the lack of response was deliberate. Not-staring. Not-talking. Just the lightest of glances, every few steps. Whenever I looked at anyone, they looked away.

I told myself that they were probably trying *not* to make a big deal of my arrival, that this was what discretion looked like—but it still felt like I'd wandered into a ballroom where everyone else was dancing a complicated waltz, twisting, spinning around me like I wasn't even there.

As I closed the distance to the archways, a girl with long black hair bucked the trend of ignoring me like a Thoroughbred shaking off an inferior rider. She watched me intently, and one by one, the girls around her did the same.

When I reached them, the black-haired girl stepped away from the group—toward me.

"I'm Thea," she said, smiling. "You must be Avery." Her voice was perfectly pleasant—borderline musical, like a siren who knew with the least bit of effort she could sing sailors into the sea. "Why don't I show you to the office?"

———

"The headmaster is Dr. McGowan. She's got a PhD from Princeton. She'll keep you in her office for at least a half hour, talking about *opportunities* and *traditions*. If she offers you coffee, take it—her own personal roast, to die for." Thea seemed well aware of the fact that we were both getting plenty of stares now. She also seemed to be enjoying it. "When Dr. Mac gives you your schedule, make sure you have time for lunch every day. Country Day uses what they call modular scheduling, which means we operate on a six-day cycle, even though we only have school five days a week. Classes meet anywhere from three to five times a cycle, so if you're not careful, you can end up in class straight through lunch on A day and B day but have practically no classes on C or F."

"Okay." My head was spinning, but I forced out one more word. "Thanks."

"People at this school are like fairies in Celtic mythology," Thea said lightly. "You shouldn't thank us unless you want to owe us a boon."

I wasn't sure how to reply to that, so I said nothing. Thea didn't seem to take offense. As she led me down a long hallway with old class portraits lining the walls, she filled the silence. "We're not so bad, really. Most of us anyway. As long as you're with me, you'll be fine."

That rankled. "I'll be fine regardless," I told her.

"Clearly," Thea said emphatically. That was a reference to the money. It had to be. Didn't it? Thea's dark eyes roved over mine. "It must be hard," she said, studying my response with an intensity that her smile did absolutely nothing to hide, "living in that house with those boys."

"It's fine," I said.

"Oh, honey." Thea shook her head. "If there's one thing the Hawthorne family isn't, it's fine. They were a twisted, broken mess before you got here, and they'll be a twisted, broken mess once you're gone."

Gone. Where exactly did Thea think I was going?

We'd reached the end of the hallway now and the door to the headmaster's office. It opened, and four boys poured out in single file. All four of them were bleeding. All four were smiling. Xander was the fourth. He saw me—and then he saw who I was with.

"Thea," he said.

She gave him a too-sweet smile, then lifted a hand to his face—
or more specifically, to his bloodied lip. "Xander. Looks like you
lost."

"There are no losers in Robot Battle Death Match Fight Club,"
Xander said stoically. "There are only winners and people whose
robots sort of explode."

I thought about Tobias Hawthorne's office—about the patents
I'd seen on the walls. What kind of genius *was* Xander Hawthorne?
And was he missing an *eyebrow*?

Thea proceeded as if that was exactly nothing to remark upon.
"I was just showing Avery to the office and giving her some insider
tips on surviving Country Day."

"Charming!" Xander declared. "Avery, did the ever-delightful
Thea Calligaris happen to mention that her uncle is married to my
aunt?"

Zara's last name was Hawthorne-Calligaris.

"I hear Zara and your uncle are looking for ways to challenge
the will." Xander gave every appearance of talking to Thea, but I
got the distinct feeling that he was really issuing a warning to me.

Don't trust Thea.

Thea gave an elegant little shrug, undaunted. "I wouldn't know."

CHAPTER 23

've slotted you into American Studies and Philosophy of Mind-fulness. In science and math, you should be able to continue on with your current course of study, assuming our course load doesn't prove to be too much." Dr. McGowan took a sip of her coffee. I did the same. It was just as good as Thea had promised it would be, and that made me wonder how much truth there was to the rest of what she'd said.

It must be hard living in that house with those boys.

They were a twisted, broken mess before you got here, and they'll be a twisted, broken mess once you're gone.

"Now," Dr. Mac—as she'd insisted on being called—continued, "in terms of electives, I would suggest Making Meaning, which focuses on the study of how meaning is conveyed through the arts and includes a strong component of civic engagement with local museums, artists, theater productions, the ballet company, the opera, and so on. Given the support the Hawthorne Foundation has traditionally provided to these endeavors, I believe you will find the course...useful."

The Hawthorne Foundation? I managed—just barely—to avoid repeating the words.

"Now, for the rest of your schedule, I will need you to tell me a bit about your plans for the future. What are you passionate about, Avery?"

It was on the tip of my tongue to tell her what I'd told Principal Altman. I was a girl with a plan—but that plan had always been driven by practicalities. I'd picked a college major that would get me a solid job. The practical thing to do now was stay the course. This school *had* to have more resources than my old one. They could help me game standardized tests, maximize the college credit I received in high school, put me in the perfect position to finish college in three years instead of four. If I played my cards right, even if Zara and her husband somehow ended up undoing what Tobias Hawthorne had done, I could come out ahead.

But Dr. Mac hadn't just asked about my plans. She'd asked what I was passionate about, and even if the Hawthorne family did manage to successfully challenge the will, I'd probably still get a payout. How many millions of dollars might they be willing to pay me just to go away? Worse came to worst, I could probably sell my story for more than enough to pay for college.

"Travel," I blurted out. "I've always wanted to travel."

"Why?" Dr. Mac peered at me. "What is it that attracts you to other places? The art? The history? The peoples and their cultures? Or are you drawn to the marvels of the natural world? Do you want to see mountains and cliffs, oceans and giant sequoia trees, the rain forest—"

"Yes," I said fiercely. I could feel tears stinging in my eyes, and I wasn't entirely sure why. "To all of it. *Yes.*"

Dr. Mac reached out and took my hand. "I'll get you a list of electives to look at," she said softly. "I understand that study abroad won't be an option for the next year, due to your rather unique circumstances, but we have some marvelous programs you might consider thereafter. You might even entertain the idea of delaying graduation a bit."

If someone had told me a week earlier that there was *anything* that could tempt me to stay in high school even a minute longer than necessary, I would have thought they were delusional. But this wasn't a normal school.

Nothing about my life was normal anymore.

CHAPTER 24

Max called me back around noon. At Heights Country Day, modular scheduling meant that there were gaps in my schedule during which I wasn't expected to be anywhere in particular. I could wander the halls. I could spend time in a dance studio, a darkroom, or *one* of the gymnasiums. When, precisely, I ate lunch was up to me. So when Max called and I ducked into an empty classroom, no one stopped me, and no one cared.

"This place is heaven," I told Max. *"Actual. Heaven."*

"The mansion?" Max asked.

"The school," I breathed. "You should see my schedule. And the classes!"

"Avery," Max said sternly. "It is my understanding that you have inherited roughly a bazillion dollars, and you want to talk about your new *school?*"

There was so much I wanted to talk to her about. I had to think to remember what she knew and what she didn't. "Jameson Hawthorne showed me the letter his grandfather left him, and it's this insane, twisty puzzle-riddle thing. Jameson's convinced that's what I am—a puzzle to be solved."

"I am currently looking at a picture of Jameson Hawthorne," Max announced. I heard a flush in the background and realized she must have been in the bathroom—at a school that wasn't as lax about student free time as this one. "Gotta say. He's faxable."

It took me a second to catch on. "Max!"

"I'm just saying, he looks like he knows his way around a fax machine. He's probably really great at dialing the numbers. I bet he's even faxed long-distance."

"I have no idea what you're even talking about anymore," I told her.

I could practically hear her grinning. "Neither do I! And I'm going to stop now because we don't have much time. My parents are freaking out about all of this. Now is not the time for me to be skipping class."

"Your parents are freaking out?" I frowned. "Why?"

"Avery, do you know how many calls I've gotten? A reporter showed up at our house. My mom's threatening to lock down my social media, my email—everything."

I'd never thought of my friendship with Max as particularly public, but it definitely wasn't a secret, either.

"Reporters want to interview you," I said, trying to wrap my mind around it. "About me."

"Have you *seen* the news?" Max asked me.

I swallowed. "No."

There was a pause. "Maybe...don't." That piece of advice spoke volumes. "This is a lot, Ave. Are you okay?"

I blew a hair out of my face. "I'm fine. I've been assured by my lawyer and my head of security that a murder attempt is highly unlikely."

"You have a bodyguard," Max said, awed. "Son of a beach, your life is cool now."

"I have a staff, servants—who hate me, by the way. The house is like nothing I've ever seen. And the family! These boys, Max. They have patents and world records and—"

"I'm looking at pictures of *all* of them now," Max said. "Come to mama, you delicious mustards."

"Mustards?" I echoed.

"Bastions?" she tried.

I let out a snort of laughter. I hadn't realized how badly I'd needed this until she was there.

"I'm sorry, Ave. I have to go. Text me but—"

"Watch what I say," I filled in.

"And in the meantime, buy yourself something nice."

"Like what?" I asked.

"I'll make you a list," she promised. "Love you, beach."

"Love you, too, Max." I kept the phone up to my ear for a second or two after she was gone. *I wish you were here.*

Eventually, I managed to find the cafeteria. There were maybe two dozen people eating. One of them was Thea. She nudged a chair out from her table with her foot.

She's Zara's niece, I reminded myself. *And Zara wants me gone.* Still, I sat.

"I'm sorry if I came on a little strong this morning." Thea glanced at the other girls at her table, all of whom were just as impossibly polished and beautiful as she was. "It's just that, in your position, I'd want to know."

I recognized the bait for exactly what it was, but I couldn't keep myself from asking. "Know what?"

"About the Hawthorne brothers. For the longest time, every boy wanted to be them, and everyone who likes boys wanted to date them. The way they look. The way they act." Thea paused. "Even just being Hawthorne-adjacent changed the way that people looked at you."

"I used to study with Xander sometimes," one of the other girls said. "Before..." She trailed off.

Before what? I was missing something here—something big.

"They were magic." Thea had the oddest expression on her face. "And when you were in their orbit, you felt like magic, too."

"Invincible," someone else chimed in.

I thought about Jameson, dropping down from a second-story balcony the day we'd met, Grayson sitting behind Principal Altman's desk and banishing him from the room with an arch of his brow. And then there was Xander: six foot three, grinning, bleeding, and talking about robots exploding.

"They aren't what you think they are," Thea told me. "I wouldn't want to live in a house with the Hawthornes."

Was this an attempt to get under my skin? If I left Hawthorne House—if I moved out—I'd lose my inheritance. Did she know that? Had her uncle put her up to this?

Coming into today, I'd expected to be treated like trash. I wouldn't have been surprised if the girls at this school had been possessive over the Hawthorne boys, or if everyone, male and female, had resented me on the boys' behalf. But this...

This was something else.

"I should go." I stood, but Thea stood with me.

"Think what you want to about me," she said. "But the last girl at this school who got tangled up with the Hawthorne brothers? The last girl who spent hour after hour in that house? She *died*."

CHAPTER 25

I left the cafeteria as soon as I'd choked down my food, unsure where I was going to hide until my next class and equally uncertain that Thea had been lying. *The last girl who spent hour after hour in that house?* My brain kept replaying the words. *She died.*

I made it down one hallway and was turning toward another when Xander Hawthorne popped out of a nearby lab, holding what appeared to be a mechanical dragon.

All I could think about was what Thea had just said.

"You look like you could use a robotic dragon," Xander told me. "Here." He thrust it into my hands.

"What am I supposed to do with this?" I asked.

"That depends on how attached you are to your eyebrows." Xander raised his one remaining eyebrow very high.

I tried to summon up a reply, but I had nothing. *The last girl who spent hour after hour in that house? She died.*

"Are you hungry?" Xander asked me. "The refectory is back that way."

As much as I hated letting Thea win, I was wary—of him, of all things Hawthorne. "Refectory?" I repeated, trying to sound normal.

Xander grinned. "It's prep school for *cafeteria*."

"Prep school isn't a language," I pointed out.

"Next you'll be telling me that French isn't one, either." Xander patted the robotic dragon on its head. It burped. A wisp of smoke rose up from its mouth.

They aren't what you think they are, I could hear Thea warning me.

"Are you okay?" Xander asked, and then he snapped his fingers. "Thea got to you, didn't she?"

I handed the dragon back to him before it could explode. "I don't want to talk about Thea."

"As it so happens," Xander said, "I hate talking about Thea. Shall we discuss your little tête-à-tête with Jameson last night instead?"

He knew that his brother had been to my room. "It wasn't a tête-à-tête."

"You and your grudge against French." Xander peered at me. "Jameson showed you his letter, didn't he?"

I had no idea whether or not that was supposed to be a secret. "Jameson thinks it's a clue," I said.

Xander was quiet for a moment, then nodded in the opposite direction from the refectory. "Come on."

I followed him because it was either that or find myself another random empty classroom.

"I used to lose," Xander said suddenly as we rounded a corner. "On Saturday mornings, when my grandfather set us to a challenge, I always lost." I had no idea why he was telling me this. "I was the youngest. The least competitive. The most apt to be distracted by scones or complex machinery."

"But...," I prompted. I could hear in his tone that there was one.

"But," Xander replied, "while my brothers were trying to take one another down in the race to the finish line, I was generously

104

sharing my scones with the old man. He was awfully chatty, full of stories and facts and contradictions. Would you like to hear one?"

"A contradiction?" I asked.

"A fact." Xander wiggled his eyebrows—*eyebrow*. "He didn't have a middle name."

"What?" I said.

"My grandfather was born Tobias Hawthorne," Xander told me. "No middle name."

I wondered if the old man had signed Xander's letter the same way he had signed Jameson's. *Tobias Tattersall Hawthorne*. He'd signed mine with initials—three of them.

"If I asked you to show me your letter, would you?" I asked Xander. He'd said that he usually came in last in their grandfather's games. That didn't mean he wasn't playing this one.

"Now, where would the fun be in that?" Xander deposited me in front of a thick wooden door. "You'll be safe from Thea in there. There are some places even she dares not tread."

I glanced through the clear pane on the door. "The library?"

"The archive," Xander corrected archly. "It's prep school for *library*—not a bad place to hang out during free mods if you're looking to get some time alone."

Hesitantly, I pushed the door open. "You coming?" I asked him.

He closed his eyes. "I can't." He didn't offer any more explanation than that. As he walked away, I couldn't shake the feeling that I was missing something.

Maybe multiple somethings.

The last girl who spent hour after hour in that house? She died.

CHAPTER 26

The archive looked more like a university library than one that belonged in a high school. The room was full of archways and stained glass. Countless shelves were brimming with books of every kind, and at the center of the room, there were a dozen rectangular tables—state of the art, with lights built into the tables and enormous magnifying glasses attached to the sides.

All the tables were empty except for one. A girl sat with her back to me. She had auburn hair, a darker red than I'd ever seen on a person. I sat down several tables away from her, facing the door. The room was silent except for the sound of the other girl turning the pages of the book she was reading.

I withdrew Jameson's letter and my own from my bag. *Tattersall.* I dragged my finger over the middle name with which Tobias Hawthorne had signed Jameson's missive, then looked at the initials scrawled on mine. The handwriting matched. Something nagged at me, and it took me a moment to realize what it was. *He used the middle name in the will, too.* What if that was the catch here? What if that was all it took to invalidate the terms?

I texted Alisa. The reply came immediately: *Legal name change, years ago. We're good.*

Xander had said that his grandfather was *born* Tobias Hawthorne, no middle name. Why tell me that at all? Deeply doubting that I would ever understand anyone with the last name Hawthorne, I reached for the magnifying glass attached to the table. It was the size of my hand. I placed the two letters side by side beneath it and turned on the lights built into the table.

Chalk one up for private schools.

The paper was thick enough that the light didn't shine through, but the magnifying glass made quick work of blowing the writing up ten times its normal size. I adjusted the glass, bringing the signature on Jameson's letter into focus. I could see details now in Tobias Hawthorne's handwriting that I hadn't been able to see before. A slight hook on his *r*'s. Asymmetry on his capital *T*'s. And there, in his middle name, was a noticeable space, twice that between any two other letters. Magnified, that space made the name appear as two words.

Tatters all. Tatters, all. "As in, he left them all in tatters?" I wondered out loud. It was a leap, but it didn't feel like much of one, not when Jameson had been so sure that there was more to this letter than met the eyes. Not when Xander had made it a point to tell me about his grandfather's lack of a middle name. If Tobias Hawthorne had legally changed his name to add in *Tattersall*, that strongly suggested he'd chosen the name himself. *To what end?*

I looked up, suddenly remembering that I wasn't alone in this room, but the girl with the dark red hair was gone. I shot off another text to Alisa: *When did TH change his name?*

Did the name change correspond to the moment he'd decided to leave his family in the billionaire version of tatters, to leave everything to me?

A text came through a moment later, but it wasn't from Alisa. It was from Jameson. I had no idea how he'd even gotten the number—for this new phone or my last.

I see it now, Mystery Girl. Do you?

I looked around, feeling like he might be watching me from the wings, but by all indications, I was alone.

The middle name? I typed back.

No. I waited, and a second text came through a full minute later. *The sign-off.*

My gaze went to the end of Jameson's letter. Right before the signature, there were two words: *Don't judge.*

Don't judge the Hawthorne patriarch for dying without ever telling his family he was sick? Don't judge the games he was playing from beyond the grave? Don't judge the way he had pulled the rug out from underneath his daughters and grandsons?

I looked back at Jameson's text, then to the letter, and read it again from the beginning. *Better the devil you know than the one you don't—or is it? Power corrupts. Absolute power corrupts absolutely. All that glitters is not gold. Nothing is certain but death and taxes. There but for the grace of God go I.*

I imagined being Jameson, getting this letter—wanting answers and being given platitudes instead. *Proverbs.* My brain supplied the alternate term, and my eyes darted back down to the sign-off. Jameson had thought we were looking for a wordplay or a code. Every line in this letter, barring the proper names, was a proverb or a slight variation thereon.

Every line except one.

Don't judge. I'd missed most of my old English teacher's lecture on proverbs, but there was only one I could think of that started with those two words.

Does "Don't judge a book by its cover" mean anything to you? I asked Jameson.

His reply was immediate. *Very good, Heiress.* Then, a moment later: *It sure as hell does.*

CHAPTER 27

We could be making something out of nothing," I said hours later. Jameson and I stood in the Hawthorne House library, looking up at the shelves circling the room, filled with books from eighteen-foot ceiling to floor.

"Hawthorne-born or Hawthorne-made, there's always something to be played." Jameson spoke with a singsong rhythm, like a child skipping rope. But when he brought his gaze down from the shelves to me, there was nothing childlike in his expression. "Everything is something in Hawthorne House."

Everything, I thought. *And everyone.*

"Do you know how many times in my life one of my grandfather's puzzles has sent me to this room?" Jameson turned slowly in a circle. "He's probably rolling in his grave that it took me this long to see it."

"What do you think we're looking for?" I asked.

"What do *you* think we're looking for, Heiress?" Jameson had a way of making everything sound like it was either a challenge or an invitation.

Or both.

Focus, I told myself. I was here because I wanted answers at least as much as the boy beside me did. "If the clue is *a book by its cover*," I said, turning the riddle over in my mind "then I'd guess that we're looking for either a book or a cover—or maybe a mismatch between the two?"

"A book that doesn't match its cover?" Jameson's expression gave no hint of what he thought of that suggestion.

"I could be wrong."

Jameson's lips twisted—not quite a smile, not quite a smirk. "Everyone is a little wrong sometimes, Heiress."

An invitation—and a challenge. I had no intention of being *a little wrong*—not with him. The sooner my body remembered that, the better. I physically turned away from Jameson to do a three-sixty, slowly taking in the scope of the room. Just looking up at the shelves felt like standing at the edge of the Grand Canyon. We were completely encircled by books, going up two stories. "There must be thousands of books in here." Given how big the library was, given how high the shelves went up, if we *were* looking for a book mismatched to its cover sleeve…

"This could take hours," I said.

Jameson smiled—with teeth this time. "Don't be ridiculous, Heiress. It could take days."

———◆———

We worked in silence. Neither one of us left for dinner. A thrill ran through my body each time I realized that I was holding a first edition. Every once in a while, I'd flip a book open to find it signed. Stephen King. J. K. Rowling. Toni Morrison. Eventually, I managed to stop pausing in awe at what I held in my hands. I lost track of time, lost track of everything except the rhythm of pulling books off shelves and covers off books, replacing the cover, replacing the book. I could hear Jameson working. I could feel him in the room, as we moved through our respective shelves, closer and closer to each other. He'd taken the upper level. I was working down below. Finally, I glanced up to see him right on top of me.

"What if we're wasting our time?" I asked. My question echoed through the room.

"Time is money, Heiress. You have plenty to waste."

"Stop calling me that."

"I have to call you something, and you didn't seem to appreciate Mystery Girl or the abbreviation thereof."

It was on the tip of my tongue to point out that I didn't call him anything. I hadn't said his name once since entering this room. But somehow, instead of offering that retort, I looked up at him, and a different question came out of my mouth instead.

"What did you mean in the car today, when you said that the last thing I needed was for anyone to see us together?"

I could hear him taking books off shelves and covers off books and replacing them both—again and again—before I got a response. "You spent the day at the fine institution that is Heights Country Day," he said. "What do you think I meant?"

He always had to be the one asking questions, always had to turn everything around.

"Don't tell me," Jameson murmured up above, "that you didn't hear any whispers."

I froze, thinking about what I had heard. "I met a girl." I made myself continue working my way through the shelf—book off, cover off, cover on, book reshelved. "Thea."

Jameson snorted. "Thea isn't a girl. She's a whirlwind wrapped in a hurricane wrapped in steel—and every girl in that school follows her lead, which means I'm persona non grata and have been for a year." He paused. "What did Thea say to you?" Jameson's attempt to sound casual might have fooled me if I'd been looking at his face, but without the expression to sell it, I heard a telltale note underneath. *He cares.*

Suddenly, I wished I hadn't brought Thea up. Sowing discord was probably her goal.

"Avery?"

Jameson's use of my given name confirmed for me that he didn't just want a response; he needed one.

"Thea kept talking about this house," I said carefully. "About what it must be like for me to live here." That was true—or true enough. "About all of you."

"Is it still a lie," Jameson asked loftily, "if you're masking what matters, but what you're saying is technically true?"

He wanted the truth.

"Thea said there was a girl and that she died." I spoke like I was ripping off a bandage, too fast to second-guess what I was saying.

Overhead, the rhythm of Jameson's work slowed. I counted five seconds of utter silence before he spoke. "Her name was Emily."

I knew, though I couldn't pinpoint how, that he wouldn't have said it if I'd been able to see his face.

"Her name was Emily," he repeated. "And she wasn't just a girl."

A breath caught in my throat. I forced it out and kept checking books, because I didn't want him to know how much I'd heard in his tone. *Emily mattered to him. She still matters to him.*

"I'm sorry," I said—sorry for bringing it up and sorry she was gone. "We should call it a night." It was late, and I didn't trust myself not to say something else I might regret.

Jameson's working rhythm stopped overhead and was replaced with the sound of footsteps as he made his way to and down the wrought-iron spiral stairs. He positioned himself between me and the exit. "Same time tomorrow?"

It suddenly felt imperative that I not let myself look at his deep green eyes. "We're making good progress," I said, forcing myself to head for the door. "Even if we don't find a way to shortcut the process, we should be able to make it through all the shelves within the week."

Jameson leaned toward me as I passed. "Don't hate me," he said softly.

Why would I hate you? I felt my pulse jump in my throat. Because of what he'd just said, or because of how close he was to me?

"There's a slight chance that we might not be done within the week."

"Why not?" I asked, forgetting to avoid looking at him.

He brought his lips right next to my ear. "This isn't the only library in Hawthorne House."

CHAPTER 28

How many libraries did this place have? That was what I focused on as I walked away from Jameson—not the feel of his body too close to mine, not the fact that Thea hadn't been lying when she'd said that there was a girl or that she'd died.

Emily. I tried and failed to banish the whisper in my mind. *Her name was Emily.* I reached the main staircase and hesitated. If I went back to my wing now, if I tried to sleep, all I would do was replay my conversation with Jameson, again and again. I glanced back over my shoulder to see if he'd followed me—and saw Oren instead.

My head of security had told me I was safe here. He seemed to believe it. But still, he trailed me—invisible until he wanted to be seen.

"Turning in for the night?" Oren asked me.

"No." There was no way I could sleep, no way I could even close my eyes—so I explored. Down one long hall, I found a theater. Not a movie theater, but something closer to an opera house. The walls were golden. A red velvet curtain obscured what had to be a stage. The seats were on an incline. The ceiling arced, and when I flipped a switch, hundreds of tiny lights came to life along that arc.

I remembered Dr. Mac telling me about the Hawthorne Foundation's support of the arts.

The next room over was filled with musical instruments— dozens of them. I bent to look at a violin with an S carved to one side of the strings, its mirror image on the other.

"That's a Stradivarius." Those words were issued like a threat.

I turned to see Grayson standing in the doorway. I wondered if he'd been following us—and for how long. He stared at me, his pupils black and fathomless, the irises around them ice gray. "You should be careful, Ms. Grambs."

"I'm not going to break anything," I said, stepping back from the violin.

"You should be careful," Grayson reiterated, his voice soft but deadly, "with Jameson. The last thing my brother needs is you and whatever this is."

I glanced at Oren, but his face was impassive, like he couldn't hear anything that passed between us. *It's not his job to eavesdrop. It's his job to protect me—and he doesn't see Grayson as a threat.*

"*This* being me?" I shot back. "Or the terms of your grandfather's will?" I wasn't the one who'd upended their lives. But I was here, and Tobias Hawthorne wasn't. Logically, I knew that my best option was to avoid confrontation, avoid *him* altogether. This was a big house.

Standing this close to Grayson, it didn't feel nearly big enough.

"My mother hasn't left her room in days." Grayson stared at and into me. "Xander nearly blew himself up today. Jameson is one bad idea away from ruining his life, and none of us can leave the estate without being hounded by the press. The property damage they've caused alone..."

Say nothing. Turn away. Don't engage. "Do you think this is easy for me?" I asked instead. "Do you think I want to be stalked by the paparazzi?"

"You want the money." Grayson Hawthorne looked down at me from on high. "How could you not, growing up the way you did?"

That was just dripping with condescension. "Like you *don't* want the money?" I retorted. "Growing up the way *you* did? Maybe I haven't had everything handed to me my entire life, but—"

"You have no idea," Grayson said lowly, "how ill prepared you are. A girl like you?"

"You don't know me." A rush of fury surged through my veins as I cut him off.

"I will," Grayson promised. "I'll know everything about you soon enough." Every bone in my body said that he was a person who kept his promises. "My access to funds might be somewhat limited currently, but the Hawthorne name still means something. There will always be people tripping over themselves to do favors for any one of us." He didn't move, didn't blink, wasn't physically aggressive in any way, but he bled power, and he knew it. "Whatever you're hiding, I'll find it. Every last secret. Within days, I'll have a detailed dossier on every person in your life. Your sister. Your father. Your mother—"

"Don't talk about my mother." My chest was tight. Breathing was a challenge.

"Stay away from my family, Ms. Grambs." Grayson pushed past me. I'd been dismissed.

"Or what?" I called after him, and then, possessed by something I couldn't quite name, I continued. "Or what happened to Emily will happen to me?"

Grayson jerked to a halt, every muscle in his body taut. "Don't you say her name." His posture was angry, but his voice sounded like it was about to crumble. Like I'd *gutted* him.

Not just Jameson. My mouth went dry. *Emily didn't just matter to Jameson.*

I felt a hand on my shoulder. *Oren.* His expression was gentle, but clearly, he wanted me to leave it alone.

"You won't last a month in this house." Grayson managed to pull himself together long enough to issue that prediction like a royal issuing a decree. "In fact, I'd lay money that you're gone within the week."

CHAPTER 29

Libby found me shortly after I made my way back to my room. She was holding a stack of electronics. "Alisa said I should buy some things for you. She said you haven't bought anything for yourself."

"I haven't had time." I was exhausted, overwhelmed, and past the point of being able to wrap my mind around *anything* that had happened since I'd moved into Hawthorne House.

Including Emily.

"Lucky for you," Libby replied, "I have nothing *but* time." She didn't sound entirely happy about that, but before I could probe further, she began setting things down on my desk. "New laptop. A tablet. An e-reader, loaded with romance novels, in case you need some escapism."

"Look around at this place," I said. "My life *is* escapism at the moment."

That got a grin out of Libby. "Have you seen the gym?" she asked me, the awe in her voice making it clear that she had. "Or the chef's kitchen?"

"Not yet." My gaze caught suddenly on the fireplace, and I found myself listening, wondering: Was anyone back there? *You won't last a month in this house.* I didn't think Grayson had meant that as a physical threat—and Oren certainly hadn't reacted as if my life were being threatened. Still, I shivered.

"Ave? There's something I have to show you." Libby flipped open my new tablet's cover. "Just for the record, it's okay if you want to yell."

"Why would I—" I cut off when I saw what she'd pulled up. It was a video of Drake.

He was standing next to a reporter. The fact that his hair was combed told me that the interview hadn't been a total surprise. The caption across the screen read: *Friend of the Grambs family.*

"Avery was always a loner," Drake said on-screen. "She didn't have friends."

I had Max—and that was all I'd needed.

"I'm not saying she was a bad person. I think she was just kind of desperate for attention. She wanted to matter. A girl like that, a rich old man..." He trailed off. "Let's just say that there were definite daddy issues."

Libby cut the video off there.

"Can I see that?" I asked, gesturing toward the tablet with murder in my heart—and probably my eyes.

"That's the worst of it," Libby assured me. "Would you like to yell now?"

Not at you. I took the tablet and scrolled through the related videos—all of them interviews or think pieces, all about me. Former classmates. Coworkers. Libby's mom. I ignored the interviews until I got to one that I couldn't ignore. It was labeled simply: *Skye Hawthorne and Zara Hawthorne-Calligaris.*

The two of them stood behind a podium at what appeared to be some kind of press conference—so much for Grayson's assertion that his mother hadn't left her room in days.

"Our father was a great man." Zara's hair whipped in a subtle wind. The expression on her face was stoic. "He was a revolutionary entrepreneur, a once-in-a-generation philanthropist, and a man who valued family above all else." She took Skye's hand. "As we grieve his passing, rest assured that we will not see his life's work die with him. The Hawthorne Foundation will continue operations. My father's numerous investments will undergo no immediate changes. While we cannot comment on the complex legalities of the current situation, I can assure you that we are working with the authorities, elder-abuse specialists, and a team of medical and legal profession-als to get to the bottom of this situation." She turned to Skye, whose eyes brimmed with unshed tears—perfect, picturesque, dramatic.

"Our father was our hero," Zara declared. "We will not allow him, in death, to become a victim. To that end, we are providing the press with the results of a genetic test that proves conclusively that, contrary to the libelous reports and speculation circulating in the tabloids, Avery Grambs is not the result of infidelity on the part of our father, who was faithful to his beloved wife, our mother, for the entirety of their marriage. We as a family are as bewildered at recent events as all of you, but genes don't lie. Whatever else this girl may be, she is not a Hawthorne."

The video cut off. Dumbfounded, I thought back to Grayson's parting shot. *I'd lay money that you're gone within the week.*

"Elder-abuse specialists?" Libby was agog and aghast beside me.

"And the authorities," I added. "Plus a team of medical special-ists. She might not have come right out and said that I'm under investigation for defrauding a dementia-ridden old man, but she sure as hell implied it."

"She doesn't get to do that." Libby was pissed—a blue-haired, ponytailed, gothic ball of fury. "She can't just say whatever she wants. Call Alisa. You have lawyers!"

What I had was a headache. This wasn't unexpected. Given the size of the fortune at stake, it was inevitable. Oren had warned me that the women would come after me in the courtroom.

"I'll call Alisa tomorrow," I told Libby. "Right now, I'm going to bed."

CHAPTER 30

T hey don't have a legal leg to stand on."

I didn't have to call Alisa in the morning. She showed up and found me.

"Rest assured, we will shut this down. My father will be meeting with Zara and Constantine later today."

"Constantine?" I asked.

"Zara's husband."

Thea's uncle, I thought.

"They know, of course, that they stand to lose a great deal by challenging the will. Zara's debts are substantial, and they won't be cleared if she files a suit. What Zara and Constantine don't know, and what my father will make very clear to them, is that even if a judge were to rule Mr. Hawthorne's latest will to be null and void, the distribution of his estate would then be governed by his prior will, and *that* will left the Hawthorne family even less than this one."

Traps upon traps. I thought about what Jameson said after the will had been read, and then I thought about the conversation I'd had with Xander over scones. *Even if you* thought *that you'd manipulated our grandfather into this, I guarantee that he'd be the one manipulating you.*

"How long ago did Tobias write his prior will?" I asked, wondering if its only purpose had been to reinforce this one.

"Twenty years ago in August." Alisa ruled out that possibility. "The entire estate was to go to charity."

"Twenty years?" I repeated. That was longer than any of the Hawthorne grandsons except Nash had been alive. "He disinherited his daughters twenty years ago and never told them?"

"Apparently so. And in answer to your query yesterday"—Alisa was nothing if not efficient—"the firm's records show that Mr. Hawthorne legally changed his name twenty years ago last August. Prior to that, he had no middle name."

Tobias Hawthorne had given himself a middle name at the same time he'd disinherited his family. *Tattersall. Tatters, all.* Given everything that Jameson and Xander had told me about their grandfather, that seemed like a message. Leaving the money to me—and before me, to charity—wasn't the point.

Disinheriting his family was.

"What the hell happened twenty years ago in August?" I asked.

Alisa seemed to be weighing her response. My eyes narrowed, and I wondered if any part of her was still loyal to Nash. To his family.

"Mr. Hawthorne and his wife lost their son that summer. Toby. He was nineteen, the youngest of their children." Alisa paused, then forged on. "Toby had taken several friends to one of his parents' vacation homes. There was a fire. Toby and three other young people perished."

I tried to wrap my mind around what she was saying: Tobias Hawthorne had written his daughters out of his will after the death of his son. *He was never the same after Toby died.* Zara had said that when she'd thought she'd been passed over for her sister's sons. I searched my mind for Skye's reply.

Disappeared, Skye had insisted, and Zara had lost it.

"Why would Skye say that Toby disappeared?"

Alisa was caught off guard by my question—clearly, she didn't remember the exchange at the reading of the will.

"Between the fire and a storm that night," Alisa said, once she'd recovered, "Toby's remains were never definitively found."

My brain worked overtime trying to integrate this information. "Couldn't Zara and Skye have their lawyer argue that the old will was invalid, too?" I asked. "Written under duress, or he was mad with grief, or something like that?"

"Mr. Hawthorne signed a document reaffirming his will yearly," Alisa told me. "He never changed it, until you."

Until me. My entire body tingled, just thinking about it. "How long ago was that?" I asked.

"Last year."

What could have happened to make Tobias Hawthorne decide that instead of leaving his entire fortune to charity, he was going to leave it to me?

Maybe he knew my mother. Maybe he knew she died. Maybe he was sorry.

"Now, if your curiosity has been sated," Alisa said, "I would like to return to more pressing issues. I believe my father can get a handle on Zara and Constantine. Our biggest remaining PR issue is..." Alisa steeled herself. "Your sister."

"Libby?" That hadn't been what I was expecting.

"It's to everyone's benefit if she lies low."

"How could she possibly lie low?" I asked. This was the biggest story on the planet.

"For the immediate future, I've advised her to stay on the estate," Alisa said, and I thought about Libby's comment that she had nothing *but* time. "Eventually, she can think about charity work, if she would like, but for the time being, we need to be able to control the narrative, and your sister has a way of...drawing attention."

I wasn't sure if that was a reference to Libby's fashion choices or her black eye. Anger bubbled up inside me. "My sister can wear whatever she wants," I said flatly. "She can do whatever she wants. If Texas high society and the tabloids don't like it, that's too damn bad."

"This is a delicate situation," Alisa replied calmly. "Especially with the press. And Libby..."

"She hasn't talked to the press," I said, as sure of that as I was of my own name.

"Her ex-boyfriend has. Her mother has. Both are looking for ways to cash in." Alisa gave me a look. "I don't need to tell you that most lottery winners find their existence made miserable as they drown in requests and demands from family and friends. You are blessedly short on both. Libby, however, is another matter."

If Libby had been the one to inherit, instead of me, she would have been incapable of saying no. She would have given and given, to everyone who managed to get their hooks in her.

"We might consider a one-time payment to the mother," Alisa said, all business. "Along with a nondisclosure agreement preventing her from talking about you or Libby to the press."

My stomach rebelled at the idea of giving money to Libby's mom. The woman didn't deserve a penny. But Libby didn't deserve to have to see her mother regularly trying to sell her out on the nightly news.

"Fine," I said, clenching my teeth, "but I'm not giving *anything* to Drake."

Alisa smiled, a flash of teeth. "Him, I'll muzzle for fun." She held out a thick binder. "In the meantime, I've assembled some key information for you, and I have someone coming in this afternoon to work on your wardrobe and appearance."

"My *what?*"

"Libby, as you said, can wear whatever she wants, but you don't have that luxury." Alisa shrugged. "You're the real story here. Looking the part is always step one."

I had no idea how this conversation had started with legal and PR issues, detoured through Hawthorne family tragedy, and ended with me being told by my lawyer that I needed a makeover.

I took the binder from Alisa's outstretched hand, tossed it on the desk, then headed for the door.

"Where are you going?" Alisa called after me.

I almost said *the library*, but Grayson's warning from the day before was still fresh in my mind. "Doesn't this place have a bowling alley?"

CHAPTER 31

t really was a bowling alley. In my house. There was a bowling alley *in my house*. As promised, there were "only" four lanes, but otherwise, it had everything you'd expect a bowling alley to have. There was a ball return. Pin-setters on each lane. A touch screen to set up the games, and fifty-five-inch monitors overhead to keep track of the score. Emblazoned on all of it—the balls, the lanes, the touch screen, the monitors—was an elaborate letter *H*.

I tried not to take that as a reminder that none of this was supposed to be mine.

Instead, I focused on choosing the right ball. The right shoes—because there were at least forty pairs of bowling shoes on a rack to the side. *Who needs forty pairs of bowling shoes?*

Tapping my finger against the touch screen, I entered my initials. *AKG.* An instant later, a welcome flashed across the monitor.

WELCOME TO HAWTHORNE HOUSE, AVERY KYLIE GRAMBS!

The hairs on my arms stood up. I doubted programming my name into this unit had been a top priority for anyone the last couple of days. *And that means...*

"Was it you?" I asked out loud, addressing the words to Tobias Hawthorne. Had one of his last acts on earth been to program this welcome?

I pushed down the urge to shiver. At the end of the second lane, pins were waiting for me. I picked up my ball—ten pounds, with a silver *H* on a dark green background. Back home, the bowling alley had offered ninety-nine-cent bowling once a month. My mom and I had gone, every time.

I wished that she were here, and then I wondered: If she *were* alive, would I even be here? I wasn't a Hawthorne. Unless the old man had chosen me randomly, unless I had somehow done something to catch his attention, his decision to leave everything to me had to have something to do with her.

If she'd been alive, would you have left the money to her? At least this time, I wasn't addressing Tobias Hawthorne out loud. *What were you sorry for? Did you do something to her? Not do something to her—or for her?*

I have a secret. . . . I heard my mom saying. I threw the ball harder than I should have and hit only two pins. If my mom had been here, she would have mocked me. I concentrated then and bowled. Five games later, I was covered in sweat, and my arms were aching. I felt good—good enough to venture back out into the House and go hunting for the gym.

Athletic complex might have been a more accurate term. I stepped out onto the basketball court. The room jutted out in an L shape, with two weight benches and a half dozen workout machines in the smaller part of the L. There was a door on the back wall.

As long as I'm playing Dorothy in Oz . . .

I opened it and found myself looking up. A rock climbing wall stretched out two stories overhead. A figure grappled with a near-vertical section on the wall, at least twenty feet up, with no harness. *Jameson.*

He must have sensed me somehow. "Ever climbed one of these before?" he called down.

Again, I thought of Grayson's warning, but this time, I told myself that I didn't give a damn about what Grayson Hawthorne had to say to me. I walked over to the climbing wall, planted my feet at the base, and did a quick survey of the available hand- and footholds.

"First time," I called back to Jameson, reaching for one of them. "But I'm a quick learner."

I made it until my feet were about six feet off the ground before the wall jutted out at an angle designed to make things difficult. I braced one leg against a foothold and the other against the wall and stretched my right arm for a handhold a fraction of an inch too far away.

I missed.

From the ledge above me, a hand snaked down and grabbed mine. Jameson smirked as I dangled midair. "You can drop," he told me, "or I can try to swing you up."

Do it. I bit back the words. Oren was nowhere to be seen, and the last thing I needed to do, alone with a Hawthorne, was go higher. Instead, I let go of his arm and braced for impact.

After I landed, I stood, watching Jameson work his way back up the wall, muscles tensing against his thin white T-shirt. *This is a bad idea,* I told myself, my heart thumping. *Jameson Winchester Hawthorne is a very bad idea.* I hadn't even realized I remembered his middle name until it popped into my head, a last name, just like his first. *Stop looking at him. Stop thinking about him. The next year is going to be complicated enough without . . . complications.*

Feeling suddenly like I was being watched, I turned to the

door—and found Grayson staring straight at me. His light eyes were narrowed and focused.

You don't scare me, Grayson Hawthorne. I forced myself to turn away from him, swallowed, and called up to Jameson. "I'll see you in the library."

CHAPTER 32

The library was empty when I stepped through the door at nine fifteen, but it didn't stay empty for long. Jameson arrived at half past nine, and Grayson let himself in at nine thirty-one.

"What are we doing today?" Grayson asked his brother.

"*We?*" Jameson shot back.

Grayson meticulously cuffed his sleeves. He'd changed after his workout, donning a stiff collared shirt like armor. "Can't an older brother spend time with his younger brother and an interloper of dubious intentions without getting the third degree?"

"He doesn't trust me with you," I translated.

"I'm such a delicate flower." Jameson's tone was light, but his eyes told a different story. "In need of protection and constant supervision."

Grayson was undaunted by sarcasm. "So it would seem." He smiled, the expression razor sharp. "What are we doing today?" he repeated.

I had no idea what it was about his voice that made him so impossible to ignore.

"Heiress and I," Jameson replied pointedly, "are following a hunch, doubtlessly wasting sinful amounts of time on what I'm sure you would consider to be nonsensical flapdoodle."

Grayson frowned. "I don't talk like that."

Jameson let the arch of an eyebrow speak for itself.

Grayson narrowed his eyes. "And what hunch are the two of you following?"

When it became clear that Jameson wasn't going to answer, I did—not because I owed Grayson Hawthorne a single damn thing. Because part of any winning strategy, long-term, was knowing when to play to your opponent's expectations and when to subvert them. Grayson Hawthorne expected nothing from me. *Nothing good.*

"We think your grandfather's letter to Jameson included a clue about what he was thinking."

"What he was thinking," Grayson repeated, sharp eyes making a casual study of my features, "and why he left everything to *you.*"

Jameson leaned back against the doorframe. "It sounds like him, doesn't it?" he asked Grayson. "One last game?"

I could hear in Jameson's tone that he wanted Grayson to say yes. He wanted his brother's agreement, or possibly approval. Maybe some part of him wanted for them to do this together. For a split second, I saw a spark of *something* in Grayson's eyes, too, but it was extinguished so quickly I was left wondering if the light and my mind were playing tricks on me.

"Frankly, Jamie," Grayson commented, "I'm surprised you still feel you know the old man at all."

"I am just full of surprises." Jameson must have caught himself wanting something from Grayson, because the light in his own eyes went out, too. "And you can leave any time, Gray."

"I think not," Grayson replied. "Better the devil you know than the devil you don't." He let those words hang in the air. "Or is it? Power corrupts. Absolute power corrupts absolutely."

My eyes darted toward Jameson, who stood eerily, absolutely still.

"He left you the same message," Jameson said finally, pushing off the doorway and pacing the room. "The same clue."

"Not a clue," Grayson countered. "An indication that he wasn't in his right mind."

Jameson whirled on him. "You don't believe that." He assessed Grayson's expression, his posture. "But a judge might." Jameson shot me a look. "He'll use his letter against you if he can."

He might have given his letter to Zara and Constantine already, I thought. But according to what Alisa had told me, that wouldn't matter.

"There was another will before this one," I said, looking from brother to brother. "Your grandfather left your family even less in that one. He didn't disinherit you *for* me." I was looking at Grayson when I said those words. "He disinherited the entire Hawthorne family before you were even born—right after your uncle died."

Jameson stopped pacing. "You're lying." His entire body was tense.

Grayson held my gaze. "She's not."

If I'd been guessing how this would go, I would have guessed that Jameson would believe me and that Grayson would be the skeptic. Regardless, both of them were staring at me now.

Grayson broke eye contact first. "You may as well tell me what you think that godforsaken letter means, Jamie."

"And why," Jameson said through gritted teeth, "would I give away the game like that?"

They were used to competing with each other, to pushing to the finish line. I couldn't shake the feeling that I didn't belong here—between them—at all.

"You do realize, Jamie, that I am capable of staying here with the two of you in this room indefinitely?" Grayson said. "As soon as I see what you're up to, you know I'll reason it out. I was raised to play, same as you."

Jameson stared hard at his brother, then smiled. "It's up to the interloper of dubious intentions." His smile turned to a smirk.

He expects me to send Grayson packing. I probably should have, but it was entirely possible that we were wasting our time here, and I had no particular objection to wasting Grayson Hawthorne's.

"He can stay."

You could have cut the tension in the room with a knife.

"All right, Heiress." Jameson flashed me another wild smile. "As you wish."

CHAPTER 33

'd known that things would go faster with an extra set of hands, but I hadn't anticipated what it would feel like to be shut in a room with *two* Hawthornes—particularly these two. As we worked, Grayson behind me and Jameson above, I wondered if they'd always been like oil and water, if Grayson had always taken himself too seriously, if Jameson had always made a game of taking *nothing* seriously at all. I wondered if the two of them had grown up slotted into the roles of heir and spare once Nash had made it clear he would abdicate the Hawthorne throne.

I wondered if they'd gotten along before Emily.

"There's nothing here." Grayson punctuated that statement by placing a book back on the shelf a little too hard.

"Coincidentally," Jameson commented up above, "*you* also don't have to be here."

"If she's here, I'm here."

"Avery doesn't bite." For once, Jameson referred to me by my actual name. "Frankly, now that the issue of relatedness has been settled in the negative, I'd be game if she did."

I choked on my own spit and seriously considered throttling him. He was baiting Grayson—and using me to do it.

"Jamie?" Grayson sounded almost too calm. "Shut up and keep looking."

I did exactly that. Book off, cover off, cover on, book reshelved. The hours ticked by. Grayson and I worked our way toward each other. When he was close enough that I could see him out of the corner of my eye, he spoke, his voice barely audible to me—and not audible to Jameson at all.

"My brother's grieving for our grandfather. Surely, you can understand that."

I could, and I did. I said nothing.

"He's a sensation seeker. Pain. Fear. Joy. It doesn't matter." Grayson had my full attention now, and he knew it. "He's hurting, and he needs the rush of the game. He needs for this to mean something."

This as in his grandfather's letter? The will? Me?

"And you don't think it does," I said, keeping my own voice low. Grayson didn't think I was special, didn't believe this was the kind of puzzle worth solving.

"I don't think that you have to be the villain of this story to be a threat to this family."

If I hadn't already met Nash, I would have pegged Grayson as the oldest brother.

"You keep talking about the rest of the family," I said. "But this isn't just about them. I'm a threat to you."

I'd inherited *his* fortune. I was living in *his* house. His grandfather had chosen me.

Grayson was right beside me now. "I am not threatened." He wasn't imposing physically. I had never seen him lose control. But the closer he came to me, the more my body threw itself into high alert.

"Heiress?"

I startled when Jameson spoke. Reflexively, I stepped away from his brother. "Yes?"

"I think I found something."

I pushed past Grayson to make my way to the stairs. Jameson had found something. *A book that doesn't match its cover.* That was an assumption on my part, but the instant I hit the second story and saw the smile on Jameson Hawthorne's lips, I knew that I was right.

He held up a hardcover book.

I read the title. *"Sail Away."*

"And on the inside..." Jameson was a showman at heart. He removed the cover with a flourish and tossed me the book. *The Tragical History of Doctor Faustus.*

"Faust," I said.

"The devil you know," Jameson replied. "Or the devil you don't."

It could have been a coincidence. We could have been reading meaning where there was none, like people trying to intuit the future in the shape of clouds. But that didn't stop the hairs on my arms from rising. It didn't stop my heart from racing.

Everything is something in Hawthorne House.

That thought beat in my pulse as I opened the copy of *Faust* in my hands. There, taped to the inside cover, was a translucent red square.

"Jameson." I jerked my eyes up from the book. "There's something here."

Grayson must have been listening to us down below, but he said nothing. Jameson was beside me in an instant. He brought his fingers to the red square. It was thin, made of some kind of plastic film, maybe four inches long on each side.

"What's this?" I asked.

Jameson took the book gingerly from my hands and carefully removed the square from the book. He held it up to the light.

"Filter paper." That came from down below. Grayson stood in the center of the room, looking up at us. "Red acetate. A favorite of our grandfather's, particularly useful for revealing hidden messages. I don't suppose the text of that book is written in red?"

I flipped to the first page. "Black ink," I said. I kept flipping. The color of the ink never changed, but a few pages in, I found a word that had been circled in pencil. A rush of adrenaline shot through my veins. "Did your grandfather have a habit of writing in books?" I asked.

"In a first edition of *Faust*?" Jameson snorted. I had no idea how much money this book was worth, or how much of its value had been squandered with that one little circle on the page—but I knew in my bones that we were onto something.

"Where," I read the word out loud. Neither brother provided any commentary, so I flipped another page and then another. It was fifty or more before I hit another circled word.

"A..." I kept turning the pages. The circled words were coming quicker now, sometimes in pairs. *"There is..."*

Jameson grabbed a pen off a nearby shelf. He didn't have any paper, so he started writing the words on the back of his left hand. "Keep going."

I did. *"A* again..." I said. *"There is* again." I was almost to the end of the book. *"Way,"* I said finally. I turned the pages more slowly now, *Nothing. Nothing. Nothing.* Finally, I looked up "That's it."

I closed the book. Jameson held his hand up in front of his body, and I stepped closer to get a better look. I brought my hand to his, reading the words he'd written there. *Where. A. There is. A. There is. Way.*

What were we supposed to do with that?

"Change the order of the words?" I asked. It was a common enough type of word puzzle.

Jameson's eyes lit up. *"Where there is a . . ."*

I picked up where he'd left off. *"There is a way."*

Jameson's lips curved upward. "We're missing a word," he murmured. *"Will.* Another proverb. Where there's a *will,* there's a way." He flicked the red acetate in his hand, back and forth, as he thought out loud. "When you look through a colored filter, lines of that color disappear. It's one way of writing hidden messages. You layer the text in different colors. The book is written in black ink, so the acetate isn't meant to be used on the book." Jameson was talking faster now, the energy in his voice contagious.

Grayson spoke up from the room's epicenter. "Hence the message *in* the book, directing us where to make use of the film."

They were used to playing their grandfather's games. They'd been trained to from the time they were young. I hadn't, but their back-and-forth had given me just enough to connect the dots. The acetate was meant to reveal secret writing, but not in the book. Instead, the book, like the letter before it, contained a clue—in this case, a phrase with a single missing word.

Where there's a will, *there's a way.*

"What do you think the chances are," I said slowly, turning the puzzle over in my mind, "that somewhere, there's a copy of your grandfather's will written in red ink?"

CHAPTER 34

I asked Alisa about the will. I half expected her to look at me like I'd lost my marbles, but the second I said the word *red*, her expression shifted. She informed me that a viewing of the Red Will could be arranged, but first I had to do something for her. That *something* ended up involving a brother-sister stylist team carting what appeared to be the entire inventory of Saks Fifth Avenue into my bedroom. The female stylist was tiny and said next to nothing.

The man was six foot six and kept up a steady stream of observations. "You can't wear yellow, and I would encourage you to banish the words *orange* and *cream* from your vocabulary, but most every other color is an option." The three of us were in my room now, along with Libby, thirteen racks of clothing, dozens of trays of jewelry, and what appeared to be an entire salon set up in the bathroom. "Brights, pastels, earth tones in moderation. You gravitate toward solids?"

I looked down at my current outfit: a gray T-shirt and my second-most-comfortable pair of jeans. "I like simple."

"Simple is a lie," the woman murmured. "But a beautiful one sometimes."

Beside me, Libby snorted and bit back a grin. I glared at her. "You're enjoying this, aren't you?" I asked darkly. Then I took in the outfit she was wearing. The dress was black, which was Libby enough, but the style would have fit right in at a country club.

I'd *told* Alisa not to pressure her. "You don't have to change how you—" I started to say, but Libby cut me off.

"They bribed me. With boots." She gestured toward the back wall, which was lined with boots, all of them leather, in shades of purple, black, and blue. Ankle-length, calf-length, even one pair of thigh-highs.

"Also," Libby added serenely, "creepy lockets." If a piece of jewelry looked like it might be haunted, Libby was *there*.

"You let them make you over in exchange for fifteen pairs of boots and some creepy lockets?" I said, feeling mildly betrayed.

"And some incredibly soft leather pants," Libby added. "Totally worth it. I'm still me, just…fancy." Her hair was still blue. Her nail polish was still black. And *she* wasn't the one the style team was focused on now.

"We should start with the hair," the male stylist declared beside me, eyeing my offending tresses. "Don't you think?" he asked his sister.

There was no reply as the woman disappeared behind one of the racks. I could hear her thumbing through another, rearranging the order of the clothing.

"Thick. Not quite wavy, not quite straight. You could go either way." This giant man looked and sounded like he should be playing tight end, not advising me on hairstyles. "No shorter than two inches below your chin, no longer than mid-back. Gentle layers wouldn't hurt." He glanced over at Libby. "I suggest you disown her if she opts for bangs."

"I'll take that under consideration," Libby said solemnly. "You'd be miserable if it wasn't long enough for a ponytail," she told me.

"Ponytail." That got me a censuring look from the linebacker. "Do you hate your hair and want it to suffer?"

"I don't hate it." I shrugged. "I just don't care."

"That is also a lie." The woman reappeared from behind the clothing rack. She had a half dozen hangers' worth of clothes in her hands, and as I watched, she hung them up, face out, on the closest rack. The result was three different outfits.

"Classic." She nodded to an ice-blue skirt, paired with a long-sleeved T-shirt. "Natural." The stylist moved on to the second option—a loose and flowing floral dress combining at least a dozen shades of red and pink. "Preppy with an edge." The final option included a brown leather skirt, shorter than any of the others—and probably tighter, too. She'd matched it with a white collared shirt and a heather-gray cardigan.

"Which calls to you?" the male stylist asked. That got another snort out of Libby. She was definitely enjoying this *way* too much.

"They're all fine." I eyed the floral dress. "That one looks like it might be itchy."

The stylists seemed to be developing a migraine. "Casual options?" he asked his sister, pained. She disappeared and re-appeared with three more outfits, which she added to the first three. Black leggings, a red blouse, and a knee-length white cardigan were paired with the *classic* combo. A lacy sea-green shirt and darker green pants joined the floral monstrosity, and an over-sized cashmere sweater and torn jeans were hung beside the leather skirt.

"Classic. Natural. Preppy with an edge." The woman reiterated my options.

"I have philosophical objections to colored pants," I said. "So that one's out."

"Don't just look at the clothes," the man instructed. "Take in the *look*."

Rolling my eyes at someone twice my size probably wasn't the wisest course of action.

The female stylist crossed to me. She walked lightly on her feet, like she could tiptoe across a bed of flowers without breaking a single one. "The way you dress, the way you do your hair—it's not silly. It's not shallow. This..." She gestured to the rack behind her. "It's not just clothing. It's a message. You're not deciding what to wear. You're deciding what story you want your image to tell. Are you the ingenue, young and sweet? Do you dress to this world of wealth and wonders like you were born to it, or do you want to walk the line: the same but different, young but full of steel?"

"Why do I have to tell a story?" I asked.

"Because if you don't tell the story, someone else will tell it for you." I turned to see Xander Hawthorne standing in the doorway, holding a plate of scones. "Makeovers," he told me, "like the recreational building of Rube Goldberg machines, are hungry work."

I wanted to narrow my eyes, but Xander and his scones were glare-proof.

"What do you know about makeovers?" I grumbled. "If I were a guy, there'd be two racks of clothing in this room, max."

"And if I were White," Xander returned loftily, "people wouldn't look at me like I'm half a Hawthorne. Scone?"

That took the wind out of my sails. It was ridiculous of me to think that Xander didn't know what it was like to be judged, or to have to play life by different rules. I wondered, suddenly, what it was like for him, growing up in this house. Growing up Hawthorne.

"Can I have one of the blueberry scones?" I asked—my version of a peace offering.

Xander handed me a lemon scone. "Let's not get ahead of ourselves."

———————➤————————

With only a moderate amount of teeth-gnashing, I ended up picking option three. I hated the word *preppy* almost as much as I disliked any claims to having an *edge*, but at the end of the day, I couldn't pretend to be wide-eyed and innocent, and I deeply suspected that any attempts to act like this world was a natural fit would itch—not physically, but under my skin.

The team kept my hair long but worked in layers and cajoled it into a bed-head wave. I'd expected them to suggest highlights, but they'd gone the opposite route: subtle streaks a shade darker and richer than my normal ashy brown. They cleaned my eyebrows up but left them thick. I was instructed on the finer points of an elaborate facial regimen and found myself on the receiving end of a spray tan via airbrush, but they kept my makeup minimal: eyes and lips, nothing more. Looking at myself in the mirror, I could almost believe that the girl staring back belonged in this house.

"What do you think?" I asked, turning to Libby.

She was standing near the window, backlit. Her hand was clutching her phone, her eyes glued to the screen.

"Lib?"

She looked up and gave me a deer-in-headlights look that I recognized all too well.

Drake. He was texting her. Was she texting back?

"You look great!" Libby sounded sincere, because she was sincere. Always. Sincere and earnest and way, way too optimistic.

He hit her, I told myself. *He sold us out. She won't take him back.*

"You look fantastic," Xander declared grandly. "You also don't

144

look like someone who might have seduced an old man out of billions, so that's good."

"Really, Alexander?" Zara announced her presence with next to no fanfare. "No one believes that Avery seduced your grandfather."

Her story—her image—was somewhere between *oozing class* and *no-nonsense*. But I'd seen her press conference. I knew that while she might care about her father's reputation, she didn't have any particular attachment to mine. The worse I looked, the better for her. *Unless the game has changed.*

"Avery." Zara gave me a smile as cool as the winter colors she wore. "Might I have a word?"

CHAPTER 35

Zara didn't speak immediately once the two of us were alone. I decided that if she wasn't going to break the silence, I would. "You talked to the lawyers." That was the obvious explanation for why she was here.

"I did." Zara offered no apologies. "And now I'm talking to you. I'm sure you can forgive me for not doing so sooner. As you can imagine, this has all come as a bit of a shock."

A bit? I snorted and cut through the niceties. "You held a press conference strongly suggesting that your father was senile and that I'm under investigation by the authorities for elder abuse."

Zara perched at the end of an antique desk—one of the few surfaces in the room *not* covered with accessories or clothes. "Yes, well, you can thank your legal team for not making certain realities apparent sooner."

"If I get nothing, you get nothing." I wasn't going to let her come in here and dance around the truth.

"You look...nice." Zara changed the subject and eyed my new outfit. "Not what I would have chosen for you, but you're presentable."

Presentable, with an edge. "Thanks," I grunted.

"You can thank me once I've done what I can to ease you through this transition."

I wasn't naive enough to believe that she'd had a sudden change of heart. If she'd despised me before, she despised me now. The difference was that now she needed something. I figured that if I waited long enough, she'd tell me exactly what that something was.

"I'm not sure how much Alisa has told you, but in addition to my father's personal assets, you have also inherited control of the family's foundation." Zara took measure of my expression before continuing. "It's one of the largest private charitable foundations in the country. We give away upward of a hundred million dollars a year."

A *hundred million dollars.* I was never going to get used to this. Numbers like that were never going to seem real. "Every year?" I asked, stunned.

Zara smiled placidly. "Compound interest is a lovely thing."

A hundred million dollars *a year* in interest—and she was just talking about the foundation, not Tobias Hawthorne's personal fortune. For the first time, I actually ran the math in my head. Even if taxes took half of the estate, and I only averaged a four-percent yield—I'd still be making nearly a billion dollars a year. *Doing nothing.* That was just wrong.

"Who does the foundation give its money to?" I asked quietly.

Zara pushed off the desk and began pacing the length of the room. "The Hawthorne Foundation invests in children and families, health initiatives, scientific advancement, community building, and the arts."

Under those headings, you could support nearly anything. *I* could support nearly anything.

I could change the world.

"I've spent my entire adult life running the foundation." Zara's lips pulled tight across her teeth. "There are organizations that rely on our support. If you intend to exert yourself, there's a right way and a wrong way to do that." She stopped right in front of me. "You need me, Avery. As much as I'd like to wash my hands of all of this, I've worked too long and too hard to see that work undone."

I listened to what she was saying—and what she wasn't. "Does the foundation pay you?" I asked. I ticked off the seconds until her reply.

"I draw a salary commensurate with the skills I bring."

As satisfying as it would have been to tell her that her services would no longer be needed, I wasn't that impulsive, and I wasn't cruel. "I want to be involved," I told her. "And not just for show. I want to make decisions."

Homelessness. Poverty. Domestic violence. Access to preventative care. What could I do with a hundred million dollars a year?

"You're young enough," Zara said, her voice almost wistful, "to believe that money solves all ills."

Spoken like a person so rich she can't imagine the weight of problems money can *solve.*

"If you're serious about taking a role at the foundation..." Zara sounded like she was enjoying saying that about as much as she would have enjoyed dumpster diving or a root canal. "I can teach you what you need to know. Monday. After school. At the foundation." She issued each part of that order as its own separate sentence.

The door opened before I could ask where exactly the foundation was. Oren took up position beside me. *The women will come after you in the courtroom,* he'd told me. But now Zara knew that she couldn't come after me legally.

And my head of security didn't want me in this room with her alone.

CHAPTER 36

The next day—Sunday—Oren drove me to Ortega, McNamara, and Jones to see the Red Will.

"Avery." Alisa met Oren and me in the firm's lobby. The place was modern: minimalist and full of chrome. The building looked big enough to host a hundred lawyers, but as Alisa walked us past a receptionist and security guard to an elevator bank, I didn't see another soul.

"You said I was the firm's only client," I commented as the elevator began to climb. "Exactly how big is the firm?"

"There are a few different divisions," Alisa replied crisply. "Mr. Hawthorne's assets were quite diversified. That requires a diverse array of lawyers."

"And the will I asked about, it's here?" My pocket held a gift from Jameson: the square of red film we'd discovered taped to the inside cover of *Faust*. I'd told him I was coming here, and he'd handed it over, no questions asked, like he trusted me more than he trusted any of his brothers.

"The Red Will is here," Alisa confirmed. She turned to Oren. "How much company did we have today?" she asked. By *company*, she meant *paparazzi*. And by *we*, she meant *me*.

"It's tapered off a little," Oren reported. "But odds are good that they'll be piled outside the door by the time we leave."

If we ended the day without at least one headline that said something along the lines of *World's Richest Teenager Lawyers Up*, I'd eat a pair of Libby's new boots.

On the third floor, we passed through another security checkpoint, and then, finally, Alisa led me to a corner office. The room was furnished but otherwise empty, with one exception. Sitting in the middle of a heavy mahogany desk was the will. By the time I saw it, Oren had taken up position outside the door. Alisa made no move to follow me when I approached the desk. As I got closer, the type jumped out at me.

Red.

"My father was instructed to keep this copy here and show it to you—or the boys—if one of you came looking," Alisa said.

I looked back at her. "Instructed," I repeated. "By Tobias Hawthorne?"

"Naturally."

"Did you tell Nash?" I asked.

A cool mask settled over her face. "I don't tell Nash anything anymore." She gave me her most austere look. "If that's all, I'll leave you to it."

Alisa never even asked what *it* was. I waited until I heard the door close behind her before I went to sit at the desk. I retrieved the film from my pocket. "Where there's a will...," I murmured, laying the square flat on the will's first page. "There's a way."

I moved the red acetate over the paper, and the words beneath it disappeared. *Red text. Red film.* It worked exactly as Jameson and Grayson had described. If the entire will was written in red, all this was going to do was make everything disappear. But if, layered underneath the red text, there was another color, then anything written in that color would remain visible.

I made it past Tobias Hawthorne's initial bequests to the Laughlins, to Oren, to his mother-in-law. *Nothing*. I got to the bit about Zara and Skye, and as I skimmed the red film over the words, they disappeared. I glanced down at the next sentence.

To my grandsons, Nash Westbrook Hawthorne, Grayson Davenport Hawthorne, Jameson Winchester Hawthorne, and Alexander Blackwood Hawthorne . . .

As I ran the film over the page, the words disappeared—but not all of them. Four remained.

Westbrook.

Davenport.

Winchester.

Blackwood.

For the first time, I thought about the fact that all four of Skye's sons bore her last name, their grandfather's last name. *Hawthorne.* Each of the boys' middle names was also a surname. *Their fathers' last names?* I wondered. As my brain wrapped itself around that, I made my way through the rest of the document. Part of me expected to see something when I hit my own name, but it disappeared, just like the rest of the text—everything except for the Hawthorne grandsons' middle names.

"Westbrook. Winchester. Davenport. Blackwood." I said them out loud, committed them to memory.

And then I texted Jameson—and wondered if he would text Grayson.

CHAPTER 37

Whoa there, kid. Where's the fire?"

I was back at Hawthorne House and headed to meet Jameson when another Hawthorne brother stopped me in my tracks. *Nash.*

"Avery just came from reading a special copy of the will," Alisa said behind me. *So much for her not telling her ex anything anymore.*

"A special copy of the will." Nash slid his gaze to me. "Would I be correct in assuming this has something to do with the gobbledygook in my letter from the old man?"

"Your letter," I repeated, my brain whirring. It shouldn't have come as a surprise. Tobias Hawthorne had left Grayson and Jameson with identical clues. *Nash, too—and probably Xander.*

"Don't worry," Nash drawled. "I'm sitting this one out. I told you, I don't want the money."

"The money is not at stake here," Alisa said firmly. "The will—"

"—is ironclad," Nash finished for her. "I believe I've heard that a time or two."

Alisa's eyes narrowed. "You never were very good at listening."

"*Listen* doesn't always mean *agree*, Lee-Lee." Nash's use of the nickname—his amiable smile and equally amiable tone—sucked every ounce of oxygen out of the room.

"I should go." Alisa turned, whip-fast, to me. "If you need anything—"

"Call," I finished, wondering just how high my eyebrows had risen at their exchange.

When Alisa closed the front door behind her, she slammed it.

"You gonna tell me where you're headed in such a hurry?" Nash asked me again, once she was gone.

"Jameson asked me to meet him in the solarium."

Nash cocked an eyebrow at me. "Got any idea where the solarium is?"

I realized belatedly that I didn't. "I don't even know *what* a solarium is," I admitted.

"Solariums are overrated." Nash shrugged and gave me an assessing look. "Tell me, kid, what do you usually do on your birthday?"

That came out of nowhere. I felt like that had to be a trick question, but I answered anyway. "Eat cake?"

"Every year on our birthdays..." Nash stared off into the distance. "The old man would call us into his study and say the same three words. *Invest. Cultivate. Create.* He gave us ten thousand dollars to invest. Can you imagine letting an eight-year-old choose stocks?" Nash snorted. "Then we got to pick a talent or interest to cultivate for the year—a language, a hobby, an art, a sport. No expenses were spared. If you picked piano, a grand piano showed up the next day, private lessons started immediately, and by midway through the year, you'd be backstage at Carnegie Hall, getting tips from the greats."

"That's amazing," I said, thinking about all the trophies I'd seen in Tobias Hawthorne's office.

Nash didn't exactly look amazed. "The old man also laid out a challenge every year," he continued, his voice hardening. "An assignment, something we were expected to create by the next birthday. An invention, a solution, a work of museum-quality art. *Something.*"

I thought about the comic books I'd seen framed on the wall. "That doesn't sound horrible."

"It doesn't, does it?" Nash said, ruminating on those words. "C'mon." He jerked his head toward a nearby corridor. "I'll show you to the solarium."

He started walking, and I had to jog to keep up.

"Did Jameson tell you about the old man's weekly riddles?" Nash asked as we walked.

"Yeah," I said. "He did."

"Sometimes," Nash told me, "at the beginning of the game, the old man would lay out a collection of objects. A fishing hook, a price tag, a glass ballerina, a knife." He shook his head in memory. "And by the time the puzzle was solved, damned if we hadn't used all four." He smiled, but it didn't reach his eyes. "I was so much older. I had an advantage. Jamie and Gray, they'd team up against me, then double-cross each other right at the end."

"Why are you telling me this?" I asked as his pace finally slowed to a near standstill. "Why tell me any of this?" About their birthdays, the presents, the expectations.

Nash didn't answer right away. Instead, he nodded down a nearby hall. "Solarium's the last door on the right."

"Thanks," I said. I walked toward the door Nash had indicated, and right before I reached my destination, he spoke up behind me.

"You might think you're playing the game, darlin', but that's not how Jamie sees it." Nash's voice was gentle enough, but for the words. "We aren't normal. This place isn't normal, and you're not a player, kid. You're the glass ballerina—or the knife."

CHAPTER 38

The solarium was an enormous room with a domed glass ceiling and glass walls. Jameson stood in the center, bathed in light and staring up at the dome overhead. Like the first time I'd met him, he was shirtless. Also like the first time I'd met him, he was drunk.

Grayson was nowhere to be seen.

"What's the occasion?" I asked, nodding to a nearby bottle of bourbon.

"Westbrook, Davenport, Winchester, Blackwood." Jameson rattled the names off, one by one. "Tell me, Heiress, what do you make of that?"

"They're all last names," I said cautiously. I paused and then decided *why the hell not.* "Your fathers'?"

"Skye doesn't talk about our fathers," Jameson replied, his voice a little hoarse. "As far as she's concerned, it's an Athena-Zeus type of situation. We're hers and hers alone."

I bit my lip. "She told me that she had four lovely conversations..."

"With four lovely men," Jameson finished. "But lovely enough for her to ever see them again? To tell us the first thing about them?"

His voice was harder now. "She's never so much as answered a question about our damned middle names, and *that*"—he picked the bourbon up off the ground and took a swig—"is why I'm drinking." He set the bottle back down, then closed his eyes, standing in the sun a moment longer, his arms spread wide. For the second time, I noticed the scar that ran the length of his torso.

Noticed each breath he took.

"Shall we go?" His eyes opened. His arms dropped.

"Go where?" I asked, so physically aware of his presence it almost hurt.

"Come now, Heiress," Jameson said, stepping toward me. "You're better than that."

I swallowed and answered my own question. "We're going to see your mother."

He took me through the coat closet in the foyer. This time, I paid close attention to the sequence of panels on the wall that released the door. Following Jameson to the back of the closet, pushing past the coats that hung there, I willed my eyes to adjust to the dark so that I could see what he did next.

He touched something. *Pulled it?* I couldn't make out what. The next thing I knew, I heard the sound of gears turning, and the back wall of the closet slid sideways. If the closet was dark, what lay beyond was even darker.

"Step where I step, Mystery Girl. And watch your head."

Jameson used his cell phone to light the way. I got the distinct feeling that was for my benefit. He knew the twists and turns of these hidden hallways. We walked in silence for five minutes before he stopped and peeked through what I could only assume was a peephole.

"Coast is clear." Jameson didn't specify what it was clear of. "Do you trust me?"

I was standing in a phone-lit passageway, close enough to feel his body's heat on mine. "Absolutely not."

"Good." He reached out, grabbed my hand, and pulled me close. "Hold on."

My arms curved around him, and the ground beneath our feet began to move. The wall beside us was rotating, and we were rotating with it, my body pressed flat against his. *Jameson Winchester Hawthorne's.* The motion stopped, and I stepped back.

We were here for a reason—and that reason had exactly nothing to do with the way my body fit against his.

They were a twisted, broken mess before you got here, and they'll be a twisted, broken mess once you're gone. The reminder echoed in my head as we stepped out into a long hallway with plush red carpet and gold moldings on the walls. Jameson strode toward a door at the end of the hall. He lifted his hand to knock.

I stopped him. "You don't need me for this," I said. "You didn't need me for the will, either. Alisa had instructions to let you see it if you asked."

"I need you." Jameson knew exactly what he was doing—the way he was looking at me, the tilt of his lips. "I don't know why yet, but I do."

Nash's warning rang in my head. "I'm the knife." I swallowed. "The fishing hook, the glass ballerina, whatever."

That *almost* took Jameson by surprise. "You've been talking to one of my brothers." He paused. "Not Grayson." His eyes roved over mine. "Xander?" His gaze flicked down to my lips and up again. "Nash," he said, certain of it.

"Is he wrong?" I asked. I thought about Tobias Hawthorne's

grandsons going to see him on their birthdays. They'd been expected to be extraordinary. They'd been expected to win. "Am I just a means to an end, worth keeping around until you know how I fit into the puzzle?"

"You *are* the puzzle, Mystery Girl." Jameson believed that. "You could tap out," he told me, "decide you can live without answers, or you could get them—with me."

An invitation. A challenge. I told myself that I was doing this because I needed to know—not because of him. "Let's get some answers," I said.

When Jameson knocked on the door, it swung inward. "Mom?" he called, and then he amended the salutation. "Skye?"

The answer came, like the tinkling of bells. "In here, darling."

Here, it became quickly apparent, was the bathroom in Skye's suite.

"Got a second?" Jameson stopped right outside the double doors to the bathroom.

"Thousands of them." Skye seemed to relish the reply. "Millions. Come in."

Jameson stayed outside the doors. "Are you decent?"

"I like to think so," his mother called back. "At least a good fifty percent of the time."

Jameson pushed the bathroom door inward, and I was greeted by the sight of the biggest bathtub I'd ever seen in my life, sitting up on a dais. I focused on the tub's claw-feet—gold, to match the moldings in the hallway—and not the woman currently in the bathtub.

"You said you were decent." Jameson did not sound surprised.

"I'm covered in bubbles," Skye replied airily. "It doesn't get any more decent than that. Now, tell your mother what you need."

Jameson glanced back at me, as if to say *and you asked why I needed the bourbon*.

"I'll stay out here," I said, turning around before I caught sight of more than bubbles.

"Oh, don't be a prude, Abigail," Skye admonished from inside the bathroom. "We're all friends here, aren't we? I make it a policy to befriend everyone who steals my birthright."

I'd never seen passive aggression quite like this.

"If you're done messing with *Avery*," Jameson interjected, "I'd like to have a little chat."

"So serious, Jamie?" Skye sighed audibly. "Well, go on, then."

"My middle name. I've asked you before if I was named after my father."

Skye was quiet for a moment. "Hand me my champagne, would you?"

I heard Jameson moving around in the bathroom behind me—presumably, fetching her champagne. "Well?" he asked.

"If you'd been a girl," Skye said, with the air of a bard, "I would have named you after myself. Skylar, perhaps. Or Skyla." She took what I could only assume was a sip of champagne. "Toby was named for my father, you know."

The mention of her long-gone brother caught my attention. I didn't know how or why, but Toby's death had somehow started this all.

"My middle name," Jameson reminded her. "Where did you get it?"

"I'd be happy to answer your question, darling." Skye paused. "Just as soon as you give me a moment alone with your delightful little friend."

CHAPTER 39

I f I'd known I was going to end up in a one-on-one conversation with a naked, bubble-covered Skye Hawthorne, I probably would have had some bourbon myself.

"Negative emotions age you." Skye shifted her position in the tub, causing water to slosh against the sides. "There's only so much one can do with Mercury in retrograde, but..." She let out a long, theatrical breath. "I forgive you, Avery Grambs."

"I didn't ask you to," I responded.

She proceeded as if she had not heard me. "You will, of course, continue to provide me a modest amount of financial support."

I was starting to wonder if this woman was legitimately living on a different planet.

"Why would I give you anything?"

I expected a sharp comeback, but all I got was an indulgent little hum, like *I* was the one being ridiculous here.

"If you're not going to answer Jameson's question," I said, "then I'm leaving."

She let me get halfway to the door. "You'll support me," she said lightly, "because I'm their mother. And I will answer your question as soon as you answer mine. What are your intentions toward my son?"

"Excuse me?" I turned to face her before I remembered, a second too late, why I'd been trying *not* to look at her the entire time I'd been in the room.

The bubbles obscured what I didn't want to see—but just barely.

"You waltzed into my suite with my shirtless, grieving son by your side. A mother has concerns, and Jameson is special. Brilliant, the way my father was. The way Toby was."

"Your brother," I said, and suddenly, I had no interest in leaving this room. "What happened to him?" Alisa had given me the gist but very few details.

"My father ruined Toby." Skye addressed her answer to the rim of her champagne glass. "Spoiled him. He was always meant to be the heir, you know. And once he was gone . . . well, it was Zara and me." Her expression darkened, but then she smiled. "And then . . ."

"You had the boys," I filled in. I wondered, then, if she'd had them *because* Toby was gone.

"Do you know why Jameson was Daddy's favorite when, by all rights, it should have been perfect, dutiful Grayson?" Skye asked. "It wasn't because my Jamie is brilliant or beautiful or charismatic. It was because Jameson Winchester Hawthorne is *hungry*. He's looking for something. He's been looking for it since the day he was born." She downed the rest of the champagne in one gulp. "Grayson is everything Toby wasn't, and Jameson is just like him."

"There's no one like Jameson." In no way had I meant to utter those words out loud.

"You see?" Skye gave me a knowing look—the same one Alisa had given me my first day at Hawthorne House. "You're already his." Skye closed her eyes and lay back in the tub. "We used to lose him when he was little, you know. For hours, occasionally for a day. We'd look away for a second, and he'd disappear into the walls. And every time we found him, I'd pick him up and cuddle him tight and know, to the depths of my soul, that all he wanted was to get lost again." She opened her eyes. "That's all you are." Skye stood up and grabbed a robe. I averted my eyes as she put it on. "Just another way to get lost. That's what she was, too."

She. "Emily," I said out loud.

"She was a beautiful girl," Skye mused, "but she could have been ugly, and they would have loved her just the same. There was just something about her."

"Why are you telling me this?" I asked.

"You," Skye Hawthorne stated emphatically, "are no Emily." She bent to pick up the champagne bottle and refilled her glass. She padded toward me, barefoot and dripping, and held it out. "I've found bubbles to be a bit of a cure all myself." Her stare was intense. "Go on. Drink."

Was she serious? I took a step back. "I don't like champagne."

"And *I*"—Skye took a long drink—"didn't choose my sons' middle names." She held the glass up, as if she were toasting me—or toasting to my demise.

"If you didn't choose them," I said, "then who did?"

Skye finished off the champagne. "My father."

CHAPTER 40

I told Jameson what his mother had told me.

He stared at me. "The old man chose our names." I could see the gears in Jameson's head turning, and then—*nothing.* "He picked our names," Jameson repeated, pacing the long hall like an animal caged. "He picked them, and then he highlighted them in the Red Will." Jameson stopped again. "He disinherited the family twenty years ago and chose our middle names—all of them but Nash's—shortly thereafter. Grayson's nineteen. I'm eighteen. Xan will be seventeen next month."

I could *feel* him trying to make this make sense. Trying to see what we were missing.

"The old man was playing a long game," Jameson said, every muscle in his body tightening. "Our whole lives."

"The names have to mean something," I stated.

"He might have known who our fathers were." Jameson considered that possibility. "Even if Skye thought she'd kept it a secret—there were no secrets from him." I heard an undertone in Jameson's voice when he said those words—something deep and cutting and awful.

Which of your secrets did he know?

"We can do a search," I said, trying to focus on the riddle and not the boy. "Or have Alisa hire a private investigator on my behalf to look for men with those last names."

"Or," Jameson countered, "you can give me about six hours to utterly sober up, and I'll show you what I do when I'm working a puzzle and I hit a wall."

Seven hours later, Jameson snuck me out through the fireplace passageway and led me to the far wing of the house—past the kitchen, past the Great Room, into what turned out to be the largest garage I'd ever seen. It was closer to a showroom, really. There were a dozen motorcycles stacked on a mammoth shelf on the wall, and twice that many cars parked in a semicircle. Jameson paced by them, one by one. He stopped in front of a car that looked like something straight out of science fiction.

"The Aston Martin Valkyrie," Jameson said. "A hybrid hypercar with a top speed of more than two hundred miles per hour." He gestured down the line. "Those three are Bugattis. The Chiron's my favorite. Nearly fifteen hundred horsepower and not bad on the track."

"Track," I repeated. "As in *racetrack*?"

"They were my grandfather's babies," Jameson said. "And now . . ." A slow smile spread across his face. "They're yours."

That smile was devilish. It was dangerous.

"No way," I told Jameson. "I'm not even allowed to leave the estate without Oren. And I can't drive a car like these!"

"Luckily," Jameson replied, ambling toward a box on the wall, "I can." There was a puzzle built into the box, like a Rubik's Cube, but silver, with strange shapes carved onto the squares. Jameson immediately began spinning the tiles, twisting them, arranging them just so. The box popped open. He ran his fingers over a plethora of keys, then selected one. "There's nothing like speed for getting out of your own head—and out of your own way." He started walking toward the Aston Martin. "Some puzzles make more sense at two hundred miles an hour."

"Is there even room for two people in that?" I asked.

"Why, Heiress," Jameson murmured, "I thought you'd never ask."

———

Jameson drove the car onto a pad that lowered us down below the ground level of the House. We shot through a tunnel, and before I knew it, we were going out a back exit that I hadn't even known existed.

Jameson didn't speed. He didn't take his eyes off the road. He just drove, silently. In the seat next to him, every nerve ending in my body was alive with anticipation.

This is a very bad idea.

He must have called ahead, because the track was ready for us when we got there.

"The Martin's not technically a race car," Jameson told me. "Technically, it wasn't even for sale when my grandfather bought it."

And technically, I shouldn't have left the estate. We shouldn't have taken the car. We shouldn't have been here.

But somewhere around a hundred and fifty miles an hour, I stopped thinking about *should*.

Adrenaline. Euphoria. Fear. There wasn't room in my head for anything else. Speed was the only thing that mattered.

That, and the boy beside me.

I didn't want him to slow down. I didn't want the car to stop. For the first time since the reading of the will, I felt *free*. No questions. No suspicions. No one staring or not staring. Nothing except this moment, right here, right now.

Nothing except Jameson Winchester Hawthorne and me.

CHAPTER 41

E ventually, the car slowed to a stop. Eventually, reality crashed down around us. Oren was there, with a team in tow. *Uh-oh*.

"You and I," my head of security told Jameson the second we exited the car, "are going to be having a little talk."

"I'm a big girl," I said, eyeing the backup Oren had brought with him. "If you want to yell at someone, yell at me."

Oren didn't yell. He did personally deposit me back in my room and indicate that we would "talk" in the morning. Based on his tone, I wasn't entirely sure that I would survive a *talk* with Oren unscathed.

I barely slept that night, my brain a mess of electrical impulses that wouldn't—couldn't—stop firing. I still had no idea what to make of the names highlighted in the Red Will, if they really were a reference to the boys' fathers, or if Tobias Hawthorne had chosen his grandsons' middle names for a different reason altogether.

All I knew was that Skye had been right. Jameson was hungry. *And so am I.* But I could also hear Skye telling me that I didn't matter, that I was no Emily.

When I did fall asleep that night, I dreamed of a teenage girl.

She was a shadow, a silhouette, a ghost, a queen. And no matter how fast I ran, down one corridor after another, I could never catch up to her.

My phone rang before dawn. Groggy and in a mood, I grabbed for it with every intention of launching it through the closest window, then realized who was calling.

"Max, it's five thirty in the morning."

"Three thirty my time. Where did you get that car?" Max didn't sound even remotely sleepy.

"A room full of cars?" I replied apologetically, and then sleep cleared from my brain enough for me to process the implications of her question. "How did you know about the car?"

"Aerial photo," Max replied. "Taken from a helicopter, and what do you mean *a room full of cars*? Exactly how big is this room?"

"I don't know." I groaned and rolled over in bed. Of course the paparazzi had caught me out with Jameson. I didn't even want to know what the gossip rags were saying.

"Equally important," Max continued, "are you having a torrid affair with Jameson Hawthorne and should I plan for a spring wedding?"

"No." I sat up in bed. "It's not like that."

"Bull fox-faxing ship."

"I have to live with these people," I told Max. "For a year. They already have enough reasons to hate me." I wasn't thinking about Skye or Zara or Xander or Nash when I said that. I was thinking about Grayson. Silver-eyed, suit-wearing, threat-issuing Grayson. "Getting involved with Jameson would just be throwing gasoline on the fire."

"And what a lovely fire it would be," Max murmured.

She was, without question, a bad influence. "I can't," I reiterated. "And besides...there was a girl." I thought back to my dream and wondered if Jameson had taken Emily driving, if she had ever played one of Tobias Hawthorne's games. "She died."

"Back the fax up there. What do you mean, she *died*? How?"

"I don't know."

"How can you not know?"

I pulled my comforter tight around me. "Her name was Emily. Do you know how many people named Emily there are in the world?"

"Is he still hung up on her?" Max asked. She was talking about Jameson, but my brain went back to that moment when I'd said Emily's name to Grayson. It had gutted him. Destroyed him.

There was a rap at my door. "Max, I have to go."

⟫━━━━━━━⟪

Oren spent more than an hour going over security protocols with me. He indicated that he would be happy to do the same thing, every morning at dawn, until it stuck.

"Point taken," I told him. "I'll be good."

"No you won't." He gave me a look. "But I'll be better."

⟫━━━━━━━⟪

My second day—and the start of my first full week—at private school shaped up much like the week before. People did their best not to stare at me. Jameson avoided me. I avoided Thea. I wondered what gossip Jameson thought we would provoke if we were seen together, wondered if there had been whispers when Emily died.

I wondered *how* she'd died.

You're not a player. Nash's words of caution came back to me, again and again, every time I caught sight of Jameson in the halls. *You're the glass ballerina—or the knife.*

"I heard that you have a need for speed." Xander pounced on me outside the physics lab. He was clearly in high spirits. "God bless the paparazzi, am I right? I also heard that you had a very special chat with my mother."

I wasn't sure if he was pumping me for information or commiserating. "Your mother is something else," I said.

"Skye is a complicated woman." Xander nodded sagely. "But she taught me how to read tarot and moisturize my cuticles, so who am I to complain?"

Skye wasn't the one who'd forged them, pushed them, set them to challenges, expected the impossible. She wasn't the one who'd made them *magic*.

"Your brothers all got the same letter from your grandfather," I told Xander, examining his reaction.

"Did they now?"

I narrowed my eyes slightly. "I know that you got it, too."

"Maybe I did," Xander admitted cheerily. "But hypothetically, if I had, and if I hypothetically were playing this game and wanted, just this once—and just hypothetically—to win..." He shrugged. "I'd want to do it my way."

"Does your way involve robots and scones?"

"What doesn't?" Grinning, Xander nudged me into the lab. Like everything at Country Day, it looked like a million dollars— figuratively. Probably more than a million dollars, literally. Curved lab tables circled the room. Floor-to-ceiling windows had replaced three of the four walls. There was colored writing on the windows— calculations in different handwritings, like scratch paper was just so passé. Each lab table came complete with a large monitor and a digital whiteboard. And that wasn't even touching on the size of the microscopes.

I felt like I'd just walked into NASA.

There were only two free seats. One was next to Thea. The

other was as far away from Thea as you could get, next to the girl I'd seen in the archive. Her dark red hair was pulled into a loose ponytail at the nape of her neck. Her coloring was stop-and-stare striking—hair *that* red, skin *that* pale—but her eyes were downcast.

Thea met my gaze and gestured imperiously toward the seat next to her. I glanced back toward the red-haired girl.

"What's her story?" I asked Xander. No one was talking to her. No one was looking at her. She was one of the most beautiful people I'd ever seen, and she might as well have been invisible.

Wallpaper.

"Her story"—Xander sighed—"involves star-crossed love, fake dating, heartbreak, tragedy, twisted familial relationships, penance, and a hero for the ages."

I gave him a look. "Are you serious?"

"You should know by now," Xander replied lightly, "I'm not the serious Hawthorne."

He plopped down in the seat next to Thea, leaving me to make my way toward the red-haired girl. She proved to be a decent lab partner: quiet, focused, and able to calculate almost anything in her head. The entire time we worked in tandem, she didn't say a single word to me.

"I'm Avery," I said, once we'd finished and it became clear that she still wasn't going to introduce herself.

"Rebecca." Her voice was soft. "Laughlin." She saw the shift in my expression when she said her last name and confirmed what I was thinking. "My grandparents work at Hawthorne House."

Her grandparents *ran* Hawthorne House, and neither one of them had seemed overly enthused about the prospect of working for me. I wondered if that was why I'd gotten the silent treatment from Rebecca.

She's not talking to anyone else, either.

"Has someone shown you how to turn in assignments on your tablet?" Rebecca asked beside me. The question was tentative, like she fully expected to be slapped down. I tried to wrap my mind around the fact that someone that beautiful could be tentative about anything.

Everything.

"No," I said. "Could you?"

Rebecca demonstrated, uploading her results with a few clicks on the touch screen. A moment later, her tablet returned to its main screen. She had a photo as her wallpaper. In it, Rebecca looked off to the side, while another, amber-haired girl laughed directly into the camera. They both had wreaths of flowers on their heads, and they had the same eyes.

The other girl wasn't any more beautiful than Rebecca— and probably less—but somehow, it was impossible to look away from her.

"Is that your sister?" I asked.

"Was." Rebecca closed the cover on her tablet. "She died."

My ears roared, and I knew, then, exactly who I was looking at. I felt, on some level, like I'd known it from the moment I'd seen her. "Emily?"

Rebecca's emerald eyes caught on mine. I panicked, thinking that I should have said something else. *I'm sorry for your loss*—or something.

But Rebecca didn't seem to find my response odd or off-putting. All she said, pulling her tablet into her lap, was "She would have been very interested to meet you."

CHAPTER 42

I couldn't get Emily's face out of my mind, but I hadn't looked at the picture closely enough to recall every detail of her features. Her eyes had been green. Her hair was strawberry blonde, like sunlight through amber. I remembered the wreath of flowers on her head but not her hair's length. No matter how hard I tried to visualize her face, the only other things I could remember were that she'd been laughing and that she'd looked right at the camera, head-on.

"Avery." Oren spoke from the front seat. "We're here."

Here was the Hawthorne Foundation. It felt like it had been an eternity since Zara had offered to show me the ropes. As Oren exited the car and opened my door, I registered the fact that, for once, there wasn't a reporter or photographer in sight.

Maybe it's dying down, I thought as I stepped into the lobby of the Hawthorne Foundation. The walls were a light silvery-gray, and dozens of massive black-and-white photographs hung on them, seemingly suspended midair. Hundreds of smaller prints surrounded the larger ones. *People.* From all over the world, captured in motion and moments, from all angles, all perspectives, diverse along every dimension imaginable—age and gender and race and culture. *People*. Laughing, crying, praying, playing, eating, dancing, sleeping, sweeping, embracing—everything.

I thought about Dr. Mac asking me why I wanted to travel. *This. This is why.*

"Ms. Grambs."

I looked up to see Grayson. I wondered how long he'd watched me taking in this room. I wondered what he'd seen on my face.

"I'm supposed to meet Zara," I said, fending off his inevitable attack.

"Zara isn't coming." Grayson walked slowly toward me. "She's convinced that you are in need of...*guidance*." There was something about the way he said that word that slid past every defense mechanism I had and straight under my skin. "For some reason, my aunt seems to believe that guidance would be best received coming from me."

He looked exactly as he had the day I'd met him, down to the color of his Armani suit. It was the same light, liquid gray as his eyes—the same color as this room. Suddenly, I remembered the coffee table book I'd seen in Tobias Hawthorne's study—a book of photographs, with Grayson's name on the side.

"You took these?" I breathed, staring at the photos all around me. It was a guess—but I'd always been a good guesser.

"My grandfather believed that you have to see the world to change it." Grayson looked at me, then caught himself staring. "He always said that I was the one with the eye."

Invest. Create. Cultivate. Nash's explanation of their childhood came back to me, and I wondered how old Grayson was the first time he held a camera, how old he was when he started traveling the world, seeing it, capturing it on film.

I wouldn't have pegged him as the artist.

Irritated that I'd been tricked into thinking about him at all, I narrowed my eyes. "Your aunt must not have noticed your tendency to make threats. I'm betting she also didn't know about the background check on my dead mother. Otherwise, there is no way she could have come to the conclusion that I'd prefer working with *you*."

Grayson's lips twitched. "Zara doesn't miss much. And as for the background checks..." He disappeared behind the front desk and reappeared holding two folders. I glared at him, and he arched a brow. "Would you prefer I kept the results of my searches from you?"

He held out one folder, and I took it. He'd had no right to do this—to pry into my life or my mom's. But as I looked down at the folder in my hand, I heard my mother's voice, clear as a bell, in my head. *I have a secret....*

I flipped open the folder. Employment records, death certificate, credit report, no criminal background, a photograph...

I pressed my lips together, trying desperately to stop looking at it. She was young in the picture, and she was holding me.

I forced my eyes to Grayson's, ready to unleash on him, but he calmly handed me the second folder. I wondered what he'd found out about me—if there was anything in this folder that could possibly explain what his grandfather had seen in me. I opened it.

Inside, there was a single sheet of paper, and it was blank.

"That's a list of every purchase you've made since inheriting. Things have been purchased for you but..." Grayson dipped his eyes toward the page. "Nothing."

"Is that what passes for an apology where you're from?" I asked him. I'd surprised him. I wasn't acting like a gold digger.

"I won't apologize for being protective. This family has suffered enough, Ms. Grambs. If I were choosing between you and any one of them, I would choose them, always and every time. However..." His eyes made their way back to mine. "I may have misjudged you."

There was something intense in those words, in the expression on his face—like the boy who'd learned to see the world *saw* me.

"You're wrong." I flipped the folder closed, turning away from him. "I did try to spend some money. A big chunk. I asked Alisa to find a way to get it to a friend of mine."

"What kind of friend?" Grayson asked. His expression shifted. "A boyfriend?"

"No." I answered. What did he care if I had a boyfriend? "A guy I play chess with in the park. He lives there. In the park."

"Homeless?" Grayson was looking at me differently now, like in all his travels, he'd never encountered anything quite like this. Like me. After a second or two, he snapped out of it. "My aunt is right. You're in desperate need of an education."

He started walking, and I had no choice except to follow, but I refused to stay in his wake, like a duckling toddling after its mother. He stopped at a conference room and held the door open for me. I brushed past him, and even that split second of contact made me feel like I was going two hundred miles an hour.

Absolutely not. That was what I would have told Max if she were on the phone. What was wrong with me? Grayson had spent most of our acquaintance threatening me. *Hating* me.

He let the conference room door close behind him, then continued walking to the back wall. It was lined with maps: first a world map, then each continent, then broken down by countries, all the way down to states and towns.

"Look at them," he instructed, nodding toward the maps, "because that is what's at stake here. Everything. Not a single person. Giving money to individuals does little."

"It does a lot," I said quietly, "for those people."

"With the resources you have now, you can no longer afford to concern yourself with the individual." Grayson spoke like this was a lesson he'd had beaten into him. *By whom? His grandfather?* "You, Ms. Grambs," he continued, "are responsible for the world."

I felt those words like a lit match, a spark, a flame.

Grayson turned to the wall of maps. "I deferred college for a year to learn the ropes at the foundation. My grandfather assigned me to make a study of modes of charitable giving, with an eye to improving ours. I was to make my pitch in the coming months." Grayson stared hard at the map that hung even with his eyes. "Now I suppose that I will be making my pitch to you." He seemed to be measuring the pace of his words. "The foundation conservatorship has its own paperwork. When you turn twenty-one, it's yours, just like everything else."

That hurt him, more than any of the terms of the will. I thought about Skye referring to him as the heir apparent, even though she insisted that Jameson had been Tobias Hawthorne's favorite. Grayson had spent his gap year dedicated to the foundation. His photographs hung in the lobby.

But his grandfather chose me. "I'm—"

"Don't say that you are sorry." Grayson stared at the wall a moment longer, then turned to face me. "Don't be sorry, Ms. Grambs. Be worthy of it."

He might as well have ordered me to be fire or earth or air. A person couldn't be worthy of billions. It wasn't possible—not for anyone, and definitely not for me.

"How?" I asked him. *How am I supposed to be worthy of anything?*

He took his time replying, and I found myself wishing that I were the kind of girl who could fill silences. The kind who laughed with abandon, flowers in her hair.

"I can't teach you how to *be* anything, Ms. Grambs. But if you're willing, I can teach you a way of thinking."

I pushed back the memory of Emily's face. "I'm here, aren't I?"

Grayson began to walk down the length of the room, passing map after map. "It might *feel* better to give to someone you know than a stranger, or to donate to an organization whose story brings a tear to your eye, but that's your brain playing tricks on you. The morality of an action depends, ultimately and only, on its outcomes."

There was an intensity in the way he spoke, the way he moved. I couldn't have looked away or stopped listening, even if I'd tried.

"We shouldn't give because we feel one way or another," Grayson told me. "We should direct our resources to wherever objective analysis says we can have the largest impact."

He probably thought he was talking over my head, but the moment he said *objective analysis*, I smiled. "You're talking to a future actuarial science major, Hawthorne. Show me your graphs."

>———◄

By the time Grayson finished, my head was spinning with numbers and projections. I could see exactly how his mind worked—and it was disturbingly like my own.

"I get why a scattershot approach won't work," I said. "Big problems require big thinking and big interventions—"

"Comprehensive interventions," Grayson corrected. "Strategic."

"But we also have to spread our risk."

"With empirically driven cost-benefits analyses."

Everyone had things they found inexplicably attractive. Apparently, for me it was suit-wearing, silver-eyed guys using the word *empirically* and taking for granted that I knew what it meant.

Get your mind out of the gutter, Avery. Grayson Hawthorne is not for you.

His phone rang, and he glanced down at the screen. "Nash," he informed me.

"Go ahead," I told him. "Take it." At this point, I needed a breather—from him, but also from *this*. Math, I understood. Projections, I could wrap my mind around. But this?

This was real. This was power. *One hundred million dollars a year.*

Grayson answered his phone and left the room. I walked the perimeter, looking at the maps on the walls, memorizing the names of every country, every city, every town. I could help all of them—or none. There were people out there who might live or die because of me, futures good or bad that might be realized because of my choices.

What right did I even have to be the one making them?

Overwhelmed, I came to a stop in front of the very last map on the wall. Unlike the others, this one had been hand-drawn. It took me a moment to realize that the map was of Hawthorne House and the surrounding estate. My eyes went first to Wayback Cottage, a small building tucked in the back corner of the estate. I remembered, from the reading of the will, that Tobias Hawthorne had given lifetime occupancy of this building to the Laughlins.

Rebecca's grandparents, I thought. *Emily's.* I wondered if the girls had come to visit them when they were small, how much time they'd spent on the estate—at Hawthorne House. *How old was Emily the first time Jameson and Grayson laid their eyes on her?*

How long ago did she die?

The door to the conference room opened behind me. I was glad that Grayson couldn't see my face. I didn't want him to know that I'd been thinking about *her*. I made a show of studying the map in front of me, the geography of the estate, from the northern forest called the Black Wood to a small creek that ran along the western edge of the estate.

The Black Wood. I read the label again, the rush of blood through my veins was suddenly deafening. *Blackwood.* And there, in smaller letters, the winding body of water was labeled, too. Not a creek. The Brook.

A brook, on the west side of the property. Westbrook.

Blackwood. Westbrook.

"Avery." Grayson spoke behind me.

"What?" I said, unable to fully tear my mind from the map—and the implications.

"That was Nash."

"I know," I said. He'd told me who was on the other end of the line before he'd answered.

Grayson laid a hand gently on my shoulder. Alarm bells rang in the back of my head. Why was he being so gentle? "What did Nash want?"

"It's about your sister."

CHAPTER 43

I thought you said you'd take care of Drake." My fingers tightened around my cell phone, and my free hand wound itself into a fist at my side. "For fun."

I'd called Alisa the moment I'd made it to the car. Grayson had followed and buckled himself into the back seat beside me. I didn't have the time or mental space to dwell on his presence beside me. Oren was driving. I was pissed.

"I *did* take care of him," Alisa assured me. "You and your sister are both in possession of temporary restraining orders. If Drake attempts to contact or comes within a thousand feet of either of you for any reason, he's facing arrest."

I forced my fingers out of the fist but couldn't manage to loosen my grip on the phone. "Then why is he at the gates of Hawthorne House right now?"

Drake was here. In Texas. When Nash had called, Libby was safely inside, but Drake was spamming her phone with texts and calls, demanding a face-to-face.

"I'll handle this, Avery." Alisa recovered almost instantly. "The firm has some contacts on the local police force who know how to be discreet."

Right now, being *discreet* wasn't my priority. My priority was Libby. "Does my sister know about this restraining order?"

"She signed the paperwork." That was a hedge if I'd ever heard one. "I'll handle it, Avery. You just lie low." She hung up, and I let the hand holding my phone drop into my lap.

"Can you drive any faster?" I asked Oren.

Libby had her own security detail. Drake wouldn't get a chance to hurt her—physically.

"Nash is with your sister." Grayson spoke for the first time since we'd entered the car. "If the gentleman so much as tries to lay a finger on her, I assure you, my brother would take pleasure in removing that finger."

I wasn't sure if Grayson was referring to separating said finger from Libby's body—or from Drake's.

"Drake isn't a gentleman," I told Grayson. "And I'm not just worried about him getting violent." I was worried about him being sweet, worried that, instead of losing his temper, he'd be so kind and tender that she'd start to question the fading bruise ringing her eye.

"If it would make you feel better, I can have him removed from the property," Oren offered. "But that might cause a bit of a scene for the press."

The press? My brain clicked into gear. "There weren't any paparazzi at the foundation." I'd noted that when we'd arrived. "They're back at the house?"

The wall around the estate could keep the press off the property, but there was nothing stopping them from congregating, legally, on a public street.

"If I were a betting man," Oren commented, "I would guess that Drake placed a few calls to reporters to ensure an audience."

There was nothing discreet about the scene that greeted us when Oren pulled up to the drive, past a verifiable horde of press. Up ahead, I could see Drake's form outside the wrought-iron gates. There were two other men standing near him. Even from a distance, I could make out their police uniforms.

And so could the paparazzi.

So much for Alisa's friends on the police force being discreet. I gritted my teeth and thought about the way Drake would guilt Libby if there was footage of him being dragged down the drive.

"Stop the car," I snapped.

Oren stopped, then turned around in his seat to face me. "I would advise you to stay in this vehicle." That wasn't advice. That was an order.

I reached for the door handle.

"Avery." Oren's tone stopped me dead in my tracks. "If you're getting out, I'm getting out first."

Remembering our little one-on-one that morning, I decided not to test him.

Beside me, Grayson unbuckled his seat belt. He reached for my wrist, his touch gentle. "Oren's right. You shouldn't go out there."

I looked down at his hand on mine, and after a heartbeat, I looked back up. "And what would you do," I said, "what lengths would you go to in order to protect *your* family?"

I had him there, and he damn well knew it. He drew his hand back from mine, slowly enough that I felt the pads of his fingers skim my knuckles. My breath coming quickly now, I opened the car door and braced myself. Drake was the biggest story the press had on the Hawthorne Heiress front because we hadn't given them anything bigger. Yet.

Chin held high, I stepped out of the car. *Look at me. I'm the story here.* I walked down the drive, back toward the street. I was wearing boots with heels and my Country Day pleated skirt. My uniform blazer pulled against my body as I walked. The new hair. The makeup. The attitude.

I'm the story here. The chatter tonight wasn't going to be about Drake. The eyes of the world weren't going to be on him. I'd keep them on me.

"Impromptu press conference?" Oren asked under his breath. "As your bodyguard, I feel compelled to warn you that Alisa is going to *kill* you."

That was Future Avery's problem. I tossed my wave-perfect hair and squared my shoulders. The roar of reporters yelling my name was louder the closer we got.

"Avery!"

"Avery, look over here!"

"Avery, what do you have to say about rumors that—"

"Smile, Avery!"

I was standing right in front of them now. I had their attention. Beside me, Oren raised a hand, and just like that, the crowd went silent.

Say something. I'm supposed to say something.

"I...ummm..." I cleared my throat. "This has been a big change."

There were a few small laughs. *I can do this.* The instant I thought those words, the universe made me pay for them. A fight broke out behind me, between Drake and the cops. I saw cameras starting to angle away from me, saw the long-distance lenses zooming in on the gates.

Don't just talk. Tell the story. Make them listen.

"I know why Tobias Hawthorne changed his will," I said loudly.

The response to that announcement was electric. There was a reason this was the story of the decade, one thing that everyone wanted to know. "I know why he chose me." I made them look at me and only me. "I'm the only one who does. I know the truth." I sold that lie for all I was worth. "And if you run a word about that pathetic excuse for a human being behind me—any of you—I will make it my mission in life to ensure that you never, ever find out."

CHAPTER 44

I didn't process the magnitude of what I'd done until I was safely inside Hawthorne House. *I told the press that I have the answers they want.* It was the first time I'd spoken to them, the first real footage anyone had of me, and I'd lied through my teeth.

Oren was right. Alisa was going to kill me.

I found Libby in the kitchen, surrounded by cupcakes. Literally hundreds of them. If she'd been an apology baker back home, the addition of an industrial-grade kitchen with triple ovens had basically taken her nuclear.

"Libby?" I approached her cautiously.

"Do you think I should go for red velvet or salted caramel next?" Libby was holding an icing bag with both hands. Blue hair had escaped her ponytail and was matted to her face. She wouldn't meet my eyes.

"She's been at it for hours," Nash told me. He stood leaning back against a stainless-steel refrigerator, his thumbs hooked through the belt loops of his well-worn jeans. "Her phone's been going off for just as long."

"Don't talk about me like I'm not here." Libby looked up from the cupcakes she was icing to narrow her eyes at Nash.

"Yes, ma'am." Nash smiled, wide and slow. I wondered how long he'd been with her—*why* he'd been with her.

"Drake is gone," I told Libby, hoping Nash would take that as his cue that he wasn't needed here. "I took care of it."

"I'm supposed to take care of you." Libby shoved her hair out of her face. "Stop looking at me like that, Avery. I'm not going to break."

"'Course not, darlin'," Nash said, from his spot leaning against the fridge.

"You..." Libby looked at him, a spark of annoyance lighting up her eyes. "You shut up."

I'd never heard Libby tell someone to shut up in her life, but at least she didn't sound fragile or hurt or in any danger of texting Drake back. I thought about Alisa saying that Nash Hawthorne had a savior complex.

"Shutting up now." Nash picked up a cupcake and took a bite out of it like it was an apple. "For what it's worth, I vote for red velvet next."

Libby turned back to me. "Salted caramel it is."

CHAPTER 45

That night, when Alisa called to read me the I-can't-do-my-job-if-you-won't-let-me riot act, she didn't allow me to get a word in edgewise. After she'd said a terse good-bye, which seemed to promise more retribution to come, I sat down at my computer.

"How bad is it?" I said out loud. The answer, it turned out, was leading-story-on-every-news-site bad.

Hawthorne Heiress Keeping Secrets.

What Does Avery Grambs Know?

I barely recognized myself in the pictures the paparazzi had taken. The girl in the photos was pretty and full of righteous fury. She looked as arrogant and dangerous as a Hawthorne.

I didn't feel like that girl.

I fully expected to get a text from Max, demanding to know what was going on, but even when I messaged her, she didn't message back. I went to close my laptop but then stopped, because I remembered telling Max that the reason I had no idea what had happened to Emily was that *Emily* was such a common name. I hadn't been able to search for her before.

But I knew her last name now. "Emily Laughlin," I said out loud. I typed her name into the search field, then added *Heights Country*

Day School to narrow the results. My finger hovered over the return key. After a long moment, I pulled the trigger.

I hit Enter.

An obituary came up, but that was it. No news coverage. No articles suggesting that a local golden girl had died by suspicious cause. No mention of Grayson or Jameson Hawthorne.

There was a picture with the obituary. Emily was smiling this time instead of laughing, and my brain soaked up all the details I'd missed before. Her hair was layered, and she wore it long. The ends curved this way and that, but the rest was silky straight. Her eyes were too big for her face. The shape of her upper lip made me think of a heart. She had a scattering of freckles.

Thump. Thump. Thump.

My head shot up at the noise, and I slammed my laptop closed. The last thing I wanted was anyone knowing what I'd just looked up.

Thump. This time, I did more than just register the sound. I flipped my bedside lamp on, swung my feet to the floor, and walked toward it. By the time I ended up at the fireplace, I was fairly certain who was on the other side.

"Do you ever use doors?" I asked Jameson, once I'd utilized the candlestick to open the passage.

Jameson cocked an eyebrow and cocked his head. "Do you *want* me to use the door?"

I felt like what he was really asking was if I wanted him to be normal. I remembered sitting beside him at high speed and thought about the climbing wall—and his hand reaching out to catch mine.

"I saw your press conference." Jameson had that expression on his face again, the one that made me feel like we were playing chess and he'd just made a move designed to be seen as a challenge.

"It wasn't so much a press conference as a very bad idea," I admitted wryly.

"Have I ever told you," Jameson murmured, staring at me in a way that had to be intentional, "that I'm a sucker for bad ideas?"

When he'd shown up here, I'd felt like I'd summoned him by searching for Emily's name, but now I saw this midnight visit for exactly what it was. Jameson Hawthorne was here, in my bedroom, at night. I was wearing my pajamas, and his body was listing toward mine.

None of this was an accident.

You're not a player, kid. You're the glass ballerina—or the knife.

"What do you want, Jameson?" My body wanted to lean toward him. The rational part of me wanted to step back.

"You lied to the press." Jameson didn't look away. He didn't blink, and neither did I. "What you told them…it *was* a lie, wasn't it?"

"Of course it was." If I'd known why Tobias Hawthorne left me his fortune, I wouldn't have been working side by side with Jameson to figure it out.

I wouldn't have lost my breath when I'd seen that map at the foundation.

"It's hard to tell with you sometimes," Jameson commented. "You're not exactly an open book." He fixed his gaze somewhere in the vicinity of my lips. His face inched toward mine.

Never lose your heart to a Hawthorne.

"Don't touch me," I said, but even as I stepped back, I could feel something—the same something I'd felt when I brushed up against Grayson back at the foundation.

A thing I had no business feeling—for either of them.

"Our thrill ride last night paid off," Jameson told me. "Getting out of my own head let me look at the puzzle with new eyes. Ask me what I figured out about our middle names."

"I don't have to," I told him. "I solved it, too. Blackwood. Westbrook. Davenport. Winchester. They're not just names. They're places—or at least, the first two are. The Black Wood. The West Brook." I let myself focus on the puzzle and not the fact that this room was lit only by lamplight and we were standing too close. "I'm not sure about the other two yet, but..."

"But..." Jameson's lips curved upward, his teeth flashing. "You'll figure it out." He brought his lips near my ear. *"We will, Heiress."*

There is no we. Not really. I'm a means to an end for you. I believed that. I did, but somehow what I found myself saying was "Feel like a walk?"

CHAPTER 46

This wasn't just a walk, and we both knew it.

"The Black Wood is enormous. Finding anything there will be impossible if we don't know what we're looking for." Jameson matched his stride, slow and steady, to mine. "The brook is easier. It runs most of the length of the property, but if I know my grandfather, we're not looking for something in the water. We're looking for something on—or under—the bridge."

"What bridge?" I asked. I caught sight of movement out of the corner of my eye. *Oren.* He stayed in the shadows, but he was there.

"The bridge," Jameson replied, "where my grandfather proposed to my grandmother. It's near Wayback Cottage. Back in the day, that was all my grandfather owned. As his empire grew, he bought up the surrounding land. He built the House but always kept up the cottage."

"The Laughlins live there now," I said, picturing the cottage on the map. "Emily's grandparents." I felt guilty even saying her name, but that didn't stop me from watching his response. *Did you love her? How did she die? Why does Thea blame your family?*

Jameson's mouth twisted. "Xander said you'd had a little chat with Rebecca," he said finally.

"No one at school talks to her," I murmured.

"Correction," Jameson replied. "Rebecca doesn't talk to anyone at school. She hasn't for months." He was quiet for a moment, the sound of our footsteps drowning out all else. "Rebecca was always the shy one. The responsible one. The one their parents expected to make good decisions."

"Not Emily." I filled in the blank.

"Emily…" Jameson sounded different when he said her name. "Emily just wanted to have fun. She had a heart condition, congenital. Her parents were ridiculously overprotective. They never let her do anything as a kid. She got a transplant when she was thirteen, and after that, she just wanted to *live*."

Not survive. Not just make it through. *Live*. I thought of the way she'd laughed into the camera, wild and free and a little too canny, like she'd known when that picture was taken that we'd all be looking at it later. At her.

I thought about the way that Skye had described Jameson. *Hungry*.

"Did you take her driving?" I asked. If I could have taken the question back, I would have, but it hung in the air between us.

"There is *nothing* that Emily and I didn't do." Jameson spoke like the words had been ripped out of him. "We were the same," he told me, and then he corrected himself. "I thought that we were the same."

I thought about Grayson, telling me that Jameson was a sensation seeker. Fear. Pain. Joy. Which of those had Emily been—for him?

"What happened to her?" I asked. My internet search hadn't yielded any answers. Thea had made it sound like the Hawthornes were somehow to blame, like Emily had died *because* she spent time at Hawthorne House. "Did she live at the cottage?"

Jameson ignored my second question and answered the first. "Grayson happened to her."

I'd known, from the moment I'd said Emily's name in Grayson's presence, that she had mattered to him. But Jameson seemed pretty clear on the fact that he'd been the one involved with her. *There is nothing that Emily and I didn't do.*

"What do you mean, Grayson happened to her?" I asked Jameson. I glanced back, but I couldn't see Oren anymore.

"Let's play a game," Jameson said darkly, his pace ticking up a notch as we hit a hill. "I'll give you one truth about my life and two lies, and it's up to you to decide which is which."

"Isn't it supposed to be two truths and one lie?" I asked. I may not have gone to many parties back home, but I hadn't grown up under a rock.

"What fun is it," Jameson returned, "playing by other people's rules?" He was looking at me like he expected me to understand that.

Understand him.

"Fact the first," he rattled off. "I knew what was in my grandfather's will long before you showed up here. Fact the second: I'm the one who sent Grayson to fetch you."

We reached the top of the hill, and I could see a building in the distance. A cottage—and between us and it, a bridge.

"Fact the third," Jameson said, standing statue-still for the span of a heartbeat. "I watched Emily Laughlin die."

CHAPTER 47

I didn't play Jameson's game. I didn't guess which of the things he'd just said was true, but there was no mistaking the way his throat had tightened when he'd said those last words.

I watched Emily Laughlin die.

That didn't tell me what had happened to her. It didn't explain why he'd told me that *Grayson* had happened to her.

"Shall we turn our attention to the bridge, Heiress?" Jameson didn't make me guess. I wasn't sure he really wanted me to.

I forced my focus to the scene in front of us. It was picturesque. There were fewer trees here to block the moonlight. I could make out the way the bridge arched the creek, but not the water below. The bridge was wooden, with railings and balusters that looked like they'd been painstakingly handmade. "Did your grandfather build this himself?"

I'd never met Tobias Hawthorne, but I was starting to feel like I knew him. He was everywhere—in this puzzle, in the House, in the boys.

"I don't know if he built it." Jameson flashed a Cheshire Cat grin, his teeth glinting in the moonlight. "But if we're right about this, he almost certainly built something *into* it."

Jameson excelled at pretense—pretending that I'd never asked him about Emily, pretending he hadn't just told me that he'd watched her die.

Pretending that what happened after midnight stayed in the dark.

He walked the length of the bridge. Behind him, I did the same. It was old and a little creaky but solid as a rock. When Jameson reached the end, he backtracked, his hands stretched out to the sides, fingertips lightly trailing the railings.

"Any idea what we're looking for?" I asked him.

"I'll know it when I see it." He might as well have said *when I see it, I'll let you know.* He'd said that he and Emily were alike, and I couldn't shake the feeling that he wouldn't have expected her to be a passive participant. He wouldn't have treated her as just another part of the game, laid out in the beginning to be useful by the end.

I'm a person. I'm capable. I'm here. I'm playing. I took my phone from the pocket of my coat and turned on its flashlight. I made my way back over the bridge, shining the beam on the railing, looking for indentations or a carving—something. My eyes tracked the nails in the wood, counting them out, mentally measuring the distance between every one.

When I finished with the railing, I squatted, inspecting each baluster. Opposite me, Jameson did the same. It felt almost like we were dancing—a strange midnight dance for two.

I'm here.

"I'll know it when I see it," Jameson said again, somewhere between a mantra and a promise.

"Or maybe I will." I straightened.

Jameson looked up at me. "Sometimes, Heiress," he said, "you just need a different point of view."

He jumped, and the next thing I knew, he was standing on

the railing. I couldn't make out the water down below, but I could hear it. The night air was otherwise silent, until Jameson started walking.

It was like watching him teeter on the balcony, all over again.

The bridge isn't that high. The water probably isn't that deep. I turned my flashlight toward him, rising from my crouched position. The bridge creaked beneath me.

"We need to look below," Jameson said. He climbed to the far side of the railing, balancing on the bridge's edge. "Grab my legs," he told me, but before I could figure out where to grab them or what he was planning to do, he changed his mind. "No. I'm too big. You'll drop me." He was back over the railing in a flash. "I'll have to hold you."

◄──────────►

There were a lot of firsts I'd never gotten around to after my mother's death. First dates. First kisses. First times. But this particular first—being dangled off a bridge by a boy who'd *just* confessed to watching his last girlfriend die—wasn't exactly on the to-do list.

If she was with you, why did you say that Grayson *happened to her?*

"Don't drop your phone," Jameson told me. "And I won't drop you."

His hands were braced against my hips. I was facedown, my legs between the balusters, my torso hanging off the bridge's edge. If he let go, I was in trouble.

The Dangling Game, I could almost hear my mom declaring.

Jameson adjusted his weight, serving as an anchor for mine. *His knee is touching mine. His hands are on me.* I felt more aware of my own body, my own skin, than I could ever remember feeling.

Don't feel. Just look. I flashed my light at the underside of the bridge. Jameson didn't let go.

"Do you see anything?"

"Shadows," I replied. "Some algae." I twisted, arching my back slightly. The blood was rushing to my head. "The boards on the bottom aren't the same boards we can see up top," I noted. "There's at least two layers of wood." I counted the boards. *Twenty-one.* I took another few seconds to examine the way the boards met up with the shore, and then I called back, "There's nothing here, Jameson. Pull me up."

———————◆———————

There were twenty-one boards beneath the bridge and, based on the count I'd just completed, twenty-one on the surface. Everything added up. Nothing was amiss. Jameson paced, but I thought better standing still.

Or I would have thought better standing still if I hadn't been watching him pace. He had a way of moving—unspeakable energy, uncanny grace. "It's getting late," I said, averting my gaze.

"It was always late," Jameson told me. "If you were going to turn into a pumpkin, it would have happened by now, Cinderella."

Another day, another nickname. I didn't want to read into that—I wasn't even sure *what* to read into that. "We have school tomorrow," I reminded him.

"Maybe we do." Jameson hit the end of the bridge, turned, and walked back. "Maybe we don't. You can play by the rules—or you can make them. I know which I prefer, Heiress."

Which Emily preferred. I couldn't keep myself from going there. I tried to focus on the moment, the puzzle at hand. The bridge creaked. Jameson kept pacing. I cleared my mind. And the bridge creaked again.

"Wait." I cocked my head to the side. "Stop." Shockingly, Jameson did as I'd commanded. "Back up. Slowly." I waited, and I listened—and then I heard the creak again.

"It's the same board." Jameson arrived at that conclusion at the same time I did. "Every time." He squatted down to get a better look at it. I knelt, too. The board didn't look different from any of the others. I ran my fingers over it, feeling for something—I wasn't sure what.

Beside me, Jameson was doing the same. He brushed against me. I tried not to feel anything and expected him to pull back, but instead, his fingers slid between mine, weaving our hands together, flat on the board.

He pressed down.

I did the same.

The board creaked. I leaned into it, and Jameson began rotating our hands, slowly, from one side of the board to the other.

"It moves." My eyes darted up toward him. "Just a little."

"A little isn't enough." He pulled his fingers slowly back from mine, feather-light and warm. "We're looking for a latch—something keeping the board from rotating all the way around."

Eventually, we found it, small knots in the wood where the board met up with the balusters. Jameson took the one on the left. I took the one on the right. Moving in synchrony, we pressed. There was a popping sound. When we met back in the middle and tested the board once more, it moved more freely. Together, we rotated it until the bottom of the board faced upward.

I shined my flashlight on the wood. Jameson did the same with his. Carved into the surface of the wood was a symbol.

"Infinity," Jameson said, tracing his thumb over the carving.

I tilted my head to the side and took a more pragmatic view. "Or eight."

CHAPTER 48

Morning came way too early. Somehow, I dragged myself out of bed and got dressed. I debated if I could get away with skipping hair and makeup but remembered what Xander had said about telling the story so no one else tells it for you.

After what I'd pulled with the press the day before, I couldn't afford to show weakness.

As I finished donning what I mentally called my battle face, there was a knock at my door. I answered it and saw the maid who Alisa had told me was "one of Nash's." She was carrying a breakfast tray. Mrs. Laughlin hadn't sent one up since my first morning at Hawthorne House.

I wondered what I'd done to deserve this one.

"Our crew deep-cleans the house from top to bottom on Tuesdays," the maid informed me, once she'd set up the tray. "If it's all right with you, I'll start in your bathroom."

"Just let me hang up my towel," I said, and the woman stared at me like I'd announced an intention to do naked yoga right there in front of her.

"You can leave your towel on the floor. We'll be laundering them anyway."

That just felt wrong. "I'm Avery." I introduced myself, even though she almost certainly knew my name. "What's your name?"

"Mellie." She didn't volunteer more than that.

"Thank you, Mellie." She stared at me blankly. "For your help." I thought about the fact that Tobias Hawthorne had kept outsiders out of Hawthorne House as much as possible. And still, there was an entire crew in to clean on Tuesdays. I shouldn't have found that surprising. It should have been more surprising that the entire crew wasn't here cleaning every day. *And yet...*

I went across the hall to Libby's room because I knew she would get exactly how surreal and uncomfortable this felt. I knocked lightly, in case she was still sleeping, and the door drifted inward, just far enough for me to catch sight of a chair and ottoman—and the man currently occupying them.

Nash Hawthorne's long legs were stretched out on the ottoman, his boots still on. A cowboy hat covered his face. He was sleeping.

In my sister's room.

Nash Hawthorne was sleeping in my sister's room.

I made an involuntary sound and stepped back. Nash stirred, then saw me. Hat in hand, he slipped out of the chair and joined me in the hallway.

"What are you doing in Libby's room?" I asked him. He hadn't been in her bed, but still. What the hell was the oldest Hawthorne brother doing keeping vigil over my sister?

"She's going through something," Nash said, like that was news to me. Like I hadn't been the one to handle Drake the day before.

"Libby isn't one of your projects," I told him. I had no idea how much time they'd spent together these past few days. In the kitchen, she'd seemed to find him irritating. *Libby doesn't get irritated. She's a gothic beam of sunshine.*

"My projects?" Nash repeated, eyes narrowing. "What exactly has Lee-Lee been telling you?"

His continual use of a nickname for my lawyer only served to remind me that they had been engaged. *He's Alisa's ex. He's "saved" who knows how many members of the staff. And he spent the night in my sister's room.*

This could not possibly end well. But before I could say that, Mellie stepped out of my room. She couldn't be done with the bathroom yet, so she must have heard us. Heard Nash.

"Mornin'," he told her.

"Good morning," she said with a smile—and then she looked at me, looked at Libby's room, looked at the open door—and stopped smiling.

CHAPTER 49

O ren met me at the car with a cup of coffee. He didn't say a word about my little adventure with Jameson the night before, and I didn't ask how much he'd observed. As he opened the car door, Oren leaned toward me. "Don't say I didn't warn you."

I had no idea what he was talking about, until I realized that Alisa was sitting in the front seat. "You're looking sedate this morning," she commented.

I took *sedate* to mean *moderately less rash and therefore less likely to evoke a tabloid scandal.* I wondered how she would have described the scene I'd stumbled across in Libby's room.

This is so not good.

"I hope you don't have plans for this weekend, Avery," Alisa said as Oren put the car in drive. "Or the next weekend." Neither Jameson nor Xander had joined us, which meant that I had absolutely no buffer, and clearly, Alisa was royally pissed.

My lawyer can't ground me, can she? I thought.

"I was hoping to keep you out of the limelight a bit longer," Alisa continued pointedly, "but since that plan has gone by the wayside, you'll be attending a pink ribbon fund raiser this Saturday night and a game next Sunday."

"A game?" I repeated.

"NFL," she said curtly. "You own the team. My hope is that scheduling some high-profile social outings will provide enough grist for the gossip mill that we can delay setting up your first sit-down interview until after we've gotten you some real media training."

I was still trying to absorb the NFL bombshell when the words *media training* put a knot of dread in my throat.

"Do I have to—"

"Yes," Alisa told me. "Yes to the gala this weekend, yes to the game next weekend, yes to the media training."

I didn't say another word in complaint. I'd stoked this fire—and protected Libby—knowing that, sooner or later, I'd have to pay the piper.

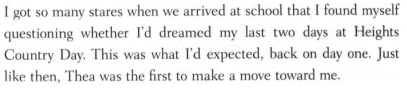

I got so many stares when we arrived at school that I found myself questioning whether I'd dreamed my last two days at Heights Country Day. This was what I'd expected, back on day one. Just like then, Thea was the first to make a move toward me.

"You did a thing," she said in a tone that highly suggested what I'd done was both naughty and delicious. Inexplicably, my mind went to Jameson, to the moment on the bridge when his fingers had woven their way between mine.

"Do you really know why Tobias Hawthorne left you every-thing?" Thea asked, her eyes alight. "The whole school's talking about it."

"The whole school can talk about whatever they want."

"You don't like me much," Thea noted. "That's okay. I'm a

hypercompetitive, bisexual perfectionist who likes to win and looks like *this*. I'm no stranger to being hated."

I rolled my eyes. "I don't hate you." I didn't know her well enough to hate her yet.

"That's good," Thea replied with a self-satisfied smile, "because we're going to be spending a lot more time with each other. My parents are going out of town. They seem to believe that, left to my own devices, I might do something ill-advised, so I'll be staying with my uncle, and I understand that he and Zara have taken up residence at Hawthorne House. I guess they're not quite ready to cede the family homestead to a stranger."

Zara had been playing nice—or at least *nicer*. But I'd had no idea that she'd moved in. Then again, Hawthorne House was so gargantuan that an entire professional baseball team could be living there and I might have no idea.

For all I knew, I might *own* a professional baseball team.

"Why would you want to stay at Hawthorne House?" I asked Thea. She was the one who'd warned me away.

"Contrary to popular belief, I don't always do what I want." Thea tossed her dark hair over her shoulder. "And besides, Emily was my best friend. After everything that happened last year, when it comes to the charms of Hawthorne brothers, I'm immune."

CHAPTER 50

When I finally got ahold of Max, she wasn't feeling chatty. I could tell that something was wrong, but not what. She didn't have a single fake expletive to share on the topic of Thea moving in, and she cut our back-and-forth short without any commentary whatsoever on the Hawthorne brothers' physiques. I asked if everything was okay. She said that she had to go.

Xander, in contrast, was more than willing to discuss the Thea development. "If Thea's here," he told me that afternoon, lowering his voice like the walls of Hawthorne House might have ears, "she's up to something."

"*She* as in Thea?" I asked pointedly. "Or your aunt?"

Zara had thrown me together with Grayson at the foundation, and now she was moving Thea into the House. I recognized someone stacking the board, even if I couldn't see the play underneath.

"You're right," Xander said. "I seriously doubt Thea *volunteered* to spend time with our family. It is possible that she fervently wishes for vultures to dine upon my entrails."

"You?" I said. Thea's issues with the Hawthorne brothers had seemed to revolve around Emily—and that meant, I had assumed, around Jameson and Grayson. "What did you do?"

"It is a story," Xander said with a sigh, "involving star-crossed love, fake dating, tragedy, penance...and possibly vultures."

I thought back to asking Xander about Rebecca Laughlin. He hadn't said anything to indicate she was Emily's sister. He'd murmured almost exactly what he'd just said about Thea.

Xander didn't let me ruminate for long. Instead, he dragged me off to what he declared to be his fourth-favorite room in the House. "If you're going to be going head-to-head with Thea," he told me, "you need to be prepared."

"I'm not going head-to-head with anyone," I said firmly.

"It is adorable that you believe that." Xander stopped where one corridor met another. He reached up—all six foot three of him—to touch a molding that ran up the corner. He must have hit some kind of release, because the next thing I knew, he was pulling the molding toward us, revealing a gap behind it. He stuck his hand into the gap behind the molding, and a moment later, a portion of the wall swung out toward us like a door.

I was *never* going to get used to this.

"Welcome to...my lair!" Xander sounded overjoyed to be saying those words.

I stepped into his "lair" and saw...a machine? *Contraption* probably would have been the more accurate term. There were dozens of gears, pulleys, and chains, a complicated series of connected ramps, several buckets, two conveyor belts, a slingshot, a birdcage, four pinwheels, and at least four balloons.

"Is that an anvil?" I asked, frowning and leaning forward for a better look.

"That," Xander said proudly, "is a Rube Goldberg machine. As it so happens, I am a three-time world champion at building machines that do simple things in overly complicated ways." He handed me a marble. "Place this in the pinwheel."

I did. The pinwheel spun, blowing a balloon, that tipped a bucket...

As I watched each mechanism set off the next, I glanced at the youngest Hawthorne brother out of the corner of my eye. "What does this have to do with Thea moving in?"

He'd told me that I needed to be prepared, then brought me here. Was this supposed to be some kind of metaphor? A warning that Zara's actions might appear complicated, even when the goal was simple? An insight into Thea's charge?

Xander cast a sideways look at me and grinned. "Who said this had anything to do with Thea?"

CHAPTER 51

That night, in honor of Thea's visit, Mrs. Laughlin made a melt-in-your-mouth roast beef. Orgasmic garlic mashed potatoes. Roasted asparagus, broccoli florets, and three different kinds of crème brûlée.

I couldn't help feeling like it was pretty revealing that Mrs. Laughlin had pulled out all the stops for Thea—but not for me.

Trying not to seem petty, I sat down to a formal dinner in the "dining room," which probably should have been called a banquet hall instead. The massive table was set for eleven. I cataloged the participants in this little family dinner: four Hawthorne brothers. Skye. Zara and Constantine. Thea. Libby. Nan. And me.

"Thea," Zara said, her voice almost too pleasant, "how is field hockey?"

"We're undefeated this season." Thea turned toward me. "Have you decided which sport you'll be playing, Avery?"

I managed to resist the urge to snort, but barely. "I don't do sports."

"Everyone at Country Day does a sport," Xander informed me, before stuffing his mouth with roast beef. His eyes rolled upward with pleasure as he chewed. "It is an actual, real requirement and not a figment of Thea's delightfully vindictive imagination."

"Xander," Nash said in warning.

"I said she was *delightfully* vindictive," Xander replied innocently.

"If I were a boy," Thea told him with a Southern belle smile, "people would just call me driven."

"Thea." Constantine frowned at her.

"Right." Thea dabbed at her lips with her napkin. "No feminism at the dinner table."

This time, I couldn't bite back the snort. *Point, Thea.*

"A toast," Skye declared out of nowhere, holding up her wineglass and slurring the words enough that it was clear she'd already been imbibing.

"Skye, dear," Nan said firmly, "have you considered sleeping it off?"

"A toast," Skye reiterated, glass still held high. "To Avery."

For once, she'd gotten my name right. I waited for the guillotine to drop, but Skye said nothing else. Zara raised her glass. One by one, every other glass went up.

Every person in this room had probably gotten the message: No good could come of challenging the will. I might have been the enemy—but I was also the one with the money.

Is that why Zara brought Thea here? To get close to me? Is that why she left me alone at the foundation with Grayson?

"To you, Heiress," Jameson murmured to my left. I turned to look at him. I hadn't seen him since the night before. I was fairly certain he'd skipped school. I wondered if he'd spent the day in the Black Wood, looking for the next clue. *Without me.*

"To Emily," Thea added suddenly, her glass still raised, her eyes on Jameson. "May she rest in peace."

Jameson's glass came down. His chair was pushed roughly back from the table. Farther down, Grayson's fingers tightened around the stem of his own glass, his knuckles going white.

"*Theadora,*" Constantine hissed.

Thea took a drink and adopted the world's most innocent expression. "What?"

Everything in me wanted to follow Jameson, but I waited a few minutes before excusing myself. Like that would keep any of them from knowing exactly where I was going.

In the foyer, I pressed my hand flat against the wall panels, hitting the sequence designed to reveal the coat closet door. I needed my coat if I was going to venture off into the Black Wood. I was sure that was where Jameson had gone.

As my hand hooked around the hanger, a voice spoke from behind me. "I'm not going to ask you what Jameson is up to. What you're up to."

I turned to face Grayson. "You're not going to ask me," I repeated, taking in the set of his jaw and those canny silver eyes, "because you already know."

"I was there last night. At the bridge." There were edges in Grayson's tone—not rough, but sharp. "This morning, I went to see the Red Will."

"I still have the decoder," I pointed out, trying not to read anything into the fact that he'd seen his brother and me at the bridge—and didn't sound happy about it.

Grayson shrugged, his shoulders pulling against the confines of his suit. "Red acetate is easy enough to come by."

If he'd seen the Red Will, he knew that their middle names were clues. I wondered if his mind had gone immediately to their fathers. I wondered if that hurt him, the way it hurt Jameson.

"You were there last night," I said, echoing back what he'd told me. "At the bridge." How much had he seen? How much did he know?

What had he thought when Jameson and I had touched?

"Westbrook. Davenport. Winchester. Blackwood." Grayson took a step toward me. "They're last names—but they are also locations. I found the clue on the bridge after you and my brother had gone."

He'd followed us there. He'd found what we'd found.

"What do you want, Grayson?"

"If you were smart," he warned softly, "you'd stay away from Jameson. From the game." He looked down. "From me." Emotion slashed across his features, but he masked it before I could tell what, exactly, he was feeling. "Thea's right," he said sharply, turning away from me—*walking* away from me. "This family—we destroy everything we touch."

CHAPTER 52

I knew from the map roughly where the Black Wood was. I found Jameson on the outskirts, standing eerily still, like he *couldn't* move. Without warning, he broke that stillness, punching furiously at a nearby tree, hard and fast, the bark tearing at his hands.

Thea brought up Emily. This is what even the mention of her name does to him.

"Jameson!" I was almost to him now. He jerked his head toward me, and I stopped, overwhelmed with the feeling that I shouldn't have been there, that I had no right to witness any of the Hawthorne boys hurting that much.

The only thing I could think to do was try to make what I'd just seen matter less. "Broken any fingers lately?" I asked lightly. *The Pretending It Doesn't Matter Game.*

Jameson was ready and willing to play. He held his hands up, grunting as he bent them at the knuckles. "Still intact."

I dragged my eyes from him and took in our surroundings. The perimeter was so densely wooded that if the trees hadn't already shed their leaves, no light would have been able to make it to the forest floor.

"What are we looking for?" I asked. Maybe he didn't consider me a real partner in this hunt. Maybe there was no real *we*—but he answered.

"Your guess is as good as mine, Heiress."

All around us, bare branches stretched up overhead, skeletal and crooked.

"You skipped school today to do *something*," I pointed out. "You have a guess."

Jameson smiled like he couldn't feel the blood welling up on his hands. "Four middle names. Four locations. Four clues—carvings, most likely. Symbols, if the clue on the bridge was infinity; numbers, if it was an eight."

I wondered what, if anything, he'd done to clear his mind between last night and entering the Black Wood. *Climbing. Racing. Jumping.*

Disappearing into the walls.

"Do you know how many trees four acres can hold, Heiress?" Jameson asked jauntily. "Two hundred, in a healthy forest."

"And in the Black Wood?" I prompted, taking first one step toward him, then another.

"At least twice that."

It was like the library all over again. Like the keys. There had to be a shortcut, a trick we weren't seeing.

"Here." Jameson bent down, then placed a roll of glow-in-the-dark duct tape in my hand, letting his fingers brush mine as he did. "I've been marking off trees as I check them."

I concentrated on his words—not his touch. Mostly. "There has got to be a better way," I said, turning the duct tape over in my hands, my eyes finding their way to his once more.

Jameson's lips twisted into a lazy, devil-may-care smirk. "Got any suggestions, Mystery Girl?"

———

Two days later, Jameson and I were still doing things the hard way, and we still hadn't found anything. I could see him becoming more and more single-minded. Jameson Winchester Hawthorne would push until he hit a wall. I wasn't sure what he would do to break through it this time, but every once in a while, I caught him looking at me in a way that made me think he had some ideas.

That was how he was looking at me now. "We aren't the only ones searching for the next clue," he said as dusk began to give way to darkness. "I saw Grayson with a map of the woods."

"Thea's tailing me," I said, ripping off a piece of tape, hyper-aware of the silence all around us. "The only way I can shake her is when she sees an opportunity to mess with Xander."

Jameson brushed gently past me and marked off the next tree over. "Thea holds a grudge, and when she and Xander broke up, it was ugly."

"They dated?" I slid past Jameson and searched the next tree, running my fingers over the bark. "Thea is practically your cousin."

"Constantine is Zara's second husband. The marriage is recent, and Xander's always been a fan of loopholes."

Nothing with the Hawthorne brothers was ever simple—including what Jameson and I were doing now. Since we'd worked our way to the center of the forest, the trees were spread farther apart. Up ahead, I could see a large open space—the only place in the Black Wood where grass was able to grow on the forest floor.

My back to Jameson, I moved to a new tree and began running my hands over the bark. Almost immediately, my fingers hit a groove.

"Jameson." It wasn't pitch-dark yet, but there was little enough light in the woods that I couldn't entirely make out what I'd found until Jameson appeared beside me, shining an extra light. I ran my fingers slowly over the letters carved into the tree.

TOBIAS HAWTHORNE II

Unlike the first symbol we'd found, these letters weren't smooth. The carving hadn't been done with an even hand. The name looked like it had been carved by a child.

"The I's at the end are a Roman numeral," Jameson said, his voice going electric. "Tobias Hawthorne the Second."

Toby, I thought, and then I heard a *crack*. A deafening echo followed, and the world exploded. Bark flying. My body thrown backward.

"Get down!" Jameson yelled.

I barely heard him. My brain couldn't process what I was hearing, what had just happened. *I'm bleeding.*

Pain.

Jameson grabbed me and pulled me toward the ground. The next thing I knew, his body was over mine and the sound of a second gunshot rang out.

Gun. Someone's shooting at us. There was a stabbing pain in my chest. *I've been shot.*

I heard footsteps beating against the forest floor, and then Oren yelled, "Stay down!" Weapon drawn, my bodyguard put himself between us and the shooter. A small eternity passed. Oren took off running in the direction the shots had come from, but I knew, with a prescience I couldn't explain, that the shooter was gone.

"Are you okay, Avery?" Oren doubled back. "Jameson, is she okay?"

"She's bleeding." That was Jameson. He'd pulled back from my body and was looking down at me.

My chest throbbed, just below my collarbone, where I'd been hit.

"Your face." Jameson's touch was light against my skin. The moment his fingertips skimmed lightly over my cheekbone, the nerves in my face were jarred alive. *Hurts.*

"Did they shoot me twice?" I asked, dazed.

"The assailant didn't shoot you at all." Oren made quick work of displacing Jameson and ran his hands expertly over my body, checking for damage. "You got hit by a couple of pieces of bark." He probed at the wound below my collarbone. "The other cut's just a scratch, but the bark's lodged deep in this one. We'll leave it until we're ready to stitch you up."

My ears rang. "Stitch me up." I didn't want to just repeat what he was saying back to him, but it was literally all my mouth would do.

"You're lucky." Oren stood, then did a quick check of the tree, where the bullet had hit. "A couple of inches to the right, and we'd be looking at removing a bullet, not bark." My bodyguard stalked past the place where the tree had been hit to another tree behind us. In one smooth motion, he produced a knife from his belt and jammed it into the tree.

It took me a moment to realize that he was digging out a bullet.

"Whoever fired this is long gone now," he said, wrapping the bullet in what appeared to be some kind of handkerchief. "But we might be able to trace this."

This, as in a bullet. Someone had just tried to shoot us. *Me.* My brain was finally catching up now. *They weren't aiming for Jameson.*

"What just happened here?" For once, Jameson didn't sound like he was playing. He sounded like his heart was beating as rapidly and viciously as mine.

"What happened," Oren replied, glancing back into the distance, "is that someone saw the two of you out here, decided you were easy targets, and pulled their trigger. Twice."

CHAPTER 53

Someone shot at me. I felt...*numb* wasn't the right word. My mouth was too dry. My heart was beating too fast. I hurt, but it felt like I was hurting from a distance.

Shock.

"I need a team in the northeast quadrant." Oren was on the phone. I tried to focus on what he was saying but couldn't seem to focus on anything, not even my arm. "We have a shooter. Gone now, almost certainly, but we'll sweep the woods just in case. Bring a med kit."

Oren hung up, then turned his attention back to Jameson and me. "Follow me. We'll stay where we have cover until the support team gets here." He led us back toward the south end of the forest, where the trees were denser.

It didn't take the team long to arrive. They came in ATVs—two of them. *Two men, two vehicles.* As soon as they pulled up, Oren rattled off coordinates: where we'd been when we were shot, the direction the bullets had come from, the trajectory.

The men didn't say anything in response. They drew their weapons. Oren climbed into the four-seat ATV and waited for Jameson and me to do the same.

"You headed back to the House?" one of the men asked.

Oren met his subordinate's eyes. "The cottage."

<hr/>

Halfway to Wayback Cottage, my brain started working again. My chest hurt. I'd been given a compress to hold on the wound, but Oren hadn't treated it yet. His first priority had been getting us to safer ground. *He's taking us to Wayback Cottage. Not Hawthorne House.* The cottage was closer, but I couldn't shake the feeling that what Oren had really been saying to his men was that he didn't trust the people at the House.

So much for the way he'd assured me—repeatedly—that I was safe. That the Hawthorne family wasn't a threat. The entire estate, including the Black Wood, was walled in. No one was allowed past the gate without a thorough background check.

Oren doesn't think we're dealing with an outside threat. I let that sink in, a heaviness in my stomach as I processed the limited number of suspects. *The Hawthornes—and the staff.*

<hr/>

Going to Wayback Cottage felt like a risk. I hadn't interacted with the Laughlins much, but they hadn't ever given me the impression that they were glad I was here. *Exactly how loyal are they to the Hawthorne family?* I thought about Alisa saying that Nash's people would die for him.

Would they kill for him, too?

Mrs. Laughlin was at home when we arrived at Wayback. *She's not the shooter,* I thought. *She couldn't have made it back here in time. Could she?*

The older woman took one look at Oren, Jameson, and me and ushered us inside. If a bleeding person being stitched up at her kitchen table was an unusual occurrence, she gave no sign of it. I wasn't sure if the way she was taking this in stride was comforting—or suspicious.

"I'll put on some tea," she said. My heart pounding, I wondered if it was safe to drink anything she gave me.

"You okay with me playing medic?" Oren asked, settling me in a chair. "I'm sure Alisa could arrange for some fancy plastic surgeon."

I wasn't okay with any of this. Everyone had been so sure that I wasn't going to get ax-murdered that I'd let my guard down. I'd pushed back the thought that people had killed over far less than what I'd inherited. I'd let every single one of the Hawthorne brothers past my defenses.

This wasn't Xander. I couldn't get my body to calm down, no matter how hard I tried. *Jameson was right next to me. Nash doesn't want the money, and Grayson wouldn't . . .*

He wouldn't.

"Avery?" Oren prompted, a note of concern working its way into his deep voice.

I tried to stop my mind from racing. I felt sick—physically sick. *Stop panicking.* I had a piece of wood in my flesh. I would have preferred *not* having a piece of wood in my flesh. *Pull it together.*

"Do what you need to do to stop the bleeding," I told Oren. My voice only shook a little.

Removing the bark hurt. The disinfectant hurt a hell of a lot more. The med kit included a shot of local anesthetic, but there was no amount of anesthetic that could alter my brain's awareness of the needle when Oren began stitching my skin back together.

Focus on that. Let it hurt. After a moment, I looked away from Oren and tracked Mrs. Laughlin's movements. Before handing me my tea, she laced it—heavily—with whiskey.

"Done." Oren nodded to my cup. "Drink that."

He'd brought me here because he trusted the Laughlins more than he trusted the Hawthornes. He was telling me that it was safe to drink. But he'd told me a lot of things.

Someone shot at me. They tried to kill me. I could be dead. My hands were shaking. Oren steadied them. His eyes knowing, he lifted my teacup to his own mouth and took a drink.

It's fine. He's showing me that it's fine. Unsure if I'd ever be able to kick myself out of fight-or-flight mode, I forced myself to drink. The tea was hot. The whiskey was strong.

It burned all the way down.

Mrs. Laughlin gave me an almost maternal look, then scowled at Oren. "Mr. Laughlin will want to know what happened," she said, as if she herself were not at all curious about why I was bleeding at her kitchen table. "And someone needs to clean up the poor girl's face." She gave me a sympathetic look and clucked her tongue.

Before, I'd been an outsider. Now she was hovering like a mother hen. *All it took was a few bullets.*

"Where is Mr. Laughlin?" Oren asked, his tone conversational, but I heard the question—and the implication underneath. *He's not here. Is he a good shot? Would he—*

As if summoned, Mr. Laughlin walked through the front door and let it slam behind him. There was mud on his boots.

From the woods?

"Something's happened," Mrs. Laughlin told her husband calmly.

Mr. Laughlin looked at Oren, Jameson, and me—in that order, the same order in which his wife had taken in our presence—and then poured himself a glass of whiskey. "Security protocols?" he asked Oren gruffly.

Oren gave a brisk nod. "In full force."

He turned back to his wife. "Where's Rebecca?" he asked.

Jameson looked up from his own cup of tea. "Rebecca's here?"

"She's a good girl," Mr. Laughlin grunted. "Comes to visit, the way she should."

So where is she? I thought.

Mrs. Laughlin rested a hand on my shoulder. "There's a bathroom through there, dear," she told me quietly, "if you want to clean up."

CHAPTER 54

The door Mrs. Laughlin had sent me through didn't lead directly to a bathroom. It led to a bedroom that held two twin beds and little else. The walls were painted a light purple; the twin comforters were quilted from squares of fabric in lavender and violet.

The bathroom door was slightly ajar.

I walked toward it, so painfully aware of my surroundings that I felt like I could have heard a pin drop a mile away. *There's no one here. I'm safe. It's okay. I'm okay.*

Inside the bathroom, I checked behind the shower curtain. *There's no one here*, I told myself again. *I'm okay.* I managed to get my cell phone out of my pocket and called Max. I needed her to answer. I needed not to be alone with this. What I got was voicemail.

I called seven times, and she didn't pick up.

Maybe she couldn't. *Or maybe she doesn't want to.* That hit me almost as hard as looking in the mirror and seeing my blood-streaked, dirt-smeared face. I stared at myself.

I could hear the echo of gunfire.

Stop. I needed to wash—my hands, my face, the streaks of

blood on my chest. *Turn on the water*, I told myself sternly. *Pick up the washcloth.* I willed my body to move.

I couldn't.

Hands reached past me to turn on the faucet. I should have jumped. I should have panicked. But somehow, my body relaxed into the person behind me.

"It's okay, Heiress," Jameson murmured. "I've got you."

I hadn't heard Jameson come in. I wasn't entirely sure how long I'd been standing there, frozen.

Jameson reached for a pale purple washcloth and held it under the water.

"I'm fine," I insisted, as much to myself as to him.

Jameson lifted the washcloth to my face. "You're a horrible liar." He ran the cloth over my cheek, working his way down toward the scratch. A breath caught in my throat. He rinsed the washcloth, blood and dirt coloring the sink, as he lifted the cloth back to my skin.

Again.

And again.

He washed my face, took my hands in his and held them under the water, his fingers working the dirt from mine. My skin responded to his touch. For the first time, no part of me said to pull away. He was so gentle. He wasn't acting like this was just a game to him—like I was just a game.

He picked the washcloth back up and ran it down my neck to my shoulder, over my collarbone and across. The water was warm. I leaned into his touch. *This is a bad idea.* I knew that. I'd always known that, but I let myself concentrate on the feel of Jameson Hawthorne's touch, the stroke of the cloth.

"I'm okay," I said, and I could almost believe that.

"You're better than okay."

I closed my eyes. He'd been there with me in the forest. I could feel his body over mine. Protecting me. I needed this. I needed *something*.

I opened my eyes, looked at him. Focused on him. I thought about going two hundred miles an hour, about the climbing wall, about the moment I'd first seen him up on that balcony. Was being a sensation seeker so bad? Was wanting to feel something other than *awful* really so wrong?

Everyone is a little wrong sometimes, Heiress.

Something gave inside of me, and I pushed him gently back against the bathroom wall. *I need this.* His deep green eyes met mine. *He needs it, too.* "Yes?" I asked him hoarsely.

"Yes, Heiress."

My lips closed over his. He kissed me back, gentle at first, then not gently at all. Maybe it was the aftereffects of shock, but as I drove my hands into his hair, as he grabbed my ponytail and angled my face upward, I could see a thousand versions of him in my mind: *Balanced on the balcony's railing. Shirtless and sunlit in the solarium. Smiling. Smirking. Our hands touching on the bridge. His body protecting mine in the Black Wood. Trailing a washcloth down my neck—*

Kissing him felt like fire. He wasn't soft and sweet, the way he had been while washing away the blood and dirt. I didn't need soft or sweet. *This* was exactly what I needed.

Maybe I could be what he needed, too. Maybe this didn't have to be a bad idea. Maybe the complications were worth it.

He pulled back from the kiss, his lips only an inch away from mine. "I always knew you were special."

I felt his breath on my face. I felt every last one of those words. I'd never thought of myself as special. I'd been invisible for so long. *Wallpaper.* Even after I'd become the biggest story in the world, it had never really felt like anyone was paying attention to *me*. The real me.

"We're so close now," Jameson murmured. "I can feel it." There was an energy in his voice, like the buzzing of a neon light. "Someone obviously didn't want us looking at that tree."

What?

He went to kiss me again, and, my heart sinking, I turned my head to the side. I'd thought... I wasn't sure what I'd thought. *That when he told me I was special, he wasn't talking about the money—or the puzzle.*

"You think someone shot at us because of a tree?" I said, the words getting caught in my throat. "Not, say, the fortune I inherited that your family would like to get their hands on? Not the billions of reasons that anyone with the last name Hawthorne has to hate me?"

"Don't think about that," Jameson whispered, cupping my cheeks. "Think about Toby's name carved into that tree. Infinity carved into the bridge." His face was close enough to mine that I could still feel his breath. "What if what the puzzle is trying to tell us is that my uncle isn't dead?"

Was *that* what he'd been thinking when someone was shooting at us? In the kitchen, as Oren took a needle to my wound? As he'd brought his lips to mine? Because if the only thing he'd been able to think about was the mystery...

You're not a player, kid. You're the glass ballerina—or the knife.

"Will you listen to yourself?" I demanded. My chest was tight— tighter now than it had been in the forest, in the thick of it all. Nothing about Jameson's reaction should have surprised me, so why did it hurt?

Why was I letting it hurt?

"Oren just pulled a chunk of wood out of my chest," I said, my voice low, "and if things had worked out a little differently, he could have been pulling out a bullet." I gave Jameson a second to reply— just one. *Nothing*. "What happens to the money if I die while the will is in probate?" I asked flatly. Alisa had told me the Hawthorne family didn't stand to benefit, but did *they* know that? "What happens if whoever fired that gun scares me off, and I leave before the year is up?" Did they know that if I left, it all went to charity? "Not everything is a game, Jameson."

I saw something flicker in his eyes. He closed them, just for an instant, then opened them and leaned in, bringing his lips painfully close to mine. "That's the thing, Heiress. If Emily taught me anything, it's that everything *is* a game. Even this. *Especially* this."

CHAPTER 55

Jameson left, and I didn't follow him.

Thea's right, Grayson whispered in the recesses of my mind. *This family—we destroy everything we touch.* I choked back tears. I'd been shot at, I'd been injured, and I'd been kissed—but I sure as hell wasn't destroyed.

"I'm stronger than that." I angled my face toward the mirror and looked myself in the eye. If it came down to a choice between being scared, being hurt, and being pissed, I knew which one I preferred.

I tried calling Max one more time, then texted her: *Someone tried to kill me, and I made out with Jameson Hawthorne.*

If that didn't garner a response, nothing would.

I made my way back into the bedroom. Even though I'd calmed down a little, I still scanned for threats, and I saw one: Rebecca Laughlin, standing in the doorway. Her face looked even paler than usual, her hair as red as blood. She looked shell-shocked.

Because she overheard Jameson and me? Because her grandparents told her about the shooting? I wasn't sure. She was wearing thick hiking boots and cargo pants, both of them spattered with mud. Staring at her, all I could think was that if Emily had been even half as beautiful as her sister was, it was no wonder Jameson could look at me and think only about his grandfather's game.

Everything is *a game. Even this.* Especially *this.*

"My grandmother sent me to check on you." Rebecca's voice was soft and hesitant.

"I'm okay," I said, and I almost meant it. I *had* to be okay.

"Gran said you were shot." Rebecca stayed in the doorway, like she was afraid to come any closer.

"Shot at," I clarified.

"I'm glad," Rebecca said, and then she looked mortified. "I mean, that you weren't shot. It's good, right, getting shot at instead of shot?" Her gaze darted nervously from me toward the twin beds, the quilts. "Emily would have told you to simplify and say that you were shot." Rebecca sounded more sure of herself telling me what Emily would have said than trying to summon an appropriate response herself. "There was a bullet. You were wounded. Emily would have said you were entitled to a little melodrama."

I was entitled to look at everyone like they were a suspect. I was entitled to an adrenaline-fueled lapse in judgment. And maybe I was entitled, just this once, to push for answers.

"You and Emily shared this room?" I said. That was obvious now, when I looked at the twin beds. *When Rebecca and Emily came to visit their grandparents, they stayed here.* "Was purple your favorite color as a kid or hers?"

"Hers," Rebecca said. She gave me a very small shrug. "She used to tell me that my favorite color was purple, too."

In the picture I'd seen of the two of them, Emily had been looking directly at the camera, dead center; Rebecca had been on the fringes, looking away.

"I feel like I should warn you." Rebecca wasn't even facing me anymore. She walked over to one of the beds.

"Warn me about what?" I asked, and somewhere in the back of my mind, I registered the mud on her boots—and the fact that she'd been on the premises, but not with her grandparents, when I'd been shot at.

Just because she doesn't feel like a threat doesn't mean she isn't one.

But when Rebecca started talking again, it wasn't about the shooting. "I'm supposed to say that my sister was wonderful." She acted like that wasn't a change of subject, like Emily *was* what she was warning me about. "And she was, when she wanted to be. Her smile was contagious. Her laugh was worse, and when she said something was a good idea, people believed her. She was good to me, almost all the time." Rebecca met my gaze, head-on. "But she wasn't nearly as good to those boys."

Boys, plural. "What did she do?" I asked. I should have been more focused on who shot me, but part of me couldn't shake the way Jameson had invoked Emily, right before walking away from me.

"Em didn't like to choose." Rebecca seemed to be picking her words carefully. "She wanted *everything* more than I wanted anything. And the one time I wanted something..." She shook her head and aborted that sentence. "My job was to keep my sister happy. It's something my parents used to tell me when we were little—that Emily was sick, and I wasn't, so I should do what I could to make her smile."

"And the boys?" I asked.

"They made her smile."

I read into what Rebecca was saying—what she'd been saying. *Em didn't like to choose.* "She dated both of them?" I tried to get a handle on that. "Did they know?"

"Not at first," Rebecca whispered, like some part of her thought Emily might hear us talking.

"What happened when Grayson and Jameson found out she was dating both of them?"

"You're only asking that because you didn't know Emily," Rebecca said. "She didn't want to choose, and neither one of them wanted to let her go. She turned it into a competition. A little game."

And then she died.

"How did Emily die?" I asked, because I might never get another opening like this one—not with Rebecca, not with the boys.

Rebecca was looking at me, but I got the general sense that she wasn't seeing me. That she was somewhere else. "Grayson told me that it was her heart," she whispered.

Grayson. I couldn't think beyond that. It wasn't until Rebecca had left that I had realized she'd never gotten around to telling me what, specifically, she *ought* to have been warning me about.

CHAPTER 56

I t was another three hours before Oren and his team cleared me to go back to Hawthorne House. I rode back in the ATV with *three* bodyguards.

Oren was the only one who spoke. "Due in part to Hawthorne House's extensive network of security cameras, my team was able to track and verify locations and alibis for all members of the Hawthorne family, as well as Ms. Thea Calligaris."

They have alibis. Grayson has an alibi. I felt a rush of relief, but a moment later, my chest tightened. "What about Constantine?" I asked. Technically, he wasn't a Hawthorne.

"Clear," Oren told me. "He did not personally wield that gun."

Personally. Reading between those lines shook me. "But he might have hired someone?" *Any of them might have,* I realized. I could hear Grayson telling me that there would always be people tripping over themselves to do favors for his family.

"I know a forensic investigator," Oren said evenly. "He works alongside an equally skilled hacker. They'll take a deep dive into everyone's finances and cell phone records. In the meantime, my team is going to focus on the staff."

I swallowed. I hadn't even met most of the staff. I didn't know exactly how many of them there were, or who might have had opportunity—or motive. "The entire staff?" I asked Oren. "Including the Laughlins?" They'd been kind to me after I'd emerged from washing up, but right now I couldn't afford to trust my gut—or Oren's.

"They're clear," Oren told me. "Mr. Laughlin was at the House during the shooting, and security footage confirms Mrs. Laughlin was at the cottage."

"What about Rebecca?" I asked. She'd left the estate right after talking to me.

I could see Oren wanting to say that Rebecca wasn't a threat, but he didn't. "No stone will be left unturned," he promised. "But I do know that the Laughlin girls never learned to shoot. Mr. Laughlin wasn't even allowed to keep a gun at the cottage when they were present."

"Who else was on the premises today?" I asked.

"Pool maintenance, a sound technician working on upgrades in the theater, a massage therapist, and one of the cleaning staff."

I committed that list to memory, then my mouth went dry. "Which cleaning staff?"

"Melissa Vincent."

The name meant nothing to me—until it did. "Mellie?"

Oren's eyes narrowed. "You know her?"

I thought of the moment she'd seen Nash outside Libby's room.

"Something I should know?" Oren asked—and it wasn't really a question. I told him what Alisa had said about Mellie and Nash, what I'd seen in Libby's room, what *Mellie* had seen. And then we pulled up to Hawthorne House, and I saw Alisa.

"She's the only person I've let past the gates," Oren assured me. "Frankly, she's the only one I intend to let past those gates for the foreseeable future."

I probably should have found that more comforting than I did.

"How is she?" Alisa asked Oren as soon as we exited the SUV.

"Pissed," I answered, before Oren could reply on my behalf. "Sore. A little terrified." Seeing her—and seeing Oren standing next to her—broke the dam, and an accusation burst out of me. "You both told me I would be fine! You swore that I was not in danger. You acted like I was being ridiculous when I mentioned murder."

"Technically," my lawyer replied, "you specified *ax*-murder. And technically," she continued through gritted teeth, "it is possible that there was an oversight, legally speaking."

"What kind of oversight? You told me that if I died, the Hawthornes wouldn't get a penny!"

"And I stand by that conclusion," Alisa said emphatically. "However..." She clearly found any admission of fault distasteful. "I also told you that if you died while the will was in probate, your inheritance would pass through to your estate. And typically, it would."

"Typically," I repeated. If there was one thing I'd learned in the past week, it was that there was nothing *typical* about Tobias Hawthorne—or his heirs.

"However," Alisa continued, her voice tight, "in the state of Texas, it is possible for the deceased to add a stipulation to the will that requires heirs to survive him by a certain amount of time in order to inherit."

I'd read the will multiple times. "Pretty sure I'd remember if there was something in there about how long I had to avoid *dying* to inherit. The only stipulation—"

"Was that you must live in Hawthorne House for one year," Alisa finished. "Which, I will admit, would be quite the difficult stipulation to fulfill if you were dead."

That was her oversight? The fact that I couldn't *live* in Hawthorne House if I wasn't alive?

"So if I die..." I swallowed, wetting my tongue. "The money goes to charity?"

"Possibly. But it's also possible that *your* heirs could challenge that interpretation on the basis of Mr. Hawthorne's intent."

"I don't have heirs," I said. "I don't even have a will."

"You don't need a will to have heirs." Alisa glanced at Oren. "Has her sister been cleared?"

"*Libby?*" I was incredulous. Had they *met* my sister?

"The sister's clear," Oren told Alisa. "She was with Nash during the shooting."

He might as well have detonated a bomb for how well *that* went over.

Eventually, Alisa gathered her composure and turned back to me. "You won't legally be able to sign a will until you turn eighteen. Ditto for the paperwork regarding the foundation conservatorship. And *that* is the other oversight here. Originally, I was focused only on the will, but if you are unable or unwilling to fulfill your role as conservator, the conservatorship passes." She paused heavily. "To the boys."

If I died, the foundation—all the money, all the power, all that potential—went to Tobias Hawthorne's grandsons. A hundred million dollars a year to give away. You could buy a lot of favors for money like that.

"Who knows about the terms of the foundation's conservatorship?" Oren asked, deadly serious.

"Zara and Constantine, certainly," Alisa said immediately.

"Grayson," I added hoarsely, my wounds throbbing. I knew him well enough to know that he would have demanded to see the conservatorship papers himself. *He wouldn't hurt me.* I wanted to believe that. *All he does is warn me away.*

"How soon can you have documents drawn up leaving control of the foundation to Avery's sister in the event of her death?" Oren demanded. If this was about control of the foundation, that would protect me—or else it would put Libby in danger, too.

"Is anyone going to ask me what I want to do?" I asked.

"I can have the documents drawn up tomorrow," Alisa told Oren, ignoring me. "But Avery can't legally sign them until she's eighteen, and even then, it's unclear if she's authorized to make that kind of decision prior to assuming full control of the foundation at the age of twenty-one. Until then..."

I had a target on my forehead.

"What would it take to evoke the protection clause in the will?" Oren changed tactics. "There *are* circumstances under which Avery could remove the Hawthornes as tenants, correct?"

"We'd need evidence," Alisa replied. "Something that ties a specific individual or individuals to acts of harassment, intimidation, or violence, and even then, Avery can only kick out the perpetrator—not the whole family."

"And she can't live somewhere else for the time being?"

"No."

Oren didn't like that, but he didn't waste time on unnecessary commentary. "You'll go nowhere without me," Oren told me, steel in his voice. "Not on the estate, not in the House. Nowhere, you understand? I was always close by. Now I get to play visible deterrent."

Beside me, Alisa narrowed her eyes at Oren. "What do you know that I don't?"

There was a single moment's pause, then my bodyguard

answered the question. "I had my people check the armory. Nothing is missing. In all likelihood, the weapon fired at Avery wasn't a Hawthorne gun, but I had my men pull the security footage from the past few days anyway."

I was too busy trying to wrap my mind around the fact that Hawthorne House had an *armory* to process the rest.

"The armory had a visitor?" Alisa asked, her voice almost too calm.

"Two of them." Oren seemed like he might stop there, for my benefit, but he pressed on. "Jameson and Grayson. Both have alibis—but both were looking at rifles."

"Hawthorne House has an *armory*?" That was all I could manage to say.

"This is Texas," Oren replied. "The whole family grew up shooting, and Mr. Hawthorne was a collector."

"A *gun* collector," I clarified. I hadn't been a fan of firearms *before* I'd almost been shot.

"If you'd read the binder I left you detailing your assets," Alisa interjected, "you'd know that Mr. Hawthorne had the world's largest collection of late nineteenth- and early twentieth-century Winchester rifles, several of which are valued at upward of four hundred thousand dollars."

The idea that anyone would pay that much for a rifle was mind-boggling, but I barely batted an eye at the price tag, because I was too busy thinking that there was a reason Jameson and Grayson had both made visits to the armory to look at rifles—one that had nothing to do with shooting me.

Jameson's middle name was *Winchester*.

CHAPTER 57

Even though it was the dead of night, I made Oren take me to the armory. Following him through twisting hallway after hallway, all I could think was that someone could hide forever in this house.

And that wasn't counting the secret passages.

Eventually, Oren came to a stop in a long corridor. "This is it." He stood in front of an ornate gold mirror. As I watched, he ran his hand along the side of the frame. I heard a *click*, and then the mirror swung out into the hallway, like a door. Behind it, there was steel.

Oren stepped up, and I saw a line of red go down over his face. "Facial recognition," he informed me. "It's really only meant as a backup security measure. The best way to keep intruders from breaking into a safe is to make sure they don't even know it's there."

Hence, the mirror. He pushed the door inward. "The entire armory is lined with reinforced steel." He stepped through, and I followed.

When I'd heard the word *armory*, I'd pictured something out of a movie: copious amounts of black and Rambo-style cartridges on the walls. What I got looked more like a country club. The walls were lined with cabinets of a deep cherry–colored wood. There was an intricately carved table in the center of the room, complete with a marble top.

"*This* is the armory?" I said. There was a rug on the floor. A plush, expensive rug that looked like it belonged in a dining room.

"Not what you were expecting?" Oren closed the door behind us. It clicked into place, and then he flipped three additional dead bolts in quick succession. "There are safe rooms scattered throughout the house. This doubles as one—a tornado shelter, too. I'll show you the locations of the others later, just in case."

In case someone tries to kill me. Rather than dwelling on that, I focused on the reason I'd come here. "Where are the Winchesters?" I asked.

"There are at least thirty Winchester rifles in the collection." Oren nodded toward a wall of display cases. "Any particular reason you wanted to see them?"

A day earlier, I might have kept this secret, but Jameson hadn't told me that he'd looked for—possibly found—the clue corresponding to his own middle name. I didn't owe him any secrecy now.

"I'm looking for something," I told Oren. "A message from Tobias Hawthorne—a clue. A carving, most likely of a number or symbol."

The etching on the tree in the Black Wood had been neither. Mid-kiss, Jameson had seemed convinced that Toby's name was the next clue—but I wasn't so sure. The writing hadn't been a match for the carving at the bridge. It had been uneven, childlike. What if Toby had carved it himself, as a kid? What if the real clue was still out there in the woods?

I can't go back. Not until we know who the shooter is. Oren could clear a room and tell me it was safe. He couldn't clear a whole forest.

Pushing back against the echo of gunshots—and everything that had come after—I opened one of the cabinets. "Any thoughts on where your former employer might have hidden a message?" I asked Oren, my focus intense. "Which gun? Which part of the gun?"

"Mr. Hawthorne rarely took me into his confidence," Oren told me. "I didn't always know how his mind worked, but I respected him, and that respect was mutual." Oren removed a cloth from a drawer and unfolded it, spreading it across the table's marble top. Then he walked over to the cabinet I'd opened and lifted out one of the rifles.

"None of them are loaded," he said intently. "But you treat them like they are. Always."

He laid the gun down on the cloth and then ran his fingers lightly over the barrel. "This was one of his favorites. He was one hell of a shot."

I got the sense that there was a story there—one he'd probably never tell me.

Oren stepped back, and I took that as my cue to approach. Everything in me wanted to shrink back from the rifle. The bullets that had been fired at me were too fresh in my own memory. My wounds still throbbed, but I made myself examine each part of the weapon, looking for something, anything, that might be a clue. Finally, I turned back to Oren. "Where do you load the bullets?"

>———◄

I found what I was looking for on the fourth gun. To load a bullet into a Winchester rifle, you cocked a lever away from the stock. On the underside of that lever, on the fourth gun I looked at, were three letters: *O. N. E.* The way it had been etched into the metal made the letters look like initials, but I read it as number, to go with the one we'd found on the bridge.

Not infinity, I thought. *Eight. And now: One.*
Eight. One.

CHAPTER 58

Oren escorted me back to my wing. I thought about knocking on Libby's door, but it was late—too late—and it wasn't like I could just pop in and say, *There's murder afoot, sleep tight!*

Oren did a sweep of my quarters and then took up position outside my door, feet spread shoulder-width apart, hands dangling by his side. He had to sleep sometime, but as the door closed between us, I knew it wouldn't be tonight.

I pulled my phone out of my pocket and stared at it. Nothing from Max. She was a night owl and two hours behind me time zone–wise. There was no way she was asleep. I DM-ed the same message I'd texted her earlier to every social media account she had.

Please respond, I thought desperately. *Please, Max.*

"Nothing." I hadn't meant to say that out loud. Trying not to feel utterly alone, I made my way to the bathroom, laid my phone on the counter, and slipped off my clothes. Naked, I looked in the mirror. Except for my face and the bandage over my stitches, my skin looked untouched. I peeled the bandage back. The wound was angry and red, the stitches even and small. I stared at it.

Someone—almost certainly someone in the Hawthorne family—wanted me dead. *I could be dead right now.* I pictured their faces, one by one. Jameson had been there with me when the shots rang out. Nash had claimed from the beginning that he didn't want the money. Xander had been nothing but welcoming. But Grayson...

If you were smart, you'd stay away from Jameson. From the game. From me. He'd warned me. He'd told me that their family destroyed everything they touched. When I'd asked Rebecca how Emily had died, it hadn't been Jameson's name she'd mentioned.

Grayson told me that it was her heart.

I flipped the shower on as hot as it would go and stepped in, turning my chest from the stream and letting the hot water beat against my back. It hurt, but all I wanted was to scrub this entire night off me. What had happened in the Black Wood. What had happened with Jameson. *All of it.*

I broke down. Crying in the shower didn't count.

After a minute or two, I got ahold of myself and turned the water off, just in time to hear my phone ringing. Wet and dripping, I lunged for it.

"Hello?"

"You had better not be lying about the assassination attempt. Or the making out."

My body sagged in relief. "Max."

She must have heard in my tone that I wasn't lying. "What the elf, Avery? What the everlasting mothing-foxing elf is going on there?"

I told her—all of it, every detail, every moment, everything I'd been trying not to feel.

"You have to get out of there." For once, Max was deadly serious.

"What?" I said. I shivered and finally managed to grab a towel.

"Someone tried to kill you," Max said with exaggerated patience, "so you need to get out of Murderland. Like, now."

"I can't leave," I said. "I have to live here for a year, or I lose everything."

"So your life goes back to the way it was a week ago. Is that so bad?"

"Yes," I said incredulously. "I was living in my car, Max, with no guarantee of a future."

"Key word: *living*."

I pulled the towel tighter around me. "Are you saying you would give up billions?"

"Well, my other suggestion involves preemptively whacking the entire Hawthorne family, and I was afraid you'd take that as a euphemism."

"Max!"

"Hey, I'm not the one who made out with Jameson Hawthorne."

I wanted to explain to her exactly how I'd let that happen, but all that came out of my mouth was "Where were you?"

"Excuse me?"

"I called you, right after it happened, before the thing with Jameson. I needed you, Max."

There was a long, pregnant silence on the other end of the phone line. "I'm doing just fine," she said. "Everything here is just peachy. Thanks for asking."

"Asking about what?"

"*Exactly.*" Max lowered her voice. "Did you even notice that I'm not calling from my phone? This is my brother's. I'm on lockdown. Total lockdown—because of you."

I'd known the last time we'd talked that something wasn't right. "What do you mean, because of me?"

"Do you really want to know?"

What kind of question was that? "Of course I do."

"Because you haven't asked about me at all since any of this happened." She blew out a long breath. "Let's be honest, Ave, you barely asked about me before."

My stomach tightened. "That's not true."

"Your mom died, and you needed me. And with everything with Libby and that bob-forsaken shipstain, you really needed me. And then you inherited billions and billions of dollars, so of course, you needed me! And I was happy to be there, Avery, but do you even know my boyfriend's name?"

I racked my mind, trying to remember. "Jared?"

"Wrong," Max said after a moment. "The correct answer is that I don't have a boyfriend anymore, because I caught *Jaxon* on my phone, trying to send himself screenshots of your texts to me. A reporter offered to pay him for them." Her pause was painful this time. "Do you want to know how much?"

My heart sank. "I'm so sorry, Max."

"Me too," Max said bitterly. "But I'm especially sorry that I ever let him take pictures of me. *Personal* pictures. Because when I broke up with him, he sent those pictures to my parents." Max was like me. She only cried in the shower. But her voice was hitching now. "I'm not even allowed to date, Avery. How well do you think that went down?"

I couldn't even imagine. "What do you need?" I asked her.

"I need my life back." She went quiet, just for a minute. "You know what the worst part is? I can't even be mad at you, because *someone tried to shoot you.*" Her voice got very soft. "And you need me."

That hurt, because it was true. I needed her. I'd always needed her more than she had needed me, because she was my friend, sin- gular, and I was one of many for her. "I'm sorry, Max."

She made a dismissive sound. "Yeah, well, the next time some- one tries to shoot you, you're going to have to buy me something really nice to make it up to me. Like Australia."

"You want me to buy you a trip to Australia?" I asked, thinking that could probably be arranged.

"No." Her reply was pert. "I want you to buy me Australia. You can afford it."

I snorted. "I don't think it's for sale."

"Then I guess that you have no choice but to *avoid getting shot at.*"

"I'll be careful," I promised. "Whoever tried to kill me isn't going to get another chance."

"Good." Max was quiet for a few seconds. "Ave, I have to go. And I don't know when I'm going to be able to borrow another phone. Or get online. Or *anything.*"

My fault. I tried to tell myself this wasn't good-bye—not forever. "Love you, Max."

"Love you, too, beach."

After we hung up, I sat there in my towel, feeling like something inside of me had been carved out. Eventually, I made my way back into my bedroom and threw on some pajamas. I was in bed, thinking about everything Max had said, wondering if I was a fundamentally selfish or needy person, when I heard a sound like scratching in the walls.

I stopped breathing and listened. There it was again. *The passageway.*

"Jameson?" I called. He was the only one who'd used this passage into my room—or at least the only one I knew of. "Jameson, this isn't funny."

There was no response, but when I got up and walked toward the passageway, then stood very still, I could have sworn I heard someone breathing, right on the other side of the wall. I gripped the candlestick, prepared to pull it and face down whoever or whatever stood beyond, but then my common sense—and my promise to Max—caught up to me, and I opened the door to the hallway instead.

"Oren?" I said. "There's something you should know."

———————————

Oren searched the passageway, then disabled its entrance into my room. He also "suggested" I spend the night in Libby's room, which didn't have passageway access.

It wasn't really a suggestion.

My sister was asleep when I knocked. She roused, but barely. I crawled into bed with her, and she didn't ask why. After my conversation with Max, I was fairly certain I didn't want to tell her. Libby's entire life had already been turned upside down because of me. Twice. First when my mom had died, then all of this. She'd already given me everything. She had her own issues to deal with. She didn't need mine.

Under the covers, I hugged a pillow tight to my body and rolled toward Libby. I needed to be close to her, even if I couldn't tell her why. Libby's eyes fluttered, and she snuggled up next to me. I willed myself not to think about anything else—not the Black Wood, not the Hawthornes, nothing. I let darkness overcome me, and I slept.

I dreamed that I was back at the diner. I was young—five or six—and happy.

I place two sugar packets vertically on the table and bring their ends together, forming a triangle capable of standing on its own. "There," I say. I do the same with the next pair of packets, then set a fifth across them horizontal, connecting the two triangles I built.

"Avery Kylie Grambs!" My mom appears at the end of the table, smiling. "What have I told you about building castles out of sugar?"

I beam back at her. "It's only worth it if you can go five stories tall!"

I woke with a start. I turned over, expecting to see Libby, but her side of the bed was empty. Morning light was streaming in through the windows. I made my way to Libby's bathroom, but she wasn't there, either. I was getting ready to go back to my room— and my bathroom—when I saw something on the counter: Libby's phone. She'd missed texts, dozens of them, all from Drake. There were only three—the most recent—that I could read without a password.

I love you.

You know I love you, Libby-mine.

I know that you love me.

CHAPTER 59

Oren met me in the hall the second I left Libby's suite. If he'd been up all night, he didn't look it.

"A police report has been filed," he reported. "Discreetly. The detectives assigned to the case are coordinating with my team. We're all in agreement that it would be to our advantage, at least for the moment, if the Hawthorne family does not realize there *is* an investigation. Jameson and Rebecca have been made to understand the importance of discretion. As much as you can, I'd like you to proceed as though nothing has happened."

Pretend I hadn't had a brush with death the night before. Pretend everything was fine. "Have you seen Libby?" I asked. *Libby isn't fine.*

"She went down for breakfast about half an hour ago." Oren's tone gave away nothing.

I thought back to those texts, and my stomach tightened. "Did she seem okay?"

"No injuries. All limbs and appendages fully intact."

That wasn't what I'd been asking, but given the circumstances, maybe it should have been. "If she's downstairs in full view of Hawthornes, is she safe?"

"Her security detail is aware of the situation. They do not currently believe she is at risk."

Libby wasn't the heiress. She wasn't the target. I was.

———◆———

I got dressed and went downstairs. I'd gone with a high-necked top to hide my stitches, and I'd covered the scratch on my cheek with makeup, as much as I could.

In the dining room, a selection of pastries had been set out on the sideboard. Libby was curled up in a large accent chair in the corner of the room. Nash was sitting in the chair beside her, his legs sticking straight out, his cowboy boots crossed at the ankles. Keeping watch.

Between them and me were four members of the Hawthorne family. *All with reason to want me dead*, I thought as I walked past them. Zara and Constantine sat at one end of the dining room table. She was reading a newspaper. He was reading a tablet. Neither paid the least bit of attention to me. Nan and Xander were at the far end of the table.

I felt movement behind me and whirled.

"Somebody's jumpy this morning," Thea declared, hooking an arm through mine and leading me toward the sideboard. Oren followed, like a shadow. "You've been a busy girl," Thea murmured, directly into my ear.

I knew that she had been watching me, that she'd probably been ordered to stick close and report back. *How close was she last night? What does she know?* Based on what Oren had said, Thea hadn't shot me herself, but the timing of her move into Hawthorne House didn't seem like a coincidence.

Zara had brought her niece here for a reason.

"Don't play the innocent," Thea advised, picking up a croissant and bringing it to her lips. "Rebecca called me."

I fought the urge to glance back at Oren. He'd indicated that Rebecca would keep her mouth shut about the shooting. What else was he wrong about?

"You and Jameson," Thea continued, like she was chiding a child. "In Emily's old room, no less. A bit uncouth, don't you think?"

She doesn't know about the attack. The realization shot through me. *Rebecca must have seen Jameson come out of the bathroom. She must have heard us. Must have realized that we . . .*

"Are people being uncouth without me again?" Xander asked, popping up between Thea and me and breaking Thea's hold. "How rude."

I didn't want to suspect him of anything, but at this rate, the stress of suspecting and not-suspecting was going to kill me before anyone else could do me in.

"Rebecca stayed the night in the cottage," Thea told Xander, relishing the words. "She finally broke her yearlong silence and texted me *all* about it." Thea acted like a person playing a trump card— but I wasn't sure what, exactly, that card was.

Rebecca?

"Bex texted me, too," Xander told Thea. Then he glanced apologetically at me. "Word of Hawthorne hookups travels fast."

Rebecca might have kept her mouth shut about the shooting, but she might as well have taken out a billboard about that kiss.

The kiss meant nothing. The kiss isn't the problem here.

"You, there. Girl!" Nan jabbed her cane imperiously at me and then at the tray of pastries. "Don't make an old woman get up."

If anyone else had spoken to me like that, I would have ignored them, but Nan was both ancient and terrifying, so I went to pick up the tray. I remembered too late that I was injured. Pain flashed like a lightning bolt through my flesh, and I sucked a breath in through my teeth.

Nan stared, just for a moment, then prodded Xander with her cane. "Help her, you lout."

Xander took the tray. I let my arm drop back to my side. *Who saw me flinch?* I tried not to stare at any of them. *Who already knew I was injured?*

"You're hurt." Xander angled his body between mine and Thea's.

"I'm fine," I said.

"You most decidedly are not."

I hadn't realized Grayson had slipped into the banquet hall, but now he was standing directly beside me.

"A moment, Ms. Grambs?" His stare was intense. "In the hall."

CHAPTER 60

I probably shouldn't have gone anywhere with Grayson Hawthorne, but I knew that Oren would follow, and I wanted something from Grayson. I wanted to look him in the eye. I wanted to know if he'd done this to me—or had any idea who had.

"You're injured." Grayson didn't phrase that as a question. "You will tell me what happened."

"Oh, I will, will I?" I gave him a look.

"Please." Grayson seemed to find the word painful or distasteful—or both.

I owed him nothing. Oren had asked me not to mention the shooting. The last time I'd talked to Grayson, he'd issued a terse warning. He stood to gain the foundation if I died.

"I was shot." I let the truth out because for reasons I couldn't even explain, I needed to see how he would react. "Shot at," I clarified after a beat.

Every muscle in Grayson's jawline went taut. *He didn't know.* Before I could summon up even an ounce of relief, Grayson turned from me to my guard. "When?" he spat out.

"Last night," Oren replied curtly.

"And where," Grayson demanded of my bodyguard, "were you?"

"Not nearly as close as I'll be from now on," Oren promised, staring him down.

"Remember me?" I raised a hand, then paid for it. "Subject of your conversation and capable individual in her own right?"

Grayson must have seen the pain the movement caused me, because he turned and used his hands to gently lower mine. "You'll let Oren do his job," he ordered softly.

I didn't dwell on his tone—or his touch. "And who do you think he's protecting me from?" I glanced pointedly toward the banquet hall. I waited for Grayson to snap at me for daring to suspect anyone he loved, to reiterate again that he would choose each and every one of them over me.

Instead, Grayson turned back to Oren. "If anything happens to her, I will hold you personally responsible."

"Mr. Personal Responsibility." Jameson announced his presence and ambled toward his brother. "Charming."

Grayson gritted his teeth, then realized something. "You were both in the Black Wood last night." He stared at his brother. "Whoever shot at her could have hit you."

"And what a travesty it would be," Jameson replied, circling his brother, "if anything happened to me."

The tension between them was palpable. Explosive. I could see how this would play out—Grayson calling Jameson reckless, Jameson risking himself further to prove the point. How long would it be before Jameson mentioned me? *The kiss.*

"Hope I'm not interrupting." Nash joined the party. He flashed a lazy, dangerous smile at his brothers. "Jamie, you're not skipping school today. You have five minutes to put on your uniform and get in my truck, or there will be a hog-tying in your future." He waited for Jameson to get a move on, then turned. "Gray, our mother has requested an audience."

Having dealt with his siblings, the oldest Hawthorne brother shifted his attention to me. "I don't suppose you need a ride to Country Day?"

"She does not," Oren replied, arms crossed over his chest. Nash noted both his posture and his tone, but before he could reply, I interjected.

"I'm not going to school." That was news to Oren, but he didn't object.

Nash, on the other hand, shot me the exact same look he'd given Jameson when he'd made the threat about hog-tying. "Your sister know you're playing hooky on this fine Friday afternoon?"

"My sister is none of your concern," I told him, but thinking about Libby brought my mind back to Drake's texts. There were worse things than the idea that Libby might get involved with a Hawthorne. *Assuming Nash doesn't want me dead.*

"Everyone who lives or works in this house is my concern," Nash told me. "No matter how many times I leave or how long I'm gone for—people still need looking after. So..." He gave me that same lazy grin. "Your sister know you're playing hooky?"

"I'll talk to her," I said, trying to see past the cowboy in him to what lay underneath.

Nash returned my assessing look. "You do that, sweetheart."

CHAPTER 61

I told Libby I was staying home. I tried to form the words to ask her about Drake's texts and came up dry. *What if Drake's not just texting?* That thought snaked its way through my consciousness. *What if she's seen him? What if he talked her into sneaking him onto the estate?*

I shut down that line of thinking. There was no "sneaking" onto the estate. Security was airtight, and Oren would have told me if Drake had been on the premises during the shooting. He would have been the top suspect—or close to it.

If I die, there's at least a chance that everything passes to my closest blood relatives. That's Libby—and our father.

"Are you sick?" Libby asked, placing the back of her hand on my forehead. She was wearing her new purple boots and a black dress with long, lacy sleeves. She looked like she was going somewhere.

To see Drake? Dread settled in the pit of my stomach. *Or with Nash?*

"Mental health day," I managed. Libby accepted that and declared it Sister Time. If she'd had plans, she didn't think twice before ditching them for me.

"Want to hit the spa?" Libby asked earnestly. "I got a massage yesterday, and it was to die for."

I almost died yesterday. I didn't say that, and I didn't tell her that the massage therapist wouldn't be coming back today—or anytime soon. Instead, I offered up the only distraction I could think of that might also distract me from all of the secrets I was keeping from her.

"How would you like to help me find a Davenport?"

According to the internet search results Libby and I pulled up, the term *Davenport* was used separately to refer to two kinds of furniture: a sofa and a desk. The sofa usage was a generic term, like Kleenex for a tissue or dumpster for a garbage bin, but a Davenport desk referred to a specific kind of desk, one that was notable for compartments and hidey-holes, with a slanted desktop that could be lifted to reveal a storage compartment underneath.

Everything I knew about Tobias Hawthorne told me that we probably weren't looking for a sofa.

"This could take a while," Libby told me. "Do you have any idea how big this place is?"

I'd seen the music rooms, the gymnasium, the bowling alley, the showroom for Tobias Hawthorne's cars, the *solarium* . . . and that wasn't even a quarter of what there was to see. "Enormous."

"Palatial," Libby chirped. "And since I'm such bad publicity, I haven't had anything to do for the past week *except* explore." That publicity comment had to have come from Alisa, and I wondered how many chats she'd had with Libby without me there. "There's a literal ballroom," Libby continued. "Two theaters—one for movies and one with box seats and a stage."

"I've seen that one," I offered. "And the bowling alley."

Libby's kohl-rimmed eyes grew round. "Did you bowl?"

Her awe was contagious. "I bowled."

Libby shook her head. "It is never going to stop being bizarre that this house has a *bowling alley.*"

"There's also a driving range," Oren added behind me. "And racquetball."

If Libby noticed how close he was sticking to us, she gave no indication of it. "How in the world are we supposed to find one little desk?" she asked.

I turned back to Oren. If he was here, he might as well be useful. "I've seen the office in our wing. Did Tobias Hawthorne have any others?"

➤━━━━━━◄

The desk in Tobias Hawthorne's other office wasn't a Davenport, either. There were three rooms off the office. *The Cigar Room. The Billiards Room.* Oren provided explanations as needed. The third room was small, with no windows. In the middle of it, there was what appeared to be a giant white pod.

"Sensory deprivation chamber," Oren told me. "Every once in a while, Mr. Hawthorne liked to cut off the world."

➤━━━━━━◄

Eventually, Libby and I resorted to searching on a grid, the same way Jameson and I had searched the Black Wood. Wing by wing and room by room, we made our way through the halls of Hawthorne House. Oren was never more than a few feet behind.

"And now...*the spa.*" Libby flung the door open. She seemed upbeat. Either that, or she was covering for something.

Pushing that thought down, I looked around the spa. We clearly weren't going to find the desk here, but that didn't stop me from taking it all in. The room was L-shaped. In the long part of the L, the floor was wooden; in the short part, it was made of stone. In the middle of the stone section, there was a small square pool built into the ground. Steam rose from its surface. Behind it, there was a glass shower as big as a small bedroom, with faucets attached to the ceiling instead of the wall.

"Hot tub. Steam room." Someone spoke up behind us. I turned to see Skye Hawthorne. She was wearing a floor-length robe, a black one this time. She strode to the larger section of the room, dropped the robe, and lay down on a gray velvet cot. "Massage table," she said, yawning, barely covering herself with a sheet. "I ordered a masseuse."

"Hawthorne House is closed to visitors for the moment," Oren said flatly, completely unimpressed with her display.

"Well, then." Skye closed her eyes. "You'll need to buzz Magnus past the gates."

Magnus. I wondered if he was the one who'd been here yesterday. If he was the one who'd shot at me—at her request.

"Hawthorne House is closed to visitors," Oren repeated. "It's a matter of security. Until further notice, my men have instructions to allow only essential personnel past the gates."

Skye yawned like a cat. "I assure you, John Oren, this massage is *essential.*"

On a nearby shelf, a row of candles was burning. Light shone through sheer curtains, and low and pleasant music played.

"What matter of security?" Libby asked suddenly. "Did something happen?"

I gave Oren a look that I hoped would keep him from answering that question, but it turned out that I was aiming that request in the wrong direction.

"According to my Grayson," Skye told Libby, "there was some nasty business in the Black Wood."

CHAPTER 62

Libby waited until we were back in the hallway to ask, "What happened in the woods?"

I cursed Grayson for telling his mother—and myself for telling Grayson.

"Why do you need extra security?" Libby demanded. After a second and a half, she turned to Oren. "Why does she need extra security?"

"There was an incident yesterday," Oren said, "with a bullet and a tree."

"A bullet?" Libby repeated. "Like, from a gun?"

"I'm fine," I told her.

Libby ignored me. "What kind of incident with a bullet and a tree?" she asked Oren, her blue ponytail bouncing with righteous indignation.

My head of security couldn't—or wouldn't—obfuscate more than he already had. "It's unclear if the shots were meant to scare Avery, or if she was a genuine target. The shooter missed, but she was injured by debris."

"Libby," I said emphatically, "*I'm fine.*"

"Shots, plural?" Libby didn't even seem like she'd heard me.

Oren cleared his throat. "I'll give you two a moment." He retreated down the hall—still in sight, still close enough to hear but far enough away to pretend he couldn't.

Coward.

"Someone shot at you, and you didn't tell me?" Libby didn't get mad often, but when she did, it was epic. "Maybe Nash is right. Damn him! I said you pretty much took care of yourself. He said he'd never met a billionaire teenager who didn't need the occasional kick in the pants."

"Oren and Alisa are taking care of the situation," I told Libby. "I didn't want you to worry."

Libby lifted her hand to my cheek, her eyes falling on the scratch I'd covered up. "And who's taking care of you?"

I couldn't help thinking about Max saying *and you needed me* again and again. I looked down. "You have enough on your plate right now."

"What are you talking about?" Libby asked. I heard her suck in a quick breath, then exhale. "Is this about Drake?"

She'd said his name. The floodgates were officially open, and there was no holding it back now. "He's been texting you."

"I don't text him back," Libby said defensively.

"You also haven't blocked him."

She didn't have a reply for that.

"You could have blocked him," I said hoarsely. "Or asked Alisa for a new phone. You could report him for violating the restraining order."

"I didn't ask for a restraining order!" Libby seemed to regret those words the second she'd said them. She swallowed. "And I don't want a new phone. All my friends have the number for this one. *Dad* has the number for this one."

I stared at her. "Dad?" I hadn't seen Ricky Grambs in two years.

My caseworker had been in touch with him, but he hadn't so much as placed a phone call to me. He hadn't even come to my mother's funeral. "Did Dad call you?" I asked Libby.

"He just...wanted to check on us, you know?"

I knew that he'd probably seen the news. I knew that he didn't have *my* new number. I knew that he had billions of reasons to want me now, when he'd never cared enough to stick around for either of us before.

"He wants money," I told Libby, my voice flat. "Just like Drake. Just like your mom."

Mentioning her mother was a low blow.

"Who does Oren think shot you?" Libby was grappling for calm.

I made an attempt at the same. "The shots were fired from inside the walls of the estate," I said, repeating what I'd been told. "Whoever shot me had access."

"That's why Oren is tightening security," Libby said, the gears in her head turning behind her kohl-lined eyes. "Essential personnel only." Her dark lips fixed themselves into a thin line. "You should have told me."

I thought about the things she hadn't told me. "Tell me that you haven't seen Drake. That he hasn't come here. That you wouldn't let him onto the estate."

"Of course I didn't." Libby went silent. I wasn't sure if she was trying not to yell at me—or not to cry. "I'm going to go." Her voice was steady—and fierce. "But for the record, *little sis*, you're a minor, and I'm still your legal guardian. The next time someone tries to shoot you, I damn well want to know."

CHAPTER 63

I knew Oren had to have heard every word of my fight with Libby, but I was also fairly certain he wouldn't comment on it.

"I'm still looking for the Davenport," I said tersely. If I'd needed the distraction before, it was downright mandatory now. Without Libby to explore with me, I couldn't bring myself to just keep wandering from room to room. *We already checked the old man's office. Where else would someone keep a Davenport desk?*

I concentrated on that question, not my fight with Libby. Not what I'd said—and what she hadn't.

"I have it on good authority," I told Oren after a moment, "that Hawthorne House has multiple libraries." I let out a long, slow breath. "Got any idea where they are?"

———◆———

Two hours and four libraries later, I was standing in the middle of number five. It was on the second floor. The ceiling was slanted. The walls were lined with built-in shelves, each shelf exactly tall enough for a row of paperback books. The books on the shelves were well-worn, and they covered every inch of the walls, except for a large stained-glass window on the east side. Light shone through, painting colors on the wood floor.

No Davenport. This was starting to feel useless. This trail hadn't been laid for me. Tobias Hawthorne's puzzle hadn't been designed with me in mind.

I need Jameson.

I cut that thought off at the knees, exited the library, and retreated downstairs. I'd counted at least five different staircases in this house. This one spiraled, and as I walked down it, the sound of piano music beckoned from a distance. I followed it, and Oren followed me. I came to the entryway of a large, open room. The far wall was filled with arches. Beneath each arch was a massive window.

Every window was open.

There were paintings on the walls, and positioned between them was the biggest grand piano I'd ever seen. Nan sat on the piano's bench, her eyes closed. I thought the old woman was playing, until I walked closer and realized that the piano was playing itself.

My shoes made a sound against the floor, and her eyes flew open.

"I'm sorry," I said. "I—"

"Hush," Nan commanded. Her eyes closed again. The playing continued, building to a crashing crescendo, and then—silence. "Did you know that you can listen to concerts on this thing?" Nan opened her eyes and reached for her cane. With no small amount of effort, she stood. "Somewhere in the world, a master plays, and with the push of a button, the keys move here."

Her eyes lingered on the piano, an almost wistful expression on her face.

"Do you play?" I asked.

Nan harrumphed. "I did when I was young. Got a bit too much attention for it, and my husband broke my fingers, put an end to that."

The way she said it—no muss, no fuss—was almost as jarring as the words. "That's horrible," I said fiercely.

Nan looked at the piano, then at her gnarled, bird-boned hand. She lifted her chin and stared out the massive windows. "He met with a tragic accident not long after that."

It sounded an awful lot like Nan had arranged for that "accident." *She killed her husband?*

"Nan," a voice scolded from the doorway. "You're scaring the kid."

Nan sniffed. "She scares that easy, she won't last here." With that, Nan made her way from the room.

The oldest Hawthorne brother turned his attention to me. "You tell your sister you're playing delinquent today?"

The mention of Libby had me flashing back to our argument. *She's talking to Dad. She didn't want a restraining order against Drake. She won't block him.* I wondered how much of that Nash already knew.

"Libby knows where I am," I told him stiffly.

He gave me a look. "This ain't easy for her, kid. You're at the eye of the storm, where things are calm. She's taking the brunt of it, from all sides."

I wouldn't call getting shot at "calm."

"What are your intentions toward my sister?" I asked Nash.

He clearly found my line of questioning amusing. "What are your intentions toward Jameson?"

Was there *no one* in this house who didn't know about that kiss?

"You were right about your grandfather's game," I told Nash. He'd tried to warn me. He'd told me exactly why Jameson had been keeping me close.

"Usually am." Nash hooked his thumbs through his belt loops. "The closer to the end you come, the worse it'll get."

The logical thing to do was stop playing. Step back. But I wanted answers, and some part of me—the part that had grown up with a mom who'd turned everything into a challenge, the part who'd played my first game of chess when I was six years old—wanted to *win*.

"Any chance you know where your grandfather might have stashed a Davenport desk?" I asked Nash.

He snorted. "You don't learn easy, do you, kid?"

I shrugged.

Nash considered my question, then cocked his head to the side. "You check the libraries?"

"The circular library, the onyx one, the one with the stained-glass window, the one with the globes, the maze..." I glanced over at my bodyguard. "That's it?"

Oren nodded.

Nash cocked his head to the side. "Not quite."

CHAPTER 64

Nash led me up two sets of stairs, down three hallways, and past a doorway that had been bricked shut.

"What's that?" I asked.

He slowed momentarily. "That was my uncle's wing. The old man had it walled off when Toby died."

Because that's normal, I thought. *About as normal as disinheriting your whole family for twenty years and never saying a word.*

Nash picked up the pace again, and finally, we came to a steel door that looked like it belonged on a safe. There was a combination dial, and below it, a five-pronged lever. Nash casually twirled the dial—left, right, left—too quick for me to catch the numbers. There was a loud clicking sound, and then he turned the lever. The steel door opened out into the hall.

What kind of library needs that kind of securit—

My brain was in the process of finishing that thought when Nash stepped through the doorway, and I realized that what lay beyond wasn't a single room. It was a whole other wing.

"The old man started construction on this part of the house when I was born," Nash informed me. The hallway around us was papered with dials, keypads, locks, and keys, all affixed to the walls like art. "Hawthornes learn how to wield a lockpick young," Nash told me as we walked down the hall. I looked in a room to my left, and there was a small airplane—not a toy. An *actual* single-person airplane.

"*This* was your playroom?" I asked, eyeing the doors lining the rest of the hall and wondering what surprises those rooms held.

"Skye was seventeen when I was born." Nash shrugged. "She made an attempt at playing parent. Didn't stick. The old man tried to compensate."

By building you . . . this.

"C'mon." Nash led me toward the end of the hall and opened another door. "Arcade," he told me, the explanation completely unnecessary. There was a foosball table, a bar, three pinball machines, and an entire wall of arcade-style consoles.

I walked over to one of the pinball machines, pressed a button, and it surged to life.

I glanced back at Nash. "I can wait," he said.

I should have stayed focused. He was leading me to the final library—and possibly the location of the Davenport and the next clue. But one game wouldn't kill me. I gave a preliminary flip of the flipper, then launched the ball.

I didn't come anywhere near the top score, but when the game was over, it prompted me for my initials anyway, and when I entered them, a familiar message flashed across the screen.

WELCOME TO HAWTHORNE HOUSE, AVERY KYLIE GRAMBS!

It was the same message I'd gotten at the bowling alley, and just as I had then, I felt the ghost of Tobias Hawthorne all around me. *Even if you* thought *that you'd manipulated our grandfather into this, I guarantee that he'd be the one manipulating you.*

Nash walked behind the bar. "Refrigerator is full of sugary drinks. What's your poison?"

I came closer and saw that he wasn't kidding when he said *full*. Glass bottles lined every shelf of the fridge, with soda in every imaginable flavor. "Cotton candy?" I wrinkled my nose. "Prickly pear? *Bacon and jalepeno?*"

"I was six when Gray was born," Nash said, like that was an explanation. "The old man unveiled this room the day my new little brother came home." He twisted the top off a suspiciously green soda and took a swig. "I was seven for Jamie, eight and a half for Xander." He paused, as if weighing my worth as his audience. "Aunt Zara and her first husband were having trouble conceiving. Skye would leave for a few months, come back pregnant. Wash, rinse, and repeat."

That might have been the most messed up thing I'd ever heard.

"You want one?" Nash asked, nodding toward the fridge.

I wanted to take about ten of them but settled for Cookies and Cream. I glanced back at Oren, who'd been playing my silent shadow this whole time. He gave no indication that I should avoid drinking, so I twisted off the cap and took a swig.

"The library?" I reminded Nash.

"Almost there." Nash pushed through to the next room. "Game room," he said.

At the center of the room, there were four tables. One table was rectangular, one square, one oval, one circular. The tables were black. The rest of the room—walls, floor, and shelves—was white. The shelves were built into three of the room's four walls.

Not bookshelves, I realized. They held games. Hundreds, maybe thousands, of board games. Unable to resist, I went up to the closest shelf and ran my fingers along the boxes. I'd never even heard of most of these games.

"The old man," Nash said softly, "was a bit of a collector."

I was in awe. How many afternoons had my mom and I spent playing garage-sale board games? Our rainy-day tradition had involved setting up three or four and turning them all into one massive game. But *this*? There were games from all over the world. Half of them didn't have English writing on the boxes. I suddenly pictured all four Hawthorne brothers sitting around one of those tables. Grinning. Trash-talking. Outmaneuvering each other. Wrestling for control—possibly literally.

I pushed that thought back. I'd come here looking for the Davenport—the next clue. *That* was the current game—not anything held in these boxes. "The library?" I asked Nash, tearing my eyes away from the games.

He nodded toward the end of the room—the one wall that wasn't covered in board games. There was no door. Instead, there was a fire pole and what appeared to be the bottom of some kind of chute. A slide?

"Where's the library?" I asked.

Nash came to stand beside the fire pole and tilted his head toward the ceiling. "Up there."

CHAPTER 65

Oren went up first, then returned—via pole, not slide. "Room's clear," he told me. "But if you try to climb up, you might pull a stitch."

The fact that he'd mentioned my injury in front of Nash told me something. Either Oren wanted to see how he would respond, or he trusted Nash Hawthorne.

"What injury?" Nash asked, taking the bait.

"Someone shot at Avery," Oren said carefully. "You wouldn't happen to know anything about that, would you, Nash?"

"If I did," Nash replied, his voice low and deadly, "it would already be handled."

"Nash." Oren gave him a look that probably meant *stay out of it*. But from what I'd been able to tell, "staying out of it" wasn't really a Hawthorne trait.

"I'll be going now," Nash said casually. "I have some questions to ask my people."

His people—including Mellie. I watched Nash saunter off, then turned back to Oren. "You knew he would go talk to the staff."

"I know they'll talk to him," Oren corrected. "And besides, you blew the element of surprise this morning."

I'd told Grayson. He'd told his mother. Libby knew. "Sorry about that," I said, then I turned to the room overhead. "I'm going up."

"I didn't see a desk up there," Oren told me.

I walked over to the pole and grabbed hold. "I'm going up anyway." I started to pull myself up, but the pain stopped me. Oren was right. I couldn't climb. I stepped back from the pole, then glanced to my left.

If I couldn't make it up the pole, it would have to be the slide.

➤————————◆

The last library in Hawthorne House was small. The ceiling sloped to form a pyramid overhead. The shelves were plain and only came up to my waist. They were full of children's books. Well-worn, well-loved, some of them familiar in a way that made me ache to sit and read.

But I didn't, because as I stood there, I felt a breeze. It wasn't coming from the window, which was closed. It came from the shelves on the back wall—*no.* As I walked closer, I discovered that it was coming from a crack between the two shelves.

There's something back there. My heart caught like a breath stuck in my throat. Starting with the shelf on the right, I latched my fingers around the top of the shelf and pulled. I didn't have to pull hard. The shelf was on a hinge. As I pulled, it rotated outward, revealing a small opening.

This was the first secret passage I'd discovered on my own. It was strangely exhilarating, like standing on the edge of the Grand Canyon or holding a priceless work of art in your hands. Heart pounding, I ducked through the opening and found a staircase.

Traps upon traps, I thought, *and riddles upon riddles.*

Gingerly, I walked down the steps. As I got farther from the light above, I had to pull out my phone and turn on the flashlight so I could see where I was going. *I should go back for Oren.* I knew that, but I was going faster now—down the steps, twisting, turning, until I reached the bottom.

There, holding a flashlight of his own, was Grayson Hawthorne.

He turned toward me. My heart beat viciously, but I didn't step back. I looked past Grayson and saw the only piece of furniture on the landing of the hidden stairs.

A Davenport.

"Ms. Grambs." Grayson greeted me, then turned back to the desk.

"Have you found it yet?" I asked him. "The Davenport clue?"

"I was waiting."

I couldn't quite read his tone. "For what?"

Grayson looked up from the desk, silver eyes catching mine in the dark. "Jameson, I suppose."

It had been hours since Jameson had left for school, hours since I'd seen Grayson last. How long had he been here, waiting?

"It's not like Jamie to miss the obvious. Whatever this game is, it's about us. The four of us. Our names were the clues. Of course we would find something here."

"At the bottom of this staircase?" I asked.

"In our wing," Grayson replied. "We grew up here—Jameson, Xander, and me. Nash, too, I suppose, but he was older."

I remembered Xander telling me that Jameson and Grayson used to team up to beat Nash to the finish line, then double-cross each other at the end of the game.

"Nash knows about the shooting," I told Grayson. "I told him." Grayson gave me a look I couldn't quite discern. "What?" I said.

Grayson shook his head. "He'll want to save you now."

"Is that such a bad thing?" I asked.

Another look—and more emotion, heavily masked. "Will you

show me where you were hurt?" Grayson asked, his voice not quite strained—but *something*.

He probably just wanted to see how bad it is, I told myself, but still, the request hit me like an electric shock. My limbs felt inexplicably heavy. I was keenly aware of every breath I took. This was a small space. We stood close to each other, close to the desk.

I'd learned my lesson with Jameson, but this felt different. Like Grayson wanted to be the one to save me. Like he *needed* to be the one.

I lifted my hand to the collar of my shirt. I pulled it downward—below my collarbone, exposing my wound.

Grayson lifted his hand toward my shoulder. "I am sorry that this happened to you."

"Do you know who shot at me?" I had to ask, because he'd apologized—and Grayson Hawthorne was not the type to apologize. *If he knew...*

"No," Grayson swore.

I believed him—or at least I wanted to. "If I leave Hawthorne House before the year is up, the money goes to charity. If I die, it goes to charity or my heirs." I paused. "If I die, the foundation goes to the four of you."

He had to know how that looked.

"My grandfather should have left it to us all along." Grayson turned his head, forcefully pulling his gaze from my skin. "Or to Zara. We were raised to make a difference, and you..."

"I'm nobody," I finished, the words hurting me to say.

Grayson shook his head. "I don't know what you are." Even in the minimal light of our flashlights, I could see his chest rising and falling with every breath.

"Do you think Jameson's right?" I asked him. "Does this puzzle of your grandfather's end with answers?"

"It ends with *something*. The old man's games always do." Grayson paused. "How many of the numbers do you have?"

"Two," I replied.

"Same," he told me. "I'm missing this one and Xander's."

I frowned. "Xander's?"

"Blackwood. It's Xander's middle name. The West Brook was Nash's clue. The Winchester was Jameson's."

I looked back toward the desk. "And the Davenport is yours."

He closed his eyes. "After you, Heiress."

His use of Jameson's nickname for me felt like it meant something, but I wasn't sure what. I turned my attention to the task at hand. The desk was made of a bronze-colored wood. Four drawers ran perpendicular to the desktop. I tested them one at a time. Empty. I ran my right hand along the inside of the drawers, looking for anything out of the ordinary. Nothing.

Feeling Grayson's presence beside me, knowing that I was being watched and judged, I moved on to the top of the desk, raising it up to reveal the compartment underneath. Empty again. As I had with drawers, I ran my fingers along the bottom and sides of the compartment. I felt a slight ridge along the right side. Eyeballing the desk, I estimated the width of the border to be an inch and a half, maybe two inches.

Just wide enough for a hidden compartment.

Unsure how to trigger its release, I ran my hand back over the place where I'd felt the ridge. Maybe it was just a seam, where two pieces of wood met. *Or maybe...* I pressed the wood in, hard, and it popped outward. I closed my fingers around the block that had just released and pulled it away from the desk, revealing a small opening. Inside was a keychain, with no key.

The keychain was plastic, in the shape of the number one.

CHAPTER 66

Eight. One. One.
        I slept in Libby's room again that night. She didn't. I asked Oren to confirm with her security team that she was okay and on the premises.

She was—but he didn't tell me where.

No Libby. No Max. I was alone—more alone than I'd been since I got here. *No Jameson.* I hadn't seen him since he'd left that morning. *No Grayson.* He hadn't lingered with me for long after we'd discovered the clue.

One. One. Eight. That was all I had to concentrate on. Three numbers, which confirmed for me that Toby's tree in the Black Wood had just been a tree. If there was a fourth number, it was still out there. Based on the keychain, the clue in the Black Wood could appear in any format, not just a carving.

Late into the night and nearly asleep, I heard something like footsteps. *Behind me? Below?* The wind whistled outside my window. Gunshots lurked in my memory. I had no idea what was lurking in the walls.

I didn't fall asleep until dawn. When I did, I dreamed about sleeping.

"I have a secret," my mom says, cheerfully bouncing onto my bed, jarring me awake. "Care to make a guess, my newly fifteen-year-old daughter?"

"I'm not playing," I grumble, pulling the covers back over my head. "I never guess right."

"I'll give you a hint," my mom wheedles. "For your birthday." She pulls the covers back and flops down beside me on my pillow. Her smile is contagious.

I finally break and smile back. "Fine. Give me a hint."

"I have a secret... about the day you were born."

I woke with a headache to my lawyer throwing open the plantation shutters. "Rise and shine," Alisa said, with the force and surety of a person making an argument in court.

"Go away." Channeling my younger self, I pulled the covers over my head.

"My apologies," Alisa said, not sounding apologetic in the least. "But you really do have to get up now."

"I don't have to do anything," I muttered. "I'm a billionaire."

That worked about as well as I expected it to. "If you'll recall," Alisa replied pleasantly, "in an attempt to do damage control after your impromptu press conference earlier this week, I arranged for your debut in Texas society to take place this weekend. There is a charity benefit that you will be attending this evening."

"I barely slept last night." I tried for pity. "Someone tried to shoot me!"

"We'll get you some vitamin C and a pain pill." Alisa was without mercy. "I'm taking you dress shopping in half an hour. You have media training at one, hair and makeup at four."

"Maybe we should reschedule," I said. "Due to someone wanting to kill me."

"Oren signed off on us leaving the estate." Alisa gave me a look. "You have twenty-nine minutes." She eyed my hair. "Make sure you're looking your best. I'll meet you at the car."

CHAPTER 67

Oren escorted me to the SUV. Alisa and two of his men were waiting inside it—and they weren't the only ones.

"I know you weren't planning on going shopping without me," Thea said, by way of greeting. "Where there are high-fashion boutiques, so there is Thea."

I looked toward Oren, hoping he'd kick her out of the car. He didn't.

"Besides," Thea told me in a haughty little whisper as she buckled her seat belt, "we need to talk about Rebecca."

———◆———

The SUV had three rows of seats. Oren and a second bodyguard sat in the front. Alisa and the third sat in the back. Thea and I were in the middle.

"What did you do to Rebecca?" Thea waited until she was satisfied that the other occupants of the car weren't listening too closely before she asked the question, low and under her breath.

"I didn't do anything to Rebecca."

"I will accept that you didn't fall into the Jameson Hawthorne trap for the *purpose* of dredging up memories of Jameson and

Emily." Thea clearly thought she was being magnanimous. "But that's where my generosity ends. Rebecca's painfully beautiful, but the girl cries ugly. I know what she looks like when she's spent all night crying. Whatever her deal is—this isn't just about Jameson. What happened at the cottage?"

Rebecca knows about the shooting. She was forbidden from telling anyone. I tried to wrap my mind around the implications. *Why was she crying?*

"Speaking of Jameson," Thea changed tactics. "He is oh so clearly miserable, and I can only assume that I owe that to you."

He's miserable? I felt something flicker in my chest—a *what-if*—but quelled it. "Why do you hate him so much?" I asked Thea.

"Why don't you?"

"Why are you even here?" I narrowed my eyes. "Not in this car," I amended, before she could mention high-fashion boutiques, "at Hawthorne House. What did Zara and your uncle ask you to come here to do?"

Why stick so close to me? What did they want?

"What makes you think they asked me to do anything?" It was obvious in Thea's tone and in her manner that she was a person who'd been born with the upper hand and never lost it.

There's a first time for everything, I thought, but before I could lay out my case, the car pulled up to the boutique, and the paparazzi circled us in a deafening, claustrophobic crunch.

I slumped back in my seat. "I have an entire mall in my closet." I shot Alisa an aggrieved look. "If I just wore something I already have, we wouldn't have to deal with this."

"*This,*" Alisa echoed as Oren got out of the car and the roar of the reporters' questions grew louder, "is the point."

I was here to be seen, to control the narrative.

"Smile pretty," Thea murmured directly into my ear.

The boutique Alisa had chosen for this carefully choreographed outing was the kind of store that had only one copy of each dress. They'd closed the entire shop down for me.

"Green." Thea pulled an evening gown from the rack. "Emerald, to match your eyes."

"My eyes are hazel," I said flatly. I turned from the dress she was holding up to the sales attendant. "Do you have anything less low-cut?"

"You prefer higher cuts?" The sales attendant's tone was so carefully nonjudgmental that I was almost certain she was judging me.

"Something that covers my collarbone," I said, and then I shot a look at Alisa. *And my stitches.*

"You heard Ms. Grambs," Alisa said firmly. "And Thea is right— bring us something green."

CHAPTER 68

We found a dress. The paparazzi snapped their pictures as Oren ushered the lot of us back into the SUV. As we pulled away from the curb, he glanced in the rearview mirror. "Seat belts buckled?"

Mine was. Beside me, Thea fastened hers. "Have you thought about hair and makeup?" she asked.

"Constantly," I replied in a deadpan. "These days, I think of literally nothing else. A girl has to have her priorities in order."

Thea smiled. "And here I was thinking your priorities all had the last name Hawthorne."

"That's not true," I said. *But isn't it?* How much time had I spent thinking about them? How badly had I wanted Jameson to mean it when he'd told me I was special?

How clearly could I still feel Grayson checking my wound?

"Your bodyguard didn't want me to come today," Thea murmured as we turned onto a long and winding road. "Neither did your lawyer. I persevered, and do you know why?"

"Not a clue."

"This has nothing to do with my uncle or Zara." Thea played with the tips of her dark hair. "I'm just doing what Emily would want me to do. Remember that, would you?"

Without warning, the car swerved. My body kicked into panic mode—fight or flight, and neither one of them was an option, strapped into the back seat. I whipped my head toward Oren, who was driving—and noticed that the guard in the passenger seat had his hand on his gun, vigilant, ready.

Something's wrong. We shouldn't have come. I shouldn't have trusted, even for a moment, that I was safe. *Alisa pushed this. She wanted me out here.*

"Hold tight," Oren yelled.

"What's going on?" I asked. The words lodged themselves in my throat and came out as a whisper. I saw a flash of movement out of my window: a car, jerking toward us, high speed. I screamed.

My subconscious was screaming at me to *run.*

Oren swerved again, enough to prevent full-scale impact, but I heard the screech of metal on metal.

Someone is trying to run us off the road. Oren laid on the gas. The sound of sirens—police sirens—barely broke through the cacophony of panic in my head.

This can't be happening. Please don't let this be happening. Please, no.

Oren roared into the left lane, ahead of the car that had attacked us. He swung the SUV around, up and over the median, sending us racing in the opposite direction.

I tried to scream, but it wasn't loud or shrill. I was keening, and I couldn't make it stop.

There was more than one siren now. I turned toward the back of the car, expecting the worst, preparing for impact—and I saw the car that had hit us spinning out. Within seconds, the vehicle was surrounded by cops.

"We're okay," I whispered. I didn't believe it. My body was still telling me that I would never be okay again.

Oren eased off the gas, but he didn't stop, and he didn't turn around.

"What the hell was that?" I asked, my voice high enough in pitch and volume to crack glass.

"That," Oren replied calmly, "was someone taking the bait."

The bait? I swung my gaze toward Alisa. "What is he talking about?"

In the heat of the moment, I'd thought that it was Alisa's fault that we were here. I'd doubted her—but Oren's response suggested that maybe I should have blamed them both.

"This," Alisa said, her trademark calm dented but not destroyed, "was the point." That was the same thing she'd said when we'd seen the paparazzi outside the boutique.

The paparazzi. Making sure we were seen. The absolute need to come dress shopping, despite everything that had happened.

Because *of everything that had happened.*

"You used me as *bait?*" I wasn't a yeller, but I was yelling now.

Beside me, Thea recovered her voice—and then some. "What the hell is going on here?"

Oren exited the highway and slowed to a stop at a red light. "Yes," he told me apologetically, "we used you—and ourselves—as bait." He glanced toward Thea and answered her question. "There was an attack on Avery two days ago. Our friends at the police station agreed to play this my way."

"Your way could have killed us!" I couldn't make my heart stop pounding. I could barely breathe.

"We had backup," Oren assured me. "My people, as well as the police. I won't tell you that you weren't in danger, but the situation being what it was, danger was not a possibility that could be eliminated. There were no good options. You had to continue living in that house. Instead of waiting for another attack, Alisa and I engineered what looked like a prime opportunity. Now, maybe we can get some answers."

First, they'd told me that the Hawthornes weren't a threat. Then they'd used me to flush out the threat. "You could have told me," I said roughly.

"It was better," Alisa told me, "that you didn't know. That *no one* knew."

Better for whom? Before I could say that, Oren got a call.

"Did Rebecca know about the attack?" Thea asked beside me. "Is that why she's been so upset?"

"Oren." Alisa ignored Thea and me. "Did they apprehend the driver?"

"They did." Oren paused, and I caught him looking at me in the rearview mirror, his eyes softening in a way that made my stomach twist. "Avery, it was your sister's boyfriend."

Drake. "Ex-boyfriend," I corrected, my voice getting caught in my throat.

Oren didn't respond to my assertion. "They found a rifle in his trunk that, at least preliminarily, matches the bullets. The police will be wanting to talk to your sister."

"What?" I said, my heart still banging mercilessly at my rib cage. "Why?" On some level, I knew—I knew the answer to that question, but I couldn't accept it.

I wouldn't.

"If Drake was the shooter, someone would have had to sneak

him onto the estate," Alisa said, her voice uncharacteristically gentle.

Not Libby, I thought. "Libby *wouldn't*—"

"Avery." Alisa put a hand on my shoulder. "If something happens to you—even without a will—your sister and your father are your heirs."

CHAPTER 69

These were the facts: Drake had tried to run my car off the road. He had a weapon that was a likely match for the bullets Oren had recovered. He had a felony record.

The police took my statement. They asked questions about the shooting. About Drake. About Libby. Eventually, I was escorted back to Hawthorne House.

The front door flew open before Alisa and I had even made it to the porch.

Nash stormed out of the house, then slowed when he saw us. "You want to tell me why I'm just now getting word that the police hauled Libby out of here?" he asked Alisa.

I'd never heard a Southern drawl sound quite like that.

Alisa lifted her chin. "If she's not under arrest, she had no obligation to go with them."

"She doesn't know that!" Nash boomed. Then he lowered his voice and looked her in the eye. "If you'd wanted to protect her, you could have."

There were so many layers to that sentence, I couldn't begin to untangle them, not with my brain focused on other things. *Libby. The police have Libby.*

"I'm not in the business of protecting every sad story that comes along," Alisa told Nash.

I knew she wasn't *just* talking about Libby, but that didn't matter. "She's not a sad story," I gritted out. "She's my sister!"

"And, more likely than not, an accessory to attempted murder." Alisa reached out to touch my shoulder. I stepped back.

Libby wouldn't hurt me. She wouldn't let anyone hurt me. I believed that, but I couldn't say it. Why couldn't I say it?

"That bastard's been texting her," Nash said beside me. "I've been trying to get her to block him, but she feels so damn guilty—"

"For what?" Alisa pushed. "What does she feel guilty for? If she's got nothing to hide from the police, then why are you so concerned about her talking to them?"

Nash's eyes flashed. "You're really going to stand there and act like we weren't both raised to treat 'never talk to the authorities without a lawyer present' like a Commandment?"

I thought about Libby, alone in a cell. She probably wasn't even *in* a cell, but I couldn't shake the image. "Send someone," I told Alisa shakily. "From the firm." She opened her mouth to object, and I cut her off. *"Do it."*

I might not hold the purse strings now, but I would someday. She worked for me.

"Consider it done," Alisa said.

"And leave me alone," I told her fiercely. She and Oren had kept me in the dark. They'd moved me around like a chess piece on a board. "All of you," I said, turning back toward Oren.

I needed to be alone. I needed to do everything in my power to keep them from planting even a seed of doubt, because if I couldn't trust Libby...

I had no one.

Nash cleared his throat. "You want to tell her about the media consultant waiting in the sitting room, Lee-Lee, or should I?"

CHAPTER 70

I agreed to sit down with Alisa's high-priced media consultant. Not because I had any intention of going through with tonight's charity gala, but because it was the one way I knew of to make sure that everyone else left me alone.

"There are three things we're going to work on today, Avery." The consultant, an elegant Black woman with a posh British accent, had introduced herself as Landon. I had no idea if that was her first name or her last. "After the attack this morning, there will be more interest in your story—and your sister's—than ever."

Libby wouldn't hurt me, I thought desperately. *She wouldn't let Drake hurt me.* And then: *She didn't block his number.*

"The three things we will be practicing today are what to say, how to say it, and how to identify things you shouldn't say and demur." Landon was poised, precise, and more stylish than either of my stylists. "Now, obviously, there is going to be some interest in the unfortunate incident that took place this morning, but your legal team would prefer you say as little on that front as possible."

That front being the second attempt on my life in three days. *Libby isn't involved. She can't be.*

"Repeat after me," Landon instructed, "*I'm grateful to be alive, and I'm grateful to be here tonight.*"

I blocked out the thoughts dogging me, as much as I could. "I'm grateful to be alive," I repeated stonily, "and I'm grateful to be here tonight."

Landon gave me a look. "How do you think you sound?"

"Pissed?" I guessed dourly.

Landon offered me a gentle suggestion. "Perhaps try sounding less pissed." She waited a moment, and then assessed the way I was sitting. "Open up your shoulders. Loosen those muscles. Your posture is the first thing the audience's brain is going to latch on to. If you look like you're trying to fold in on yourself, if you make yourself small, that sends a message."

With a roll of my eyes, I tried to sit up a little straighter and let my hands fall to my sides. "I'm grateful to be alive, and I'm grateful to be here tonight."

"No." Landon gave a shake of her head. "You want to sound like a real person."

"I am a real person."

"Not to the rest of the world. Not yet. Right now you're a spectacle." There was nothing unkind in Landon's tone. "Pretend you're back home. You're in your comfort zone."

What was my comfort zone? Talking to Max, who was MIA for the foreseeable future? Crawling into bed with Libby?

"Think of someone you trust."

That hurt in a way that should have hollowed me out but left me feeling like I might throw up instead. I swallowed. "I'm grateful to be alive, and I'm grateful to be here tonight."

"It seems forced, Avery."

I ground my teeth. "It *is* forced."

"Does it have to be?" Landon let me marinate in that question for a moment. "Is no part of you grateful to have been given this opportunity? To live in this house? To know that no matter what happens, you and the people you love will always be taken care of?"

Money was security. It was safety. It was knowing that you could screw up without screwing up your life. *If Libby did let Drake onto the estate, if he's the one who shot at me—she couldn't have known that's what was going to happen.*

"Aren't you grateful to be alive, after everything that's happened? Did you *want* to die today?"

No. I wanted to live. Really live.

"I'm grateful to be here," I said, feeling the words a little more this time, "and I'm grateful to be alive."

"Better, but this time...let it hurt."

"Excuse me?"

"Show them that you're vulnerable."

I wrinkled my nose at her.

"Show them that you're just an ordinary girl. Just like them. That's the trick of my trade: How real, how vulnerable, can you seem without letting yourself actually be vulnerable at all?"

Vulnerable wasn't the story I'd chosen to tell when they'd been designing my wardrobe. I was supposed to have an edge. But sharp-edged girls had feelings, too.

"I'm grateful to be alive," I said, "and I'm grateful to be here tonight."

"Good." Landon gave a little nod. "Now we're going to play a little game. I'm going to ask you questions, and you're going to do the one thing you absolutely must master before I let you out of here to go to the gala tonight."

"What's that?" I asked.

"You're *not* going to answer the questions." Landon's expression was intent. "Not with words. Not with your face. Not at all—unless and until you get a question that you can, in some way, answer with the key message we've already practiced."

"Gratitude," I said. "Et cetera, et cetera." I shrugged. "Doesn't sound hard."

"Avery, is it true that your mother had a long-standing sexual liaison with Tobias Hawthorne?"

She almost got me. I almost spat out the word *no*. But somehow, I refrained.

"Did you stage today's attack?"

What?

"Watch your face," she told me, and then, without losing a beat: "How is your relationship with the Hawthorne family?"

I sat, passive, not allowing myself to so much as think their names.

"What are you going to do with the money? How do you respond to the people calling you a con woman and a thief? Were you injured today?"

That last question gave me an opening. "I'm fine," I said. "I'm grateful to be alive, and I'm grateful to be here tonight."

I expected accolades but got none.

"Is it true that your sister is in a relationship with the man who tried to kill you? Is she involved with the attempt on your life?"

I wasn't sure if it was the way she'd snuck the questions in, right after my previous answer, or how close to the quick the question cut, but I snapped.

"*No.*" The word burst from my mouth. "My sister had *nothing* to do with this."

Landon gave me a look. "From the top," she said steadily. "Let's try again."

CHAPTER 71

After my session with Landon, she dropped me off in my bedroom, where my style team awaited. I could have told them that I wasn't going to the gala, but Landon had gotten me thinking: What kind of message would that send?

That I was afraid? That I was hiding away—or hiding something? That Libby was guilty?

She's not. That was what I kept telling myself, over and over again. I was halfway through hair and makeup when Libby let herself into my bedroom. My stomach muscles clenched, my heart jumping into my throat. Her face was streaked with running makeup. She'd been crying.

She didn't do anything wrong. She didn't. Libby hesitated for three or four seconds, then threw herself at me, catching me up in the biggest, tightest hug of my life. "I'm sorry. I am so, so sorry."

I had a moment—exactly one—where my blood ran cold.

"I should have blocked him," Libby continued. "But for what it's worth, I just put my phone in the blender. And then I turned the blender on."

She wasn't apologizing for aiding and abetting Drake. She was apologizing for not blocking his number. For fighting with me when I'd wanted her to.

I bowed my head, and a set of hands immediately lifted my chin back up as the stylists continued their work.

"Say something," Libby told me.

I wanted to tell her that I believed her, but even saying the words felt disloyal, like an acknowledgment that I really hadn't been sure until now. "You're going to need a new phone," I said.

Libby gave a strangled little laugh. "We're also going to need a new blender." She swiped the heel of her right hand across her eyes.

"No tears!" the man making me up barked. That was aimed at me, not Libby, but she straightened, too. "You want to look like the picture we were given, correct?" the man asked me, aggressively working some mousse through my hair.

"Sure," I replied. "Whatever." If Alisa had given them a picture, that was one less decision for me to make, one less thing to think about.

Like the current billion-dollar question: If Drake had shot at me, and Libby hadn't let him onto the estate—who had?

———◆———

An hour later, I stood facing the mirror. The stylists had braided my hair, but it wasn't just a braid. They'd divided my hair in half and then each half into thirds. Each third had been bisected, and one half was wound around the other, giving the hair a spiraling, ropelike look. Tiny, transparent hair ties and an ungodly amount of hair spray had held that in place as they'd begun to French-braid my hair on each side. I had no idea what exactly had happened next, other than the fact that it had hurt like hell and required all four of my stylists' hands plus one of Libby's, but the final braid wrapped around my head to frame one side of my face. The coils were multicolored, showing off my lowlights and the natural blonde streaks in my ashy-brown hair. The effect was hypnotizing, like nothing I'd ever seen.

The makeup was less dramatic—natural, fresh, understated everywhere but the eyes. I had no idea what witchcraft they'd invoked, but my charcoal-lined eyes looked twice their normal size, and *green*—a true green, with flecks that looked more gold than brown.

"And the pièce de résistance..." One of the stylists slipped a necklace around my neck. "White gold and three emeralds."

The jewels were the size of my thumbnail.

"You look beautiful," Libby told me.

I looked nothing like myself. I looked like someone who belonged at a ball, and still, I almost backed out of going to the gala. The one thing that kept me from throwing in the towel was Libby.

If there was ever a time for me to control the narrative, it was now.

CHAPTER 72

O ren met me at the top of the stairs.

"Have the police gotten anything out of Drake?" I asked. "Has he admitted to the shooting? Who is he working with?"

"Deep breath," Oren told me. "Drake has more than implicated himself, but he's trying to paint Libby as the mastermind. That story doesn't add up. There is no security footage of him entering the estate, and there would be if, as he claims, Libby had let him through the gate. Our best guess at the moment is that he came in through the tunnels."

"The tunnels?" I repeated.

"They're like the secret passages in the house, except they run under the estate. I know of two entrances, and they're both secure."

I heard what Oren left unsaid. "There are two that you know of—but this is Hawthorne House. There could be more."

On my way to a ball, I should have felt like a fairy-tale princess, but my horse-drawn carriage was an SUV identical to the one that Drake had side-swiped this morning. Nothing said *fairy tale* like an attempted assassination.

Who knows the location of the tunnels? That was the question of the hour. If there were tunnels that Hawthorne House's head of security didn't even know about, I seriously doubted that Drake had come across them on his own. Libby wouldn't have known about them, either.

So who? Someone very, very familiar with Hawthorne House. *Did they reach out to Drake? Why?* That last question was less of a mystery. After all, why commit murder yourself when there was someone else out there willing and ready to do it for you? All someone would have had to know was that Drake existed, that he'd already gotten violent once, that he had every reason to hate me.

Within the walls of Hawthorne House, none of that was a secret.

Maybe his accomplice had sweetened the pie by telling him that if anything happened to me, Libby stood to inherit.

They let a felon do the dirty work—and take the fall. I sat in my bulletproof SUV in a five-thousand-dollar dress and a necklace that probably could have paid for at least a year of college, wondering if Drake's capture meant that the danger was over—or if whoever had given him tunnel access had other plans for me.

"The foundation purchased two tables for tonight's event," Alisa told me from the front seat. "Zara was loath to part with any seats, but since it's technically *your* foundation, she didn't have much of a choice."

Alisa was acting like nothing had happened. Like I had every reason to trust her, when it felt like reasons not to were stacking up.

"So I'll be sitting with them," I said without expression. "The Hawthornes."

One of whom—at *least* one of whom—might still want me dead.

"It's to your advantage if everything appears friendly between you." Alisa had to realize how ridiculous that sounded, given the context. "If the Hawthorne family accepts you, that will go a long way toward squelching some of the less seemly theories as to why you inherited."

"And what about the unseemly theories that one of them—*at least* one—wants me dead?" I asked.

Maybe it was Zara, or her husband, or Skye, or even Nan, who'd more or less told me that she'd killed her husband.

"We're still on high alert," Oren assured me. "But it would be to our benefit if the Hawthornes didn't realize that. If the conspirator's hope was to pin things on Drake—and Libby—let them think they've succeeded."

Last time around, I'd blown the element of surprise. This time, things would be different.

CHAPTER 73

A very, look over here!"

"Any comment about the arrest of Drake Sanders?"

"Can you comment on the future of the Hawthorne Foundation?"

"Is it true that your mother was once arrested for solicitation?"

If it hadn't been for the *seven* rounds of practice questions I'd been put through earlier, that last one would have gotten me. I would have answered, and my answer would have contained expletives, plural. Instead, I stood near the car and waited.

And then the question I'd been waiting for came. "With everything that's happened, how do you feel?"

I looked directly at the reporter who'd asked that question. "I'm grateful to be alive," I said. "And I'm grateful to be here tonight."

\>=———————=\<

The event was held in an art museum. We entered on the upper floor and descended a massive marble staircase into the exhibit hall. By the time I was halfway down, everyone in the room was either staring at me or not-staring in a way that was worse.

At the bottom of the stairs, I saw Grayson. He wore a tuxedo exactly the way he wore a suit. He was holding a glass—clear, with clear liquid inside. The moment he saw me, he froze in place, as suddenly and fully as if someone had stopped time. I thought back to standing with him at the bottom of the hidden staircase, to the way he'd looked at me, and on some level, I thought that was the way he was looking at me now.

I thought I'd taken his breath away.

Then he dropped the glass in his hand. It hit the floor and shattered, shards of crystal spraying everywhere.

What happened? What did I do?

Alisa nudged me to keep moving. I finished descending the stairs as the waitstaff hurried over to clean up the glass.

Grayson stared at me. "What are you doing?" His voice was guttural.

"I don't understand," I said.

"Your hair," Grayson choked out. He lifted his free hand to my braid, his fingers nearly touching it before he pulled them into a fist. "That necklace. That dress..."

"What?" I said.

The only word he managed in reply was a name.

———◆———

Emily. It was always Emily. Somehow, I made my way to the bathroom without looking too much like I was running away. I fumbled to tear my phone out of the black satin handbag I'd been given, unsure what I was planning to do with the phone once I got it out. Someone stepped up to the mirror beside me.

"You look nice," Thea said, casting a glance sidelong at me. "In fact, you look *perfect*."

I stared at her, and comprehension dawned. "What did you do, Thea?"

She glanced down at her own phone, hit a few buttons, and a moment later, I had a text. I hadn't even realized she had my number.

I opened the text and the picture attached, and all of the blood drained from my face. In this photo, Emily Laughlin wasn't laughing. She was smiling at the camera—a wicked little smile, like she was on the verge of a wink. Her makeup was natural, but her eyes looked unnaturally large, and her hair . . .

Was exactly like mine.

"What did you do?" I asked Thea again, more accusation this time than question. She'd invited herself along on my shopping trip. She was the one who'd suggested I wear green—just like Emily wore in this photo.

Even my necklace was eerily like hers.

I'd assumed, when the stylist had asked if I wanted to look like the picture, that Alisa was the one who'd supplied it. I'd assumed it was a photo of a model. *Not a dead girl.*

"Why would you do this?" I asked Thea, amending my question.

"It's what Emily would have wanted." Thea pulled a tube of lipstick out of her purse. "If it's any consolation," she said, once she was finished turning her lips a sparkling ruby red, "I didn't do this to *you*."

She'd done it to *them*.

"The Hawthornes didn't kill Emily," I spat. "Rebecca said that it was her heart."

Technically, she'd said that *Grayson* had said it was her heart.

"How sure are you that the Hawthorne family isn't trying to kill *you*?" Thea smiled. She had been there this morning. She'd been shaken. And now she was acting like this was all a joke.

"There is something fundamentally wrong with you," I said.

My fury didn't seem to penetrate. "I told you the day we met that the Hawthorne family was a twisted, broken mess." She stared at the mirror a moment longer. "I never said that I wasn't one, too."

CHAPTER 74

I took off the necklace and stood holding it in front of the mirror. The hair was a bigger problem. It had taken two people to put it up. It would take an act of God for me to get it down.

"Avery?" Alisa stuck her head into the bathroom.

"Help me," I told her.

"With what?"

"My hair."

I reached back and started pulling at it, and Alisa caught my hands in hers. She transferred my wrists to her right hand and flipped a lock on the bathroom door with her left. "I shouldn't have pushed you," she said, her voice low. "This is too much, too soon, isn't it?"

"Do you know who I look like?" I asked her. I shoved the necklace in her face. She took it from my hands.

She frowned. "Who you look like?" That seemed like an honest question from a person who didn't like asking questions she didn't already know the answers to.

"Emily Laughlin." I couldn't keep from cutting a glance back to the mirror. "Thea dressed me up just like her."

It took Alisa a moment to process that. "I didn't know." She paused, considering. "The press won't, either. Emily was just an ordinary girl."

There was nothing ordinary about Emily Laughlin. I didn't know when I'd come to believe that. The moment I'd seen her picture? My conversation with Rebecca? The very first time Jameson had said her name, or the first time I'd said it to Grayson?

"If you stay in this bathroom much longer, people will take note," Alisa warned me. "They already have. For better or worse, you need to get out there."

I'd come tonight because in some twisted way I'd thought that putting on a happy face would protect Libby. I'd hardly be here if my own sister had tried to have me killed, would I?

"Fine," I told Alisa through gritted teeth. "But if I do this for you, I want your word that you'll protect my sister in any way you can. I don't care what your deal is with Nash, or what Nash's is with Libby. You don't just work for me anymore. You work for her, too."

I saw Alisa swallowing back whatever it was she really wanted to say. All that exited her mouth was: "You have my word."

———————

I just had to make it through dinner. A dance or two. The live auction. Easier said than done. Alisa led me to the pair of tables that the Hawthorne Foundation had purchased. At the table on the left, Nan was holding court among the white-haired set. The table on the right was half-filled with Hawthornes: Zara and Constantine, Nash, Grayson, and Xander.

I made a beeline for Nan's table, but Alisa sidestepped and gently steered me to the seat directly next to Grayson. Alisa took the next chair over, leaving only three open seats—at least one of which I assumed was for Jameson.

Beside me, Grayson said nothing. I lost the battle not to flick my eyes in his direction and found him staring straight ahead, not looking at me—or anyone else at the table.

"I didn't do this on purpose," I told him under my breath, trying to keep the expression on my face normal for the benefit of our audience, partygoers and photographers alike.

"Of course not," Grayson replied, his tone stiff, the words rote.

"I'd take the braid out if I could," I murmured. "But I can't do it myself."

His head tilted down slightly, his eyes closing, just for a moment. "I know."

I was overcome then by the mental image of Grayson helping Emily take down her hair, his fingers working the braid out, bit by bit.

My arm bumped Alisa's wineglass. She tried to catch it but didn't move fast enough. As the wine stained the white tablecloth red, I realized what should have been obvious right from the beginning, from the moment the will had been read.

I didn't belong here in this world—not at a party like this, not sitting beside Grayson Hawthorne. And I never would.

CHAPTER 75

made it through dinner without anyone trying to kill me, and Jameson never showed. I told Alisa that I needed some air, but I didn't go outside. I couldn't face the press again this soon, so I ended up in another wing of the museum instead, Oren playing shadow behind me.

The wing was closed. The lights were dim, and the exhibit rooms were blocked off, but the corridor was open. I walked down the long hall, Oren's footsteps trailing mine. Up ahead, there was a light shining, bright against all its surroundings. The cord blocking off this exhibit room had been moved to one side. Stepping past it felt like stepping out of a dark theater and into the sun. The room was bright. Even the frames on the paintings were white. There was only one person in the room, wearing a tuxedo without the jacket.

"Jameson." I said his name, but he didn't turn. He was standing in front of a small painting, looking at it intently from three or four feet away. He glanced at me as I walked toward him, then turned back to the painting.

You saw me, I thought. *You saw the way they did my hair.* The room was quiet enough that I could hear the beating of my own heart. *Say something.*

He nodded toward the painting. "Cézanne's *Four Brothers*," he said as I came to stand beside him. "A Hawthorne family favorite, for obvious reasons."

I made myself look at the painting, not at him. There were four figures on the canvas, their features blurred. I could make out the lines of their muscles. I could practically *see* them in motion, but the artist hadn't been aiming for realism. My eyes went to the gold tag under the painting.

Four Brothers. Paul Cézanne. 1898. On loan from the collection of Tobias Hawthorne.

Jameson angled his face back toward mine. "I know you found the Davenport." He arched an eyebrow. "You beat me to it."

"So did Grayson," I said.

Jameson's expression darkened. "You were right. The tree in the Black Wood was just a tree. The clue we're looking for is a number. *Eight. One. One.* There's just one more."

"There is no *we*," I said. "Do you even see me as a person, Jameson? Or am I just a tool?"

"I might have deserved that." He held my gaze a moment longer, then looked back at the painting. "The old man used to say that I have laser focus. I'm not built to care about more than one thing at a time."

I wondered if that thing was the game—or *her*.

"I'm done, Jameson." My words echoed in the white room. "With you. With whatever this was." I turned to walk away.

"I don't care that you're wearing Emily's braid." Jameson knew exactly what to say to make me stop. "I don't care," he repeated, "because *I don't care about Emily*." He let out a ragged breath. "I broke up with her that night. I got tired of her little games. I told her I was done, and a few hours later, she died."

I turned back, and green eyes, a little bloodshot, settled on mine. "I'm sorry," I said, wondering how many times he'd replayed their last conversation.

"Come with me to the Black Wood," Jameson pleaded. He was right. He had laser focus. "You don't have to kiss me. You don't even have to like me, Heiress, but please don't make me do this alone."

He sounded raw, real in a way that he never had before. *You don't have to kiss me.* He'd said that like he wanted me to.

"I hope I'm not interrupting."

In unison, Jameson and I looked toward the doorway. Grayson stood there, and I realized that from his vantage point, all he would have seen of me when he'd walked into the room was the braid.

For a moment, Grayson and Jameson stared at each other.

"You know where I'll be, Heiress," Jameson told me. "If there's any part of you that wants to find me."

He brushed past Grayson on his way out the door. Grayson watched him go for the longest time before he turned back to me. "What did he say, when he saw you?"

When he saw my hair. I swallowed. "He told me that he broke up with Emily the night she died."

Silence.

I turned back to look at Grayson.

His eyes were closed, every muscle in his body taut. "Did Jameson tell you that I killed her?"

CHAPTER 76

After Grayson left, I spent another fifteen minutes in the gallery—alone—staring at Cézanne's *Four Brothers* before Alisa sent someone to find me.

"I agree," Xander told me, even though I hadn't said anything for him to agree with. "This party sucks. The socialite-to-scone ratio is pretty much unforgivable."

I wasn't in the mood for scone jokes. *Jameson says he broke up with Emily. Grayson claims that he killed her. Thea is using me to punish them both.* "I'm out of here," I told Xander.

"You can't leave yet!"

I gave him a look. "Why not?"

"Because…" Xander waggled his lone eyebrow. "They just opened up the dance floor. You want to give the press something to talk about, don't you?"

⋙━━━━━⋘

One dance. That was all I was giving Alisa—and the photographers— before I got the hell out of here.

"Pretend I'm the most fascinating person you've ever met," Xander advised as he escorted me onto the dance floor for a waltz.

He held a hand out for mine, then curved his other arm around my back. "Here, I'll help: Every year on my birthday, from the time I was seven until I was twelve, my grandfather gave me money to invest, and I spent it all on cryptocurrency because I am a genius and not at all because I thought *cryptocurrency* sounded kind of cool." He spun me once. "I sold my holdings before my grandfather died for almost a hundred million dollars."

I stared at him. "You what?"

"See?" he told me. "Fascinating." Xander kept right on dancing, but he looked down. "Not even my brothers know."

"What did your brothers invest in?" I asked. All this time, I'd been assuming that they'd been cut off with *nothing*. Nash had told me about Tobias Hawthorne's birthday tradition, but I hadn't thought twice about their "investments."

"No idea," Xander said jauntily. "We weren't allowed to discuss it."

We danced on, the photographers snapping their shots. Xander brought his face very close to mine.

"The press is going to think we're dating," I told him, my mind still spinning at his revelation.

"As it so happens," Xander replied archly, "I excel at fake dating."

"Who exactly did you fake date?" I asked.

Xander looked past me to Thea. "I am a human Rube Goldberg machine," he said. "I do simple things in complicated ways." He paused. "It was Emily's idea for Thea and me to date. Em was, shall we say, *persistent*. She didn't know that Thea was already with someone."

"And you agreed to put on a show?" I asked incredulously.

"I repeat: I am a human Rube Goldberg machine." His voice softened. "And I didn't do it for Thea."

Then for who? It took me a moment to put it together. Xander had mentioned fake dating *twice* before: once with respect to Thea, and once when I'd asked him about Rebecca.

"Thea and Rebecca?" I said.

"Deeply in love," Xander confirmed. *Thea called her painfully beautiful.* "The best friend and the younger sister. What was I supposed to do? They didn't think Emily would understand. She was possessive of the people she loved, and I knew how hard it was for Rebecca to go against her. Just once, Bex wanted something for herself."

I wondered if Xander had feelings for her—if fake dating Thea had been his twisted, Rube Goldberg way of saying that. "Were Thea and Rebecca right?" I asked. "About Emily not understanding?"

"And then some." Xander paused. "Em found out about them that night. She saw it as a betrayal."

That night—the night she died.

The music came to an end, and Xander dropped my hand, keeping his other arm around my waist. "Smile for the press," he murmured. "Give them a story. Look deep into my eyes. Feel the weight of my charm. Think of your favorite baked goods."

The edges of my lips turned up, and Xander Hawthorne escorted me off the dance floor to Alisa. "You can go now," she told me, pleased. "If you'd like."

Hell yes. "You coming?" I asked Xander.

The invitation seemed to surprise him. "I can't." He paused. "I solved the Black Wood." That got my full attention. "I could win this." Xander looked down at his fancy shoes. "But Jameson and Grayson need it more. Head back to Hawthorne House. There'll be a helicopter waiting for you when you get there. Have the pilot fly you over the Black Wood."

A helicopter?

"Where you go," Xander told me, "they'll follow."

They, as in his brothers. "I thought you wanted to win," I said to Xander.

He swallowed. Hard. "I do."

CHAPTER 77

'd only halfway believed Xander when he'd promised me a helicopter, but there it was, on the front lawn of Hawthorne House, blades still. Oren wouldn't let me step foot aboard until he'd checked it over. Even then, he insisted on taking the pilot's spot. I climbed in the back and discovered Jameson already there.

"Order a helicopter?" he asked me, like that was a perfectly normal thing to do.

I buckled myself into the seat next to him. "I'm surprised you waited for liftoff."

"I told you, Heiress." He gave me a crooked smile. "I don't want to do this alone." For a split second, it was like the two of us were back at the racetrack, barreling toward the finish line, then outside the helicopter, a flash of black caught my eye.

A tuxedo. Grayson's expression was impossible to read as he climbed on board.

Did Jameson tell you that I killed her? The echo of the question was deafening in my mind. As if he'd heard it, Jameson's head whipped toward Grayson. "What are you doing here?"

Xander had said that where I went, both of them would follow. *Jameson didn't follow me*, I reminded myself, every nerve in my body alive. *He got here first.*

"May I?" Grayson asked me, nodding toward an empty seat. I could feel Jameson staring at me, feel him willing me to say no.

I nodded.

Grayson sat behind me. Oren checked to make sure we were secure, then turned on the rotor. Within a minute, the sound of the blades was deafening. My heart jumped into my throat as we took to the air.

I'd enjoyed my first time on an airplane, but this was different— it was more. The noise, the vibration, the heightened sense that almost nothing separated me from the air—or the ground. My heart was beating, but I couldn't hear it. I couldn't hear myself think—not about the way Grayson's voice had broken as he'd asked that question, not about the way Jameson had told me that I didn't *have* to kiss him or like him.

All I could think about was looking down.

As we flew over the edge of the Black Wood, I could make out the twisted tangle of trees down below—too dense for sunlight to shine through. But when my gaze shifted toward the center of the forest, the trees thinned out, opening to a clearing in the very center. Jameson and I had been nearing the clearing when Drake had started taking shots. I'd noted the grass, but I hadn't *seen* it, not the way I was seeing it now.

From overhead, the clearing, the lighter ring of trees surrounding it, and the dense outer forest formed what looked like a long, skinny letter *O*.

Or a zero.

By the time the copter touched down, I felt like I was getting ready to burst out of my skin. I hopped out before the blades had fully stopped, adrenaline-fueled and giddy.

Eight. One. One. Zero.

Jameson bounded toward me. "We did it, Heiress." He stopped right in front of me, lifting his hands, palm up. Drunk on the high of the helicopter, I did the same, and his fingers locked through mine. "Four middle names. Four numbers."

Kissing him had been a mistake. Holding his hands now was a mistake—but I didn't care.

"Eight, one, one, zero," I said. "That's the order we discovered the numbers in—and the order of the clues in the will." Westbrook, Davenport, Winchester, and Blackwood, in that order. "A combination, maybe?"

"There are at least a dozen safes in the House," Jameson mused. "But there are other possibilities. An address . . . coordinates . . . and there's no guarantee that the clue isn't scrambled. To solve it, we may have to reorder the numbers."

An address. Coordinates. A combination. I closed my eyes, just for a second, just long enough for my brain to put another possibility into words. "A date?" All four clues were numbers; they were also single digits. For a combination lock or coordinates, I would have expected some two-digit entries. But a date . . .

The one or the zero would have to go at the front. 1-1-0-8 would be 11/08. "November eighth," I said, and then I ran through the rest of the possibilities. *08/11.* "August eleventh." *01/18.* "January eighteenth."

Then I hit the last possibility—the last date.

I stopped breathing. This was too big of a coincidence to be a coincidence at all.

"Ten-eighteen—October eighteenth." I sucked in a breath. Every nerve in my body felt like it was alive. "That's my birthday."

I have a secret, my mother had told me on my fifteenth birthday, two years ago, days before she'd died, *about the day you were born....*

"No." Jameson dropped my hands.

"Yes," I replied. "I was born on October eighteenth. And my mother—"

"This isn't about your mother." Jameson balled his fingers into fists and stepped back.

"Jameson?" I had no idea what was going on here. If Tobias Hawthorne had chosen me because of something that had happened the day I was born, that was big. *Huge.* "This could be it. Maybe his path crossed my mom's while she was in labor? Maybe she did something for him while she was pregnant with me?"

"Stop." The word cracked like a whip. Jameson was looking at me like I was unnatural, like I was broken, like the sight of me could turn stomachs, including and especially his.

"What are you—"

"The numbers are not a date."

Yes, I thought fiercely. *They are.*

"This can't be the answer," he said.

I stepped forward, but he jerked back. I felt a light touch on my arm. *Grayson.* As gentle as his touch was, I got the distinct sense that he was holding me back.

Why? What had I done?

"Emily died," Grayson told me, his voice tight, "on October eighteenth, a year ago."

"That sick *son of a bitch*," Jameson cursed. "All of this—the clues, the will, her—all of it for *this*? He just found a random person born on that day to send a message? *This* message?"

"Jamie—"

"Don't talk to me." Jameson swung his gaze from Grayson to me. "Screw this. I'm done."

As he stalked away into the night, I called after him. "Where are you going?"

"Congratulations, Heiress," Jameson called back, his voice dripping with everything but felicitations. "I guess you had the good fortune of being born on the right day. Mystery solved."

CHAPTER 78

There had to be more to the puzzle than this. There *had* to be. I couldn't just be a random person born on the right calendar date. *That can't be it.* What about my mother? What about her secret—a secret she'd mentioned on my fifteenth birthday, a full year before Emily had died? And what about the letter Tobias Hawthorne had left me?

I'm sorry.

What had Tobias Hawthorne had to apologize for? *He didn't just randomly select a person with the right birthday. There has to be more to it than that.*

But I could still hear Nash telling me: *You're the glass ballerina—or the knife.*

"I'm sorry." Grayson spoke again beside me. "It's not Jameson's fault that he's like this. It's not Jameson's fault..." The invincible Grayson Hawthorne seemed to be having trouble talking. "...that this is how the game ends."

I was still wearing my clothes from the gala. My hair was still in Emily's braid.

"I should have known." Grayson's voice was swollen with

emotion. "I *did* know. The day that the will was read, I knew that all of this was because of me."

I thought of the way Grayson had shown up at my hotel room that night. He'd been angry, determined to figure out what *I* had done.

"What are you talking about?" I searched his face and eyes for answers. "How is this because of you? And don't tell me you killed Emily."

No one—not even Thea—had called Emily's death a murder.

"I did," Grayson insisted, his voice low and vibrating with intensity. "If it weren't for me, she wouldn't have been there. She wouldn't have jumped."

Jumped. My throat went dry. "Been where?" I asked quietly. "And what does any of this have to do with your grandfather's will?"

Grayson shuddered. "Maybe I was meant to tell you," he said after a long while. "Maybe that was always the point. Maybe you were always meant to be equal parts puzzle...and penance." He bowed his head.

I'm not your penance, Grayson Hawthorne. I didn't get the chance to say that out loud before he was talking again—and once he started, it would have taken an act of God to stop him.

"We'd always known her. Mr. and Mrs. Laughlin have been at Hawthorne House for decades. Their daughter and granddaughters used to live in California. The girls came to visit twice a year—once with their parents at Christmastime, and again in the summer, for three weeks, alone. We didn't see much of them at Christmas, but in the summers, we all played together. It was a bit like summer camp, really. You have camp friends, who you see once a year, who have no place in your ordinary life. That was Emily—and Rebecca. They were so different from the four of us. Skye said it was because they were girls, but I always thought it was because there were only two of them, and Emily came first. She was a force of nature, and their parents were always so worried she'd overexert herself. She was allowed to play cards with us, and other quiet, indoor games—but she wasn't allowed to roam outside the way we did, or to run.

"She'd get us to bring her things. It became a bit of a tradition. Emily would set us on a hunt, and whoever found what she'd requested—the more unusual and hard to find, the better—won."

"What did you win?" I asked.

Grayson shrugged. "We're brothers. We didn't have to win anything in particular—just *win*."

That tracked. "And then Emily got a heart transplant," I said. Jameson had told me that much. He'd said that afterward, she wanted to *live*.

"Her parents were still protective, but Emily had lived in glass cages long enough. She and Jameson were thirteen. I was fourteen. She'd breeze in for the summers, the consummate daredevil. Rebecca was always after us to be careful, but Emily insisted that her doctors had said that her activity level was only limited by her physical stamina. If she *could* do it, there was no reason she *shouldn't*. The family moved here permanently when Emily was sixteen. She and Rebecca didn't live on the estate, the way they had during visits, but my grandfather paid for them to attend private school."

I saw where this was going. "She wasn't just a summer camp friend anymore."

"She was everything," Grayson said—and he didn't exactly say it like it was a compliment. "Emily had the entire school eating out of the palm of her hand. Maybe that was our fault."

Even just being Hawthorne-adjacent changed the way that people looked at you. Thea's statement came back to me.

"Or maybe," Grayson continued, "it was just because she was

Em. Too smart, too beautiful, too good at getting what she wanted. She had no fear."

"She wanted you," I said. "And Jameson, and she didn't want to choose."

"She turned it into a game." Grayson shook his head. "And God help us, we played. I want to say that it was because we loved her— that it was because of *her*, but I don't even know how much of that was true. There's nothing more Hawthorne than *winning*."

Had Emily known that? Used it to her advantage? Had it ever hurt her?

"The thing was . . ." Grayson choked. "She didn't just want us. She wanted what we could give her."

"Money?"

"Experiences," Grayson replied. "Thrills. Race cars and motor-cycles and handling exotic snakes. Parties and clubs and places we weren't supposed to be. It was a rush—for her and for us." He paused. "For me," he corrected. "I don't know what it was, exactly, for Jamie."

Jameson broke up with her the night she died.

"One night, I got a call from Emily, late. She said that she was done with Jameson, that all she wanted was me." Grayson swal-lowed. "She wanted to celebrate. There's this place called Devil's Gate. It's a cliff overlooking the Gulf—one of the most famous cliff-diving locations in the world." Grayson angled his head down. "I knew it was a bad idea."

I tried to form words—any words. "How bad?"

He was breathing heavily now. "When we got there, I headed for one of the lower cliffs. Emily headed for the top. Past the dan-ger signs. Past the warnings. It was the middle of the night. We shouldn't have been there at all. I didn't know why she wouldn't let me wait until morning—not until later, when I realized she'd lied about *choosing* me."

Jameson had broken up with her. She'd called Grayson, and she hadn't been in the mood to *wait*.

"Cliff diving killed her?" I asked.

"No," Grayson said. "She was fine. *We* were fine. I went to grab our towels, but when I came back...Emily wasn't even in the water anymore. She was just lying on the shoreline. Dead." He closed his eyes. "Her heart."

"You didn't kill her," I said.

"The adrenaline did. Or the altitude, the change in pressure. *I don't know.* Jameson wouldn't take her. I shouldn't have, either."

She made decisions. She had agency. It wasn't your job to tell her no. I knew instinctively that no good could come of saying any of that, even if it was true.

"You know what my grandfather told me, after Emily's funeral? *Family first.* He said that what happened to Emily wouldn't have happened if I'd put my family first. If I'd refused to play along, if I'd chosen my brother over her." Grayson's vocal cords tensed against his throat, as if he wanted to say something else but couldn't. Finally, it came. "That's what this is about. One-zero-one-eight. October eighteenth. The day Emily died. Your birthday. It's my grandfather's way of confirming what I already knew, deep down.

"All of this—all of it—is because of me."

CHAPTER 79

When Grayson left, Oren escorted me back to the house. "How much did you hear?" I asked him, my mind tangled with thoughts and emotions I wasn't sure I was ready to handle.

Oren gave me a look. "How much do you want me to have heard?"

I bit at the inside of my lip. "You knew Tobias Hawthorne. Would he have picked me to inherit just because Emily Laughlin died on my birthday? Did he decide to leave his fortune to a random person born on October eighteenth? Hold a lottery?"

"I don't know, Avery." Oren shook his head. "The only person who ever really knew what Tobias Hawthorne was thinking was Mr. Hawthorne himself."

I made my way back through the halls of Hawthorne House, back toward the wing I shared with my sister. I wasn't certain that either Grayson or Jameson would ever speak a word to me again. I didn't know what the future held, or why the idea that I might have been chosen for a completely trivial reason felt like such a punch to the gut.

How many people on this planet shared my birthday?

I stopped on the stairs, in front of the portrait of Tobias Hawthorne that Xander had shown me what felt like a lifetime ago. I racked my mind now, as I'd done then, for any memory, any moment in time when my path had crossed with the billionaire's. I looked Tobias Hawthorne in the eye—Grayson's silver eyes—and silently asked him *why*.

Why me?

Why were you sorry?

I pictured my mother playing I Have A Secret. *Did something happen the day I was born?*

I stared at the portrait, taking in every wrinkle on the old man's face, every hint to personality in his posture, even the muted color in the background. *No answers.* My eyes caught on the artist's signature.

Tobias Hawthorne X. X. VIII

I looked back at the old man's silver eyes. *The only one who ever really knew what Tobias Hawthorne was thinking was Mr. Hawthorne himself.* This was a self-portrait. And the letters next to the name?

"Roman numerals," I whispered.

"Avery?" Oren said beside me. "Everything okay?"

In Roman numerals, *X* was ten, *V* was five, and *I* was one.

"Ten." I put my finger under the first X, then moved it to the rest of the letters, reading them as a single unit. "Eighteen."

Remembering the mirror that had hidden the armory, I reached behind the portrait's frame. I wasn't sure what I was feeling for until I found it. A button. *A release.* I pushed it, and the portrait swung outward.

Behind it, on the wall, was a keypad.

"Avery?" Oren said again, but I was already bringing my fingers up to the keypad. *What if the numbers aren't the final answer?* The possibility caught me in its jaws and wouldn't let go. *What if they're meant to lead to the next clue?*

I brought my index finger to the keypad and tried the obvious combination. "One. Zero. One. Eight."

There was a beep, and then the top of the step below me began to rise, revealing a compartment underneath. I ducked down and reached inside. There was only one thing in the hollowed stair: a piece of stained glass. It was purple, in the shape of an octagon, with a tiny hole in the top, through which a sheer, shimmering ribbon had been threaded. It looked almost like a Christmas ornament.

As I held the stained glass up by the string, my eyes caught on the underside of the panel. Etched into the wood was the following verse.

Top of the clock
Meet me at high
Tell the late day hello
Wish the morning good-bye
A twist and a flip
What do you see?
Take them two at a time
And come find me

CHAPTER 80

I didn't know what I was supposed to do with the stained-glass ornament or what to make of the words written under the stair, but as Libby helped me let my hair down that night, one thing was perfectly clear.

The game wasn't over.

———◆———

The next morning, with Oren in my wake, I went in search of Jameson and Grayson. I found the former in the solarium, shirtless and standing in the sun.

"Go away," he said when I opened the door, without even looking to see who it was.

"I found something," I told him. "I don't think the date is the answer—at least, not all of it."

He didn't reply.

"Jameson, are you listening to me? I *found something*." For what little time I'd known him, he'd been driven, obsessed. What I held in my hand should have engendered at least a glimmer of curiosity, but when he turned to face me, his eyes dull, all he said was "Toss it over with the rest."

I looked, and in a nearby trash can, I saw at least half a dozen stained-glass octagons, identical to the one that I held, right down to the ribbon.

"The numbers ten and eighteen are everywhere in this god-forsaken house." Jameson's voice was muted, his manner contained. "I found them scratched onto a panel on my closet floor. That little purple bugger was underneath."

He didn't bother gesturing to the trash can or specifying which piece of stained glass he was referring to.

"And the others?" I asked.

"Once I started looking for the numbers, I couldn't stop, and once you see it," Jameson said, his voice low, "you can't unsee it. The old man thought he was so smart. He must have hidden hundreds of those things, all over the house. I found a chandelier with eighteen crystals in the outer circle and ten in the middle—and a hidden compartment down below. There are eighteen stone leaves on the fountain outside, and ten finely drawn roses in its bowl. The paintings in the music room . . ." Jameson looked down. "Everywhere I look, everywhere I go, another reminder."

"Don't you see," I told him fiercely. "Your grandfather couldn't have done this all after Emily died. You would have noticed—"

"Workmen in the house?" Jameson said, finishing my sentence. "The great Tobias Hawthorne added a room or wing to this place every year, and in a house this size, something is always needing to be replaced or repaired. My mother was always buying new paintings, new fountains, new chandeliers. We wouldn't have noticed a thing."

"Ten-eighteen isn't the answer," I insisted, willing his eyes to mine. "You have to see that. It's a clue—one he didn't want us to miss."

Us. I'd said *us*—and I meant it. But that didn't matter.

"Ten-eighteen is answer enough," Jameson said, turning his back on me. "I told you, Avery: I'm not playing anymore."

━━━━━━━━━━━━

Grayson was harder to find. Eventually, I tried the kitchen and found Nash instead.

"Have you seen Grayson?" I asked him.

Nash's expression was guarded. "I don't think he wants to see you, kid."

The night before, Grayson hadn't blamed me. He hadn't lashed out. But after he'd told me about Emily, he'd walked away.

He'd left me alone.

"I need to see him," I said.

"Give it some time," Nash advised. "Sometimes, you gotta excise a wound before it can heal."

━━━━━━━━━━━━

I ended up back on the staircase to the East Wing, back in front of the portrait. Oren got a call, and he must have decided the threat to me was contained enough now that he didn't need to watch me mope around Hawthorne House all day. He excused himself, and I went back to staring at Tobias Hawthorne.

It had seemed like fate when I'd found the clue in this portrait, but after talking to Jameson, I knew that it wasn't a sign—or even a coincidence. The clue I'd found had been one of many. *You didn't want them to miss this*, I addressed the billionaire silently. If he really had done all of this after Emily's death, his persistence seemed cruel. *Did you want to make sure that they wouldn't forget what happened?*

Is this whole twisted game just a reminder—an incessant reminder—to put family first?

Is that all I am?

Jameson had said, right from the beginning, that I was special. I hadn't realized until now how badly I'd wanted to believe that he was right, that I wasn't invisible, wasn't wallpaper. I wanted to believe that Tobias Hawthorne had seen something in me that had told him I could do this, that I could handle the stares and the limelight, the responsibility, the riddles, the threats—all of it. I wanted to matter.

I didn't want to be the glass ballerina or the knife. I wanted to prove, at least to myself, that I was *something*.

Jameson may have been done with the game, but I wanted to win.

CHAPTER 81

Top of the clock
Meet me at high
Tell the late day hello
Wish the morning good-bye
A twist and a flip
What do you see?
Take them two at a time
And come find me

I sat on the steps, staring at the words, then worked through the rhyme line by line, turning the piece of stained glass over in my hands. *Top of the clock.* I pictured a clock's face in my head. *What's at the top?*

"Twelve." I rolled that over in my mind. *The number at the top of a clock is twelve.* Like dominos, that set off a chain reaction in my mind. *Meet me at high . . .*

High what?

"Noon." That was a guess, but the next two lines seemed to confirm it. Noon happened in the middle of the day, when you said good-bye to the morning and hello to what came after.

I moved on to the second half of the riddle . . . and I got nothing.

A twist and a flip
What do you see?
Take them two at a time
And come find me

I focused on the stained glass. Was I supposed to twist it? Flip it? Did we need to assemble *all* of the pieces somehow?

"You look like you swallowed a squirrel." Xander plopped down on the stairs next to me.

I definitely did *not* look like I'd swallowed a squirrel, but I was guessing that was Xander's way of asking if I was okay, so I let it go. "Your brothers don't want anything to do with me," I said quietly.

"I guess my kind gesture of sending you all to the Black Wood together exploded." Xander made a face. "To be fair, most of my gestures end up exploding."

That startled a laugh out of me. I tilted the step in his direction. "The game's not over," I told him. He read the inscription. "I found it last night, after the Black Wood." I held up the stained glass. "What do you make of this?"

"Now, where," Xander said thoughtfully, "have I seen something that looks like that?"

CHAPTER 82

I hadn't been back in the Great Room since the reading of the will. Its stained-glass window was tall—eight feet high to only three feet wide—and the lowest point was even with the top of my head. The design was simple and geometric. In the topmost corners were two octagons, the exact size, shade, color, and cut as the one in my hand.

I craned my neck to get a better look. *A twist and a flip...*

"What do you think?" Xander asked me.

I cocked my head to the side. "I think we're going to need a ladder."

———◆———

Perched high on the ladder, with Xander holding it down below, I pressed my hand against one of the stained-glass octagons. At first, nothing happened, but when I pushed on the left side, the octagon rotated—seventy degrees, and then something stopped it.

Does that qualify as a twist?

I turned the second octagon. Pressing left and right didn't do anything, but pushing at the bottom did. The glass flipped a hundred and eighty degrees and then some, before locking into place.

I made my way back down to Xander, who was holding the

ladder, unsure what I'd accomplished. *"A twist and a flip,"* I recited. *"What do you see?"*

We stepped back, taking in the wide view. Sun shone through the window, causing diffused colored lights to appear on the Great Room Floor. The two panels I'd turned, in contrast, cast purple beams. Eventually, those beams crossed.

What do you see?

Xander squatted at the spot where the beams of light met on the floor. "Nothing." He tested the floorboard. "I was expecting it to pop out, or to give..."

I went back to the riddle. *What do you see?* I saw the light. I saw the beams crossing....When that didn't go anywhere, I went farther back in the poem—all the way to the top.

"Noon," I remembered. "The first half of the riddle described noon." The gears in my brain turned faster. "The angle of the beams must depend at least a little on the angle of the sun. Maybe the *twist* and the *flip* only show you what you need to see at noon?"

Xander chewed on that for a second. "We could wait," he said. "Or..." He dragged out the word. "We could cheat."

We spread out, testing the surrounding floorboards. It wasn't that long until noon. The angles couldn't change that much. I tapped the heel of my hand against board after board. *Secure. Secure. Secure.*

"Find anything?" Xander asked me.

Secure. Secure. Loose. The board beneath my hand wasn't wiggling, but it had more give than the others. "Xander—over here!"

He joined me, placed his hands on the board, and pressed. The board popped up. Xander removed it, revealing a small dial underneath. I turned the knob, not sure what to expect. The next thing I knew, Xander and I were sinking. The floor around us was sinking.

When it stopped, Xander and I weren't in the Great Room

anymore. We were underneath it, and directly in front of us was a set of stairs. I was going to go out on a limb and guess that this was one of the entrances to the tunnels that Oren *didn't* know about.

"Take the stairs two at a time," I told Xander. "That's the next line." *Take them two at a time and come find me.*

CHAPTER 83

I had no idea what would have happened if we hadn't descended the stairs two at a time, but I was glad we hadn't found out.

"Have you ever been in the tunnels?" I asked Xander, once we'd made it uneventfully down.

Xander was silent long enough to make the question feel loaded. "No."

Concentrating, I took in my surroundings. The tunnels were metal, like a giant pipe or something out of a sewer system, but they were surprisingly well lit. *Gaslights?* I wondered. I'd lost any sense of how far down we were. Up ahead, the tunnels spread out in three directions.

"Which way?" I asked Xander.

Solemnly, he pointed straight ahead.

I frowned. "How do you know?"

"Because," Xander replied jauntily, "that's what he said." He gestured near my feet. I looked down and yelped.

It took me a moment to realize that there were gargoyles at the bottom of the stairs, a match for the ones in the Great Room, except that the gargoyle on the left had one hand—and one finger—extended, pointing the way.

Come find me.

I started walking. Xander followed. I wondered if he had any idea what we were walking toward.

Come find me.

I remembered Xander telling me that even if I'd thought that I had manipulated Tobias Hawthorne, the old man would have been the one manipulating me.

He's dead, I told myself. *Isn't he?* That thought hit me hard. The press certainly thought Tobias Hawthorne had died. His family seemed to believe it. But had they actually seen his body?

What else could it mean? *Come find me.*

———◆———

Five minutes later, we hit a wall. There was nowhere else to go, nothing to see, no turns we could have taken since we'd started down this path.

"Maybe the gargoyle *lied.*" Xander sounded like he was enjoying that statement a little too much.

I pushed against the wall. *Nothing.* I turned back. "Did we miss something?"

"Perhaps," Xander said thoughtfully, "the gargoyle lied!"

I looked back the way we'd come. I walked the path back slowly, taking in every detail of the tunnel. *Bit. By bit. By bit.*

"Look!" I told Xander. "There."

It was a metal grate, built into the tunnel floor. I ducked down. There was a brand name engraved on the metal, but time had worn away most of the letters. The only ones that were left were *M* . . .

And *E*.

"Come find *me*," I whispered. Squatting down, I grabbed the grate with my fingers and pulled. Nothing. I pulled again, and this time the grate popped up. I fell backward, but Xander caught me.

The two of us stared down into the hole below.

"It is possible," Xander whispered, "that the gargoyle was telling the truth." Without waiting for me, he lowered himself into the hole—and dropped. "You coming?"

If Oren knew I was doing this, he would kill me. I dropped down and found myself in a small room. *How far underground are we now?* The room had four walls, three of them identical. The fourth was made of concrete. Three letters had been carved into the cement.

A. K. G.

My initials.

I walked toward the letters, mesmerized, and then I saw a red laser-like light pass over my face. There was a beep, and then the concrete wall split in two, like an elevator opening. Behind it was a door.

"Facial recognition," Xander said. "It didn't matter which one of us found this place. Without you, we wouldn't have been able to get past the wall."

Poor Jameson. He'd gone to all that effort to keep me close, then ditched me before I could play my part. *The glass ballerina. The knife. The girl with the face that unlocks the wall that reveals the door that…*

"That what?" I stepped forward to examine the door. There were four touch pads, one in each corner of the door. Xander hit one to wake it up, and an image of a fluorescent hand appeared.

"Uh-oh," Xander said.

"What *uh-oh*?" I asked.

"This one has Jameson's initials on it." Xander moved on to the next one. "Grayson's. Nash's." At the last one, he paused. "Mine."

He placed his hand flat on the screen. It made a beeping sound, and then I heard what sounded like a deadbolt being thrown.

I tried the door's handle. "Still locked."

"Four locks." Xander winced. "Four brothers."

My face had been needed to get this far. Their hands were required to go farther.

CHAPTER 84

Xander left me to guard the room. He said that he would be back—with his brothers.

Easier said than done. Jameson had made his feelings clear. Grayson had made himself very hard to find. Nash had never gotten sucked in to their grandfather's game in the first place. *What if they don't come?* Whatever was behind this door, it was what Tobias Hawthorne had wanted us to find. *October eighteenth* wasn't the answer—not in its entirety.

Out of all the people in the world with my birthday, why me? What was the billionaire sorry for? *There are too many pieces*, I thought. *I can't fit it together—any of it.* I needed help.

Overhead, there were footsteps. Abruptly, the sound stopped.

"Xander?" I called. No response. "Xander, is that you?"

More footsteps—coming closer. *Who else knows about this tunnel?* I'd been so intent on finding answers and following this to its end that I'd almost forgotten: Someone in Hawthorne House had given Drake access to the tunnels.

These tunnels.

I pressed my back against the wall. I could hear someone moving directly overhead. The footsteps stopped. A figure appeared above me, backlit and looming over my only exit from this space. *Female. Pale.*

"Rebecca?"

CHAPTER 85

A very." Rebecca stared down at me. "What are you doing down there?" She sounded perfectly normal, but all I could think was that Rebecca Laughlin had been on the estate the night Drake had shot at me. She didn't have an alibi, because when we'd arrived at Wayback Cottage, she wasn't there, and neither of her grandparents knew where she was. She'd said something about *warning* me.

The next day, Rebecca had looked—according to Thea—like she'd been crying. *Why?*

"Where were you," I asked her, my mouth going dry, "the night of the shooting?"

Rebecca closed her eyes. "You don't know what it's like," she said softly, "to have your entire life revolve around one person, and then you wake up one day, and that person is gone."

That wasn't an answer to my question. I thought about Thea telling me that she was only doing what Emily would have wanted. *What would Emily have wanted Rebecca to do to me?*

Xander needed to get back here—quick.

"It was my fault, you know," Rebecca said up above, her eyes still closed. "Emily was taking huge risks. I told our parents. They grounded her, forbade her from seeing the Hawthornes. But Em had her ways. She convinced our mom and dad that she was done acting out. They didn't lift the ban on the boys, but they did start letting her hang out with Thea again."

"Thea," I repeated, "who you were secretly dating."

Rebecca's eyelids shot open. "Emily found us together that afternoon. She was...*angry*. As soon as she got me alone, she told me that what Thea and I had wasn't love, that if Thea *really* loved me, she never would have pretended to be with Xander. Emily said..." Rebecca was caught up in memory now, fully. *Violently.* "She told me that Thea loved her more—and she would prove it. She asked Thea to cover about the cliff diving. I begged Thea not to, but she said that after everything, we owed it to Em."

Thea had covered for Emily the night she had died.

"Most of the things Emily talked the boys into, she *could* do, but even professional cliff divers don't jump from the top of Devil's Gate. It would have been dangerous for anyone, but that much adrenaline, that much cortisol, a change in altitude and pressure, with *her* heart?" Rebecca was speaking so softly now that I wasn't sure she truly remembered I was listening. "I'd tried telling my parents what she was doing, and that didn't work. I'd tried begging Thea, and she'd chosen Emily over me. So I decided to go to Jameson. He was the one who was supposed to take her to Devil's Gate."

Rebecca's head dipped, deep red hair falling into her face. Thea was right—Rebecca Laughlin was beautiful. But right now she didn't look quite right.

"I had a voice recording," she said softly, "of Emily talking. She used to tell me everything the boys did with her and for her and to her. She liked to keep score." Rebecca paused, and when she spoke again, her voice was sharper-edged. "I played the recording for Jameson. I told myself that I was doing it to protect my sister, to keep him from taking her to the cliffs. But the truth was, she'd taken Thea away from me."

So you took something away from her, I thought. "Jameson broke up with her," I said. He'd told me that much.

"If he hadn't," Rebecca replied, "maybe she wouldn't have needed to push things so much. Maybe she would have relented and jumped from one of the lower cliffs. Maybe it would have been okay." Her voice got even softer. "If Emily hadn't caught Thea and me together that afternoon, if she hadn't seen our relationship as such a betrayal—she might not have needed to jump at all."

Rebecca blamed herself. Thea blamed the boys. Grayson took the weight of all of it onto himself. *And Jameson...*

"I'm sorry." Rebecca's apology jarred me from my thoughts. Her tone told me she wasn't talking about Emily anymore. She wasn't talking about something that had happened over a year ago.

"Sorry for what?" I asked. *What are you doing down here, Rebecca?*

"It's not that I have anything against you. But it's what Emily would have wanted."

She is not well. I had to find a way out of here. I had to get away from her.

"Emily would have hated you for stealing their money. She would have hated the way they look at you."

"So you decided to get rid of me," I said, stalling for time. "For Emily."

Rebecca stared at me. "No."

"You knew about the tunnels, and somehow, you told Drake..."

"*No,*" Rebecca insisted. "Avery, I wouldn't do that."

"You said it yourself. Emily would have wanted me gone."

"I'm *not* Emily." The words were guttural.

"Then what were you apologizing for?" I asked.

Rebecca swallowed. "Mr. Hawthorne told me about the tunnels one summer when I was little. He showed me all the entrances, said I deserved something that was just mine. A secret. I come down here when I need to get away—sometimes when I'm visiting my grandparents, but since Emily died, things are pretty awful at home, so sometimes I enter from the outside."

I waited. "And?"

"The night of the shooting, I saw someone else in the tunnels. I didn't say anything, because Emily wouldn't have wanted me to. I owed her, Avery. After what I did—*I owed her.*"

"Who did you see?" I asked. She didn't answer. "Drake?"

Rebecca met my eyes. "He wasn't alone."

"Who else was there?" I waited. *Nothing.* "Rebecca, who else was in the tunnel with Drake?"

Who would Emily have wanted her to protect?

"One of the boys?" I asked, feeling like the ground was crumbling beneath me.

"No," Rebecca said quietly. "Their mother."

CHAPTER 86

Skye?" I tried to wrap my mind around that. She'd never seemed like a threat, the way Zara had. Passive-aggressive, sure, and petty. But violent?

We're all friends here, aren't we? I could hear her declaring. *I make it a policy to befriend everyone who steals my birthright.*

I could see her holding out a glass of champagne and telling me to drink.

"Skye was down here with Drake the night of the shooting," I said, making myself confront the implications head-on. "She gave him access to the estate, probably even pointed him toward the Black Wood."

Toward me.

"I should have told someone," Rebecca said softly. "After the shooting, as soon as I realized what I'd seen—I should have spoken up."

"Yes." That word was razor sharp—and spoken by someone other than me. "You should have." Overhead, Grayson stepped into view.

Rebecca turned to face him. "It was your mother, Gray. I *couldn't—*"

"You could have told me," Grayson said quietly. "I would have taken care of it, Bex."

I doubted Grayson's method of *taking care of it* would have involved turning his mother over to the police.

"Drake tried again," I said, glaring daggers at Rebecca. "You know that, right? He tried to run us off the road. He could have killed me—and Alisa and Oren and *Thea*."

Rebecca made a garbled sound the second I said Thea's name.

"Rebecca," Grayson said, his voice low.

"I know," Rebecca said. "But Emily wouldn't have wanted..."

"Emily's gone." Grayson's tone wasn't harsh, but his words took Rebecca's breath away. "Bex." He made her look at him. "Rebecca. I'll take care of this. I promise you: Everything is going to be fine."

"Everything is *not* fine," I told Grayson.

"Go," he murmured to Rebecca. She went, and we were alone.

Grayson lowered himself slowly into the hidden room. "Xander said you needed me."

He'd come. Maybe that would have meant more if I hadn't just had that conversation with Rebecca.

"Your mother tried to have me killed."

"My mother," Grayson said, "is a complicated woman. But she's family."

And he would choose family over me, every time.

"If I asked you to let me handle this," he continued, "would you? I can guarantee that no more harm will come to you or yours."

How exactly he could guarantee anything was unclear, but there was no doubt that he believed he could. *The world bends to the will of Grayson Hawthorne.* I thought about the day I'd met him, how sure he'd seemed of himself, how invincible.

"What if I play you for it?" Grayson asked when I didn't reply.

"You like a challenge. I know you do." He stepped toward me. "Please, Avery. Give me a chance to make this right."

There was no making this right—but all he'd asked for was a chance. *I don't owe him that. I don't owe him anything. But—*

Maybe it was the expression on his face. Or the knowledge that he'd already lost everything to me once. Maybe I just wanted him to see me and think about something other than October eighteenth.

"I'll play you for it," I said. "What's the game?"

Grayson's silver eyes held mine. "Think of a number," he told me. "One to ten. If I guess it, you let me handle the situation with my mother my way. If I don't..."

"I turn her in to the police."

Grayson took half a step toward me. "Think of a number."

The odds were in my favor here. He only had a 10 percent chance of guessing correctly. I had a 90 percent chance that he would get it wrong. I took my time choosing. There were certain numbers that people defaulted to. Seven, for instance. I could go for an extreme—one or ten, but those seemed like easy guesses, too. Eight was on my brain, from the days we'd spent solving the numerical sequence. Four was the number of Hawthorne brothers.

If I wanted to keep him from guessing, I needed to go for something unexpected. No rhyme, no reason.

Two.

"Do you want me to write the number down?" I asked.

"On what?" Grayson asked softly.

I swallowed. "How do you know that I won't lie about my number if you get it right?"

Grayson was quiet for a few seconds, then spoke. "I trust you."

I knew, with every fiber of my being, that Grayson Hawthorne didn't trust easily—or much. I swallowed. "Go ahead."

He took at least as much time generating his guess as I had choosing my number. He looked at me, and I could feel him trying to unravel my thoughts and impulses, to solve me, like one more riddle.

What do you see when you look at me, Grayson Hawthorne?

He made his guess. "Two."

I turned my head toward my shoulder, breaking eye contact. I could have lied. I could have told him that he was wrong. But I didn't. "Good guess."

Grayson let out a ragged breath, and then I felt him gently turning my face back toward his. "Avery." He almost never used my given name. He gently traced the line of my jaw. "I won't let anyone hurt you ever again. You have my word."

He thought he could protect me. He *wanted* to. He was touching me, and all I wanted was to let him. Let him protect me. Let him touch me. Let him—

Footsteps. The clattering above pushed me into taking a step back from him, and a few moments later, Xander and Nash climbed down into the room.

I managed to look at them—not Grayson "Where's Jameson?" I asked.

Xander cleared his throat. "I can report that some very colorful language was used when I requested his presence."

Nash snorted. "He'll be here."

We waited—five minutes, then ten.

"You might as well unlock yours," Xander told the others. "Your hands, if you please."

Grayson went first, then Nash. After the touch pads scanned their hands, we heard the telltale sound of deadbolts being thrown, one after the other.

"Three locks down," Xander murmured. "One to go."

Another five minutes. Eight. *He's not coming*, I thought.

"Jameson isn't coming," Grayson said, like he'd lifted the thought from my mind as easily as he'd guessed my number.

"He'll be here," Nash repeated.

"Don't I always do what I'm told?"

We looked up—and Jameson jumped. He landed between his brothers and me, going almost to the ground to absorb the shock. He straightened, then met their eyes, one at a time. *Nash. Xander. Grayson.*

Then, me. "You don't know when to stop, do you, Heiress?" That didn't exactly feel like an indictment.

"I'm tougher than I look," I told him. He stared at me for a moment longer, then turned to the door. He placed his hand flat on the pad that bore his initials. The last deadbolt was thrown, and the door was released. It creaked open—an inch, maybe two. I expected Jameson to reach for the door, but instead, he walked back to the opening and jumped, catching its sides with his hands.

"Where are you going?" I asked him. After everything it had taken to get to this point, he couldn't just walk away.

"To hell, eventually," Jameson answered. "Probably to the wine cellar, for now."

No. He couldn't just leave. He was the one who had dragged me into this, and he was going to see it through. I jumped to catch onto the opening overhead, to go after him. I felt my grip slipping. Strong hands grabbed me from beneath—*Grayson.* He pushed me upward, and I managed to climb out and to my feet.

"Don't leave," I told Jameson.

He was already walking away. When he heard my voice, he stopped but didn't turn back.

"I don't know what's on the other side of that door, Heiress, but I do know that the old man laid this trap for me."

"Just for you?" I said, an edge working its way into my voice. "That's why it required all four brothers' hands and my face to get this far?" Clearly, Tobias Hawthorne had meant for *all* of us to be here.

"He knew that any game he left, I would play. Nash might say screw it, Grayson might get bogged down in legalities, Xander might be thinking about a thousand and one other things—but *I would play.*" I could see him breathing—see him *hurting.* "So, yes, he meant this for me. Whatever is on the other side of that door..." Jameson drew in another ragged breath. "He knew. He knew what I did, and he wanted to make sure I never forgot."

"What did he know?" I asked.

Grayson appeared beside me and repeated my question. "The old man knew what, Jamie?"

Behind me, I could hear Nash and Xander climbing into the tunnel, but my mind barely registered their presence. I was focused—wholly, intensely—on Jameson and Grayson.

"Knew what, Jamie?"

Jameson turned back to face his brother. "What happened on ten-eighteen."

"It was my fault." Grayson strode forward, taking Jameson's shoulders in his hands. "I'm the one who took Emily there. I knew it was a bad idea, and I didn't care. I just wanted to win. I wanted her to love *me.*"

"I followed you that night." Jameson's statement hung in the air for several seconds. "I watched the two of you jump, Gray."

All of a sudden, I was back with Jameson, headed for the West Brook. He'd told me two lies and one truth. *I watched Emily Laughlin die.*

"You followed us?" Grayson couldn't make sense of that. "Why?"

"Masochism?" Jameson shrugged. "I was pissed." He paused. "Eventually, you ran off to get the towels, and I..."

"Jamie." Grayson dropped his hands to his sides. "What did you do?"

Grayson had told me that he'd left to get the towels, and when he'd gotten back, Emily was lying on the shore. *Dead.*

"What did you do?"

"She saw me." Jameson turned from his brother to look at me. "She saw me, and she smiled. She thought she'd won. She thought she still had me, but I turned and walked away. She called my name. I didn't stop. I heard her gasp. She was making this little strangling sound."

I brought my hand to my mouth in horror.

"I thought she was playing with me. I heard a splash, but I didn't turn around. I made it probably a hundred yards. She wasn't calling after me anymore. I glanced back." Jameson's voice broke. "Emily was hunched over, crawling out of the water. I thought she was *pretending.*"

He'd thought she was manipulating him.

"I just stood there," Jameson said dully. "I didn't do a damn thing to help her."

I watched Emily Laughlin die. I thought I was going to be sick. I could see him, standing there, trying to show her that he wasn't hers anymore, trying to resist.

"She collapsed. She went still, and she *stayed still.* And then you came back, Gray, and I left." Jameson shuddered. "I hated you for taking her there, but I hate myself more because I let her die. I stood there, and *I watched.*"

"It was her heart," I said. "What could you have—"

"I could have tried CPR. I could have done *something.*" Jameson swallowed. "But I didn't. I don't know how the old man knew, but he cornered me a few days later. He told me that he knew I'd been there and asked whether I felt culpable. He wanted me to tell you, Gray, and I wouldn't. I said that if he was so damn set on you knowing that I'd been there, he could tell you himself. But he didn't. Instead...he did this."

The letter. The library. The will. Their middle names. The date of my birth—and Emily's death. The numbers, scattered all over the estate. The stained glass, the riddle. The passage down into the tunnel. The grate marked M. E. The hidden room. The moving wall. The door.

"He wanted to make damn sure," Jameson said, "that I never forgot."

"No," Xander blurted out. The others turned to look at him. "That's not what this is," he swore. "He wasn't making a point. He wanted us—all four of us—together. Here."

Nash put a hand on Xander's shoulder. "The old man could be a real bastard, Xan."

"*That's not what this is*," Xander said again, his voice more intense than I'd ever heard it—like he wasn't speculating. Like he *knew*.

Grayson, who hadn't said a word since Jameson's confession, spoke up now. "What precisely are you saying, Alexander?"

"The two of you were walking around like ghosts. You were a robot, Gray." Xander was speaking quickly now—almost too quickly for the rest of us to follow. "Jamie was a ticking time bomb. You hated each other."

"We hated ourselves more," Grayson said, his voice like sandpaper.

"The old man knew he was sick," Xander admitted. "He told me, right before he died. He asked me to do something for him."

Nash's eyes narrowed. "And what was that?"

Xander didn't answer. Grayson's eyes narrowed. "You had to make sure we played."

"It was my job to make sure you saw this to the end." Xander looked from Grayson to Jameson. "Both of you. If either of you stopped playing, it was my job to draw you back."

"You knew?" I said. "All this time, you knew where the clues led?"

Xander was the one who'd helped me find the tunnel. He was the one who'd solved the Black Wood. Even back at the very beginning . . .

He told me that his grandfather didn't have a middle name.

"You helped me," I said. He'd *manipulated* me. Moved me around, like a lure.

"I told you that I am a living, breathing Rube Goldberg machine." Xander looked down. "I warned you. Kind of." I thought of the moment he'd taken me to see the machine he'd built. I'd asked him what it had to do with Thea, and his response had been *Who said this had anything to do with Thea?*

I stared at Xander—the youngest, tallest, and arguably most brilliant Hawthorne. *Where you go*, he'd told me back at the gala, *they'll follow.* All this time, I'd thought that Jameson was the one who was using me. I'd thought that he'd kept me close for a reason.

It had never once occurred to me that Xander had his reasons, too.

"Do you know why your grandfather chose me?" I demanded. "Have you known the answer all this time?"

Xander held his hands up in front of his body, like he thought I might throttle him. "I only know what he wanted me to know. I have no idea what's on the other side of that door. I was only supposed to get Jamie and Gray here. *Together.*"

"All four of us," Nash corrected. "Together." I remembered what he'd said in the kitchen. *Sometimes you gotta excise a wound before it can heal.*

Was that what this was? Was that the old man's grand plan? Bring me here, spur them into action, hope that the game let the truth come out?

"Not just the four of us," Grayson told Nash. He looked back toward me. "Clearly, this was a game for five."

CHAPTER 87

We dropped back down into the room, one at a time. Jameson laid his hand flat against the door and pushed it inward. The cell beyond was empty, except for a small wooden box. On the box, there were letters—golden letters etched into golden tiles that looked like they'd come out of the world's most expensive game of Scrabble.

The letters on the box spelled out my name: AVERY KYLIE GRAMBS.

There were four blank tiles, one before my first name, one after my last, and two separating the names from each other. After everything that had just happened—Jameson's confession, then Xander's—it seemed wrong that this should come down to me.

Why me? This game might have been designed to bring Jameson and Grayson back together, to bring secrets to the surface, to bleed out poison before it turned to rot—but somehow, for some reason, it ended with me.

"Looks like it's your rodeo, kid." Nash nudged me to the box.

Swallowing, I knelt. I tried to open the box, but it was locked. There was no spot for a key, no combination pad.

Above me, Jameson spoke. "The letters, Heiress."

He just couldn't help himself. Even after everything, he couldn't stop playing the game.

I reached tentatively for the *A* in *Avery*. It came off the box. One by one, I peeled off the other letters and the blank tiles, and I realized *this* was the trigger for the lock. I stared at the pieces, nineteen of them total. *My name.* That clearly wasn't the combination to unlock the box. *So what is?*

Grayson dropped down beside me. He organized the letters, vowels first, consonants in alphabetical order.

"It's an anagram," Nash commented. "Rearrange the letters."

My gut response was that my name was just my name, not an anagram of anything, but my brain was already sifting through the possibilities.

Avery was easy to turn into words, two of them, just by adding the space that had been in front of the name to split it. I placed the tiles back on the top of the box, pushing each one into place with a click.

A very . . .

I put another space after *very*. That left two blank tiles and all the letters from my middle and last names.

Kylie Grambs, arranged according to Grayson's method, read: *A, E, I, B, G, K, L, M, R, S, Y.*

Big. Balm. Bale. I started pulling words out, seeing what each of them left me with, and then I saw it.

All at once, I saw it.

"You have got to be kidding me," I whispered.

"What?" Jameson was 100 percent in this now, whether he wanted to be or not. He knelt next to Grayson and me as I put the letters up, one by one.

Avery Kylie Grambs—the name I'd been given the day I was

born, the name that Tobias Hawthorne had programmed into the bowling alley and the pinball machine and who knew how many other places in the House—became, reordered, *A very risky gamble.*

"He kept saying that," Xander murmured. "That no matter what he planned, it might not work. That it was…"

"*A very risky gamble,*" Grayson finished, his gaze making its way to me.

My name? I tried to process that. *First my birthday, now my name.* Was that it? Was that *why?* How had Tobias Hawthorne even found me?

I snapped the last blank tile into place, and the box's lock disengaged. The lid popped open. Inside, there were five envelopes, one with each of our names.

I watched as the boys opened and read theirs. Nash swore under his breath. Grayson stared at his. Jameson let out a broken little laugh. Xander shoved his into his pocket.

I turned my attention from the four of them to my envelope. The last letter Tobias Hawthorne had sent to me had explained nothing. Opening this one, I expected clarity. *How did you find me? Why tell me you're sorry? What were you sorry for?*

There was no paper inside my envelope, no letter. The only thing it contained was a single packet of sugar.

CHAPTER 88

I *place two sugar packets vertically on the table and bring their ends together, forming a triangle capable of standing on its own. "There," I say. I do the same with the next pair of packets, then set a fifth across them horizontal, connecting the two triangles I built.*

"Avery Kylie Grambs!" My mom appears at the end of the table, smiling. "What have I told you about building castles out of sugar?"

I beam back at her. "It's only worth it if you can go five stories tall!"

In my dream, that was where the memory had ended, but this time, holding the sugar in my hand, my brain took me one step further. *A man eating in the booth behind me glances back. He asks me how old I am.*

"Six," I say.

"I have some grandsons at home who are just about your age," he says. "Tell me, Avery, can you spell your name? Your full name, like your mom said a minute ago?"

I can, and I do.

"I met him," I said quietly. "Just once, years ago—just for a moment, in passing." Tobias Hawthorne had heard my mom say my full name. He'd asked me to spell it.

"He loved anagrams more than scotch," Nash said. "And he was a man who *loved* a good scotch."

Had Tobias Hawthorne mentally rearranged the letters in my full name right in that moment? Had it amused him? I thought about Grayson, hiring someone to dig up dirt on me. On my mother. Had Tobias Hawthorne been curious about us? Had he done the same?

"He would have kept track of you," Grayson said roughly. "A little girl with a funny little name." He glanced at Jameson. "He must have known her date of birth."

"And after Emily died..." Jameson was looking at me now—only at me. "He thought of you."

"And decided to leave me his entire fortune because of *my name*?" I said. "That's insane."

"You're the one who said it, Heiress: He didn't disinherit us *for* you. We weren't getting the money anyway."

"It was going to charity," I argued. "And you're telling me that on a whim, he wiped out the will he'd had for twenty years? That's—"

"He needed something to get our attention," Grayson said. "Something so unexpected, so bewildering, that it could only be seen—"

"—as a puzzle," Jameson finished. "Something we couldn't ignore. Something to wake us up again. Something to bring us here—all four of us."

"Something to purge the poison." Nash's tone was hard to read.

They'd known the old man. I hadn't. What they were saying—it made sense to *them*. In their eyes, this hadn't been a whim. It had been a very risky gamble. *I* had been a very risky gamble. Tobias Hawthorne had bet that my presence in the House would shake things up, that old secrets would be laid bare, that somehow, some-way, one last puzzle would change everything.

That, if Emily's death had torn them apart, I could bring them back together.

"I told you, kid," Nash said beside me. "You're not a player. You're the glass ballerina—or the knife."

CHAPTER 89

O ren met me the moment I stepped foot into the Great Room. That he'd been waiting made me wonder why he'd left my side in the first place. Had it really been a phone call— or had Tobias Hawthorne left him with instructions to let the five of us finish the game alone?

"Do you know what's down there?" I asked my head of security. He was more loyal to the old man than he was to me. *What else did he ask you to do?*

"Besides the tunnel?" Oren replied. "No." He made a study of me, of the boys. "Should I?"

I thought about what had happened down there while Xander was gone. About Rebecca and what she had told me down below. About Skye. I looked at Grayson. His eyes caught mine. There was a question there, and hope, and something else I couldn't name.

All I told Oren was "No."

>———◄

That night, I sat at Tobias Hawthorne's desk, the one in my wing. In my hands, I held the letter he'd left me.

Dearest Avery,
I'm sorry.
—*T. T. H.*

I'd wondered what he was sorry for, but I was starting to think I'd had things reversed. Maybe he hadn't left me the money as an apology. Maybe he was apologizing for leaving me the money. *For using me.*

He'd brought me here for *them.*

I folded the letter in half and then in half again. This—all of it—had nothing to do with my mom. Whatever secrets she'd been keeping, they predated Emily's death. In the grand scheme of things, this entire life-changing, mind-blowing, headline-grabbing chain of events had nothing to do with *me.* I was just a little girl with a funny little name, born on the right day.

I have some grandsons at home, I could hear the old man telling me, *who are just about your age.*

"This was always about them." I said the words out loud. "What am I supposed to do now?" The game was over. The puzzle was solved. I'd served my purpose. And I'd never felt so insignificant in my life.

My eyes were drawn to the compass built into the desk's surface. As I had my first time in this office, I turned the compass, and the panel on the desk popped up, revealing the compartment underneath. I traced my finger lightly over the *T* etched into the wood.

And then I looked down at my letter—at Tobias Hawthorne's signature. *T. T. H.*

My gaze traveled back to the desk. Jameson had told me once that his grandfather had never purchased a desk without hidden compartments. Having played the game, having lived in Hawthorne House—I couldn't help seeing things differently now. I tested the wood panel on which the *T* had been etched.

Nothing.

Then I placed my fingers in the *T*, and I pushed. The wood gave. *Click.* And then it popped back up into place.

"*T*," I said out loud. And then I did the same thing again. Another *click.* "*T*." I stared at the panel for a long time before I saw it: a gap between the wood and the top of the desk, at the base of the *T*. I pushed my fingers underneath and found another groove—and above it a latch. I unhooked the latch, and the panel rotated counterclockwise.

With a ninety-degree turn, I was no longer looking at a *T*. I was looking at an *H*. I pressed all three bars of the *H* at the same time. *Click.* A motor of some kind was engaged, and the panel disappeared back into the desk, revealing another compartment underneath.

T. T. H. Tobias Hawthorne had intended for this to be my wing. He'd signed my letter with initials, not his name. And those initials had unlocked this drawer. Inside, there was a folder, much like the one that Grayson had shown me that day at the foundation. My name—my full name—was written across the top.

Avery Kylie Grambs.

Now that I'd seen the anagram, I couldn't unsee it. Unsure what I would find—or even what I was expecting—I lifted the folder out and opened it. The first thing I saw was a copy of my birth certificate. Tobias Hawthorne had highlighted my date of birth—and my father's signature. The date made sense. But the signature?

I have a secret, I could hear my mother saying. *About the day you were born.*

I had no idea what to make of that—any of it. I flipped to the next page and the next and the next. They were full of pictures, four or five a year, from the time I was six.

He would have kept track of you, I could hear Grayson saying. *A little girl with a funny little name.*

The number of pictures went up significantly after my sixteenth birthday. *After Emily died.* There were so many, like Tobias Hawthorne had sent someone to watch my every move. *You couldn't risk everything on a total stranger,* I thought. Technically, that was exactly what he'd done, but looking at these pictures, I was overwhelmed with the sense that Tobias Hawthorne had done his homework.

I wasn't just a name and a date to him.

There were shots of me running poker games in the parking lot and shots of me carrying way too many cups at once at the diner. There was a picture of me with Libby, where we were laughing, and one where I was standing with my body between hers and Drake's. There was a shot of me playing chess in the park and one of me and Harry in line for breakfast, where all you could see was the back of our heads. There was even one of me in my car, holding a stack of postcards in my hands.

The photographer had caught me dreaming.

Tobias Hawthorne hadn't known me—but he'd known *about* me. I might have been a very risky gamble. I might have been a part of the puzzle and not a player. But the billionaire had known that I could play. He hadn't entered into this blindly and hoped for the best. He'd plotted, and he'd planned, and I'd been a part of that calculation. Not just Avery Kylie Grambs, born on the day that Emily Laughlin had died—but the girl in these photos.

I thought about what Jameson had said, that first night when he'd stepped from the fireplace into my room. Tobias Hawthorne left me the fortune—and all he'd left them was *me.*

CHAPTER 90

Early the next morning, Oren informed me that Skye Hawthorne was leaving Hawthorne House. She was moving out, and Grayson had instructed security that she wasn't to be allowed back on the premises.

"Any idea why?" Oren gave me a look that strongly suggested that he knew that I knew something.

I looked at him, and I lied. "Not a clue."

➤━━━━◄

I found Grayson in the hidden staircase, with the Davenport. "You kicked your mother out of the House?"

That wasn't what I'd expected him to do, when he'd won our little wager. For better or worse, Skye was his mother. *Family first.*

"Mother left of her own volition," Grayson said evenly. "She was made to understand it was the better option."

Better than being reported to the police.

"You won the bet," I told Grayson. "You didn't have to—"

He turned and took a step up so that he was standing on the same stair as me. "Yes, I did."

If I were choosing between you and any one of them, he'd told me, *I would choose them, always and every time.*

But he hadn't.

"Grayson." I was standing close to him, and the last time we'd stood together on these stairs, I'd bared my wounds—literally. This time, I found my hands rising to *his* chest. He was arrogant and awful and had spent the first week of our acquaintance dead set on making my life hell. He was still half in love with Emily Laughlin. But from the first moment I'd seen him, looking away had been nearly impossible.

And at the end of the day, he'd chosen me. *Over family. Over his mother.*

Hesitantly, I let my hand find its way from his chest to his jaw. For a single second, he let me touch him, and then he turned his head away.

"I will always protect you," he told me, his jaw tight, his eyes shadowed. "You deserve to feel safe in your own home. And I'll help you with the foundation. I'll teach you what you need to know to take to this life like you were born to it. But this...us..." He swallowed. "It can't happen, Avery. I've seen the way Jameson looks at you."

He didn't say that he wouldn't let another girl come between them. He didn't have to.

CHAPTER 91

I went to school, and when I came home, I called Max, knowing that she probably didn't even have her phone. My call got sent to voicemail. "This is Maxine Liu. I've been sequestered in the technological equivalent of a virtual convent. Have a blessed day, you rotten scoundrels."

I tried her brother's phone and got sent to voicemail again. "You have reached Isaac Liu." Max had commandeered *his* voicemail as well. "He is an entirely tolerable younger brother, and if you leave a message, he will probably call you back. Avery, if this is you, stop trying to get yourself killed. You owe me Australia!"

I didn't leave a message—but I did make plans to see what it would take for Alisa to send the entire Liu family first-class tickets to Australia. I couldn't travel until my time in Hawthorne House was up, but maybe Max could.

I owed her.

Feeling adrift and aching from what Grayson had said and the fact that Max wasn't there to process it with, I went looking for Libby. We seriously needed to get her a new phone, because a person could get lost in this place.

I didn't want to lose anyone else.

I might never have found her, but when I got close to the music room, I heard the piano playing. I followed the music and found Libby sitting on the piano bench beside Nan. They both sat with their eyes closed, listening.

Libby's black eye had finally faded away. Seeing her with Nan made me think about Libby's job back home. I couldn't ask her to just keep sitting around Hawthorne House every day, doing nothing.

I wondered what Nash Hawthorne would suggest. *I could ask her to put together a business plan. Maybe a food truck?*

Or maybe she would want to travel, too. Until the will exited probate, I was limited as to what I could do—but the fine people at McNamara, Ortega, and Jones had reason to want to stay on my good side. Eventually, the money would be mine. Eventually, it would exit the trust.

Eventually, I'd be one of the richest and most powerful women in the world.

The piano music ended, and my sister and Nan looked up and saw me. Libby did her best mother-hen impression.

"Are you sure you're okay?" she asked me. "You don't look okay."

I thought about Grayson. About Jameson. About what I'd been brought here to do. "I'm fine," I told Libby, my voice steady enough that I could almost believe it.

She wasn't fooled. "I'll make you something," she told me. "Have you ever had a quiche? I've never made a quiche."

I had no real desire to try one, but baking was Libby's way of showing love. She headed for the kitchen. I went to follow, but Nan stopped me.

"Stay," she ordered.

There was nothing to do but obey.

"I hear my granddaughter is leaving," Nan said tersely after letting me sweat it for a bit.

I considered dissembling, but she'd pretty much proven she wasn't the type for niceties. "She tried to have me killed."

Nan snorted. "Skye never did like getting her hands dirty herself. You ask me, if you're going to kill someone, you should at least have the decency to do it yourself and do it right."

This was probably the strangest conversation I'd ever had in my life—and that was saying something.

"Not that people are decent nowadays," Nan continued. "No respect. No self-respect. No grit." She sighed. "If my poor Alice could see her children now...."

I wondered what it had been like for Skye and Zara, growing up in Hawthorne House. What it had been like for Toby.

What twisted them into this?

"Your son-in-law changed his will after Toby died." I studied Nan's expression, wondering if she'd known.

"Toby was a good boy," Nan said gruffly. "Until he wasn't."

I wasn't sure quite what to make of that.

Her hands went to a locket around her neck. "He was the sweetest child, smart as a whip. Just like his daddy, they used to say, but oh, that boy had a dose of me."

"What happened?" I asked.

Nan's expression darkened. "It broke my Alice's heart. Broke all of us, really." Her fingers tightened around the locket, and her hand shook. She set her jaw, then opened the locket. "Look at him," she told me. "Look at that sweet boy. He's sixteen here."

I leaned down to get a better look, wondering if Tobias Hawthorne the Second had resembled any of his nephews. What I saw took my breath away.

No.

"That's Toby?" I couldn't breathe. I couldn't think.

"He was a good boy," Nan said gruffly.

I barely heard her. I couldn't tear my eyes away from the picture. I couldn't speak, because I knew that man. He was younger in the picture—much younger—but that face was unmistakable.

"Heiress?" A voice spoke up from the doorway. I looked to see Jameson standing there. He looked different than he had the past few days. Lighter, somehow. Marginally less angry. Capable of offering a lopsided little half smile to me. "What's got your pants in a twist?"

I looked back down at the locket and sucked in a breath that scalded my lungs. "Toby," I managed. "I know him."

"You what?" Jameson walked toward me. Beside me, Nan went very still.

"I used to play chess with him in the park," I said. "Every morning." *Harry.*

"That's impossible," Nan said, her voice shaking. "Toby's been dead for twenty years."

Twenty years ago, Tobias Hawthorne had disinherited his family. *What is this? What the hell is going on here?*

"Are you sure, Heiress?" Jameson was right beside me now. *I've seen the way Jameson looks at you*, Grayson had said. "Are you absolutely certain?"

I looked at Jameson. This didn't feel real. *I have a secret*, I could hear my mother telling me, *about the day you were born. . . .*

I reached for Jameson's hand and squeezed hard. "I'm sure."

EPILOGUE

Xander Hawthorne stared down at the letter, the way he had every day for a week. On the surface, it said very little.

> *Alexander,*
>> *Well done.*
>> *Tobias Hawthorne*

Well done. He'd gotten his brothers to the end of the game. He'd gotten Avery there, too. He'd done exactly as he'd promised— but the old man had made him a promise, too.

When their game is done, yours will begin.

Xander had never competed the way his brothers did—but oh, how he'd wanted to. He hadn't been lying when he'd told Avery that, just once, he wanted to win. When they'd made it to the final room, when she'd opened the box, when he'd torn open his envelope, he'd been expecting...*something.*

A riddle.

A puzzle.

A clue.

And all he'd received was this. *Well done.*

"Xander?" Rebecca said softly beside him. "What are we doing here?"

"Sighing melodramatically," Thea sniped. "Obviously."

That he'd gotten both of them here, in the same room, was a feat. He wasn't even sure why he'd done it, other than the fact that he needed a witness. *Witnesses.* If Xander was being honest with himself, he'd brought Rebecca because he wanted her there, and he'd brought Thea because if he hadn't...

He would have been alone with Rebecca.

"There are many types of invisible ink," Xander told them. In the past few days, he had held a match to the back of the page, heating its surface. He'd bought a UV light and gone to town. He'd tried every way he knew of unmasking a hidden message on a page, except for one. "But there's only one kind," he continued evenly, "that destroys the message after it's revealed."

If he was wrong about this, it was over. There would be no game, no winning. Xander didn't want to do this alone.

"What exactly do you think you're going to find?" Thea asked him.

Xander looked down at the letter one last time.

Alexander,
   Well done.
   Tobias Hawthorne

Perhaps the old man's promise had been a lie. Perhaps, to Tobias Hawthorne, Xander had only been an afterthought. But he had to try. He turned to the tub beside him. He filled it with water.

"Xander?" Rebecca said again, and her voice nearly undid him.

"Here goes nothing." Xander laid his letter gingerly on the surface of the water, then pressed down.

At first, he thought he'd made a horrible mistake. He thought nothing was happening. Then, slowly, writing appeared, on either side of his grandfather's signature. *Tobias Hawthorne*, he'd signed it, *no middle name*, and now the reason for that omission was clear.

The invisible ink darkened on the page. To the right of the signature, there were only two letters, equating to one Roman numeral: *II*. And to the left, there was a single word: *Find*.

Find Tobias Hawthorne II.

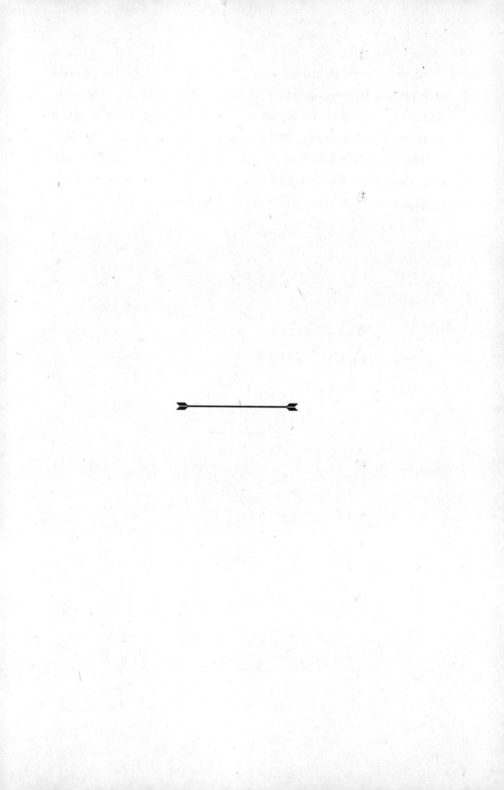

ACKNOWLEDGMENTS

Writing this book was a challenge and a joy, and I am so thankful to the incredible teams (plural!) that have supported me through every step of the process. I worked with two fantastic editors on this project. I am so grateful to Kieran Viola for recognizing that *this* was absolutely the book I needed to write next and for helping me bring Avery, the Hawthorne brothers, and their world to life. Lisa Yoskowitz then guided the book to publication, and her passion and vision for this project, along with her market savvy and grace, have made the process a dream. Any author would be lucky to work with either one of these editors; I am incredibly blessed to have gotten to work with both!

Huge thanks go out to the entire team at Little, Brown Books for Young Readers, especially Janelle DeLuise, Jackie Engel, Marisa Finkelstein, Shawn Foster, Bill Grace, Savannah Kennelly, Hannah Koerner, Christie Michel, Hannah Milton, Emilie Polster, Victoria Stapleton, and Megan Tingley. Special thanks go out to my publicist, Alex Kelleher-Nagorski, whose enthusiasm for this project has made my day more than once; to Michelle Campbell, for her incredible outreach to librarians and teachers; and to Karina Granda, for her work on the most beautiful cover I have ever seen! I am also in awe of and indebted to artist Katt Phatt, who created the incredible artwork on the cover. Thank you to Anthea Townsend, Phoebe Williams, and the entire team at Penguin Random House UK for their passion for and work on this project, and the team at Disney • Hyperion, who saw the potential in this book in 2018, when it was just a four-page proposal.

Elizabeth Harding has been my agent since I was in college, and I could not ask for a wiser, more incredible advocate! To my entire team at Curtis Brown—thank you, thank you, thank you. Holly Frederick championed TV rights for this book. Sarah Perillo did incredible work on foreign rights (in the midst of a pandemic, no less!). Thank you also to Nicole Eisenbraun, Sarah Gerton, Maddie Tavis, and Jazmia Young. I appreciate you all so much!

I'm immensely grateful for the family and friends who saw me through the writing of this project. Rachel Vincent sat across from me at Panera once a week, told me that I could do this, was always available for brainstorming, and made me smile even when I was stressed enough to want to cry. Ally Carter is always there through the highs and lows of publishing. My colleagues and students at the University of Oklahoma have been supportive in so many ways. Thank you, all!

Finally, thank you to my parents and husband, for endless support, and to my kids, for letting me get enough sleep to write this book.